FARRAR
STRAUS
GIROUX

# FIELDWORK

# fIELDWORK

## MISCHA BERLINSKI

FARRAR, STRAUS AND GIROUX
*New York*

FARRAR, STRAUS AND GIROUX
19 Union Square West, New York 10003

Library of Congress Cataloging-in-Publication Data
Berlinski, Mischa, 1973–
    Fieldwork / Mischa Berlinski.— 1st ed.
        p.   cm.
    ISBN-13: 978-0-374-29916-3 (hardcover : alk. paper)
    ISBN-10: 0-374-29916-1 (hardcover : alk. paper)
    1. Thailand—Fiction.   2. Women anthropologists—Fiction.
3. Missionaries—Fiction.   4. Indigenous peoples—Fiction.   I. Title.

PS3602.E75825F54 2007
813'.6—dc22

                                                    2006016214


Designed by Gretchen Achilles

www.fsgbooks.com


1   3   5   7   9   10   8   6   4   2

FOR MY MOTHER AND FATHER

*The main achievement of religion, as compared with animism, lies in the psychic binding of the fear of demons. Nevertheless, the evil spirit still has a place in the religious system as a relic of the previous age.*

FREUD

PART ONE

A GOOD STORY

ONE

## "GOOD *GOD*, NO"

WHEN HE WAS A YEAR out of Brown, my friend Josh O'Connor won a Thai beach vacation in a lottery in a bar. He spent two weeks on Ko Samui, decided that Thailand was home, and never left. That was at least ten years ago, and since then, Josh has done just about every sort of odd job a foreigner in Thailand can do: He taught English for a while, and was part owner of a nightclub in Phuket. He was a stringer for one of the wire agencies, and he took a few photos now and again for Agence France-Presse. Josh played the trumpet in the marching band in high school, and he parlayed the experience into a few years as the frontman for a Thai ska band called the King's Men. He founded a dating agency. He worked for a time for an environmental group attempting to stop construction of a large dam across the Mekong, and when the effort failed, he wrote publicity materials for a cement exporter. He hinted that many years ago, in a moment of real financial desperation, he smuggled a pound of hashish in his belly back to the States. I'm not sure that I entirely believe the story, but it was consistent with everything I know about Josh. Yet to see him, one would have no idea of his adventurous spirit: he was neither tall nor short but decidedly round; he was chubby-cheeked, curly-haired, and round-nosed, with bulging eyes and an over-sized head. He had thick lips and a gap between his two front teeth which whistled very slightly when he spoke and made his speech nervous and breathy. His body was pear-shaped, with an enormous, protruding posterior: when he walked, he waddled like a duck; and when he laughed, as he did often, his whole body shook. "I'm attractive," Josh once told me, "to a lady who likes herself a *big* man." As it happened, there were a lot of little Thai ladies who *did* like themselves a big man, and Josh was never lonely. He was one of the happiest men I've ever met. It was Josh's conceit that he could order a meal better than any other *farang* in the kingdom.

I first met Josh when I was on vacation just out of college and backpacking through Malaysia and Indonesia, long before Rachel and I moved to Thailand. Josh and I were staying at the same hotel in Penang. He was on a visa run, down from Bangkok. Within about five minutes of spotting me in the hotel bar, Josh had sat himself down next to me and, in admirably direct fashion, informed me of his plans to start a pornographic production company in Vietnam. He had the funding, he said, contacts in the government, and an *unbelievable* star. These plans, like so many Josh O'Connor plans, eventually came to nothing, but his account was sufficiently compelling that whenever I'm in Bangkok, I always give him a call.

Now I was down from Chiang Mai, writing an article for a Singaporean arts magazine about an up-and-coming Thai sculptor, and Josh and I agreed to meet just after sundown in front of the Ratchawat market. I spent a long, sultry afternoon teasing a few good quotations out of my sculptor; then, just as the streetlights across Bangkok were flickering on, a motorcycle taxi deposited me in front of the 7-Eleven opposite the market, where Josh was already waiting for me, a goofy smile on his chubby face.

Plastic tables packed the narrow sidewalk. The sting of frying chili peppers made my eyes water, and from the market, now closing for the day, the sweet smells of jasmine, lilies, incense, and lemongrass mingled with the smells of rotting fish, molding durian, sweat, car exhaust, and garbage. On the corner, two competing noodle men served up bowls of *guoy tieo* in a ginger-and-coriander sauce; a little farther down the road, the curry lady had set up shop with huge vats of green curry and red, a jungle curry, a *panang* curry, and a spicy fish soup. A pretty girl cut up fresh mangoes and served them over sticky rice in a coconut sauce.

There was somebody who grilled skewers of chicken over a small open flame and which he served with a peanut sauce.

But we were there for the fish family. All of the other vendors were ordinary, Josh said, nothing special, run-of-the-mill, the kind of stuff you'd find outside the market of any two-bit town from Isaan to the Malay border. But the fish lady and family, *boy howdy*, they were something else. "The prime minister's nephew told me about this place," Josh said, gesturing at the fish stall. Rows of silvery fish sprawled on a bed of ice, black-eyed, rainbow-gilled, and healthy-looking, as if they had just swum up minutes ago and were only resting; and below them massed ranks of clams, mussels, oysters, and ominous black anemones. "It's better than the Oriental Hotel."

We sat down, and Josh ordered for us. Twice our waiter walked away from the table, and twice Josh called him back to order still *more* food. Josh was at ease in his domain, leaning back in his chair like a pasha. It was August, the trailing end of the rainy season, when everything oozes. Josh pulled a piece of toilet paper from the roll on the table and gently blotted his face and hands, then opened his satchel and pulled out a half-empty bottle of Johnny Walker Black.

Josh was a natural raconteur, but he wasn't much for the old give-and-take of normal conversation: he asked after my day and listened to my reply with a distracted air, nodding occasionally, until he could be patient no longer. "That's just great," he interrupted. He took another slurp from his drink. "You know, I'm glad you're in town. I need someone who really knows the up-country."

This was Josh's subtle way of forming a segue from conversation to monologue: in all his years in Thailand, Josh had come to know the north far better than I did. There was hardly a corner of the kingdom that Josh didn't know, where he wouldn't be greeted by the abbot of the Buddhist temple—or by the madam of the best bordello—with a huge smile.

I waited to hear what Josh had to say. He paused for a second, as if gathering his strength. He leaned his heavy forearms on the plastic table. He pouted his heavy lips and flared his nostrils. He strained his round neck from side to side. Then he *launched* his story. There is no other way to describe it: a Josh O'Connor story is like a giant cruise ship leaving port, and when you make a dinner date with Josh O'Connor, you know in advance that you are going to set sail. It's part of the deal. It's a design feature, not a bug.

"Do you remember Wim DeKlerk?" Josh began.

He didn't wait for me to reply. In any case, I did remember Wim: he was a functionary at the Dutch embassy, and a drinking buddy of Josh's. The last time I was in Bangkok, I took Josh and Wim home from Royal City Avenue in a taxi, both of them singing Steely Dan songs at the top of their lungs. They were celebrating a stock tip that Josh had passed on to Wim from the prime minister's nephew. Apparently, Wim had made a killing.

"Well, about a year ago, I got a call from Wim. Some lady in Holland had called *him*, asking if he knew anybody who would go and visit her niece up at Chiang Mai Central Prison. This woman—the niece, not the lady in Holland, the niece is named Martiya, her aunt is Elena, both of them are van der Leun, are you following all this?—her uncle had just died, and the niece, Martiya, has inherited some money. Wim tells me the aunt wants somebody to go up there and take care of the details, you know, look this Martiya in the eye, explain what happened, make sure she understands everything. The aunt is about a zillion years old, doesn't want to travel, the niece won't reply to her letters, so she wants somebody to take care of this in person. Wim asks if I want to do it."

The story didn't surprise me: I remembered Wim telling me about his job at the embassy. Every day, he had told me, a worried parent called him from Amsterdam looking for a detective to help track down a child lost in the island rave culture; or a textile importer from Utrecht would call, asking him to recommend a crackerjack accountant to go over a potential business partner's books. Offering advice to Dutch people on how to get things done in Thailand was his specialty. Once, he told me, he had even helped a circus in Maastricht get an export permit for an elephant.

"Of course I said yes," Josh said.

That's why I always call Josh when I'm in Bangkok. Things like this *really* happen to him.

"So I give this woman in Holland a buzz before I go up to Chiang Mai," Josh continued. "She doesn't know anything. Last time she saw her niece, the niece was a little girl. Hadn't spoken to her in years. She hadn't gotten a letter from her in over ten years, not since she went to prison. In any case, she was from a distant branch of the van der Leun family. The niece grew up in California, had been there since she was little and was now an American. Before she went to jail, she lived in a village out near the Burmese border. You know that area? Southeast of Mae Hong Son?"

"Not really," I said.

"*Nobody* lives out there but the tigers. What was she doing out there? The aunt in Holland, she doesn't know. I figure she's one of those kids, got caught up in drug smuggling. 'How long was she up there?' I ask. Turns out the niece's been in Thailand since forever. Maybe since the seventies. And she's no kid, the woman's over fifty years old. *Strange*, I think. 'When's your niece getting out of prison?' I ask. Long pause on the phone. 'Fifty years,' the aunt says. 'So what's your niece doing in prison?' Long pause on the phone. Like she doesn't want to tell me. 'She is a murderer,' the woman finally says, in a thick Dutch accent. What do you say to that? I said, 'Who'd she kill?' Long pause on the phone. She doesn't know. That's all this Elena van der Leun can tell me. She wants me to go and tell her niece that her uncle is dead."

Josh paused as the waiter arrived at our table with a steaming cauldron of *tam yam guum*. The young waiter lit a paraffin candle under the tureen, and Josh served me and then himself. The soup was, as Josh had promised, delicious, delicately flavored with lime, cilantro, ginger, and lemongrass; the shrimp, which that very morning had been frolicking in the Gulf of Thailand, were huge and tender, with an explosive touch of sea salt. Josh ate the very hot soup with vigorous splashing movements of his spoon, and only when he had finished his first bowl and was reaching to refill it did he pick up the story again.

Several weeks after his talk with Elena van der Leun, Josh found himself in the waiting room of Chiang Mai Central Prison. Josh told me that he had been in Chiang Mai for three or four days, enjoying the luxury of his expense account, before he finally steeled himself to the task at hand: Josh was a generous man, but he did not like to be presented too directly with the misery of others, a squeamishness which made him regret having accepted Wim's offer. He had dreaded the visit, and day after day had done no more than note the location of the prison on the map, then distract himself from his unpleasant chore with a stiff drink, then another, after which the days dissolved into a blur. The morning of his prison visit, realizing that he could put off his errand no longer, he had awakened early and dressed himself neatly. He wore linen slacks and a white shirt, which when he left the hotel was crisply pressed but by the time he arrived at the prison was damp with sweat. A low sky like wet cement hid the hills which ring Chiang Mai.

"Oh man, I did not want to be there," Josh said. "I got out of that tuk-tuk, told the driver to wait for me, and it was like they were going to lock me up inside, that's what I felt like. Like I was never going to get out of there. *Bang!* The first gate closes behind me. *Bang!* The second gate closes behind me. *Bang!* That's the third gate."

Josh thumped hard on the table with every *bang*, and the other diners turned their heads.

"You ever been in a Thai jail?" Josh asked.

"No."

"The one here in Bangkok, it's a real shithole," Josh said knowingly. "Not a nice place. But this one in Chiang Mai, it wasn't bad. It wasn't what I expected."

Indeed, he said, the room in which the guards installed Josh could have been the waiting room for any provincial government ministry. Only the bars on the windows and the guard behind the heavy wooden desk betrayed the purpose of the place; that and a pervasive smell of urine and vomit. A large portrait of the king in full military regalia hung next to a clock whose loud ticks echoed through the room with impossible slowness. There were a half-dozen round metal tables, and at each table four plastic stools. Josh settled his tremendous bulk onto a stool much too small for a man of his size.

"I was the only *farang* in the room," Josh said. "There were just a couple of other people. A few hill-tribers, I don't know, maybe they were Hmong, or Dyalo, I can never remember all the costumes. They had that scared look people down from the hills always have. I remember one of them asked me if I had a cigarette, so I gave him one. There was some guy with tattoos up and down his arms, Buddhist sutras—you know, the way the gangsters have. Scary-looking dude. And some women, Thai women, chatting with each other, but looking around like they didn't want to be there. I guess *nobody* wants to be there."

Josh sat in the waiting room, which if not as horrible as he had imagined was certainly not cheerful, and reflected on the woman he was to meet. How was he to inform this stranger that her uncle was dead? Was this her last link to the world of the living? Josh wondered: What had brought Martiya van der Leun to this pass? A quick Internet search had revealed nothing about Martiya, and again, Josh thought it strange that *anyone* could have disappeared so thoroughly; even Josh, hidden as he was in Bangkok, turned up on the Internet if you Googled him, associated with articles he had written, photos he had taken, and the results of a couple of races he had run with the Hash House Harriers in much leaner days.

In the dossier of papers which Elena van der Leun had sent Josh, there was a photograph of Martiya as a young woman. While he sat in the waiting room, Josh pulled the picture out of the dossier and looked it over. The photograph, the only one that Elena could provide, was almost a quarter century old. It showed a slender, small-breasted young woman holding a long knife and leaning over a birthday cake. She was of indeterminate ethnic origin: her cheekbones were high and Asian, but her long black hair was curly and fell over her shoulders and neck. She was not looking straight at the camera, but it was nevertheless possible to see that she had keen, mischievous eyes, light blue and enormously round. Her lips were full and red, and her skin china-pale. It was not a beautiful face, Josh said, but expressive, intelligent, and curious.

"Do you still have the photo?" I interrupted.

"I sent it back to the family," he said. He refilled my drink, and his own.

With thoughts of the woman he was to meet, Josh occupied a half hour until the prisoners were allowed to enter. Then the iron doors of the antechamber swung open, and one by one the women who had been waiting on the other side wandered into the room, where they paired themselves with their guests. In other Thai prisons, Josh knew, the prisoners would have been made to enter the room on their knees as a sign of humility, but not here. The first woman to walk into the room was no older than a girl, a delicate-featured girl who might have been pretty but for the bruises. Wearing light-blue cotton prison pajamas, she spotted the man with the tattoos and raised her hands to him in the traditional Thai bow and nodded slightly. Because he did not rise from his stool, as she approached his table she was forced to bend over to keep her head below his, as good manners demanded. Without a smile or a hint of tenderness, she sat beside him and the two began to talk. Then two women came out hand in hand. They regarded the waiting room with wary eyes. Josh heard a burst of speech in some alien language from the tribeswomen behind him, and the two prisoners replied in the same strange tongue. The visitors and the hosts embraced unabashedly and settled themselves on the plastic stools, sitting cross-legged. They spoke to one another in low, urgent voices.

"She was the last one to come into the room," Josh said. "I knew her from the photo—but she looked bad. I think she must have been in her middle fifties—she was my mom's age. But this was an old woman."

Many years in the northern Thai sun had destroyed that delicate skin which Josh had admired in the picture. The dark hair had turned gray, and the once-sensual lips were cracked and thin. Yet the woman who approached Josh still had the faraway air of a handsome woman. She was not dressed in prison pajamas, like the others, but in a hand-woven tunic in the tribal style. She had white string tied tightly around each of her wrists; this was her only ornamentation. Martiya carried herself straight-backed and head-high. Josh had not expected such a small woman.

Seeing Josh, and realizing quickly that he was the anonymous stranger who had summoned her from her cell, Martiya came over and sat down, not waiting for an invitation. Had he doubted the woman's identity, her eyes would have resolved all doubts: How many women in a prison in northern Thailand could have had such striking blue eyes? She glowered at Josh, and Josh for once was at a loss for words under her intense stare.

"Ms. van der Leun . . ." he finally said.

The woman interrupted him straightaway. She spoke very slowly. "*Christ*, can't you people just leave me alone?"

Josh had prepared for this interview carefully, but this was not a re-action he had anticipated. He said, "Ms. van der Leun, I think you might have made a mistake."

Again, Martiya interrupted him. "I'm *not* the one who might have made the mistake here, buddy. You people are driving me nuts." She looked at Josh with open contempt. She took in his large body, his damp shirt, his uncombed hair. "My God, you are disgusting," she said.

Josh looked at me. "I had figured she might have gone a little, you know, cuckoo, from her time in prison, or maybe she'd beg and plead with me to take her home. I'd already decided how to handle that. I was going to be gentle but firm, and give her the name of a friend of mine who's a lawyer. But the way this woman was staring at me, I was pretty glad there was a table between us."

To Martiya, he said, "I'm sorry, but just who do you think I am?"

"*They* sent you, didn't they?"

"They?"

"You're not a missionary?"

Josh was not without a certain sense of irony, and suddenly the ten-sion of the visit, the heat of the day, and now this furious but intensely proud little woman all seemed to him absurd. He began to laugh. He couldn't help himself, he told me.

"Oh no," Josh said. "You got it all wrong, sister. I'm here to give you money."

He said this with such enthusiasm that Martiya smiled back, despite herself. She ran a hand through her gray hair. The fight left her. In a mildly embarrassed voice, she explained to Josh the source of her confu-sion. One of the evangelical societies working in the north of Thailand had conceived the project of converting the prisoners to Christianity. Who needed the Lord's blessing more? Twice a year, every year for the last ten years, she had been summoned to the visiting room, only to find the same bearded, middle-aged man—"the same bozo," she said—informing her that the Lord had forgiven her for her crimes and sins, if only she would accept Him. She had asked the missionaries to leave her alone, she said, but they were relentless. "I thought you were one of *them*."

Josh shook his head. "No," he said.

He had decided beforehand to be direct. He told her that her aunt, Elena van der Leun, had hired him, and that her uncle had died. Martiya had inherited some money, Josh said, and he was there to arrange the details of the bequest.

Martiya was silent for a minute. She looked around the room. "I haven't seen Uncle Otto since I was nine years old," she said. "He knew how to ride a horse. He was a wonderful horseman. He promised he'd buy me a horse when I was twelve. I guess he just did."

Martiya sat quietly for a long while. She picked idly at the string tied around her right wrist. Then she spoke. The vast bulk of the money— not much by occidental standards, a small fortune in a Thai prison—was to be given to a charity which aided the hill tribes, the rest deposited in her prison bank account. Then, with all the authority of a corporate executive late for a tee time, rather than a prisoner condemned to life, Martiya rose from her seat and extended her hand. The appointment was over.

Josh had one last thought. "Would you like me to call your lawyer?" he asked. "Money can change a lot of things here. Maybe he can . . ."

Martiya smiled at Josh. "I can't leave now. I'm only beginning to understand how it *really* works around here. And where would I go?"

She thanked Josh for his time and walked back through the metal door into the dark prison hallway.

"It's a true story," Josh said. "It happened just like that."

By now, the sidewalk where we were eating was full. All of the tables had been taken, families eating together. A tuk-tuk painted with a picture of an elephant passed on the street, then another with a picture of a blue-skinned Hindu god. A pineapple vendor strolled by absentmindedly, leaving behind him a dark trail of melting ice, the bell on his little cart ringing out a cheerful tune. A few old ladies sat on the stoop, chewing betel and spitting black on the sidewalk, and inside one of the Chinese shop-houses, I could see a half dozen young men in tank tops working late, stripping down motorcycle engines.

The prime minister's nephew had been right: the meal was spectacular. Josh had ordered thin delicate noodles for us, which came to the table draped in a sweet peanut sauce, and a steaming yellow crab curry with saffron. We had clams stir-fried with the tiny roasted chilies the Thais call "rat-shit peppers." We ate until we thought we would burst. Then an enormous whole fish arrived at the table, bathed in a caramelized orange sauce. I groaned, but when Josh flaked the fish off the bone with a surprisingly dexterous motion of his plump wrist and feathered it onto my plate, I ate the fish too. "Here, you've got to have the cheek, it's the best part," Josh said.

I wanted to know why Josh had told me this story, but he was incapable of conversing and eating at the same time. Only when he had scraped the last grain of rice off of his plate, sighed contentedly, and refilled his glass did his attention return to the interrupted narrative.

His work at the prison completed, Josh returned to Bangkok by the night train. He wrote the family in Holland, and made the appropriate arrangements for the dispersal of the inheritance according to Martiya's wishes. He had done his job.

"But I couldn't stop thinking about her," Josh said. "So I did some looking around. I went to the library and looked through back issues of the *Bangkok Times*. I couldn't find anything. I thought about her all the time."

Josh told me that Martiya remained on his mind for almost a month after his visit to Chiang Mai. Then slowly, his visit to Chiang Mai Central Prison was assimilated into his stock of drinking stories. He regularly won a healthy round of laughter as he recounted her saying, "My God, you are disgusting." I had laughed at that point in his recital also. It was hard to imagine that anyone could confuse Josh with a missionary. That he knew so little of this wry old murderess only added to the drama of the tale.

Then Martiya came back into his life.

Almost a year after his visit to the Chiang Mai prison, Josh received another call from Wim at the Dutch embassy. Now the story was approaching the present time: this was only several weeks before our dinner. A package had arrived for him at the embassy; the return address, in neat Thai lettering, M. VAN DER LEUN, C/O CHIANG MAI CENTRAL PRISON, etc. Josh asked Wim to send it over. He supposed it was something to do with the inheritance. But when the envelope arrived, it was larger than Josh had expected. He opened the package cautiously and found two small manuscripts, each about fifty handwritten pages, densely covered on both sides of the page. The manuscripts had been bound with white twine. The first one was entitled "Notes Toward a Political Anthropology of Prison Life in Northern Thailand"; the second, "The Economic Organization of a Thai Women's Prison."

There was also a cover letter. Josh fished around in his bag, brought out an envelope, extracted a folded piece of paper, and handed it to me. I unfolded it.

*Chiang Mai Central Prison*
*Chiang Mai*

*Dear Mr. O'Connor:*

*I have never properly thanked you for your visit, or apologized for my anger. Please accept my gratitude now, and my apologies.*

*Paper! Pens! Stamps! What is a would-be scholar's life without them? Your assistance has made it possible for me to complete my research. I have been penniless for such a long time, and I can not tell you the frustration I suffered not being able to complete the attached manuscripts, for lack of these basic necessities. Now I must call on you one more time. I would like to see both of the attached manuscripts published. They must, of course, be properly typed, which is impossible for me in my present circumstances, as you can imagine. The "Notes," etc., are intended for the Southeast Asian Journal of Social Science; the paper entitled "Economic Organization," etc., I'd like to see sent to Ethnology. It will be necessary to explain the conditions under which the papers have been written as they both lack a scholarly apparatus. If the papers are accepted, please keep whatever modest fees may result as a token of my appreciation.*

*I thank you, in advance, for your time: I have no one else at all to
whom I might entrust these documents. It is a melancholy thought.*


*Yours most sincerely,*
*Martiya van der Leun*


I read the letter, and then I read it again. Bangkok, the noisy street, the
market stench, the passing cars—all these faded away for a moment. I
looked at the signature on the letter. It was a messy, almost violent
scrawl, the only unclear words on the page. Otherwise her handwriting
was a series of fluid, graceful loops.

"That's really something," I said.

"Isn't it?" Josh agreed.

"What were the manuscripts like?"

"That's the thing. They were terrific. I opened up the envelope and I
spent the whole evening reading them. When I was in college, there was
this girl, she was an anthropology major, you know? and anyhow, I ended
up taking a couple of anthropology classes—just Anthro 101, and then a
seminar on the Hindus of the Himalayas—but the point is, even I could
see right away that this woman—Martiya, not the girl in college—
Martiya was a serious anthropologist. I mean, I don't know if she was a
professional, but I thought what she wrote was excellent."

"So tell me already, who *is* this woman?" I asked. I was still waiting
for the punch line to the story.

"That's the thing," Josh said. "That's just it. The next morning, I
decided to find out more. I was just curious, I'd been curious all year. I
called up the prison, and I figured either I would talk to one of the prison
administrators or I'd go back up to Chiang Mai and see her again. But
when I got the warden on the phone, he hemmed and hawed for a minute
and then he told me that Martiya was dead."

"She was *dead?*" I still had the letter in my hand, and I looked down
at it. The ink was light blue and sharp against the page.

"Yeah, that's the thing. The warden told me that she was dead. She
killed herself. She ate a ball of opium and killed herself."

"Wow," I said.

Josh nodded. His face was creased in a gesture of unexpected dignity.

Josh looked at me over his glass of whiskey. He thought that there was a good story here, he said, something for somebody who lived in the North. He didn't have the time to pursue it himself, but he knew that I did. He was offering me the story as a gift. "Maybe you can write it up for the *Times*."

"Maybe you're right." I had one more question for Josh. "What did you do with the manuscripts?"

"I did just what she asked. I sent them off a week ago."

Josh had nothing more to tell me about Martiya van der Leun, and I had no more questions. He didn't say it, but I think that he had been troubled by the news of Martiya's death. Martiya's letter remained on the table between us, and from time to time I glanced at it.

A little later, the bill arrived at our table. Josh offered to pay, but looked very relieved when I insisted.

# TWO

# THE PENDULUM-EDGE
## OF THE SOUL

WHEN JOSH FIRST TOLD ME about Martiya van der Leun, Rachel and I had been living in Thailand for almost exactly a year. The two of us came to Thailand not long after the Internet start-up in San Francisco where I had been working went out of business; Rachel had just graduated from college. We were bored and heading fast toward broke, when Rachel found an article on the Internet about how to find a job teaching in international schools around the world. The chief requirements for such posts apparently were a native command of English and a healthy pulse. "I've got that," Rachel said, and like a migrating swallow, her résumé flew to the farthest corners of the globe: to an oddly luxurious all-boys boarding school in Uganda, which asked that all the teachers make a personal commitment to Christ ("I'm willing," Rachel said. "Did you *see* the pool?"); to a delightful all-girls school in Switzerland; to Tajikistan, where, the school's Web site said, the security situation had stabilized dramatically in recent months; and to Thailand. A week later, the headmaster of the Water Lily International School in Chiang Mai called at three in the morning to offer Rachel a position as a first-grade teacher; she accepted immediately and announced that we were moving to Asia. I bought a copy of *Thai Made Simple* and began to study. Three months later we were in Chiang Mai, Thailand's second city, way up in the wild North.

We arrived in Chiang Mai strongly under the influence of the English travel writer Norman Lewis, whose elegant memoirs we had read before leaving California. Chiang Mai, Lewis wrote, was the "most delectable of Oriental towns," which "remained beneath a thin veneer of development Thailand's most pleasing city."

> The roofs of old Chiengmai, curling at the eaves, lay upon the city like autumn leaves, and from these arose the spires of many temples, spreading the faintest of haloes into the misted sky.

When I read this to Rachel, she said, "Wow," and then said, "Go on." I did:

> There could have been no more poetic scene than the line-up soon after dawn of the archers with their crossbows, members of a clan enjoying the privilege of shooting at the stationary outlines of fish in the intensely green waters. All these men in their ancient garb presented roughly identical features to the rising sun as they muttered a prayer at the instant of releasing an arrow.

*No more poetic scene*, my bony pink ass: all that lay upon the city when *we* arrived was a thick layer of smog; the "intensely green waters" of the river Ping were the color of chocolate milk; and when I asked after the archer caste, I was informed that such a social class did not exist, and even if it did, the polluted waterway which bisected the city nowadays supported no life whatsoever. Old Chiang Mai in the years since Lewis's visit had been encased in concentric rings of concrete, Chinese-style shop-houses whose roofs did not curl at the eaves. In the antique town center, a large number of automotive dealerships showcased a splendid variety of Japanese motorcycles, pickup trucks, and tires.

We were looking for a gabled teak house of the sort that Lewis so admired, but our real estate agent, a nervous little woman recommended by one of Rachel's colleagues at the school, refused to show us such houses. I suppose it was as if a wealthy but naïve Japanese tourist had arrived in New York and tried to rent an apartment in one of the exotic housing projects of the South Bronx. Such accommodations, she insisted, would be entirely unsuitable. A teak house would not have air-conditioning, and we would sweat. There would be big, big bugs and things that crawled and crept. What we needed, our agent insisted, was a modern *concrete* house, and it was in a modern concrete house in a suburb of modern concrete houses that we were eventually installed. Only the many temples matched the grandeur of Lewis's description, and from certain vantage points when the smog receded under the force of the late-monsoon winds, we conceded grudgingly that if we squinted we could see in the sky fuzzy rings like cigarette smoke which might be called haloes. These rings, we later learned, were produced by the burning of garbage.

Our disgruntlement with Chiang Mai persisted intensely for a month or so, until we installed a badminton court on our crabgrass lawn. From a local sporting goods dealer we bought a net, a pair of rackets, and a shuttlecock. To a warped and decaying mango tree we tied one end of the net, and the other end of the net we proposed to affix to a bamboo stake. But we were unable to cut the bamboo properly and were on the verging of retiring back to the house in failure when a very short, round-faced woman with enormous ears wearing a sarong and carrying a machete as long as her arm came running up to us. She was screeching violently. I wondered for a second if we were not perhaps interfering with a sacred bamboo grove. The creature was precisely the size and shape and almost the color of Yoda, an impression intensified by her village dialect of Thai, which seemed curiously to invert what *Thai Made Simple* had said was standard Thai word order. "Baiyom am I!" she howled. "Cut you I will!" In lunatic miscomprehension, Rachel and I reared back. But our fears were misplaced, as with a flashing whack of her rusting machete the Baiyom thing hacked into shape just the bamboo pole we needed. We had made our first friend.

In the Thai culture, we learned, hacking down a bamboo pole together is tantamount to a dinner invitation, as that evening to our surprise Baiyom arrived at the door of our house leading a delegation of neighbors. They came not from the other large concrete houses but from the simple one-room shacks beside the main road. On a low tray of woven bamboo Baiyom carried a bowl of cold cucumber soup, a spongy chili omelette, and a low mound of rice. The troupe settled themselves on the floor of the empty living room of our new home and admired the elegance of the concrete walls and plastic parquet flooring. One wall of the living room had been covered by the house's owner with floor-to-ceiling wallpaper depicting some alpine setting—cows, pines, snowy peaks. The scene elicited a low buzz of excited wonder from our new neighbors. They also inspected our bedroom and our bathroom, the guest bedroom and the kitchen, opened up all the closets, and tested the cooling properties of the refrigerator by touching the metal grilles. The group stayed until the early hours of the morning, singing folk songs, applauding loudly when we managed to lisp the simple three-word chorus, and asking repeatedly how much we paid in rent.

Everything the guidebooks had told us of Thai manners and gentility, Baiyom that evening proved wrong: the guidebooks had told us that one never demonstrates the soles of the feet in Thailand, but Baiyom stretched herself out full length on our parquet floor, her broad-bottomed calloused feet on open display. The fey and delicate Thai nature? Baiyom at the end of the meal let out a series of long belches, her little lips distended. "A good home this is," Baiyom declared. "Happy you are. Good fun we are making." The next evening, the group came again, and then the next; the heavy fog of our discontent lifted. To be persistently grumpy around these people just seemed churlish.

Rachel's school proved also, if not a disappointment, then a surprise: it was one of those odd institutions which sprout up so often in Thailand—places in every detail familiar from a Western analogue, but somehow unsettlingly *wrong*. About a third of the students were Thai, the sluggish scions of very wealthy families determined to give their children a Western education; these kids tended to arrive at around eleven, their homework carefully prepared by their Anglophone servants. Most of these kids had flunked out of Chiang Mai's other, *better*, international school. Another third were the children of employees of the American consulate, and the rest the offspring of elderly occidental retirees and their obscenely young Thai wives. Parents' Day at the school always had a strange vibe, as the blissed-out old-timers and the mustachioed DEA agents working the Golden Triangle exchanged soothing remarks on how well the kids were doing in the new environment this year, while the Thai parents congregated in the corners of the gymnasium and looked snooty.

But if the kids and their parents were a weird bunch, the faculty was a whole lot weirder, a haphazard collection of perhaps eighteen expatriates, all of them in Chiang Mai for no apparent reason other than that they had just run out of space. There was an Australian gym teacher who insinuated slyly that his days down under were *well and good done, mate*; and the American from Vermont with a shaggy red beard who came to Thailand after it was discovered that his doctorate in sociology had been the product of plagiarism. He taught the kindergarten by means of a formal lecture, as if in memory of lost glory. He sat his class down, and explained briskly the history of the alphabet since the days of the Phoenicians. The kids sat in patient rows with big eyes, and understood nothing at all, until someone started to fidget and someone else started to cry. Mr. Robert from Missouri composed poetry in Thai, and was considering becoming a Buddhist monk; failing that, he said, he would devote himself in his old age to the Four Idyllic Occupations—reading, farming, fishing, and the gathering of firewood. There was an English teacher from Massachusetts who, if given half an opportunity, would discuss in extraordinary detail the inheritance he was expecting. He had already calculated the estate tax. He loathed the heat in Thailand and heavily spiced foods. I asked him once why he stayed. "I would go home, if *only* Mother would buy me a ticket," he said, with an air of Oriental fortitude. The Water Lily School was the kind of place where the stories all started "I was just coming for a year, to do something different, and I'm still here!" There is something about the life as a foreigner in Thailand that draws those who find themselves unwilling or unable to think about their 401(k)s; and in the leisure, freedom, and isolation that the Far East provides, these types swing inexorably toward the pendulum-edges of their souls.

But who am I to criticize? I was supporting myself, a little like Josh but with perhaps a touch less brio, by all manner of odd jobs: a Thai mogul paid me—don't even ask how this came about—to write summaries of American business books. This was the year that I learned how to motivate my employees and keep my supply chains supple and fluid, like jungle creepers. From time to time, I wrote features about colorful Chiang Mai characters for an English-language Bangkok newspaper, which, thinking that its audiences might prefer an authentic voice of

Asia, published me under the nom de plume Somchai Wannapongsi; and *Executive*, a men's lifestyle magazine, hired me as their critic: I was the car critic, although I did not even have a driver's license; I was the music critic, although I cannot carry a tune; and I was the men's bespoke suit critic, although I am a—but perhaps enough said.

Our life was easy, calm, and cheap; we stayed the year in Chiang Mai, and I convinced Rachel to stay another. A new class of first-graders sat in the very small plastic desks and learned all about telling time. I wrote about the substantial advantages of double breasting and single piping. We got by.

Then Josh told me about Martiya van der Leun and my soul, too, began to swing.

Such is the power of a good story.

My hotel in Bangkok was quiet owing to the celebration of the Queen's Birthday. A mimeographed note had been slipped under my door: "On Thursday Aug 12, Her Majesty Queen Sirikit is highly adored by all Thai citizens who splendidly celebrate her Birthday each year." As a result, the notice continued, not all of the hotel's normal services would be available: room service was closed; the hotel astrologer, normally on hand between two and five in the afternoon, would not be offering readings; and the Tivoli Café would not lay out the usual breakfast buffet of waffles and congee. Although the notice did not mention it, the operator who handled outgoing long-distance calls was also unavailable. This was a cause of some frustration to me, as I had decided when I left Josh to call Elena van der Leun, Martiya's aunt in Holland, that very evening and follow up on his story. *Executive* ran a true-crime piece almost every month, and I thought that if I could figure out who Martiya had killed, I could pitch the story while still in Bangkok. But every time I picked up the rotary phone that connected me with the old-fashioned hotel switchboard, the line rang endlessly, and I imagined the telephone operator slipping off hand in hand with the astrologer to lay a wreath of orchids at one of Bangkok's numerous royal shrines. I spent the evening in the hotel bar, watching an Elvis look-alike competition held in the queen's honor.

The next morning, I got Martiya's aunt on the phone. It was the first of several conversations. Elena van der Leun spoke to me warily at first, her very excellent English cloaked in a sharp Dutch accent. She had a throaty old voice, cured by a lifetime of cigarettes, so that everything she said sounded a little like two pieces of sandpaper being rubbed together. She had plenty of time to linger by the phone and chat. There was only one ground rule for our conversations: Elena van der Leun told me that she did not know the details of her niece's crime, and she did not wish to speculate. This, of course, was what I most wanted to know. But, the crucial point aside, she was eager to talk.

So much in Martiya's dramatic life, Elena insisted, could be explained by the simple fact that her parents were not happy together. "A child needs the happy family," Elena declared. "It is the base." But Martiya's base was unstable: her mother and father met and married impetuously before the war, passed difficult wars apart, and after the war were unable to recapture the intensity of emotion that had brought them together. When Martiya was born, in 1947, in a small village in the central highlands of Celebes, a large island in the Indonesian archipelago now called Sulawesi, both parents looked to the child to reinvigorate a dying marriage. The rainy season in central Sulawesi can last as long as six months, and all winter long the family was trapped together in a cottage on the edge of a great ebony forest. The family paid local villagers to haul their water and cut their cassava and taro. They bought rice at the market. Areta van der Leun read novels. Piers van der Leun kept busy with his tape recordings and verb charts and lexicons. Areta van der Leun paced the corners of the house wearing an old lava-lava. Martiya's base teetered and then toppled.

The Dutch are widely known for their linguistic gifts, but Piers van der Leun was extraordinary even by Dutch standards. Piers spent a summer in Sweden as a young child, Elena recalled, and came back speaking perfect Swedish. "My brother could look at the map of Kenya and speak Swahili," Elena said. He was educated as a linguist at the University of Leiden, and then, like many young Dutch men of his generation, joined the colonial administration in Indonesia. The colonial government in Jakarta took care to survey and record all of the minor languages of their vast holdings, on the sound principle that even the smallest ethnic rivalry can easily flare up into a matter of sufficient gravity to involve the local government: on joining the colonial service, Piers, at his own request, was given the task of mastering the half dozen tribal languages known collectively as the Uma, spoken in the southern portion of Kulawi District of the island of Sulawesi, not far from the mighty Lariang River.

The languages were fiendishly difficult, and mastering them required all of Piers's gifts: they were beautiful subtle things, which he pieced together preposition by preposition, verb by verb. In the hut which the colonial administrator provided him, he kept enormous tables of nouns, pronouns, and a provisional grammar. He invented an alphabet, and in a shorthand of his own devising transcribed hours of their speech. The loneliness of the jungle suited him: he sent back to Holland rhapsodic letters describing the exoticism of the native customs, and the ecstasy of their shamanic visions. When the old newspapers from Amsterdam finally arrived by post and Piers read accounts of Europe tottering on the brink of another war, he thought of his gentle tribesmen and the beautiful languages in which they conducted endless philosophical debates, and he would smoke his pipe and write a long letter to his sister. In one letter, he wrote, "I am where I want to be. How many men can say that?"

Elena van der Leun later sent me photographs of Piers taken when he was in his early thirties, some time before he met Areta, well before the war. Piers is standing in what I took to be the jungle, a tall man stooped beside a tree dripping with vines. He has a pipe in his mouth, and a wisp of smoke is visible beside his ear. He has a handsome, round face. His eyes are gentle but weak. If this description is vague, so was the face: it is the face of a smiling man with a calm and easy interior life, a man who cannot even *imagine* a woman who simply will not stop crying. Not long after the picture was taken, Piers van der Leun's uncomplicated life as a bachelor scholar came to an end. Even in the most remote corner of Kulawi District, one cannot escape the world.

In the fall of 1938, Piers was invited to a general colloquium on the Australasian languages at the University of Jakarta. The field of ethnolinguistics was in its infancy, and every man at the conference table felt himself a pioneer. Piers presented a paper on the language of the Tobaku villagers, and argued that similarities between the language of the To-baku and the language of the Pipikoro implied a common ancestral tongue. His work was received enthusiastically, and after the presentation he found himself in long conversation with a Malaysian linguist, one of the few Asians at the conference, who was fascinated by Piers's methodology. Eleven months later, Piers married the Malaysian linguist's eldest daughter.

"I only met her after the war, and of course she looked so tired," recalled Elena van der Leun. "Her hair was gray already and she was too thin. But she must have been a lovely little thing before the war. It was possible to see that, even after what she had gone through. Piers wrote me letters about her and I could imagine the silk black hair and the delicate features and the white skin—Martiya had her mother's skin. She had very large round eyes, particularly for an Oriental. I think somewhere in her past there must have been white blood, since Martiya has blue eyes.

"Piers wrote me long letters about Areta—I don't have them anymore, but I remember. He was just mad for her. He had been invited up to Sabah State by her father, where he met her, and then they wrote each other every day. It was not something one did very often in those days, marry a native woman, but Piers, he did not care. She was a student of English literature—Malaysia was an English colony at the time, you know, not one of ours—and the two of them spoke always in English. He told me that she just chattered away about any old thing. He said he was falling in love with a singing bird. It was the only time in his life that I heard Piers say something so romantic."

There was a strange hiss on the telephone line and Elena said, "Do you hear me?" and I said, "Yes," and Elena went on. "I think he must have been quite exciting for her too. Piers in those days was tall and quite adventurous, and for a girl who had spent her entire life in Penang reading *novels*, the idea of living in the jungle with tribesmen must have been very exciting. The two of them were married and spent almost a year together. I think it was for Piers a very happy time. That's why they spent so long in the jungle later, because they always—"

Elena paused and started to cough. I could hear another cigarette being lit. I admired her ability to smoke and cough at the same time.

"And the war came." Elena sighed. "We had such a hard war here in Holland, but it must have been worse there. Because of his languages Piers was assigned to some sort of unit doing I don't know what. He spent most of the war in a Japanese prison camp. He was very lucky to live. And Areta's family was almost entirely dead after the war. I don't know what she did to survive. She certainly never told me, I don't think she ever told Piers. After the war, they found each other and he took her back here to Utrecht. You need to let go of bad things, and I don't think she ever let go of her bad things. Don't you think you need to let go of bad things?"

"Yes, yes, I think so," I said. How could I say anything else? "You need to let go of bad things."

"*Of course you do.* In any case, we were very poor here after the war, there wasn't even always enough to eat, but we took them in. Piers couldn't work he was so thin and tired, and Areta didn't work. Piers would go off to the library in the morning, just to get away of the house, and when he'd come back Areta would be waiting for him near the door. She would not say a word, just wait for him—as if she couldn't bear to be out of his sight for a minute. Piers as a boy had a dog like that once, but I don't think he realized how his wife waited for him. But then, whatever he'd say, she'd start a fight, a terrible fight. I remember one time she made *rijsttafel* for him for lunch as a surprise. He came back from the library, as usual, and in those days he looked so pale even after just a morning out. She ran to him with her usual excitement at his arrival, she was frantic, and announced proudly that she had made lunch for him.

"Piers said something to her. I don't know what he said, but it didn't suit her. I think he had eaten at the university. Areta looked at my brother with those huge round eyes. The disappointment went far beyond lunch. She had made all morning cooking for another man, a man that she had once loved, and my poor brother had taken his body. She was furious with this man who had stolen her lover. And she had nothing else in all the world, absolutely nothing else. She took the plate of *rijsttafel* and let it drop on the ground. Not angry, the plate just fell from her arms as if she forgot how to carry it. What a mess. Then she went to her bedroom and closed the door. When Piers went out that afternoon, she came out of her room and started waiting for him again by the door.

"Piers, he had no idea what to do. He tried talking to her and then shouting at her. Had he been a different sort of man he might have hit her. It might have done her some good. But he wasn't *that* sort of man. I said to send her away, but he couldn't. Piers felt he had a responsibility toward Areta, but I don't think he loved her anymore, at least not the way he used to. He was too tired for that kind of love, we all were. She was too."

"Was Piers still affectionate with her?" I asked. "She must have been very lonely."

"*Of course* she was lonely . . ." Elena van der Leun's voice flashed with irritation, and I realized that I had just taken the wrong side in a half-century-old family quarrel. But after a second Elena spoke again. "Piers was not a man very skilled with a woman. It was clear to us, and it must have been clear to her, that he wasn't as passionate about her as he once was. Who would have been? Finally, Piers got well enough to think about work. The university awarded him a grant to return to Indonesia and continue his studies, and he accepted. Areta seemed happy about the move. She spoke about how excited she was to get back to the East. We were sad to see Piers go, but not sorry to say goodbye to the couple. Six months later, Martiya was born."

Not long ago, I spent five days on an old barge floating down the Mekong toward the ancient holy city of Luang Prabang, alone with a Lao crew, the only other passenger a Dutch electrical engineer named Dirk, another tourist. I spoke no Lao and would have been content with silence, but day after day I was forced to endure long lectures on the Dutch welfare state, and the superiority of Dutch electro-engineering, Dutch social policy, Dutch drug policy, Dutch foreign policy, and Dutch policing to their American counterparts. An immensely wide, open sky filled the night; the river rushed on to Vietnam and the South China Sea from mystical Tibetan headwaters; and life would have been strange and weird and wonderful, altogether thrilling, if only Dirk had stopped prattling on about the ease with which a competent Dutch engineer (such as himself) could hook up a generator and set running lights aboard the boat. Before Areta is entirely dismissed as lunatic, hysterical, or wicked, let it be said in her defense that the practical, kindly Dutch can be _unbearably_ irritating, as everyone who has had intercourse with them will testify. Irritation over time, more so even than cruelty, can mount to madness.

Poor Areta! Installed in that damp little hut in a Tobaku village on the edge of the ebony forest, did Piers lecture her on the temporal sequence of conditional clauses in Tole'e? Did he whistle tunelessly while he wrote in his lexicon of Pipikoro words, as the rain hemmed them in like prison bars? Did he suggest she take long walks and learn the native names of flowers? I tried to find somebody who could testify to what _she_ might have suffered over the next few years, trapped in a cabin on the edge of the wilderness with what everyone described as a _very nice_ Dutch man. But there was no one. Her father was murdered by the Japanese. A few relatives survived the war, but they didn't survive the turmoil of independence and the Communist purges. Perhaps there is someone else somewhere out there who personally remembers Areta van der Leun besides her sister-in-law Elena, but I could not find that last remaining witness.

Martiya van der Leun always told friends that she had a wonderful early childhood in the jungle village. Every woman was her mother, and every lap was open to her. Her stories are like all early childhood stories, disjointed, dreamlike. She had a dog named Pue', which means ghost. He was a black dog and very fluffy. Once, she stole a coconut from a little boy and ran into the forest to hide. Pue' was with her, and she grew very scared. She spent a night alone in the forest with Pue', and the village headman found her in the morning. Then the shaman was called, to see if she was really alive or had died in the night and was only a spirit. Everyone in the village was very happy that she was alive and not a phantom, and there was a feast, and the villagers ate the big pig that she had loved. Once, she cut her toe and her father and mother took her to the hospital in Palu. In Palu, she had ice cream for the first time, and cried because she wasn't allowed to bring ice cream home to her friends in the village.

Every year there were six months hard rain, and even Martiya knew her mother was unhappy. Her father smoked a pipe and wrote lexical tables and then wandered to the village headman's house to drink rice whiskey or palm wine; her mother paced the house. She dressed Martiya in all her clothes and played frantic games of dress-up: she told Martiya the terrifying story of Sita and Ravana, and kidnapped Martiya from the veranda to the bedroom. They put Pue' in a cape and called him Rama, but Pue' was too dirty to be allowed in the house, and Sita was forced to rescue herself. Areta never learned Uma well and took Martiya with her to the big village down the road to negotiate on market day. Areta would smoke clove cigarettes and give Martiya a fistful of rupiah. The five-year-old girl would wander from market stall to market stall, buying cassava and taro and chili peppers and eggs. She handed over all her money to the Chinese merchant, who took what he wanted and handed her back the rest. Her mother had told her not to buy from the Chinese, but the Chinese always gave her a piece of sugarcane. The merchants all knew that she was the *tuan's* child and always charged her white man's prices. She would walk with her mother under the huge umbrella in the rain back home, their sandaled toes slipping in the mud. Areta sometimes told Martiya about the house in Penang in which she grew up, with hardwood floors covered in rugs and an entire library of books and a globe that spun on a copper base. A real English house! Her father was a sultan's brother! Once, as a child, Areta had decided that she wished to play the gamelan. Her father arranged lessons for her. Her teacher was old and Hindu, and arrived at the house dressed in a perfectly white dhoti. Although she was not a Hindu, of course, he began every lesson with a Sanskrit prayer, which she repeated, and he kissed the instrument before playing. Areta became quite competent at the gamelan. Now, of course, she would not remember the fingerings, but she hoped that Martiya would have the opportunity to play an instrument—not one of the crude pipes they played in the village, but something with which she might make real music.

Piers was increasingly concerned about his wife, Elena told me. He offered to take her back to Holland, but she refused: she detested the cold and she did not wish to bear the guilt of separating Piers from his work. "She did not like us," added Elena, a touch of bitterness in the old woman's scratchy voice. "It was too clear that she did not like our family." Her family's house in Malaysia had been destroyed. Areta hatched wild schemes: the family should go to Spain, she said. There was a copy of *Don Quixote* in her trunk of books. Or Morocco. Someplace it never rained. Piers wrote a letter to the university in Singapore, but there was no position available. Then, for a long while, the tone of Piers's letters changed. Areta had calmed herself, he wrote. Once again, she chattered about any old thing. She had started to learn the village songs. They had agreed that by the time Martiya was old enough for school, they would leave the village. Piers speculated that all the previous years of hysteria had been mourning for her family and lost world. Perhaps now the mourning had come to an end.

When Martiya was six years old, Areta died by drowning in the low river where the villagers bathed. Some speculated that she had slipped; others said that the pockets of her dress had been weighed down by heavy stones. It was the onset of the rainy season and the river was swollen high. Piers wrote to his sister that the villagers held a festival of darkness. A buffalo was slaughtered to ensure that the dead would have good eating and leave the living in peace. Two birds held in a bamboo cage were released. Martiya watched them circle over the village twice and fly off into the ebony forest.

A year after her death, Piers accepted a position as professor of linguistics at the University of California at Berkeley. He and Martiya packed up the little hut. They gave away almost everything to the villagers, even Areta's books, which were accepted gravely but with utter incomprehension by the Tobaku villagers, who, lacking a script for their own language, had little use for a hardcover edition of *Pride and Prejudice* on India paper.

Elena van der Leun told me one more thing: when Martiya left the village, she spoke Uma like a native. Within several years, she remembered the language only in occasional dreams. But for the rest of her life, if asked to state her ethnicity, either on a form or by someone curious about the origins of her round eyes, black hair, and flat features, she would always respond that she was *topo'uma*—a user of the Uma language, the same response any villager who lived near the mighty Lariang River in southern Kulawi District would have given.

# THREE

# "FOR *NIXON*?"

I GOT BACK TO CHIANG MAI and wrote my piece about the sculptor, then for the *Bangkok Times* I wrote fifteen hundred words about a jazz trio that played nightly in the lobby of the Amari Hotel. I phoned both the Dutch and the American consulates, looking for details into Martiya's case, but neither consul had much to tell me: official records of both governments were sealed; the personnel who might have recalled details of her case had long since transferred to new posts. She must have been represented by a lawyer at trial, I figured, but I had no idea how to find him; I called another lawyer, who informed me that the details of legal proceedings in Thailand are not available to the public. Elena van der Leun had told me all that she could: her biography of Martiya ended effectively at age six, with Martiya's arrival in California. Piers spent the rest of his career at Berkeley, but Elena did not know much beyond that: there had been a fight over an inheritance; Martiya had been very far away. I let the story slide.

Martiya's story interested me, but Thailand was full of strange stories and inexplicable mysteries: one morning when I woke up, from my balcony I found a troupe of elephants marching through the neighborhood, led by a wiry mahout; a baby elephant looked at me with huge, curious eyes; and then the elephants disappeared from view past the bend in the road that led toward the Westin Hotel. I couldn't explain the elephants either, or why they were walking around my middle-class Chiang Mai suburb. That fall, Rachel explained to chubby Morris how to add up numbers, even big ones, and she tried to teach Maria how to tell time, who found the whole business so tricky that for a while just looking at a clock was an invitation to tears. When the class arrived at the unit on families, Najda, a little angel who took great delight in ratting out the wrongdoings of the other children, gravely explained to Miss Rachel that she lived with her mommy from Thailand and her *other* mommy from Malaysia and her daddy from America all in the same house; the situation, Najda explained with precocious tact, was "very sensitive." There was a haunted house for Halloween, until the third-graders got too rambunctious and stepped on the papier-mâché ghosts and had to have a time-out; on the first full moon in November, like everyone in Thailand, we thanked the spirits of the waters by decorating hearts-of-palm *kratong* with flowers, incense, and candles and setting them adrift on the muddy-brown river.

The rainy season tapered off and the cool season began: the cool season is northern Thailand's spring, and Chiang Mai was filled with flowers—glorious orange trumpet, which snaked along the garden wall, and aromatic hibiscus, a half-dozen varieties of lily, and everywhere delicate golden lantana, tender clumps of brilliant red and orange, climbing up telephone poles and sprouting miraculously in the sewage-occluded gutters. Rachel wore frangipani in her hair, until told that in Thailand that flower was reserved for mourning. Then for about two weeks in early December, the city was overwhelmed by butterflies taking advantage of the brief interval between the pounding rain of the monsoon and the punishing sun of the hot season to mate and die.

But Josh's vivid description of Martiya, the idea of a murdering anthropologist carefully constructing field notes while in a Thai prison, and the only white woman who could rightfully call herself *topo'uma*—all these lingered with me. On Friday afternoons, I picked Rachel up at school with the motorcycle. School let out at half past two; the last lingering thunderstorms of the monsoon broke at three; and by four the roads were dry enough to drive. We'd head out into the hills. We took the ring road past the fast-food restaurants and the large open lots where vendors sold spirit houses and giant bronze Buddhas; past Carrefour, the mammoth French *hypermarché*; past one mall, then the other. Then, just at the edge of the first rice paddies, we passed the prison where Josh had met Martiya and Martiya had died. Seeing the squat building with the limp, rain-drenched Thai flag inspired in me an indistinct sense of guilt, like the time my grandmother gave me an amaryllis that I forgot to water.

In December, Rachel and I went back to her family's house in Seattle for Christmas. Her whole family was there, all of her sisters, and the twins. Every day it rained, except for the day it hailed, and the sky lay close to the ground like a coffin lid. Rachel's father took me aside to ask, man to man, when I was going to get a real job. Martiya's story gave me an excuse to escape. Just after the New Year, I flew down to California.

Piers van der Leun today can be found on the twelfth floor of Dwinelle Hall of the University of California at Berkeley, where he stands guard in the early mornings, surrounded by the other linguists emeriti who have their photographs on the wall outside of the secretary's office. All the dead linguists gather here in the early mornings to smoke their pipes and drink honeyed tea and babble in all the world's languages. One mentions reciprocal constructions in Bantu, and another replies that a similar grammatical structure is found, oddly enough, in Ojibwe. Their incorporeal forms drift down the hallway and settle in the department lounge, where the former authority on the phonology of the Indo-Turkic languages laments the difficulty of returning to his fieldwork. All the ghosts nod companionably: they know how difficult it is to discipline oneself in the afterlife, now that time is no longer an issue and tenure guaranteed. The recently arrived specialist in computational linguistics spills his coffee, and when the graduate students, caught in their own particular netherworld between life and death, arrive later in the day, they find the dark puddle and wonder who might have made such a mess.

Piers and Martiya van der Leun left Sulawesi in 1954, and Piers spent the remainder of his career at Berkeley. I learned this from Piers's obituary, published in the *Daily Californian*, May 1987. The van der Leuns lived in a Craftsman house on elm-shaded Etna Street. Piers continued his research, returning every other year to Indonesia, but passed most of his days on the twelfth floor of Dwinelle Hall, revising his verb tables and refining his lexicon. The lexicon was published in 1967, and was praised by a reviewer in the *Bulletin of Oriental Linguistics* as a "significant step forward in Australasian linguistics." From his old office, one can see the Bay Bridge and San Francisco; a bay view was a mark of status and distinction within the department.

I visited the former chairman of the department of linguistics, who, despite advanced age, still kept office hours. He greeted me with a strange exuberance when I knocked on his door, and I had the impression that very few people visited him between two and four on Wednesdays. He had bulging black eyes. He recalled Piers van der Leun and Martiya, but I began to doubt the quality (if not the quantity) of his memories when he referred to Piers as an Indo-Europeanist, and Swiss. If the former chairman's other recollections are accurate, Piers played tennis quite a bit and introduced Martiya to the game. The university in the 1950s, the former chairman digressed, was an entirely different place from the university today: young ladies wore tennis skirts and young men dressed neatly, often with a tie, carrying their tennis rackets over their shoulders as they left the fraternity house, but of course wearing white shorts on the courts as university regulations demanded. Occasionally, someone might show up in class still wearing tennis clothes. This was frowned upon, but nobody saw the need *officially* to forbid the act.

A long silence passed, which I assumed the former chairman spent in the organization of his unruly memories. I glanced around his office. One wall was covered in books, another in photographs, many of them showing the chairman shaking the hands of famous people—I would have asked the chairman how he came to meet both Ronald Reagan and Frank Sinatra, but I was afraid that he would have no more idea than I did.

Martiya *perhaps* attended the local junior high school, then Berkeley High School, then *might* have matriculated at the university. The former chairman had remarkable tufts of hair protruding from his magisterial, elephantine ears. He suggested I speak with his daughter, "my oldest girl," who had known Martiya slightly better, the two having graduated hypothetically in the same class at high school. The former chairman asked me which university I was associated with, and looked at me blankly when I explained that I was interested in the life of Martiya van der Leun. "Ah, yes," he said finally. "Wasn't she old Piers van der Leun's daughter?" When I said goodbye, he wished me luck on my grant application. A quick Internet search revealed that the former chairman had a linguist's mastery of the grammars of *all* the Indo-European languages, and had published new results within the last year.

The chairman's daughter lived in Boston. When I got her on the phone, she confirmed the general outlines of Martiya's career—it is amazing the things people will tell a polite stranger—and then said something about it being the crazy time of the year, with the holidays and all. Martiya's name came brightly to her lips, as if Martiya had been one of those high school personalities it is impossible to forget. Every high school has one. Martiya had indeed graduated in her class at Berkeley High and then matriculated at UC Berkeley. A cell phone was ringing in the background, and I could hear a small child crying. "I've got to *run*," she said. She took my e-mail address and, to my surprise, wrote me the next day, just a few lines suggesting that I speak with Martiya's college boyfriend Tim Blair, today a professor of English at San Francisco State University.

A lot of journalism is like this: I felt a little like the baton in a relay race of faulty memories and distant recollections. But Tim Blair remembered Martiya very, very well. I could sense it even over the telephone. "Holy shit," he murmured when I told him that Martiya was dead, a suicide in a Thai jail. He invited me to coffee at his house on Potrero Hill.

Tim Blair and I sat in his book-lined study. There were rectangular piles of handwritten papers on the floor around his desk ("Don't mind my ball and chain," he said, gesturing at the papers ruefully. "I'll get this thing out of here one of these days") and photographs of his sons on the wall. Tim Blair settled himself onto a leather couch covered with an afghan, and I was assigned to an easy chair. He stroked his silver beard slowly; his mustache dangled across his upper lip. He was one of those men with a well-formed skull suited to baldness, the kind of skull that under *exceedingly* different circumstances might have made an excellent calabash, smoothly rounded and long in the forehead with a deep bowl sufficient for a good many draughts of palm wine. There was something just a little aggressive about Tim Blair and the way he hunched his elbows on his knees. He chewed his pink lower lip.

"Tell me," I finally said, the "tell me" an interrogatory trick—I was relying here on Barbara Walters's *How to Talk to Practically Anyone About Practically Anything*—to win my subject's trust. "Tell me," I repeated, making good focused Barbara-counseled eye contact, "how did you come to know Martiya?"

Tim Blair looked at me severely for a second. I thought that perhaps I had mispronounced her name. He crossed his legs and cracked his knuckles. I had a small notebook balanced on my knee. "You know she voted for Nixon, don't you?" he said finally. "Christ, man, that blew me away."

"Nixon?" I wasn't sure where all this was going, but I wrote "Nixon" in my notebook, and underlined it.

"Twice."

*"Twice?"*

"She voted for the bastard *twice*."

I added an exclamation mark after the word "Nixon."

Tim continued, "Hell, she was just a shade shy of the goddamn John Birch Society. She said that her granddad was killed by Communists and she didn't want to see all of Southeast Asia red. She was the kind of kid who got pretty heated up about politics. We'd walk through campus and she just went after the peace protesters."

He uncrossed his legs and leaned back into the sofa. "One time, I remember, we were in the Anthropology Department lounge and this guy was talking about the Montagnards in Vietnam, and he was running off at the mouth, attacking American policy, calling it genocide and all that. She went after him. 'Why the hell do you think the Hmong are fighting *for us*?' she asked him. 'Do you think they're stupid? Do you think they don't know what's in their best interests?' He just looked at her blankly, this guy, staring at this dark-haired girl, saying what you just did not say in the Anthropology Department at Berkeley in those days. She was vicious and smart, and that was sexy." Tim lingered on the word "sexy." "I was the idiot who was running off at the mouth. That's how I met her, that's when I fell for her. *Boom!* She never held it against me that I was an idiot. But she really believed what she was saying. She said that the first thing the Communists were going to do when they took over was to drag all the indigenous people down from their villages and put them on communal farms. Or shoot 'em. And it was true. It was the first thing they did."

Tim continued without further prompting. I scribbled as quickly as I could. In college, Tim and Martiya were both anthropology majors. They were together, hardly a minute apart, most of their junior and senior years. Tim made clear that it was all a long time ago, and yet the memories of his time with Martiya were still charged, perhaps precisely because it *was* a long time ago and these were the memories of his youth. Every now and then I interrupted Tim, asking him for details about their time together, looking for something that would make Martiya come to life. But those novelistic touches were in his telling hazy and indistinct. For reasons Tim could not quite articulate, a course in the ethnology of southern India was a particularly romantic memory. They took a lot of naps on the college lawns, and when they woke up they spent long hours playing with her hair. "Being with Martiya, you got to realize that it was kind of like a ménage à trois. Her damned hair had a will of its own. One day it's flat and the next it's big, and everything about her changed, depending on the hair."

"How so?"

"She wasn't ever very subdued, but when the hair was flat, she'd be more thoughtful. But when the hair was big, she was a real hell-raiser. When the hair was big, she'd say, 'Let's get in the car and drive.' When the hair was flat, you'd find her in the library."

"Why do you think Martiya was in the Anthropology Department?" I asked.

He furrowed his brow. "In those days, anthro was for a lot of folks who didn't feel at home anywhere else. It wasn't a big department, and it had a personal atmosphere. Everyone knew everyone else. All the professors would have parties, and I guess it's one of the few places on campus where Martiya could find people who really got how she had been raised. She was kind of a celebrity in the department, and I think she liked that. Also, she was curious. One of the most curious people I've ever met. There aren't that many curious people out there."

I wrote "Martiya—curious" in my notebook.

Tim puckered his lips. "I'm not sure 'curious' is the best way to put it, actually," he said. Reluctantly, I added a question mark to the word. "Martiya was a self-improver. Ambitious. She bought the *Norton Anthology of English Literature* and read her way through it, fifty pages a day, from one end to the other. Then she got on this poetry-memorizing thing where she tried to memorize fifty lines of poetry a week. Then it was swimming—she hadn't learned to swim as a kid and she decided she needed to know how to swim. Soon she was swimming laps three-quarters of an hour every day."

The phone rang and Tim got up to answer it. His wife was on the line, and he said, "Hi, babe," and "Uh-huh," and "Okey-dokey," and "He said *that*?" and "Sonovabitch," and "I've got to go, we'll talk when you get home." He didn't mention that he was talking to a journalist about his ex-girlfriend. Then he hung up and sat down again. "The van der Leuns, big influence on me," he said. I had the impression that much of what Tim was telling me now had been prepared before my arrival, as if the night before he had lain awake thinking. Piers van der Leun was a "distracted elderly scholar type, you know, really from another generation," slightly ill at ease in California, especially in a California where the tennis whites to which he had so proudly accustomed himself were no longer the epitome of style. Martiya was "passionately devoted to her father." Although she lived in her own apartment on the north side of the campus, she stopped by her father's office almost every day in the late afternoon, and he would take her to the faculty lounge for coffee. Sometimes Tim would be invited. "My dad, he was the kind of guy who talked about nothing but baseball and union politics," Tim said. "Don't get me wrong. I love baseball, still union." Tim threw an imaginary baseball to emphasize his loyalties. "But these two, they'd spend hours talking about grammars and lexicons and Chomsky and poetry and politics—I never heard people talk like that. And Professor van der Leun would ask my opinion about all sorts of things, and then he'd kind of hang on my response, as if there was nothing more important in the world than my opinion, this little twenty-year-old twerp from Modesto."

Tim and Martiya went for long drives up the California coast. Tim had an old Pontiac that he could barely keep running, and a chocolate Lab named Chocolate, and they'd drive north, as far as they could go in a weekend. Knowing that you are happy when you are happy is a rare gift, and Tim knew how happy he was.

" 'All life's grandeur / Is something with girl in summer,' " Tim Blair said.

"I'm sorry?"

"Robert Lowell. It's true. You're too young to know it. You'll see."

The couple drove along the coast and bought sharp cheddar cheese from an old cheese-maker in Point Reyes and white wine from a vineyard in Sonoma, then wandered—sometimes ending up on the banks of the Russian River, other times going as far north as Mendocino. Once they stopped on a bluff over the Pacific, near a grove of gnarled cypress trees, and spread a blanket out on the golden grass. "Do you see that itty-bitty little island over there?" Martiya asked, pointing far, far off in the distance, to the other side of the Pacific.

"Yep."

"No, not the big one. The really itty-bitty one."

"Oh, the little one. I was looking at the big one."

"No, the big one's Java. You see all those lights? That's Jakarta. The little one is Sulawesi. That's where I was born."

"Oh, I was looking at Borneo."

"You're looking towards Japan. That's Borneo *there*."

They were together a little over two years. After graduation, Piers van der Leun gave his daughter a small sum of money, to use as she wished. She announced her intention to travel around the world, and explained to Tim her intention to travel alone. "I thought it was crazy, this little girl wanting to go around the world by herself. But she was insistent. Piers asked me to talk to her, to change her mind. She told me not to wait for her. She was a powerfully determined girl. I never really knew why it was over. I guess now when I look back on it, I was too boring for her—she couldn't imagine ever living in a house like this one." He waved his hand in a broad arc which encompassed the bay windows and the hardwood floor covered in an old Persian carpet, the coved ceiling, and the family photos. Thirty years after the fact, Tim Blair was still explaining to himself why his college girlfriend left him. Through the windows I could see the bay, covered in whitecaps stirred up by a winter breeze.

"Tim Blair—too boring," I wrote in my notebook.

"I got postcards and letters from her all year long, even though we'd broken up," Tim said. "I got letters from the craziest places—from eastern Turkey and Afghanistan and the far northeast provinces of India. I didn't write her back, because I never knew where she was going to be, so it was a kind of one-way conversation. All that year, I was dying for her just to write that she loved me and missed me, but she never did: she would just write these long letters about the people that she saw and the places she went, and how fucking *interesting* it was. I didn't give a shit. Then the letters started to peter out, and I stopped missing her so much.

"I went to grad school on the East Coast, and, once, I came back to Berkeley for a conference—this was, oh, about two, three years later. I gave her a call, and we went out for coffee. She was enrolled in the Ph.D. program in the Department of Anthropology, and she was all excited because she had been awarded a grant to study some tribe in the north of Thailand. God, I can't believe she was still in Thailand."

Tim pointed to a picture on the wall. It was hidden by a bookcase, and I had to stand up to see it clearly. It was a portrait of himself thirty years earlier. There was a strapping young man in a T-shirt. He had shoulder-length curly hair. He had a goofy smile and was standing in a flower-filled pasture. Martiya, he said, had taken that picture.

"What does she look like now?" he asked me. "I mean, before she . . ."

"I didn't meet her." I told him what Josh O'Connor had told me.

"She had beautiful lips."

I paused a second. I looked down at my notes. There was something I wanted to clarify. "For *Nixon?*" I said. "Really?"

"Twice."

Tim heard from Martiya one more time. About fifteen years ago, he said, she wrote to him. The letter was postmarked Thailand. Memories of their time together made up the bulk of the letter. The tone was tender, even affectionate. She was living in a tribal village in northern Thailand: her research had been fruitful. She had been productive. She had to tell someone, she said: she had met a man and was madly in love. Her

current happiness, Martiya told Tim, reminded her of their time together, and having no one with whom she might share these memories,
she had decided to write to Tim himself. She hoped that he was equally
happy.

Josh O'Connor had told me that Martiya had been in prison the past
ten years. Tim Blair reported that she was a free woman, madly in love,
as of fifteen years ago. Not long after she mailed this letter, by the time
line I was constructing, Martiya had killed someone.

# FOUR

# "HELL YES, I REMEMBER MARTIYA VAN DER LEUN"

THE SWIDDEN, which had lain fallow all through the fall, again lay fallow. In Berkeley, I had tried to find Martiya's graduate thesis adviser, Joseph Atkinson, but he was, the department secretary said, a sick man, in and out of the hospital. I sent him an e-mail anyway, and received no response. I went back to Seattle, and Rachel and I went back to Thailand. It had been gray with a sleety rain when we left the States, but on the lawn outside the Chiang Mai airport, the airport employees were drinking whiskey, eating sticky rice, and playing the guitar.

The cool season came over Chiang Mai, and the Thai girls wore light cotton sweaters and shivered, although I was still comfortable in a T-shirt and shorts. It was a quiet winter. My editor at *Executive* asked if I wanted to write some film reviews. I saw no reason to be a snob. Rachel ate an omelette which did not agree with her and spent a week in the hospital, where the mysterious Dr. Bahn guided her recovery. Every morning, the Indian-born physician swept into her room, glanced at her chart, and settled himself into the chair beside her bed. He took Rachel's damp, green hand, and as he asked her the usual questions about her symptoms, continued to hold the limb sympathetically. He stayed at her bedside for almost an hour, and for the duration of his visit, her nausea abated. Her illness he treated as merely a manifestation of a deeper spiritual ailment, the cure for which, ideally, was the adoption of the Hindu rites of his childhood—that and antibiotics. He looked into Rachel's pale-blue eyes and talked—about Thai Buddhism, which in his view was nothing other than Hinduism itself in an elemental form about how animals recover from illness in the forest; about the forest and its sad destruction; and about the recent death of his father, and the beauty of the experience, despite its exceptional sorrow. The ghost of his father, he told us, was not yet at peace, and never left him.

"He's here, in this room?" asked Rachel.

"Oh yes," Dr. Bahn said. This was not something that should concern us: his father had been a most lovely man.

Rachel got better, and we took her class to the zoo. At the Chiang Mai zoo, feeding the animals is encouraged, and we bought bananas for the monkeys, peanuts for the elephants, and ice cream for the first-graders. Morris was thrilled. "My mother," Morris said, in the fluent mélange of his father's English and his mother's Thai that he spoke when excited, "she tell me I'm no allowed eat ice cream. She say, 'Morris, you too fat!' " We got the ice cream from Dairy Queen, and Morris looked at his Blizzard with huge, passionate eyes. "I love you, Miss Rachel," he said finally.

Warm, easy winter days passed. Rachel and I started taking yoga lessons from an Austrian named Gunther, a former chef from Linz, who offered courses in a gazebo in his flower-strewn backyard, which was patrolled by a domesticated duck named Donut. Gunther had a great rivalry with the other German-speaking yoga teacher in Chiang Mai, a Bavarian who called himself Vivekananda. "Of course Vivekananda is very good yoga teacher," Gunther said, rubbing Donut's beak. "But I do not so much like his spirit."

Then one day in late January, we woke up sweating. The cool season was over, just like that, and not long after, Martiya's story broke open, like a coconut struck by a machete. Martiya's graduate adviser, Joseph Atkinson, had written me back. "Dear Mischa Berlinski," he began. "Hell yes, I remember Martiya van der Leun."

Rachel, like many women, had total faith in her ability to spot a romance, based on little more than a tender tone of voice or a lingering glance. She was convinced that Martiya van der Leun and her former professor were once lovers.

Handsome, dark-eyed, tall, a dramatic scar across his neck, the celebrated hero of numerous adventures in the African bush, Joseph Atkinson was a man of about sixty when a pretty undergraduate named Martiya van der Leun enrolled in his senior honors seminar. The seminar, entitled "Games People Play," was a semester-long examination of the role of play in human society. All human societies, Atkinson observed, from the Inuit to the French to the Pygmy, play; it was a fundamental human institution. But what do human beings consider play? It is not an easy word to define. The course considered work as a form of play, and play as a form of work; the games of children and the games of adults; games with consequences like baccarat, and games without, like tag; formal games like baseball, and informal games like hide-and-seek; games that mimicked war and games that mimicked daily life, as when children played house. Martiya wrote a long paper for Atkinson on the games children played in the Pipikoro villages of southern Sulawesi, drawing from her own experiences as a child. The notable feature of Pipikoro play, Martiya wrote, was the extreme complexity of the games played by even the youngest Pipikoro children: her catalogue of the rules of *makulu* ran to over thirty pages. Atkinson thought that with substantial revisions, the paper might be suitable for publication. Martiya visited him during office hours. Atkinson wrote that Martiya was small and vivacious: she had very pretty feet, and in warm weather she wore open-toed sandals; she was feminine but not womanly. She asked him about the Doyo, the tribal people he had studied in Africa. *Really?* The *only* white man? She asked him what it was like to have dengue fever, and what tribal warfare was like. She even asked him about faculty meetings.

Rachel had been brushing her teeth as I read her Atkinson's letter, and she rinsed her mouth from the tap. "God knows only a lover would be interested in a faculty meeting," she said, spitting into the sink. "She was hot for him."

"You think?"

"Absolutely."

Rachel's logic had a certain force, and I imagined the sun-splashed sexually charged afternoons in the professor's study, as the small, vivacious undergraduate with pretty feet interrogated the learned but still manly professor. Did she play idly with her hair while Atkinson described the Doyo death rituals? Were there tribal masks on the wall? Did a woven kente cloth cover the couch? When she came by his office, did she perch herself daintily on the very edge of his couch and say, "Professor Atkinson, tell me a little about your work?"

Although he published only a handful of books—*The Doyo Way of Life*; *Water, Wind, and Rain*; *The Life of Ralupeda, Doyo Shaman*—Atkinson's influence dominated generations of anthropologists, including Martiya's. Anthropologists talk of the "school of Atkinson" as they talk of the school of Malinowski, or Evans-Pritchard, or Lévi-Strauss; and every freshman taking Anthropology 101 learns to construct the complicated Atkinson kinship groups. Atkinson wrote a vigorous, masculine prose, which is how I came to imagine the man himself. I wasn't surprised to learn that Atkinson, even at a place so filled with strangeness as Berkeley, was well known for his carefully cultivated eccentricities, as when he showed up for the initial meeting of the survey course in cultural anthropology, a lecture attended by nearly eight hundred startled undergraduates, wearing nothing but a handsome, three-foot long embroidered penis sheath. On another occasion, campus police were summoned on reports of a tall, nearly naked man wandering near Sather Gate with a finely honed spear. The situation was *not* calmed when Atkinson coolly explained that he was hunting the dean of students. Atkinson's e-mails to me were typically time-stamped around four in the morning California time, and I imagined him wrapped in a tattered bathrobe that exposed his bony knees, sitting at his computer, unable to fall back to sleep. The Internet makes possible some strange friendships. Atkinson made clear to me that for reasons of literary vanity, he did not wish to see his letters published, but I was free, he said generously, to summarize their contents.

From the first, Rachel disliked Atkinson. She thought he was an egotist and arrogant, but then, I countered silently, no one without a certain egotism can spend so long in the West African jungle. I liked Atkinson's forthright prose, and I admired the way that he had defied his father in order to pursue a scholarly career: Atkinson's father, a Chicago commodities broker, sent him to London in the early 1930s to learn the tea trade; but Atkinson promptly enrolled in the celebrated doctoral program in anthropology at the London School of Economics under the legendary Bronislaw Malinowski, and reconciled with his father only after Atkinson's older brother died in combat in the South Pacific.

In his middle twenties, Atkinson went to live with the Doyo in French West Africa for five years, and emerged finally with the book that won him a professorship at Yale, where he spent almost two decades before moving to California. He wrote books about West Africans filled with hard midwestern facts. He described and described again the Doyo—how they married, how they died, how they made millet beer, and how they fought their tribal wars; famously, he himself fought in a Doyo tribal war, and emerged with a scar across his neck and upper body. Atkinson made sure the handsome silver eel-shaped wound was showing in the publicity photos on the back of all his books. Those photos, taken when Atkinson must have been in his early fifties, showed a large, well-muscled man with tight curly hair, silver at the temples, wearing an open-necked shirt. His eyes were hooded, toughening up a face that otherwise might have been delicate. His ridged arms were crossed at the chest, and his hands were large and strong. "He's not *my* type," Rachel said, looking at the picture. "But I can see what Martiya saw in him."

After she graduated, Tim Blair had told me and Atkinson confirmed, Martiya decided to travel. "Things were over with Atkinson," Rachel said. She twirled a strand of her long hair meditatively. "Martiya must have had the affair with Atkinson, saw that things weren't going anywhere, and left. It explains why she broke up with the bald guy in San Francisco too."

"You think?"

"She saw the writing on the wall. What do you do when you're twenty-three with a guy who's almost sixty? It was a we're-both-moving-on-but-we-care-for-each-other breakup, not an I-hate-you-how-could-you get-my-sister-pregnant breakup," she said.

Rachel's elegant hypothesis was consistent with the facts: from the road, Martiya wrote to Atkinson as she had written to Tim, long letters describing the Second-Class Waiting Room of the Udaipur train station; or the Kurdish wedding to which she had been invited. Atkinson told me that when she came back to Berkeley, Martiya asked him what he thought she should do with herself. Atkinson loved giving young people advice: he told Martiya that her curiosity and intelligence would make her a superior scholar in any number of disciplines, but in his opinion, *kiddo*, she was a natural anthropologist. Martiya followed her professor's counsel and enrolled in the Ph.D. program in the Department of Anthropology, where Martiya asked Atkinson to supervise her doctoral thesis.

"Well, naturally," Rachel said. "She wasn't *stupid*."

Martiya had originally intended to write her doctoral thesis on the Pipikoro. She knew the language, she argued, and her childhood intimacy with the people would allow her to present the culture vividly. But Sulawesi was politically unstable in the early 1970s, which made grants hard to come by. Joseph Atkinson, too, was opposed to her plans: the Pipikoro were not an unknown people in scholarly circles; her own father's research there had been significant. He proposed instead that she study the Dyalo of northern Thailand. No ethnographic portrait of the Dyalo existed. A detailed description of their way of life would prove a valuable contribution to the literature and a good place to start a career. Atkinson told her: "Listen, don't be a martyr. Thailand is a great place to do research. The food is good. The climate's swell. There are lots of flowers and butterflies. Nobody's going to try to *eat* you." Martiya won a research fellowship to study the Dyalo, largely on the strength of his letter of recommendation.

"Uh-huh," Rachel said knowingly.

While still in Berkeley, Martiya prepared for her time with the Dyalo as best she could. Very little guidance was typically offered to graduate students at UC Berkeley in the Department of Anthropology before they set out to do fieldwork. I spoke by telephone with Lee Cheng, who in 1967 set out from Wheeler Hall to study Saharan nomads, today the L. Stein Professor in the Department of Anthropology at Columbia University. "The philosophy really was that the field was something you did on your own," he said. "The department had the attitude that nothing much could prepare you for anthropological fieldwork, and if you couldn't do fieldwork, then you had no business being an anthropologist.

It was a real rite of passage." If you couldn't figure out how to get out to the jungle, the desert, or the savannah; if you couldn't figure out what to ask the natives; if you couldn't figure out how to build rapport with recalcitrant and suspicious locals—perhaps, the department implied, it was time to think about a nice career in sociology, where the data were unlikely to carry a spear. A story circulated in the department about the grad student who asked her hoary and accomplished adviser for his counsel on the field. The professor handed her a copy of the thickest ethnography on his shelf, one of the magisterial works of Kroeber. "I send thee forth, that thou might do likewise," he solemnly intoned. An elderly professor much interested in the Australian aborigines advised Martiya to pay particular attention to forbidden animals and eldest daughters: long years of scholarship, he continued, and a lifetime in the field had taught him that these were the soft spots of tribal, nay, *human* culture itself. "Don't do what I did and act like an old animal around the forbidden daughters," he said with a sad, greasy chuckle. Atkinson advised her to bring a bottle of tequila, a shot of which, he said, inevitably made everyone just a little more easy when discussing incest taboos, a perennial topic of anthropological inquiry.

There was no anthropological literature on the Dyalo, but in the vast holdings of Wheeler Library she found a slim memoir by a Welsh traveler named Swinton who had lived with the Dyalo in the first half of the century in the remote wilds of China's southern Yunnan Province. He offered a very brief description of the people: the Dyalo, Swinton reported, were found in small villages across southern China, northern Burma, and northern Thailand; Swinton estimated that there were perhaps a hundred thousand Dyalo speakers in the world. The Dyalo, he said, were slash-and-burn farmers and fiercely independent. To emphasize his point, Swinton told a story of a village in which the headman had been shot by his subjects with hunting rifles after he overstepped the bounds of his modest office. The Dyalo had no written language, although Dyalo poetry was subtle and beautiful. Swinton wrote, "The Dyalo language, reflecting the thinking of the Dyalo people, has neither a word for 'love,' nor 'sin,' nor 'salvation.' In Dyalo, it is impossible to 'forgive' someone. It is a brutally honest language." Swinton noted the Dyalo custom of selling their daughters into marriage, and Swinton wrote that the Dyalo were obsessed with spirits and ghosts, which they reckoned existed all about them in great numbers.

When Martiya herself went off to live with the Dyalo in the fall of 1974, she had very little more than this description to go on.

Joseph Atkinson and I gossiped about Martiya through February and into early March, as the very hot season came over Chiang Mai and the grinning, good-natured elephant outside the Westin Hotel turned brown. The hotel's gardener watered the topiary daily but was unable, as the days grew warmer, to keep the animal green: first the elephant's trunk, rearing high, changed color, then his massive, drooping ears. Day by day, the line of brown drifted southward across his mighty back. Finally, only the tail, protected during the searing hours of the late afternoon by the long shadow of the hotel itself, kept its original winter hue. Hot! Every visit to the Westin, every new letter from Atkinson, saw the hotel doorman, dressed in elaborate silken costumes appropriate to the court of great King Chulalongkorn, swing open the heavy glass doors with ever less alacrity, the pained look on his smooth face suggesting that all that movement in the heat was an affront to common sense. My underwear clung damply to my butt.

But inside the hotel it was cool, dark, carpeted, and quiet, which was why I liked to read my e-mail there in the morning: in the Westin, my otherwise sluggish thoughts seemed fresh, like sprigs of winter mint. I had made friends with perky pretty little Gai, the receptionist at the Business Service Center, and she let me check my e-mail there for free, when her boss, Miss Tong, wasn't looking. Gai considered Miss Tong's insistence on charging a *regular* customer unseemly. What, after all, was friendship for? Miss Tong, Gai said bitterly, was *kee nieo*—literally translated, a sticky shit. That this is a grave insult in Thailand says a considerable amount about the Thai character to those inclined to consider the Freudian themes of anal expulsion and retention.

Joseph Atkinson wasn't my only correspondent, of course: my mother wrote me; Josh found a job managing Thailand's first *gelateria*. My editor at *Executive* wondered if I would be interested in writing a couple of thousand words about a vineyard in Loei Province, the first in

Thailand. *Of course* I would, my interest in viticulture being long-standing. But Joseph Atkinson's e-mails were the ones that I clicked open first and read over and over again.

I always printed out Atkinson's letters for Rachel to read, before exchanging a conspiratorial smile with Gai and strolling homeward. Midway between the Westin and my house, not far from the 7-Eleven, where I stopped to drink a mango Slurpee, there was a hospital, and on the façade of the hospital hung a hand-painted canvas sign at least two stories high advertising discounts on plastic surgery. I no longer recall the text of the advertisement, but the face depicted there struck me. It was the face of a young woman, with the pale skin favored in the Thai ideal, long dark hair, and eyes as round as Meyer lemons. As was typical of Thai commercial art, the woman was neither entirely Asian nor occidental, but in-between, her face bearing the drama of Western features but none of their vulgarity. She was the product of a surgeon with the deftest touch. It was this woman's face that in my imaginings I associated with Martiya.

From the field, Martiya wrote Atkinson still more long letters. Martiya's first letters from Thailand were ebullient, he said. They made him recall his own early days in Africa, when, leaving behind gloomy London and snowbound Chicago, he first saw the land the Doyo called the Beautiful Kingdom of the Yellow Sun. Atkinson was proud to have urged her to go. She wrote exuberantly of the beauty of Thailand: the flooded lime-green rice paddies bordered by swaying palms; coconuts, mangoes, and durian for sale by the side of the road; the ornate temples with flashing mirrored roofs; wandering Buddhist monks with shaved heads in saffron robes; the cut galangal in bushels drying in the midday sun, the humid air earthy, like a root; and the sleepy, sweating water buffalo reluctantly plowing the fields. Her descriptions of Thailand, Atkinson admitted, were clichéd, but no less touching for the fact.

Atkinson gave Martiya a letter of introduction to an elderly Thai anthropologist at the University of Chiang Mai. He treated her intention to live in a Dyalo village as a silly eccentricity. He had been able to study the Karen adequately, he maintained, on visits that lasted at most a day or two, and she would not find tribal living to her taste. Did she realize, he asked, that the Dyalo had neither electricity nor running water?

And the food! One need not even mention the food. The thatched roof of a Dyalo hut would leak in the rainy season. The Dyalo themselves smelled bad, although this would be less oppressive to a *farang*. Martiya was persistent, however, and her Thai host eventually conceded: if she insisted on wandering down the path of folly, the least he could do would be to recommend a guide. In this way she was introduced to a young Dyalo man named Vinai, who spoke a rough-and-ready English in addition to his native Dyalo and fluent Thai.

Choosing the right village is an essential part of the anthropological adventure, and for almost three months Martiya and her guide wandered the mountains of northern Thailand. They traveled by motorbike and on foot, first along the paved arteries which pulsed out from Chiang Mai, then branching onto the network of dirt roads which led from village to village. Where the roads ended, they walked, along paths which, Vinai maintained, had once been the migratory routes of wild elephants. Martiya got a sense of the new world in which she found herself. The Akha, she learned, wore silver headdresses, and exposed their twins, thinking them possessed by evil spirits. Karen virgins dressed in white. The Hmong lived at the summits of the mountains, and while the Hmong greatly admired the Yao, they enslaved the Lahu. The Hmong had grown rich as opium traders and the Lahu were often opium-addicted. The primitive Mrabri no one ever saw: they had never learned to build houses and drifted through the jungle like ghosts, taking shelter every night under makeshift lean-tos. Under every T'ai Lue house there was a loom. The Lua were sullen and stared at Martiya suspiciously. Everyone, her guide said, admired the poetry of the Lisu and the quality of their singing. The Mao were quiet folk and, like the Swiss, spoke slowly. Martiya and Vinai roamed from the Burmese to the Lao border, looking for the ideal village to study. In the end, Martiya settled herself in a Dyalo village called Dan Loi, not far from the Burmese border, and set to work.

The field did to Martiya what the field always does: it scoured her and revealed the person underneath the encrusted layers of culture and ingrained habit and prejudice. Martiya came back to Berkeley three years later, tanned and strong, and began to write. She showed a few of the chapters of her doctoral thesis to Atkinson. They were superb, he said, absolutely superb. First-rate analysis, a deep connection with the subject, and intensely well observed. But Martiya wasn't convinced: she complained that she hardly *knew* the Dyalo and was being asked to write their definitive story. Every graduate student—every *good* grad student, Atkinson qualified—feels that way, but Martiya for some reason felt it more keenly than most. Atkinson told her that he understood, that it was only after he had defended his Doyo village from a raid by a neighboring tribe, actually holding a spear in his hand, that he felt he understood the people, that he could write about them.

"So what should I do?" Martiya asked.

*Write the thesis, kiddo. It's just three hundred pages of blah-blah-blah.*

After about a year, she told him she wanted to go back to Thailand. She needed more data. Atkinson told her that he couldn't oppose this idea more profoundly. "Are you nuts?" he asked. She left nevertheless.

She never finished the doctoral thesis. He never heard from her again.


Not long after my e-mails with Atkinson had tapered off, the phone rang in the middle of the night. My first thought wasn't that someone was dead or needed my kidney—I just cursed Rachel's Grandma Irene. I don't think Grandma Irene ever really bought into the outlandish notion that as the sun was rising over the Puget Sound, the same sun, harsher and so much hotter, had long since set over the rice paddies of the Golden Triangle. She called us at all hours of the night.

But I was wrong. It turned out someone *was* dead.

The fan blew hot air across our damp backs. Our first hot season in Thailand, Rachel had asked me if we were growing apart, because I didn't hold her in the night anymore. "It's got to be a zillion degrees, Rachel, are you crazy?" I said. She looked at me doubtfully. That night, I held on to her tightly, breathing hotly on her neck. She pushed me away, and now we slept, during the hot season, on far sides of the bed. I was having a dream when the phone rang, a complicated one—interpret it as you will—in which I had just gotten a job as a waiter in a French café and needed to acquire a waiter's suit with a vest and tailcoat. No tailor in

Chiang Mai would make it for me. I licked my lips when the phone rang, and for a second I wasn't sure if it wasn't the tailor from the dream calling me back.

"Hello?" I think I said. I wasn't taking notes.

On the other end of the line there was a woman's voice. "Mischa?" the voice said. "Mischa Berlinski? It's Karen!" She said it like back in college, we were once best friends. "Karen Leon! Martiya's friend!" the voice added.

"Karen," I said. Karen Leon was an anthropologist from Texas to whom Joseph Atkinson had suggested I write. In my e-mail I had included my phone number and invited her to call me.

"I just got back to Austin and I read your e-mail and I had to call *right away*. How *is* Martiya? I wrote her and she never wrote back, and I wrote *again* and I've been *so* worried."

A very long pause circumnavigated the world.

"Don't you know?" I said, and then I thought: How could she?

"Know what?"

"I guess you don't know."

"No," she said. Her voice dropped a register, from trumpet to trombone.

"She's dead." If she'd called in the morning, I might have been more gentle.

"Oh," Karen said. It was almost a groan.

I didn't know where to begin. "She killed herself. In jail. She ate a ball of opium."

"*That* killed her?"

"Yes." It didn't seem like enough. "That's what I was told."

"Well, are you sure or not?"

I felt a little defensive. "Yes, I'm sure," I said. "She's dead."

"Oh."

One of my neighbor's fighting cocks crowed, and from Texas, I heard a car alarm. The sounds must have crossed each other somewhere under the Pacific.

"It's hard news," I said.

"It's just so . . ."

"I was shocked too," I added. It seemed like the right thing to say. "Did you know . . . did you know Martiya well?"

"Oh, yes. I mean, no. I mean, I haven't seen her in years. But we were once close, before . . ." Her voice drifted off. My neighbor's fighting cock crowed again, and a dog barked.

"Would you like to talk about Martiya sometime?" I asked. In the letter I had sent to Karen I had explained that I was a journalist interested in the story of Martiya van der Leun, but no more than that. "It's just that she had so many people who admired her here, and I want to get her story straight. I mean, maybe when you've had a little time to—"

"They admire her? Really? After what happened?"

"I don't really know what happened," I admitted.

"Don't you *know*? I thought that's what you were writing about."

"No, I don't know."

"I can't believe you don't know."

"I don't," I insisted.

"Martiya *killed* someone," Karen said. The intimate excitement had returned to her voice. "Martiya shot a missionary named David Walker. From a whole family of missionaries. She shot him in the back two times with a hunting rifle."

"Do you know why she shot him?"

There was a long pause on the line, and then Karen said, "That's why I was calling *you*."

# FIVE

# WHAT A MURDER MEANS

THE VICTIM'S FAMILY was easy to track down: *everyone* in Chiang Mai seemed to know them.

Waiting for Rachel to finish class one afternoon, I mentioned the Walkers to Mr. Tim, the headmaster at the school. Mr. Tim was a fat Canadian with a straggly beard and a nervous, high-pitched laugh who had come to Chiang Mai after leaving his wife and the walk-in closet in which he had been encaged; every morning over coffee during second-period break, he recounted to the teachers the passionate details of his love affair with a stunningly lovely but stormy transvestite accountant named Saroi. I don't know precisely the attraction to a homosexual of a man who looks like a woman, even a beautiful woman. Come to think of it, I'm not sure why a beautiful transvestite would be attracted to an obese Canadian either. In any case, Mr. Tim was a favorite of students and staff alike: kids sent to his office for discipline were allowed to help themselves from a sack of lemon candy that Mr. Tim kept in his desk; no teacher ever complained that Mr. Tim was overzealous in the examination of curricula or student progress.

"*Interesting* people," he said. He didn't know the Walkers himself, but his counterpart at Chiang Mai's other, better, international school, with whom he maintained a collegial contact, did. Mary Walker, a grandchild of the Walker clan, had been in the fourth grade there several years earlier. The poor child stuttered, and her folks were in his office all the time. They struck him as nice quiet people. At Thanksgiving they made him a sweet potato pie—"Heaven knows where they found sweet potatoes *here!*"—and that little girl, he said she was just lovely to look at. The other kids were so mean to her on account of her stutter. But there was something not right with the parents. They were very *serious* people. Mr. Tim's voice grew low and conspiratorial. He didn't believe that they were missionaries *at all.* "Somebody told me that the family actually worked for the CIA—and I *believe* it."

"Really!" I exclaimed.

"Oh yes!" said Mr. Tim. "Now, I don't know all the details of the story, but once, Mary got into a fight with another girl, whose father was—Persian? I think her mother was—Norwegian? Strange couple. NGO people. In *any* case, Mary walloped the other girl but good. The other girl deserved it. The father, this Persian man, he came into the school furious, and made some kind of silly, hot-blooded remark about Americans, and somehow this got back to the Walkers. One week later, the Thai authorities *deported* him. And then Mary stopped coming to class, and her parents sent the school a note saying that they had decided that Mary would do better at home. Then somebody told me that the Walkers were the last Americans to leave China after the revolution, and somebody *else* told me that they used to live in Burma, and, well, it just all made sense to me."

It made sense to me too.

Gunther the yoga teacher knew all about the Walkers: he, too, had heard stories. Sometimes at the end of a yoga session, Gunther's wife would bring out cups of hot ginger tea and we would sit in the gazebo, gossiping. On hearing the Walker name, he stiffened. "I haff never met them," Gunther said. "But I hear so many things. I do not like this kind of Christian who liff in a big house with so many servants, and then tell the people how they must liff. Is that for you to be Christian?" Gunther looked at me severely. I shook my head. Gunther himself lived in a big house with many servants and told many people how they must live, but it did not seem the right moment to mention that. He breathed deeply to a *chakra* three fingers below his belly button and continued: an Episcopalian pastor from Delaware with a bad back several years earlier had

taken one of his classes, and this man, Gunther said, had known someone who had known the Walkers very well indeed. "He tells me that the
Walkers give the Christians money and medicine but let the people who
are not Christian alone. I do not like this spirit so much at all. I teach
yoga, luff, and compassion to everyone who come here." Gunther looked
at me again. "So you still like the Walkers so much?" he said. I sipped my
tea and protested meekly that I had never even met them.

From Thai and *farang* alike I heard stories, often improbable and
sometimes mutually impossible. Our landlady, an elderly Thai who
stopped by weekly to oversee the gardener, told me in a hushed whisper
that she had heard that an earlier generation of Walkers had once commanded a guerrilla army of anti-Communist Christian converts in southern China: she used an unfamiliar Thai word to describe the Walkers,
which, when I looked it up in the dictionary, I found meant warlord, or
anyone resistant to the rule of the king, and hence outside the boundaries of civilization itself. A parent at the school had heard that they
were the most generous philanthropists in the north of Thailand. According to a development worker I met by chance in a bar, they lived in
ostentatious wealth offered up by pious contributors in humble clapboard
churches across the Midwest. All my informants agreed that the Walkers
had been in Asia a very long time, but details varied: the Walkers had
lived, some said, in China; others said in Burma, in Laos, in Thailand.
Nobody knew the details. Everyone seemed to have met or heard a story
about a different Walker, and I couldn't keep the names straight. I was
told that the Walkers were the nicest people you could hope to meet, the
real salt of the earth, doing God's work; I was also told that the Walkers
were opportunistic, fanatical, power-mad neocolonialists. They were at
once a huge family riven by dissension, and they were close-knit. All I
knew was that Martiya van der Leun shot the scion of the family two
times in the back with a hunting rifle.

I had never met a missionary before, and so contradictory was the
impression produced by all these stories that I had little idea what to expect. I had grown up in Manhattan. The only serious Christian I had
ever met was my co-op's handyman, a black man named Leon who was
born again when I was about eleven after he went to a revival meeting in
New Jersey. The phrase "born again" had confused me considerably at

the time, and played on my imagination in horrific ways. All through my childhood and adolescence, Leon and I were friends, and I recall that once, after Kristin Skamanga dumped me, he told me in a serious voice, "It don't matter about that little girl, 'cause Jesus loves you—you know? He loves you with all His heart."

Beyond Leon, I knew no Christians who took their faith seriously. The missionary himself was a figure only from the short stories of Somerset Maugham, and I had imagined that the missionaries were faded relics of an earlier time, like Maugham's colonial administrators who drank gin slings on the veranda overlooking the jungle at the Club. An appointment to meet real missionaries like the Walkers thus struck me as intensely exotic, as if I had been invited to visit Bhutan. The stories about the Walkers, like the stories about Martiya, thrilled me: I hoped that they were all true.

Later, when I came to know the Walkers well, I decided that they were stranger, far stranger, than those who had traded rumors and spun idle gossip imagined.

Asking a mother about her murdered son is a delicate operation, like removing a stray lash from a child's eye. I had Mrs. Walker on the phone and was just starting to probe gently when she cut me off. "Oh, honey, you're here in Chiang Mai?" she asked. "Then you just come by the Mission one of these days and we'll talk. There'll be someone around. There always is."

Norma Walker said to drive north along the palm-fringed winding river road, past the Baptist church, then to take a right at the bar called Brasserie. "Do you know the place?" I certainly did: Rachel and I drank tequila there sometimes on Thursday nights when a long-haired guitarist named Tuk played note-perfect Jimi Hendrix and Santana covers with his backup band, the Tukables. I didn't mention the tequila on the phone. Norma Walker said that not long past the bar there would be a noodle stand on the left and another on the right. The compound was down the red dirt road just past the second noodle stand. I said that I'd be there the next day at one.

I arrived early. The cement wall surrounding the Walker compound was topped with broken glass; a discreet brass placard beside the closed gate read: SOUTH CHINA CHRISTIAN MISSION. At the end of the alley, a tuk-tuk driver had parked his rickshaw under the shade of a banyan tree and was asleep, sprawled in the back of his carriage. I could hear his snores.

From the outside, the compound had looked huge. But when I rolled back the front gate of the compound along its rusted track and stepped inside, the place was disappointingly gray and dusty, almost dingy. A pair of trailers sat on cement blocks along one wall; and along the other wall there was a large concrete house painted a pale chewing-gum pink. An exterior staircase led to the house's second story, and then to its third—but the third story did not yet exist. Sturdy metal poles sprouted from the flat roof like antennae. The staircase simply wandered heavenward. Only a flowering jacaranda relieved the melancholy hot-season severity of the place, and snow-white blossoms drifted limply over the dead grass and dried mud. On the front stoop of the house, a small black cat with yellow eyes was licking her paws. I knocked on the door and wiped my forehead with my sleeve. I waited a moment and knocked again.

A voice sang out from the other side of the door, "Oh, Tom, just let yourself in." It was Mrs. Walker's voice.

Tom, Mischa—close enough. I slipped off my sandals and arranged them neatly beside the other shoes: the rubber sandals, the tennis shoes, the mud-caked leather work boots, the worn-down flip-flops, and the knee-high galoshes. I opened the unlocked door and stepped into the house.

An old woman looked up at me from a couch set at an angle to the front door. She was fleshy, and just slightly more of her pink-gray skin slipped out from under her faded blue housedress than I was meant to see: hints of puffy knees expanded to puffy calves lined with varicose trails leading down to puffy ankles. A puffy face rested on a puffy neck. Only her pale-green eyes were sharp, but they were very sharp, and they looked me up and down critically. "Oh, you are not Tom Riley *at all*," she concluded, after a considerable period of judgment.

"No," I admitted, and to cover the silence which fell over the room, I added, idiotically, "I'm sorry."

"Don't be sorry," the woman replied evenly. "I'm not Tom Riley either, after all."

Having established to our mutual satisfaction that my failure to be Tom Riley implied no moral fault, she paid me no further mind, as if expecting that I knew the routine around here.

"I'm so sorry to bother you," I finally said. "But I called yesterday. I'm Mischa Berlinski. And you must be Mrs. Walker."

"I am," the woman said. "Only, you can call me Nomie. Everyone does."

"Okay, Nomie," I obliged. I was *still* standing in the doorway, so I added, "I was going to come at one."

"Then you're right on time," Nomie said. "Don't mind me if I don't get up. Mr. Walker will be with you in a moment. You just make yourself comfortable right there."

She gestured to a couch opposite her own, and closing the door behind me, I took my place. On the phone the day before, I had indicated no preference as to which of the Walkers received me.

On the couch beside Nomie there was a ball of bright-blue yarn, which the old woman began to play with, spooling out several inches of thread, wrapping it around her thick fingers, and then rolling the yarn back onto the skein. She was not a woman to whom I would have otherwise applied the adjective "kittenish." She seemed absorbed in the operation, but she must have noticed me staring at the ball, because she said, "The doctor told me this would be good for the arthritis."

"Does it help?"

"I'm not sure just yet, but I do pray for some relief."

There were no portraits of family, no bookshelves on the whitewashed walls. The only furniture was the fake-leather couch where Nomie sat, the fake-leather couch on which I had installed myself, and a wooden rocking chair. In the far corner there was an upright piano, its closed lid supporting a small tank in which three large goldfish swam frantic laps, like athletes in training for a goldfish Olympiad.

"Can I offer you a cool glass of orange Tang?" Nomie asked.

For the first and only time in my adult life, I was seized by the desire for a cool glass of orange Tang. I was aware suddenly that my throat was desperately parched, and I didn't just want but *needed* a cool glass of orange Tang. "That would absolutely hit the spot," I said.

Nomie looked down at the ball of yarn in her hand, which she continued to knead. Then she spoke very loudly in an utterly foreign language. It was a language with *sounds* I had never heard before, like whale song, or Martian. Her voice swooped and glided, and she inserted vowels and diphthongs which seemed to come from the deepest recesses of her gullet. The only word I understood was "Tang," pronounced like the Chinese dynasty.

There was a pause and then a sympathetic feminine voice shouted out, "Okey-dokey, Grandma." A few seconds later, a young woman entered the room, carrying a tray of glasses and a tall glass pitcher beaded with perspiration. She set the tray down on the coffee table. "Cool Tang!" she said.

The young woman poured me a glass of orange Tang from the pitcher. "Thank you," I said. I took a sip, and for a second my mouth was flooded with long-forgotten memories of kindergarten. "You know, I had forgotten how much I like Tang."

"I'm so glad! We like it too," she said with a giddy, musical laugh. She had the kind of face one finds smoothing out the virgin sheets of an unruffled bed in an Ikea catalogue, unthreatening to women but nevertheless appealing to men, with short dark hair sensibly cut and light-blue eyes. She sat down on the far couch, then turned toward Nomie. "Grandma, have you seen Tom Riley lately?" she asked.

"I thought *he* was Tom Riley, at first."

"He was supposed to be here ages ago. We were talking about going to the zoo. I wanted to see the monkeys." The young woman turned back to me. "I forgot my manners! Grandpa says I should just put them on a little chain. I'm Judith."

The couches were close enough that by standing up and leaning far forward we could shake hands. Nomie explained that I was there to meet with Mr. Walker.

"But didn't Grandpa go to Burma this morning?" Judith asked.

"No, he's going to Mandalay *tomorrow*, so it's lucky that you came today," Nomie said. "But you can't keep Mr. Walker too long because he needs a rest in the afternoons."

Mandalay! I thought about asking if I could go too. "I hope you don't mind my prying," I said, "but what is Mr. Walker going to do in Mandalay? Does he go often?"

Nomie stopped kneading the ball of yarn.

"Why, he's going to preach, of course!" Nomie said, in the same voice that she might have used to declare that books have pages—or the universe a Maker. It was almost certainly the first time in my life that I had heard anyone use the word "preach" in a wholly literal sense. It was a pleasant shock to discover that these missionaries were, in fact, missionaries, like the first sight of palm trees in the tropics. "We hold a Bible conference there every few months, and if Mr. Walker didn't go . . ." Her voice drifted off. "I don't go on those trips myself anymore because of the arthritis, but Mr. Walker!"

A gentle knock on the front door interrupted Nomie.

"Tom!" Judith said.

Nomie cleared her throat. "Tom Riley, don't you make me move from this spot one more time," she said. "You just let yourself in."

Tom let himself in. He took a step into the room and closed the door behind him.

"Whew!" he said. "It is . . ."—he paused, and we all waited— ". . . *hawt* out there!"

He was a large man, a *very* large man, tall, with immensely broad shoulders and thick legs. He would have been big anywhere, but in Thailand he was mammoth.

"But you should be used to it!" protested Judith. "You're from Tennessee!"

"All I know is that I'm *hawt*."

"Have some Tang," Nomie said.

"I'd love some," Tom said. He bent over and took a glass of Tang from the tray. He righted himself slowly, and I reckoned to myself that the little glass of Tang was going to do nothing to quench this big man's big thirst. But he took a sip with the utmost delicacy, licked his lips, and declared, "That's better."

Tom now noticed me for the first time. "I'm Tom Riley," he said.

His hand swallowed up my own in a surprisingly gentle handshake. "It's really great to meet you," he added, in a voice as soft as his grasp. He took the seat next to me on the couch, sinking deep into the cushions, and as if he had sat in the prow of a canoe in which I occupied the stern, I felt myself rising up.

"Tom is staying with us a little while," Nomie explained. "He's helping Mr. Walker with his Bible."

"Tom's a linguist from Tennessee," Judith added. "He knows more about the Dyalo than pretty much anyone."

Tom's huge face reddened. "Don't believe everything these folks tell you. There's not a heck of a lot I can tell a Walker about the Dyalo."

Judith said, "Really, Tom! Just the other day you were telling us about those . . . those agglut . . . aggluttin . . ."

"Agglutinating pronouns."

"Exactly! They were so interesting. Mischa, you have to ask Tom about them someday. He'll tell you about them for hours. Hours and hours and hours."

Tom looked at his very large bare feet. He said, "I've come here to learn from the Walkers, not the other way around."

The modest declaration hung in the air a moment, until Nomie glanced at her watch and cluck-clucked. "Well, you're surely not going to learn about lunch if we don't get things moving around here," she said. "Judith, honey, why don't you go and hunt down your granddad while we talk? Now that Tom's here, I have a feeling the boys will be wanting to eat soon."

Judith got up and scampered away down the hallway. She was humming. Nomie continued to turn the ball of wool in her hands. "Mr. Walker gets to working, he just loses his sense of time," she said. "And he just loves the Psalms. A peace comes over him when he reads the Psalms."

"I see it in the work," Tom said.

"It's beautiful work," added Nomie.

"Ah-men," Tom said.

"But what exactly is Mr. Walker *doing* with the Psalms?" I asked.

Tom looked at me. "Why, don't you know?"

"Now, Tom!" Nomie said. "Not everyone is in the Mission Community, not *everyone* follows the work." Those people who didn't, her voice implied, were of distinctly marginal importance.

"I suppose, but . . ."

Nomie looked up from the blue ball of wool. "Mr. Walker is translating the Bible into Dyalo," she said. "Line by line and word by word. It's his life's work. It's his legacy. His father got it All started, and his brother Samuel did so much of the Work, but they've gone Home now, and Mr. Walker is Finishing Up." I have capitalized at my own discretion, but believe me—she really spoke that way. It was something in the way she looked upward as she spoke that offered the emphasis.

"He's doing a beautiful job," Tom added. "He's an artist."

Nomie's mouth opened slightly. "Oh no, Tom. He's Inspired. Like his father and his brother."

"Yes, but Mr. Walker is a great man, and it takes nothing from the Lord to admit it," Tom said defiantly. He turned to me. "The Dyalo didn't even have an alphabet before Mr. Walker's father gave them one. Can you imagine? Mr. Walker's father invented an alphabet for the Dyalo. She's a beauty. Wonderful vowels."

"Tom should know! Alphabets are Tom's specialty," Nomie said.

Tom looked modestly at the ground, and then at his watch. I was on the verge of saying "Oh, really? A specialist in alphabets?" and asking "What brings you here to Thailand?" but was preempted by the strains of "Nearer My God to Thee," coming from the vicinity of Tom's groin. It was his cell phone. "Hey, Bill," he said. Then he stood up from the couch and, covering the mouthpiece, said, "Y'all excuse me? I'll wash up a little before lunch." Tom walked slowly down the hall, still talking to Bill on the phone.

As soon as Tom Riley had left the room and his heavy footsteps could be heard ascending a flight of unseen stairs, Nomie looked at me. "Tom's been with us now, I don't know how long," she said in a low, confidential voice. "Maybe five months, even. He came here to make Fellowship with us, and *he won't leave*. You can't *believe* how much he eats! But we get all types here. He wants to set out on a Mission himself, and he's been here learning. The man has a wonderful way with the languages, but he's just so darn big! He frightens the people. You know how the Dyalo are. I told him that he should make a mission to *Africa*, but he said he had heard about us and he has his heart set on the Dyalo." She chuckled softly. "But he loves Jesus so much, and he's got so much good heart, sometimes God chooses the oddest vehicles."

She paused. I think she expected me to say something like "Amen" or "That He does!" but I stayed silent. Something in my silence encouraged her, and she continued: "The oddest vehicles! Who would have ever thought that He would have chosen me? Why, I remember when I met Mr. Walker for the first time! I was twenty-one years old, and he came to speak in 1956 at the Wheaton Bible College, where I was a student. He was older than me, almost thirty-five, but he was the handsomest man I had ever seen, with the saddest greenest eyes! Mr. Walker started talking about his childhood in Tibet and in China and his family's work with the Dyalo, and I whispered to my girlfriend Evangeline, who was here to visit just last year, I said to her, 'Evangeline, *that* is the man I am going to love and marry.' I'll bet half the girls in that auditorium were whispering that, but the Lord heard *me*, and now he's *mine*. One year later there I was in Burma, married to Mr. Walker, with a baby on the way! I must say, it is a very good thing the Lord gives us memory but not foresight, because I really don't know if I would have become a Walker if I'd known what was in store! When Mr. Walker came to speak that day, I don't believe that I had ever once *thought* of spending my life in the Orient and Burma and Thailand and places like that. I had never even *heard* of the Dyalo. Now here I am in Thailand with five beautiful Dyalo babies, and fifteen Dyalo grandchildren!"

Nomie's mention of her family reminded me why I was there. I started to construct a sentence around the name "David Walker" and found myself lacking a verb of adequate sensitivity. I debated "murdered," "killed," "passed away," and "died." Later, I learned that the Walkers preferred to say that he had been "called Home." I didn't say anything at all. I imagined Nomie wondered at her unusual guest who had phoned her out of the blue, come to her house, and drunk her Tang in silence! But really, I had no idea at what strange things Nomie wondered: there was some weirdness in the Walker way that made the normal conversational forays seem weak and ineffective, even inappropriate. It was like talking to royalty, or to the very wealthy, or the very beautiful.

The silence was broken by the entrance into the living room of a man who I presumed was Mr. Walker. He was a man of perhaps—who can tell with old people?—eighty?—old, gray, and not entirely steady on his bare feet. Yet tomorrow he was going to Mandalay! He walked slowly to the rocking chair, and with a deliberate motion turned himself in a half circle, gripped the railings of the chair, and hovered himself down. Then, turning to me, he extended his hand across his body, and I rose halfway off the couch to shake it. His large hand was calloused and strong. "Thomas Walker," he murmured in a low voice.

"It's very nice to meet you," I said.

"Glad to have you here," he replied.

Installed comfortably in his rocking chair, Mr. Walker seemed a more solid presence than he was on his feet. His dark-green eyes were the color of drying moss; they flickered alertly behind heavy square-rimmed glasses. His hair was gray but thick, cut short, and held in place with oil. His light-gray skin was very cleanly shaved, and I wondered idly for a second how he shaved the jowls: Did he shave down one side of the jowl, arrive at the cleft, and mount back up the other side, like a moun-taineer? Mr. Walker wore a checked buttoned-up shirt and a pair of shiny brown polyester slacks which rode up high on his waist. He had the se-vere, serious, grave, and melancholy air of the midwestern farming stock from which I later learned he came. He was not a large man, but he dom-inated the room in a way that big Tom Riley hadn't.

Mr. Walker began to rock. Nomie placed the ball of wool in her lap. Outside the window, the slow thump of construction began from some-where far away. From down the hall, I heard the clink of metal pans and the sizzle of something frying. I could think of no way at all to introduce the subject of their son and why Martiya might have killed him. I had no excuse for being here except that I was very curious and thought that if the story was good I could sell it: I would summarize their grief in two thousand words, peddle it to the *Bangkok Times* or *Executive*, and then the story of their son's death would line the birdcages of Bangkok's better families. The Walkers sat implacably, organically, rocking slowly, adjust-ing themselves, as if my presence there were no more notable than one of the dark, buzzing flies that came in from the garden—until finally Mr. Walker asked his wife if Tom Riley would be at home for lunch.

"I *think* so. He's just gone to wash up."

"And Bill? Did you hear from Bill?"

"He called this morning. He's busy as a guy can be, and Margaret is sick. But he's got the hymnals all ready for tomorrow."

"It's a good thing Tom decided to go to Burma. Need somebody to carry those boxes!" Mr. Walker said.

Mr. and Mrs. Walker laughed.

"Is Preacher Matthew going to be taking the jeep?" Mrs. Walker asked.

"Why?" said Mr. Walker. "Why should he take the jeep?"

"Well, honey, if he's going up to Chiang Rai and Dok Rao to witness, he'll need the jeep."

"We'll worry about that when I get back," said Mr. Walker decisively. He turned to me. "And you, young man, what can we do for you? Can we help you with something?"

It was the most natural question in the world.

I hesitated a moment, then told them why I was there. I confessed everything—about Josh O'Connor and his visit with Martiya van der Leun, how I had spoken subsequently with Martiya's family and friends. I told the Walkers that I wanted to know the final pieces of Martiya's story, and I babbled out an apology for the imposition.

When I was done, the room was silent again. Mr. Walker rocked in his chair slowly once or twice. He looked at me, and then at the ground, and then his eyes fell on his wife. Nomie picked up her ball of wool and placed it beside her. Then she stood herself up from the couch.

"We do not say the name of that woman in this house," she said, and, moving slowly on her puffy legs, left the darkened room.


Mr. Walker insisted that I stay for lunch.

"Nomie's a fiery woman, but she'd be just crushed if you didn't eat with us," Mr. Walker said. "Her bark is worse than her bite." There was a distinctly doubtful note in his voice.

Mr. Walker led me into the dining room, where Nomie and a slight Asian woman were setting the table. Like the living room, the dining room was austere, bare but for a long table surrounded by high-backed chairs. Nomie smiled at me as I entered, and I did my best to smile back. "Mischa, this is Ah-Mo, our helper," she said, and turning toward Ah-Mo, she made what I assumed was the inverse introduction in what I assumed was Dyalo.

"Ah-Mo doesn't speak any English," Nomie said. I started to speak to Ah-Mo in my clumsy Thai, but Nomie added, "She also hasn't learned any Thai yet. Ah-Mo is Dyalo. She's here from Burma. She's a refugee."

Ah-Mo was the first Dyalo I had met, and her unusual face held me entranced for a moment. No one knows where the Dyalo come from, but some speculate Tibet—and there was to her face a Tibetan air: she was flat-featured but round-eyed, with thin, elegant lips. I wished I could talk with her: it is always difficult to read very foreign faces, but there was something keen and witty in the way she looked at me, as if she'd have a million good stories about these people, if only we could brew up some barley tea and chat. Judith must have seen me staring at Ah-Mo. Standing beside me, she whispered, "How old do you think Ah-Mo is?"

"Maybe thirty?" I whispered back.

"She's over fifty," Judith said. "Isn't that *amazing*?"

"Wow."

"It's because there's no pollution in the mountains."

"Do all the Dyalo look like her?"

Judith looked shocked. "*Oh my*, no," she said. "Only the Christians."

I was on the verge of asking from what unpleasantness Ah-Mo had fled when Nomie waved me to a place at the table. When we were all arranged, there were six of us: Mr. and Mrs. Walker, Judith, Tom Riley, who had mysteriously appeared from the stairwell and was greeted with almost rapturous pleasure by the entire Walker family, Ah-Mo, and myself. Mr. Walker asked Judith to say grace, and Judith Walker again spoke in that utterly strange language. Everyone at the table folded their hands in front of their chins and closed their eyes. Judith must have been very grateful for the food because grace went on a very long time. Then Mr. Walker decided he wanted to bless the food, too, because he started talking in Dyalo also. This was the signal that we were all supposed to hold hands. Ah-Mo's dry little hand reached out for mine on the left, and on the other side I found Tom Riley's enormous whale fin of a palm. Yet it was Ah-Mo who held my hand tighter.

Conversation over lunch—midwestern with Oriental accents: baby corn fried in a wok with bacon; an omelette served over rice with cheese, chili peppers, and tomatoes—was general: travel plans were made; the health of people whose names I did not recognize discussed—they all seemed to be getting better, thank the Lord (which was not a reflexive phrase at all but an actual opportunity for those seated around the table to bow their heads and murmur for a moment), all except someone named Susie, who apparently was not doing so well; construction would begin soon on the Ministry Center. This was missionary shop talk, and after the first half hour or so, it was boring.

At one point, Judith leaned across the table and touched my forearm.

"Mischa, are you a Christian?" she asked.

"No," I said. I shifted uncomfortably in place and said that I was Jewish.

All of the Walkers and Tom Riley turned in my direction and stared, as if I had announced that I was pregnant with triplets, all except Ah-Mo, who hadn't understood a word. She just kept eating.

Finally, Judith said, "How wonderful! We *love* to meet Jewish people. You know, Jewish people are God's chosen people."

Judith stared at me. "No, it's *true*," she insisted, and at that moment, Mr. Walker, who had been momentarily distracted, asked his wife to pass the milk, and the conversation drifted back to the pastor from Terre Haute who would be coming next week to make fellowship.

After Nomie's explosion, *I* certainly wasn't going to be the dang fool who introduced Martiya's name back into conversation. Lunch had lulled me: the day was warm, my eyes were heavy. I had organized my life around the principle that nothing came between me and my naps—not murderous anthropologists, not fiery-tempered missionaries—and for all of Nomie's protestations that Mr. Walker liked to take himself a little rest in the afternoons, the man seemed to me altogether too wide awake: these missionaries, I concluded sadly, were not the napping type. They were decidedly of the this-life-is-short-so-let's-get-something-done type. So it was with excitement and drowsiness mingled in equal measure that I accepted when at the end of the long meal Mr. Walker invited me to join him in his study.

Mr. Walker led me to his study and then left me alone in it for a moment, as he recalled another question for his wife. I am a snoop when it comes to people's books, and I studied his while I waited. His library wasn't large, and it was clearly the collection of a man with a narrowly centered but deeply researched set of interests. There were at least a half dozen translations of the Bible into English, from the King James to the New Revised Standard, as well as editions of the Old and New Testament in the original Greek and Hebrew. There were Greek and Hebrew dictionaries and grammars. Every book of the Bible had a thick, leather-bound commentary. These formed an imposing shelf unto themselves. There were books arguing against Darwinian theories of evolution, and a smaller number of books supporting the theory. There was a book entitled *Apocalypse Tomorrow*, the thickest of a long series of tomes which to judge by their bright-red covers seemed to be arguing that the end was very nigh. There were a few Tom Clancy novels with well-cracked spines.

Mr. Walker returned to the office after a minute and closed the door behind him. He circumnavigated his desk, then sank down with a grunt. He folded his hands into narrow steeples and brought them to rest in front of his mouth. He stared at me very seriously.

"I didn't want you to leave without an answer to your question," he said. "It's just that Nomie, she gets so upset."

"I understand," I said. "It's natural. I'm sorry I—"

"Do you know how they found Davy?" he asked.

"Davy?"

"My son," Mr. Walker said.

"No," I said. "No, I don't know how they found him."

Mr. Walker didn't say anything for so long that I began to think that I had offended him too. "When Davy fell from the bridge," he began, "he fell a long way, but the doctor said, the doctor said he probably survived that. His left arm wasn't broken, it was shattered, like a windowpane. His leg was broken, too, but not so bad. She left him for two days, and then she shot him from behind. That was the worst part, her leaving him. Two days."

The only noise in the room was the hum of the air conditioner.

"He was just thirty," Mr. Walker continued. "So when Mrs. Walker . . . Mrs. Walker—I don't think I've ever met a better Christian than my Nomie. She wrote to Martiya in prison, she sent her food even, and clothing. She *forgave* her. I think she genuinely forgave Martiya, because she knew Martiya—she knew that it wasn't Martiya who killed her baby. But . . . but until you lose a child—you don't know what a murder means. How do you act like a good Christian when someone does something like that to your boy?"

Mr. Walker's voice was deep, and he spoke softly, and when he wanted to emphasize something, he spoke softer still, so that when he told me that Mrs. Walker was a good Christian woman, I was leaning on the edge of my chair, straining to catch his words. Mr. Walker stared at me a moment, and I realized with a start that his question wasn't rhetorical. He was waiting for an answer.

"I don't know," I said. "I don't know how you act like a good Christian."

"Fair enough. You don't know what a murder means." It wasn't an accusation, just a simple statement of fact. Mr. Walker fingered the Greek dictionary lying open on his desk. "It's a rough, rough business we're in. I have a friend here who's a *phu yai*, a policeman, and goes after the worst kind of men—drug dealers and men who put hill-tribe women in cages and sell 'em in Bangkok like pigs, I've seen it, rough business— but I sometimes think we Walkers chose the roughest line of work there is. I always wonder if David really knew how rough it is, if we prepared him. My parents knew, and my brothers and sisters, and Mrs. Walker, and I think even the other kids knew that it was a rough business—but David, he was such a likable guy. Everyone liked him. Charming as heck. I don't think he ever really understood how cruel and vicious and cunning and resourceful the *forces* keeping the Dyalo in bondage were, how they were prepared to stop at nothing to keep the Dyalo enslaved."

I had no idea whatsoever what Mr. Walker was talking about. I nodded and crossed my legs. He unfolded his long fingers and spread them out on his desk.

"We used to have her in this house, did you know that?"

"I had no idea."

"Oh yes, she was here all the time. She had so many questions, and we might not be *scholars*, but we know the Dyalo better than anyone. She stayed right in this house, and she'd ask us all those questions for her *research*. She'd ask why the Dyalo think pregnant women can't use iron knives and we'd tell her, or why the Dyalo think it's shameful for the man and his wife to plant the rice in the field together. We'd tell her, 'Well, gosh, that's simple, you see it's like this,' and she'd say, 'Gosh, you people *are* Dyalo!' and Mrs. Walker would say, 'Four generations—you get used to folks!' But Mrs. Walker was wrong about that. We're not Dyalo, and God made people as mysterious as He is. You don't get to know anyone."

A phone rang and rang again. Mr. Walker stopped talking for a second, and when Nomie shouted, "Honey, it's for you, it's Khun Nirawat," he picked up the cordless phone which was sitting on his desk and began to speak in Thai. Excellent, fluid Thai—the kind of Thai I'd be lucky to have if I stayed in Thailand another thirty years. He raised a finger to say that he'd just be a minute. Something on the other end of the line made him chuckle. After a minute or two, he hung up the phone and his face grew serious again. "The Dyalo aren't foolish, you know," he declared, almost aggressively.

"I didn't think they were," I said, almost defensively.

"It was the hardest thing for that woman to understand. We understood that the Dyalo people . . . the Dyalo had certain *needs*, and the Dyalo recognized that we understood those needs. Do you understand what I'm telling you?"

Mr. Walker spoke so calmly, so reasonably, that I was sure that when I thought it over later it would all make sense. I nodded. Mr. Walker seemed satisfied with this response.

"The Dyalo would tell her that they were in bondage—*bondage!*—to the demons, and she'd write in her little notebook, 'The Dyalo have a rich hierarchical system of animistic spirit worship.' She didn't believe them. But *we* knew what was going on, because we've been here so long. Back when we first came, family after family asked us, 'Two thousand years! Why did it take you so long to come with God's word? To bring us this Good News? We were orphans and slaves to the forces of darkness! Our fathers have died, our grandfathers all died in bondage—and they died without hearing this Word.' Foolish people don't talk like that, you know—people *know* when they're slaves, and I tell you, brother, no man wants to live in chains."

"*Of course* not," I said. We sat for a second. I started to worry that my response had been condescending, so I asked, "What did you tell them?"

"Tell who?"

"The Dyalo. The Dyalo who wanted to know why you didn't come faster."

"I always said that *we* Walkers had come just as quickly as *we* could, and we didn't know why the others hadn't come sooner. But we were heartbroken, all of us, just heartbroken, that the Word didn't come much earlier, in time for all their forefathers to hear. When we told the Dyalo that they didn't need to be slaves, that they could be free—why! they'd *come over* to us, whole families, whole villages." Mr. Walker's green eyes were bright. "We warned her, we warned Martiya when she came that the evil spirits in the hills are dangerous, but she didn't believe us. We told her that the Deceiver was in those mountains and she needed to take precautions. We told her it was all right here"—he tapped the Bible. " 'For we wrestle not against flesh and blood, but against principalities, against powers, against the rulers of the darkness of this world, against spiritual wickedness in high *places*.' That's in Ephesians, and we read that to her, and she smiled politely, and she wrote in her notebook, and then she shot our boy."

He paused for a moment.

"She pulled the trigger, but make no mistake, it was the demons who killed him," he finally said. "I think she got into those hills and slowly but surely the demons mastered her. I think the demons who wanted, who were *desperate*, to keep the Dyalo in bondage murdered David." I must have looked at him strangely because he added, "It happens, you know—we've been here a long time and we've seen it."

A moment later, Mrs. Walker came into the study and with hardly more than a look made it clear that it was time for Mr. Walker to take his rest. I thanked the Walkers and went outside. The black cat was dozing on the stoop of the house, and the tuk-tuk driver was still snoozing under the banyan tree.

PART TWO

# THE STORY
# THE WALKERS TOLD
# OF THEMSELVES

# ONE

# THE GATES OF GOLD

THERE WAS SIMPLY NO TELLING what would come out of a Walker mouth at any time. Anna Walker, Judith Walker's cousin, told me that before the Flood, it had *never* rained. We ended up having a long conversation about whether this was possible, because wouldn't you need rain after the Fall but before the Flood when Man was forced to plow the Earth? I'm not entirely sure I got the better of the argument. Ruth-Marie Walker was not the only Walker to refer to biblical characters in precisely the same tone of voice that one might use to describe the neighbors who let their dog run loose: "I can't talk about Saul, he just gets me so frustrated." She was referring to *that* Saul, mighty king of Israel. James Walker, David Walker's brainy cousin, used in a single sentence the words "eschatological" and "dispensationalist," and I had to ask him what they meant. I asked Sarah Walker, Thomas Walker's sister, what she might have done with her life had she not been a missionary. She paused a second, and, wrinkling her nose, told me that she always had regretted turning down a position once while on home furlough working at a perfume counter in the mall. She said she thought she had a really good sense of smell. Thomas Walker told me that he expected the world to end within a generation. "Those living close to the Light, close to the Lord, will be saved," he said. He did not even bother to ask whether I was living close to the Light, close to the Lord.

Over the course of the next several weeks, I ran from one Walker to the next. I met in their homes with Walkers who lived in Chiang Mai, and ran up a big phone bill calling other Walkers who lived in the States. It was a large family, in continual motion: there was always another cousin stopping by the big pink house, or a sister coming in from China, or a granddaughter from the border of Laos and Vietnam introducing the new baby to her grandparents, or an uncle in Terre Haute whom nobody had bothered to mention before but *of course* I should get in touch with. I introduced myself to each of the newcomers, and proposed that we spend a few minutes talking. I felt the collector's passion: I wanted to talk at least a little with as many of the Walkers as I could.

In my notebook I made a genealogical table to keep track of the Walkers. At the top of the table were Raymond Walker, the family patriarch, and his wife, Laura: they were the first generation of Walkers to hear the call from God and head east; and then, arranged in neat boxes below, were Thomas Walker and his brother, Samuel, and their two sisters, Sarah and Helena. This was the generation born in China. Each of these was connected by a wavy line to a spouse; beside Mr. Walker, I wrote in Nomie's name. Then vertical lines led down to what Nomie always called the "kids," her children and her nieces and her nephews. This was the generation born in northern Burma, for the most part, and almost everyone in this generation, too, was married, wavy lines again joining Walker blood to the newcomers. This was David Walker's generation, and I marked his box in red. He was the third of Nomie and Thomas Walker's five children. He was at the very center of my chart. Then below the "kids" were Raymond and Laura Walker's thirty-four great-grandchildren, where David Walker's children would have been— Judith Walker's generation. David Walker died at thirty; had he lived, he would now have been middle-aged, with a family of his own.

Nomie showed me a photo from the last family reunion. They had held it right in the compound, and there must have been sixty or seventy Walkers gathered there. In the photograph, the Walkers were arranged on risers in massed ranks, and I recognized in the background the pink cement Walker house. The lawn, which now was mud, was greener then. "That's Mr. Walker's daddy—the Lord called him Home, oh, six, seven years ago," Nomie Walker said, pointing to Raymond Walker, a very slight old man at the center of the frame. He was leaning on a cane. "Laura was already gone at the time. And there's Mr. Walker's brother, Samuel, who was here in Thailand until he passed on two years ago, and his sister Helena, who lives just down in Hang Dong, and his other sister Sarah—she was just here visiting last year, we had such a good time." Her finger skimmed quickly over the photograph, hovering over each face as she spoke. "And then there are the kids . . ." Everyone was wearing T-shirts with the family motto "Jesus Wins All," written in English and the Dyalo script that Raymond Walker invented. I spotted Judith Walker in the photo, and her brother and sisters and cousins—handsome, clean-cut children and adolescents, the kind of kids who say "Yes, ma'am" and "No, sir." The family spilled out over the borders of the photograph, so that at the far margins of the frame, some of the Walkers leaned back in to be included in the shot. Only David was missing.

The Walkers were unfailingly helpful, even Nomie, who, so long as I didn't mention Martiya, was happy to tell me stories about what it was like in the old days; but as so often happens, it was an outsider, Big Tom Riley, who told me most of the story in the end.* The linguist from Tennessee was my translator out of Walkerese into something I could understand. The Walkers tended to dwell obsessively on details: an afternoon with Nomie and Thomas could devolve into endless bickering over whether the house in Xian-Hu had a thatch or wattle roof, and whether the big flood was in '33 or '34. But Tom Riley knew the Walker story well, having passed many long evenings in the company of one or another of the Walkers as they went from lonely Dyalo village to lonely Dyalo village, preaching—and in preaching, like war, you get to know folks.

Tom and I took to meeting in the mornings at an American-style diner in the center of Chiang Mai specializing in big breakfasts. The place was air-conditioned, with large plate-glass windows, hanging ferns, pink vinyl booths, and neat, uniformed waitresses with name tags in English and Thai, who would sidle up to our table and be shocked to find

---

*In addition to my talks with the Walkers and Tom Riley, my understanding of missionary life on the Tibetan-Chinese border and in Burma has been immeasurably enriched by the extraordinary memoirs of the late Gertrude Morse, *The Dogs May Bark: But the Caravan Moves On* (Joplin: College Press, 1998).

Tom address them fluently in the vernacular. He was, after all, a professional linguist. He'd order himself four eggs, double bacon, hash browns, and a pot of hot coffee, which by Thai standards is simply a mountain of food, and I would order a short stack of pancakes. The restaurant was filled by nine with the expat retirees, who left their young Thai wives at home and spent the long mornings lingering over coffee and the *Bangkok Times*, contemplating how to pass another long day of self-imposed Oriental exile. Sometimes Tom and I would stay talking all through the morning, until the lunch hour arrived and the place filled up with hip young Thais who thought of an American-style diner as ethnic dining, a taste of the exotic West.

In 1934, the Salween River, which tumbles down in white water out of the high mountains of Tibet, overflowed her boundaries, together with her tributaries, and the river valley where the Walker family lived and tended to the spiritual needs of the Dyalo people was flooded. The great river rose in only hours, and everything was lost but what the Walkers had on their backs. The first and only dictionary of the Dyalo language was carried off downstream, floating beside Raymond Walker's first translation of the gospels into Dyalo and the family Bible in which the Walker genealogy had been recorded. So when I asked about the family before old Raymond Walker, the Walkers of today just shrugged and waved their hands: the past was downstream, lost in the flood.

What they knew was this: they were of Scotch and Irish stock and maybe a little German—nobody really knew anymore—and they had always been wanderers. Raymond Walker was only five when his family left Sayre, Oklahoma, in 1901 and staked a claim in the Indian Territory near Tulsa, but his parents hadn't been born in Sayre, and his grandparents had been born only God Himself knew where to the east, the generations one after another in constant motion westward. The Walkers had drifted all through the nineteenth century, all across a huge continent, and probably would have kept drifting if first they hadn't run out of empty country, or if the Great War hadn't come. But the war *did* come, and Raymond Walker was the first Walker in a very long time to go eastward, to northern France, where he served as a medic, and when he came back to Oklahoma, he no longer wanted to teach school, which had been his childhood ambition.

Raymond Walker's first idea when he came home after the war was to start a business breeding registered, pedigreed Dalmatians. But an epidemic of distemper made the dogs weak and trembling in their paws and thin, and they had to be shot, and Raymond lost all the money he had invested in a beautiful bitch and stud. Raymond figured that the animals' deaths were a sign from God lest Raymond grow distracted from the plan that he had formulated in northern France. Then Raymond proposed to take his new wife, a pretty nurse named Laura, on a mission to convert the Tibetans. Nobody in Tulsa thought this a particularly fine idea: of course the Tibetans needed saving, same as everyone else, but Raymond and Laura had responsibilities in Tulsa. Raymond's father, who ran a grocery store, was ailing, his mother was always in tears, and his brother drank. And round-faced, giggling Laura Walker, they said she wouldn't last a month in China: she was pale and sickly as a child, and couldn't tolerate even a feather out of place. They asked: Why would Raymond Walker of all people want to be a missionary, anyway? It was true that when he was eleven he had won a medal for having memorized more Scripture than any other boy in town, but someone in town won that medal every year, and you didn't see the others heading off to *China*. The people in Tulsa wondered if Raymond had got religion along with Laura, but at the wedding Laura's folks were mystified too: *they* had thought it was all Raymond's fault and were shocked to find that the Walkers seemed like such normal people, if maybe a little high-strung. But Raymond and Laura were of age, no one could stop them from heading off— in truth, no one really tried—and Raymond's experience as a medic and Laura's experience as a nurse made them attractive as volunteer missionaries. Their applications to the United Missionary Society were accepted, and they left for China in the fall of 1921, as very junior members of a missionary expedition to the Sino-Tibetan border, under the leadership of the celebrated Dr. Morris Chester, member of the National Geographic Society and one of the very few white men to have penetrated the interior of the closed kingdom of Tibet. Not long after the steamship *Maiden of the East* left San Francisco for Yokohama, the first stage in what would be a six-month voyage to the Tibetan frontier, Raymond and Laura Walker conceived their son Thomas.

Every morning on the *Maiden of the East*, Raymond and Laura, habituated to country hours, rose at dawn and sang hymns together, a pleasure they would indulge through good times and terrible until separated by Laura's death at the age of eighty-six; then, closing the hymnal, they picked up the Bible and read together, book by book, as the screws of the ship took them farther and farther from Tulsa. Dr. Chester prepared them for the hardships of inner China, delivering long lectures in his stateroom which emphasized equally the majesty of Chinese culture and the savagery of Chinese life; Mrs. Chester, a large, almost square woman dressed in the Victorian style with pince-nez and a hat embroidered with silk flowers, took Laura Walker aside every morning to discuss the particular problems of feminine hygiene and etiquette in a tropical climate. Dr. Chester then spent an hour offering rudimentary instruction in the Chinese language, and then another hour in Tibetan, so that after twenty-three days at sea Raymond and Laura could recite the Lord's Prayer in both tongues. Dr. Chester remarked to Mrs. Chester that the Walkers had an excellent ear for the tones. Every night, Raymond and Laura danced in the ship's ballroom. When the ship stopped in Japan, the Walkers ate in a restaurant where they sat on the floor, and they visited a Buddhist temple where they saw people worship idols for the first time. Dr. Chester explained that this was only a foretaste of the darkness of spiritual life on the Tibetan border. The *Maiden of the East* stopped in Shanghai, and the Walkers saw the junks on the Yangtze River, so many hundreds with their sails unfurled, each manned by hundreds of coolies, and Raymond calculated that the *floating* population alone in Shanghai Harbor was greater than the population of Tulsa, perhaps more than all the American men dead in the war.

"And none of these people are Christian?" Raymond asked Dr. Chester, standing on the deck of the ocean liner. "None of them know?" The idea staggered the imagination. He imagined the population of the entire world spread out along the length of a teetering balance. Before, he had supposed that the job of the missionary was to hunt out the unsaved remnants of humanity awaiting salvation; now he realized that the balance tilted heavily toward universal damnation. It was an awesome thought. To Raymond, heathenism was like some terrible but easily cured disease, and the notion that the healing medicine was warehoused in his own land, stored away in huge forgotten boxes, crates, and vials sufficient to change the lives of millions, while here, no one even *knew* there was a cure—this was a thought so disturbing that Raymond had to pace along the deck.

Dr. Chester found Raymond's excitement to spread the Gospel touching, and reminiscent of his own passion as a young man. He laughed. "None of them know," Dr. Chester said.

Then the party changed ships and went by small French coastal steamer to Haiphong in northern French Indochina. The food on the steamer was unfortunately rather rich, with buttery French sauces, which combined with Laura's pregnancy and the rocking motion of the vessel to make her more than a touch queasy, so that she was very glad to arrive in Haiphong, where there was so much to do. Mrs. Chester, with her formidable talents for organization and her ability to command the respect of even the most cunning merchant, took charge of the provisioning. They needed to buy supplies sufficient for a mission of five years, and although the *secteur français*, where the missionaries stayed, was lovely, with its café-lined boulevards and shady banyan trees, it was better to buy from the Chinese merchants in the squalid harbor, which they visited in a rickshaw pulled by a swaybacked coolie. They bought sugar, paper, lead pencils, Bibles and hymnals by the dozen, medicines of every sort, canned meats, sardines, canned vegetables, canned pears, peaches, apricots, nectarines, and tangerines, wool blankets, bolts of cotton and wool, and thousands of tapered wax candles.

When the provisions had been acquired and safely stowed in two dozen large steamer trunks, the missionaries traveled four days by narrow-gauge railway into the southern heart of China's Yunnan Province. The lower-class carriages of the train had no toilets, and the Chesters instructed the Walkers that it was best not to look up and down the tracks when the train came to a halt. For the first time, the Walkers saw the emerald-green rice paddies and the banana trees and the palms:

in the heat of the day, steam rose from the fields and the roofs of houses.

The party arrived after the long train journey in the Chinese provincial capital of Kunming, where, in order to accommodate Laura's pregnancy, Dr. Chester ordered the construction of a large sedan chair to be carried by six coolies. When Laura's pregnancy had been revealed to the entire traveling party, Dr. Chester and Mrs. Chester had smiled knowingly at one another. "It always happens first thing when a young couple gets out in the Mission Field," said Mrs. Chester.

"Usually happens shipboard," added Dr. Chester with a wink.

"God gives you a gift because you gave your life to Him," said Mrs. Chester, thoughtfully. "He gave us our first one just like you, the day we set sail for the Orient, more than forty years ago."

For the next two months, Laura was carried westward in the sedan chair, along narrow mountain paths. Because of the dangers of brigands, it was necessary for the missionaries to travel accompanied by a retinue of mercenary soldiers. Since the coolies who carried Laura's chair were opium addicts, every few hours they insisted that the caravan stop so that they could lie by the side of the road on their straw mats, pull out long bamboo pipes from their satchels, and smoke. The opium tended to make them hardy walkers but inattentive, and Laura was frightened, as her bearers sometimes closed their eyes and like packhorses dozed even as they marched along. Whenever they arrived at a small inn for the night, Laura thanked God for having delivered her safely this far.

The caravan mounted higher into the mountains, and stealthily the soldiers defected back toward China, leaving the party more and more isolated. The days grew colder, and Laura was grateful to Dr. Chester for the shearling coats he had insisted they have made for the ladies in Kunming. Along the road as they approached Tibet, they passed elaborately enrobed Buddhist lamas with enormous hats on their heads, chanting over and over, "Om mani padme hom." Laura asked Dr. Chester what they were saying, and Dr. Chester replied that the prayer, although widely used, was meaningless and sadly futile, but a demonstration of both the deep spiritual desire and capacity of the people, if only they knew to Whom they ought to direct their prayers. Raymond, for his part as he rode along toward Tibet, passed his days reciting in his own head sermon after sermon in which he told whoever would listen about the glorious vision he had had in France. With every footstep, Raymond was more moved by his own preaching.

Dr. Chester rode on his horse at the head of the caravan. To amuse himself along the journey he read the scores of symphonies, which he positioned under the pommel of the saddle, trusting his horse to know the route. While in the flatlands leading out of Kunming, the habit had struck the Walkers as innocuous, but when they approached the mountainous country of the headwaters of the Mekong and Yangtze rivers, both Raymond and Laura began to fear for Dr. Chester, as the rocky path grew narrower and the cliff alongside fell away more steeply. In many places the road itself, hardly wide enough for a horse under the best of conditions, had fallen away and the path was maintained only by the careful positioning of a rotting wooden board. Under ideal circumstances, every such makeshift bridge would have necessitated a stop and a careful examination of the soundness of the passage. But Dr. Chester seemed oblivious to the dangers, and indeed his excitement at the music he was reading seemed only to increase as the road narrowed. Then the Walkers began to fear for themselves, for Dr. Chester, by virtue of his position as rider of the lead horse, determined the pace of the entire caravan, and Dr. Chester's speed was largely governed by the subtle, unconscious signals he gave his horse in response to the tempo of the music that he studied. Nothing could distract him from his music, and the caravan flew heedlessly along those rocky heights. When they arrived at the squalid Chinese inn to spend the night, Mrs. Chester confronted her husband: "Mr. Chester, I insist for the sake of those that we have in our care, as well for my own safety, that tomorrow you pass your time with something *adagio*."

For two months, Laura's world was the inside of her sedan chair. She grew accustomed to the sway of the chair up on the men's shoulders as they trudged along like beasts; and she memorized every detail of the thin wood floor and walls of woven bamboo. The windows were covered with thick woven curtains which she raised and lowered to protect herself from the harsh mountain rains and wind. After a week of travel, she was sufficiently habituated to the rhythmic motions of the chair that she was even able to take pen in hand and write letters to her sister. Laura had always been close to her sister, only three years younger than she, but now, separated by half a world, the last barriers of sisterly reticence tumbled and the letters became a clear reflection of her thoughts.* Laura wrote that as a young girl she had fantasized idly about the life of a princess, and now she was being toted across China princess-style. Yet after a week or two the novelty of the experience diminished, and she reflected that to the men carrying her she was merely baggage. The thought bothered her, and she discussed the matter one evening with Dr. Chester. "Are you not, my dear, carrying your baby just as these men carry you?" he asked. Laura admitted that she was, although she was uncertain precisely what Dr. Chester's point was: Dr. Chester had a way of making you see things in a new light without explaining anything. In the afternoons, with the heavy curtains closed, the sedan chair grew warm and the swaying made Laura sleepy. Travel, Laura wrote, seemed to be a matter of submission to an endless series of rocking and swaying motions: the ship on the ocean, the train passing through the endless tunnels of northern Indochina and over the high bridges with their views of the deep jungle gorges, and now being carried toward Bantang, the city on the Tibetan border where Dr. Chester had promised that the traveling, for the moment, would end, where she could wait for her baby to arrive. What a strange place to be born! thought Laura. By the time you read this, she wrote to her sister, I will probably have *had* a baby, and then it will be many more months before I can read *your* letters telling me how happy you are for me. So I better accept your congratulations now! she added, and then, overcome by a superstitious chill, knocked three times on the bamboo walls of the sedan, and wondered if bamboo was a kind of wood.

Sometimes Laura thought about Bantang. It would be, she imagined, a grand white city, with gold trim, and crisp triangular flags flapping in the mountain breezes along the outer ramparts, against a sky whose blueness made her eyes ache; and after the monotonous foods of the caravan, she dreamed also of the delicious foods she would try when invited, as she surely would be, to the governor's palace. There, seated on a silk

---

*I was able to read these lovely letters thanks to the kindness of the children of Sarah Howard, Laura's sister, of Topeka, Kansas.

cushion, she would explain her mission to the governor (Dr. Chester gallantly translating) and sip the delicately spiced mutton soup, dip a piece of barley bread in the sauce of the boiled pheasant, and with a very straight proud back recount to the wide-eyed foreigners the very many wonders of life in Oklahoma and the glories of the God who inspired their travels.

The caravan had traveled on foot for almost two months, and it had been five months since the party had made their departure from America, when Dr. Chester announced to the traveling missionaries that, God willing, they would arrive that day at Bantang. They arrived in Bantang that night, God having been willing, and were warmly welcomed by the other permanent missionaries at the station, the MacLyons of Nebraska, who would both be dead of typhoid within a year.

The Walkers had been in Bantang for almost a week when Raymond asked Laura if she was happy there. This was one of the things she liked about Raymond: so many men didn't even know to ask such simple, sensitive questions. She wanted to tell Raymond about the overwhelming strangeness of the place, and about how the size of the mountains scared her and made her feel small and worried for their baby. She didn't complain about Bantang, although it had been something of a disappointment: nowhere near as big and glamorous as Tulsa even, this place was like the Indian country, with its dun-colored clay houses and narrow alleyways in which could be found the occasional corpse of a dog, a cat, or even a donkey. One thought consoled Laura: the women around here were unlikely, she reckoned, to catch Raymond's eye, as their faces were smeared black with honey and dirt, as was the Tibetan custom, and their hair reeked with the smell of rancid butter. She didn't tell Raymond any of these things, reserving her complaints for her sister. She only told Raymond that usually when she prayed at night, she felt a calm come over her and she knew that Jesus was listening to her; but here she had been praying harder the last week than she had ever prayed before, and the sweet sensation hadn't come. This sweet sensation was Christianity to Laura. It was, she thought, the sweetness of being loved. She adored the sweet sensation, and the notion that there were those in the world who did not know that sweetness kept her awake at night, as if she heard

the cries of motherless children. This was why when Raymond had proposed a mission to China, she had accepted. Raymond assured her that
the sweetness would return, and he was right.

The Walkers had been in Bantang a little over three months when
Laura gave birth to Thomas Walker. She had been secretly afraid that the
place where he was born would influence the appearance of her child, and
that he would be small, with an Asiatic aspect; but he was of a normal size,
and pink. Dr. Chester, an amateur phrenologist, studied the boy's skull and
said that he would be intelligent and of a passionate nature, a brave servant of Christ. To celebrate the birth, the missionaries of Bantang made
strawberry ice cream with ice brought down from the mountains.

Every family tells stories of origins and beginnings, and the story that
the Walkers tell of themselves begins here, with the long voyage to the
Orient, the caravan ride from Kunming, and the Mission Station at Bantang. Although the great flood of 1934 wiped out the written record of
family history, the decisive psychological break had been made already,
the day the *Maiden of the East* pulled leisurely out of the harbor into the
Pacific and set sail in the direction of the evening sun.

If the folks in Tulsa really didn't know why Raymond Walker was heading off to China to save souls, it was because they weren't listening, for if
there was one thing Raymond Walker liked to do, it was witness the
Gospel. You couldn't stop the man. For the rest of his life, he told anyone who wanted to listen, and plenty who didn't, the story of how he
got right with God. He told the story in sermons, in speeches, and in
friendly informal discourses, which he delivered in stone churches,
wooden chapels, and on the slopes of tall mountains, where with his own
hands he had cleared an open field of rocks so the people could come and
listen. Raymond felt that if all the moments of his life were to be listed in
order of importance, that moment in France when he cleared his books
with God would stand undisputed at the head.

This was the story that he told.

In the war, a moment had come when he had been in a trench and
left for dead: his unit had retreated, and when he awoke, he was alone
with glistening, gray corpses on either side of him. It was a clear, cold

night lit by a harvest moon, and Raymond lost all hope of living. Even his fear retreated under the certainty of death. And then the miracle happened, and what else could it be called but a miracle? He heard the angels singing. They sang to him *a cappella*, welcoming him to Heaven, the most pure and lovely sound he had ever heard. They were singing a hymn that he knew from childhood, a tender hymn that he had heard on his mother's lips and many times had sung himself. The angels were singing in four-part harmony. The deep, throaty bass angels sang like the Negro choir he had heard in Tulsa one time, the fundament, the support, the rainbow and reliable anchor that is the promise of God; the tenor angels, hovering above the basses, augmenting, enriching, offering an open hand if only one will accept it; the altos, lovely, incandescent, and maternal; and above all the soprano angels, whose voices were as pure and piercing as morning light. They sang:

> There were ninety-and-nine that safely lay
> In the Shelter of the fold.
> But one was out on the hills far away,
> Far off from the gates of gold.
> Away on the mountains wild and bare,
> Away from the tender Shepherd's care,
> Away from the tender Shepherd's care.

Raymond thought he was being welcomed to Heaven. The angels sang to him for hours as he lay immobile in a bloody trench, his limp hand lying in the remains of another man's gut, and when he woke up sometime later, very much alive, he could not deny that he had heard the angels singing and he understood the meaning of their song.

No, if the folks in Tulsa found Raymond's motivations for becoming a missionary mysterious, it certainly wasn't for lack of effort on his part to explain things: when Raymond tried to explain to his father that he was a changed man, his father asked if he wanted to get himself involved in real estate, because he knew a man in Oklahoma City who was looking for a junior partner; and when Raymond talked about things with his mother, she gave him a strange pained look. It was a frustrating time. The only one who had really listened was the pretty nurse with the round cheeks at the VA hospital where Raymond went twice weekly to treat his injured shoulder, and the two of them sat talking for hours in the hospital's rose garden. When he had told her about the angels, her eyes had grown misty, and Laura had smiled and said, "That must have been lovely. I wish I had heard the angels." *Lovely*—that was just the word Raymond had been looking for. He said, "It was. It was lovely." Then they got to talking more, and Raymond told her what he hadn't told anybody else: that he had been turning things over in his head, slowly thinking it through, and the only explanation he could come up with for everything he'd seen was that the world was in the midst of the Final Battle. The end was coming, just like in prophecy, and it wouldn't be long now before God judged each and every man. He admitted that the spectacle of the nations turning upon each other in this awful combat had shaken him to his core: the combatants were men who had been given the gift of the Gospel and then squandered it. He had gone back and read Daniel and Revelation, and things were just so clear to him, what was coming, the terrible Day when every man would be judged fairly. He hadn't been living right, he confessed to Laura. He hadn't been living right at all, he said, and by the things he had seen, the giant explosions, he knew that the world *could* end. It was a distinct possibility. And Laura said that when you saw a cyclone coming, you closed the blinds, put the family in the root cellar, and warned the neighbors.

And so Raymond found himself standing on those hillsides in Tibet and China and the Dyalo country, staring out at the weathered tribal faces. What hard lives these gentle people faced! He had come, he told them, to tell them the terrible Good News: that they would be judged soon, and judged hard, but judged by a God who delighted to love them and help them. He had come as fast as he could with his wife and his children from the white man's land to tell them to take precautions: the river of time was rising, and their homes would soon be flooded, and their rice fields washed away. But there was a way out, Raymond Walker added. He could lead them to the high ground.


It is an unfortunate fact which every traveler eventually comes to know, but there is no place in this world so exotic, so remote, or so beautiful that boredom does not eventually set in; and the Walkers after two years in Bantang, which although exotic and remote was not beautiful, were bored.

The death of the MacLyons had been a hard blow for the young couple: the MacLyons had been of the Walkers' generation, and the four young missionaries had been great friends, a buoyant counterweight to the staid gravity of the older Chesters. At night, Mary MacLyon had brought out a harmonica and Stan MacLyon a banjo, and the foursome had stomped and hooted their way through a hundred familiar tunes, whereas the Chesters retired early to bed. From the moment the Walkers arrived in Bantang, Stan and Raymond had started to plan an evangelizing tour into the mountain villages, while Mary and Laura discussed repainting the interior of the gloomy Mission. The foursome had taken to eating their meals together late at night by the light of wax candles, and although the Chesters were, of course, invited to eat with them, the invitation was inevitably declined on account of Dr. Chester's indigestion should he dine late. Stan and Mary were the sort always willing to tell another joke, or stay up an hour longer, or put together a skit, or bring home strangers they found on the streets of Bantang. After Thomas was born, Mary insisted on waking up with the baby as often as Raymond and Laura; Mrs. Chester, by contrast, had no particular skill in dandling a baby, and Thomas tended to cry when she walked into the room. When the MacLyons prayed, they rocked on the balls of their feet, and shouted and wept; they closed the Bible after daily readings bathed in a sheen of sweat. Stan had an odd and wonderful gift: he could see the faces of Old Testament characters in the faces of the people of Bantang. The dissolute tax collector with his anxious hooded eyes fingering his official seal *was* crazy old Saul playing with his javelin, once Stan MacLyon pointed it out. The Walkers found Stan and Mary's wild, passionate, mystical faith exhilarating.

When the Chesters prayed, on the other hand, it was a sober thing: Dr. Chester read passages from Scripture, Mrs. Chester said "Amen," and Dr. Chester in his meticulous way gave commentary. The Chesters of course were wonderful missionaries, but they had been manning this particular Mission Station now for almost thirty years. In their youth, they had had great adventures: as a young man, Mr. Chester had dreamed that he would live his life on muleback, spreading the Gospel, his wife on another mule, their worldly possessions on a third. Mrs. Chester had been wooed by this dream, and for many years they had so lived. Dr. Chester had explained the Gospel to the Dalai Lama himself, and Mrs. Chester had raised four children in this inhospitable and almost savage country, of whom three survived. After Mrs. Chester broke her hip, the Chesters had established the permanent Mission Station at Bantang, and nursed the station through famine, revolution, and civil war. In their day, they had seen two dozen young missionaries come and go through Bantang station, every single one of them devoted Christians, and the Chesters had come to realize that success as a missionary was not so much a question of exuberance as endurance. Sometimes they found themselves slightly wearied by the young people. Something of the mentality of the Chinese Mandarin had worn off on them: Dr. Chester admitted that he was less eager to proselytize as he grew older, although no less eager to see his faith spread, and Mrs. Chester, on her last home furlough, had shocked the ladies of a number of midwestern Christian congregations by saying that in her humble opinion, if lacking, of course, the grandeur of the Christian faith, Tibetan Buddhism nevertheless seemed to contain a number of truths. Dr. Chester looked forward to the completion of his translation of the Bible into Tibetan, which he had promised the Dalai Lama he would personally present to His Holiness in Lhassa, and he harbored a secret hope, a new dream for his old age: that in exchange for this great labor, the Dalai Lama would allow the Chesters to remain as permanent guests in the interior of Tibet. This would be their retirement, which they would pass together in dignified conversation with the Buddhist monks about the meaning of the universe.

The Walkers and MacLyons all had noted how remarkably affectionate the Chesters were. Dr. Chester was silver-haired, with a neatly trimmed silver mustache and round cheeks which turned red in the mountain cold; talking to Laura, Mrs. Chester more than once confessed herself guilty of the sin of pride when she considered her good fortune in being the possessor of this still-handsome man. Mrs. Chester dressed only in the dreariest of black dresses, which covered her completely from her thick neck to her heavy ankles, and yet she never appeared in public in season without the fresh gardenia or lotus in her lapel that Mr. Chester had picked for her that very morning from the flowery little garden he tended behind the Mission. After forty years of marriage, the Chesters still wandered the small city hand in hand, Mrs. Chester's fine hand reaching out of her long robes to find Dr. Chester's heavy paw. Holding hands was considered mildly vulgar in Chinese eyes, but neither member of the couple was willing to forgo this innocent pleasure simply to placate local custom. The Chesters were content chiefly with each other's company: if the stories Dr. Chester repetitively told bored the younger missionaries of the station, in Mrs. Chester's eyes there was no more thrilling raconteur than her husband; and Dr. Chester was deaf to any audience's stifled yawns when his wife pressed him, *Morris, please*, to continue.

The Walkers had been in Bantang a year when the MacLyons died of typhoid, one after the other, the onset of Mary's illness and Stan's death only three weeks apart. They were buried under matched headstones which read: GONE FOR THE GLORY OF CHRIST.

Now the late-night meals by wax candle ended. Everyone agreed that it made more sense to eat together at a reasonable hour; and Laura Walker gave up her attempts to redecorate the Mission, as Raymond was blind to her improvements—the improvised curtains she had sewn from Chinese silk, the fresh vases of lilies and Tibetan roses she set out—and Mrs. Chester was wholly uninterested in her suggestions: having lived in this clay house now so very many years, she declared that she saw little reason to change it. During the long voyage to Bantang and the first year in the Mission, Dr. Chester's lectures on Tibetan life and customs had fascinated the Walkers, but after eighteen months, the Walkers noticed that Dr. Chester had begun to repeat himself. More than once he had talked about the particular way in which a single Tibetan woman might be married at once to several brothers, and more than once Mrs. Chester had made the same mild joke, "Dr. Chester, I should certainly not have liked being married to *your* brothers. That is more than a woman deserves." Laura wondered more than once if she needed to chuckle again. The evenings at the Mission Station grew intolerably long. Dr. Chester for his relaxation read from his pile of musical scores, but when Laura begged him actually to make music, he replied that unless there was a symphony orchestra handy, he was lacking an instrument. Dr. Chester found his own joke intolerably droll. Mrs. Chester was the type of woman who enjoyed novels, which she read slowly and thoughtfully, and then passed on to Laura, who despite her most valiant efforts simply could not see the attraction of the medium: she could never persuade herself that the comings and goings of imaginary characters were worthy of her attention.

The long evenings were not preceded by thrilling days. The Walkers chafed under the daily routine prescribed by Dr. and Mrs. Chester. It was hardly the high drama of saving souls that they had hoped for. Every morning, Raymond and Laura studied the Chinese language for two hours and the Tibetan for another two. This, they admitted, was a necessary duty, and after two years of study, Dr. Chester decided that both members of the couple were competent to deliver their first sermons. Laura chose to preach on "Sin, Salvation, and God's Love," Raymond on "Christian Prayer and Values." Laura had worked hard all her life, but here in Bantang, domestic affairs occupied far less of her time than she was used to, for the Mission employed a number of Chinese and Tibetan helpers who, having given up their families to gain their souls, needed employment, which the tender-hearted Chesters could not refuse them. This legion of servants occupied themselves with the daily household chores—with the goats (the Mission had a flock of over one hundred) and the chickens, the cooking, the clothes, the cleaning, and drawing fresh water from the well. In the afternoons, Laura accompanied Mrs. Chester on a round of the city's Christian charitable institutions: the small hospital, the orphanage, and the school. At the hospital, Laura sat by the bedside of the sick; at the orphanage, she introduced and led the games of her childhood, touch-tag and hide-and-seek; and at the school, she delivered every day a brief lesson on Christian living. These were assignments that she might have accepted happily were it not for Mrs. Chester's constant stream of advice. Laura was not the type of woman who frequently allowed herself the luxury of harsh thoughts, but she did admit shyly to her husband that when Mrs. Chester was stricken with a mild fever and spent three weeks in bed recuperating, the days had passed more easily.

One incident in particular set Laura against Mrs. Chester. It was the Walkers' second spring in Bantang, and on a day when the mountain air was remarkably clear and the sky a deep cobalt blue, Mrs. Chester, enchanted by the season, proposed to Laura that in place of their usual rounds, they visit a village some five or six miles from town where an old Christian woman lived, one of the first Chinese converts of the region. They set out in the early morning, but the village proved farther from Bantang than Mrs. Chester had recalled, and the two women did not arrive until well after noon. They took a long tea with the old Christian woman and did not set out on the road back until late afternoon.

Now, the roads around Bantang were generally safe by daylight but not without danger at night, and the two women walked quickly. They were halfway back to Bantang when they passed a small tribal woman crouched beside the road. The small woman made a cooing sound at them and smiled. Her teeth were stained black with betel nut, and her lips were the color of tar. The woman gestured at Mrs. Chester and Laura. She spoke to them in Chinese with a tribal accent as thick as Laura's midwestern drawl: "The wind has whispered me stories of the white folk in Bantang, but the wind has never told me what you do here."

Laura was not confident in her Chinese, and she deferred to Mrs. Chester, who explained that she and her husband had come from the white man's land across the endless seas to teach the people about Jesus, His Love, Sin, and Salvation.

The tribal woman, still squatting by the road, frowned. "Teach me, then," she said. "If you've come this far, I owe you my ears."

Mrs. Chester looked around. They were on a dark patch of road, and the sun was fast approaching the mountain horizon. There was still another hour's walk to the outskirts of town. Dr. Chester would be anxious. "We don't have the time to teach you just now," she said. "We must teach you another day."

The woman listened with a cocked head, then spat blood-red betel juice on the side of the road. "Don't tell me you've come all this way to teach *me* and then say you don't have time," she replied.

Mrs. Chester and Laura returned home safely that night. Laura recounted the incident to Raymond, and they agreed that Laura should find the tribal woman at once the next morning and explain the Gospel to her. But the next day the road was empty, and Laura couldn't help feeling that a woman of greater faith and integrity than herself would have insisted on teaching the woman by the side of the road, no matter the hour of day or night or the danger.

For his part, Raymond found himself relegated to a position as Dr. Chester's clerical assistant. Great volumes of mail from well-wishers and the inquisitive arrived by the weekly post for Dr. Chester, alerted to the work by his dispatches in *National Geographic*, and he would deposit these with Raymond, asking him to draft replies, so that Dr. Chester could continue work on his translation. Raymond prepared responses which ended either, depending on the formality of the communication and the intended audience: "Yours in the Hope of His Coming" (meant for well-wishers, general curious questions and requests, people with whom Dr. Chester did not have a close personal relationship); "Yours in the Service of Christ" (or, alternatively, "Yours in the Joy of His Service," meant for other missionaries and members of the clergy); or simply "Yours in Christ," a salutation which Dr. Chester felt appropriate to use only with the most intimate of his epistolary partners. At the end of the day, Raymond left the letters for Dr. Chester to sign. The Missionary Society required a lengthy written report every three months, and an accounting of the Mission Station's finances, and pounding these out on the Mission's portable typewriter was also made part of Raymond's responsibilities. Raymond was not a good typist. "Accounting is a part of evangelism," Dr. Chester said, seeing Raymond struggle with the books. "We pray for money to continue our work, and our Lord expects us to husband carefully His gifts." When Raymond took Dr. Chester aside after a year in Bantang and explained his desire to engage in a more *active* evangelism, Dr. Chester proposed that Raymond preach in the afternoons in front of the market. The market in Bantang was not a large one, and very quickly the traders in barley, sheep, yak meat, salt, and tea grew accustomed to the sight in the late afternoons of the lean, handsome American standing on a crate, stammering his way through an incomprehensible speech in poor Tibetan.

The most frustrating thing for the Walkers about their life in Bantang was that the size of the Christian community there held steady. Those who would be converted in this small city, it seemed, had been converted. Later in life, Raymond Walker would say that there was no better preparation for missionary life than to be assigned the task of tilling a stony mission field, but at the time the effort did not amuse him at all—the long wearisome unproductive days in which he wandered the streets of Bantang, cornering everyone who would listen. It bothered Raymond intensely that everywhere around him were souls to be won for Christ and that he did not possess the means to win them. Dr. Chester did not seem to care, or to realize the profound urgency of the moment.

One night Raymond had a dream. He was in a train station, and enormous queues of Chinamen streamed past him to board an old steam train. Raymond stopped one of them and asked him the destination of the train. The Chinaman, old and wizened, replied that it was the train to Hell. The destination was confirmed by the cry of a huge Negro porter: "Hell Express! All aboard!" Raymond tried to hold the old Chinaman back, but in his dream his limbs lost force and the man slithered easily from Raymond's hand. Raymond grasped at an old woman headed for the platform, and she, too, slipped from his hands and climbed aboard the train, which bulged with humanity, limbs protruding from the windows and doors. Then the terrible thing happened. In the great shuffling crowd, Raymond himself was swept aboard. "This is the train to Hell!" he cried. "Let me down!" But Raymond could not pass through the crowds, and he awoke in a sweat just before the train steamed out of the station.

The next morning, Raymond told Dr. Chester that he was ready to leave Bantang. He wanted to travel to the faraway tribal villages to spread the Word—the trip he had planned with Stan MacLyon. Dr. Chester, hardly bothering to look up from the page of Tibetan characters he was proofreading, forbade the expedition: with a wave of his soft, pink hand, he explained that the roads and hills were filled with robbers, brigands, and warring factions, and he would not allow the young father to take such risks, not when he was performing valuable service to God in the Mission itself. Something in Dr. Chester's response provoked the younger man, who remembered the way his father had looked past him when he had explained the angelic choir.

"You *forbid* me?" His voice was tight, and he plucked at a cuff link to keep his hands from sweeping all of Dr. Chester's papers—his translation of the Bible, his mountain of correspondence, his notes for *National Geographic*—off his desk.

"I must," said Dr. Chester, taking off his round spectacles, then wearily rubbing the bridge of his nose. "You leave me no choice. I will not have a widow and orphan here at Bantang station to suit your wandering fancy."

"You mean that you will not have your correspondence unanswered, that the Gospel might be spread," replied Raymond.

Raymond stormed out of Dr. Chester's small office and plunged himself into the tumult of the market. That evening the merchants and traders remarked to one another that the white man had been even more agitated than usual.

For almost a week, Raymond did not bother with his usual duties at the Mission. Dr. Chester's papers lay in a muddle, and the younger missionary, in open defiance, set about putting together a small caravan to tour the neighboring villages. He took his morning tea at the market and spent his days in town. Dr. Chester, for his part, was furious also—furious that the authority he had veritably built with his own hands at the Mission Station was denied. Dr. Chester was not a large man, and he was no longer young, but when angry in his past he had confronted other men larger than himself and frightened them. Now, late at night, Dr. Chester imagined confronting Raymond Walker.

It was the wives who finally eased the tensions, as so often in these cases. *With Thomas so very little, did Raymond really want to leave her just now?* Laura asked her husband. *Wasn't Dr. Chester himself equally impatient as a young man?* Mrs. Chester asked the doctor. *Dr. Chester was obviously unsettled by the zeal of a younger man,* consoled Laura. *Think how difficult it must be to enter the Mission field in the shadow of a giant,* soothed Mrs. Chester. Then in the subtle way of wives, each commanded her mate to make peace. One afternoon Dr. Chester found Raymond in the market, and that evening the foursome ate dinner together again. The next day, Raymond returned to the typewriter.

All winter, a tenuous peace held at the Mission. Raymond did not renew his demands, and Laura held her tongue as Mrs. Chester explained the proper way to fold a sheet or soothe a fevered brow. But the underlying tensions remained: neither Walker admitting it to the other (but both admitting it to their grandchildren many years later, who in turn told me), both Raymond and Laura began to pray for deliverance from the Mission at Bantang. They asked God to allow them to be of greater use to Him and His Kingdom, and God answered their prayers in His terrible ironic fashion.

Half a year after Raymond Walker and Dr. Chester quarreled, the Grand Tigi of Gartok, the lord of eastern Tibet, invited the Walkers and the Chesters to preach the Word at his court. The Tigi had heard rumors of the fascinating work in which the missionaries were engaged; now he wished to discuss these vital spiritual matters with the foreigners himself.

Such an invitation was of the most extraordinary and rare nature. Bantang lay on the Tibetan frontier, but the interior of Tibet was a closed nation. The last white man to visit Lhassa had been Dr. Chester, almost ten years earlier, and as far as anyone knew, Laura would be only the second white woman to enter the kingdom at all, following in Mrs. Chester's footsteps. Thomas's visit would be unique. Dr. Chester organized the preparations: the appropriate gifts for the Grand Tigi, the retinue of guards to shepherd the group safely across the border, the hardy ponies, and of course early versions of the Tibetan New Testament to distribute to the curious. (These books had only recently arrived from the printer in Shanghai, and the fortuitous coincidence of their arrival and the invitation to the interior of Tibet, the missionaries agreed, was surely proof of the Lord's desire that His Word be spread.) For several weeks, the Mission was in high excitement as the work approached. But only two days before the party was supposed to set out from Bantang, Dr. Chester received a message by courier: Père Antoine, the Catholic missionary who worked to the southwest, was desperately ill with influenza. Normally this would have been a job for Raymond, as the junior missionary at the station, but Dr. Chester offered in his typical gallant fashion to tend Père Antoine in Raymond's place. Dr. Chester insisted that the Walkers travel on as planned, lest the missionary party, setting out too late in the year, find itself unable to reach Tibet, hidden behind the great wall erected annually by the first of the Himalayan snowfalls.

Only Mrs. Chester did not support this arrangement.

"Dr. Chester," she said, "don't you perhaps think that Raymond ought to accompany you on your visit to Père Antoine? The hills, you know . . ."

She brought up the subject over the breakfast shared by the four missionaries, and this was her mistake: had she been alone with Dr. Chester, perhaps she might have found a small hole in the iron wall of his pride; in front of Raymond, any admission of weakness was unthinkable. Dr. Chester looked up from his bowl of rice, his round spectacles steamed over. "I do believe, Mrs. Chester, that I *will* have some of that excellent chutney after all," he said.

"I'm quite serious, Dr. Chester. I heard just last week from one of the ladies at the—"

"That chutney, if you please."

"Dr. Chester!"

Dr. Chester sat up straight in his chair. He was still in his pale silk dressing gown. "Mrs. Chester," he said finally, "I do believe we must recall that we are here to spread the Gospel. Raymond is not here to keep track of these old bones"—he patted his sternum—"but to make sure that the Word is spread."

Mrs. Chester knew that there was no appeal to this decision. She shot a distressed glance at the end of the table, where Raymond seemed quite fascinated by the oily swirls of his tea and Laura was much occupied suddenly with feeding Thomas, who was himself quite busy with a piece of toast. The matter was settled. The next morning, with little Thomas holding on tight to the pommel of Raymond's saddle and Laura secure on her mule, the party set out for Tibet as planned.

Now for the first time the Walkers would be alone in the Orient, in Tibet!—that most mysterious of lands, with the opportunity to spread their faith in the manner of their own choosing. From the start it was a journey of miracles. The most dangerous portion of the voyage was certainly the four-day journey from Bantang to the Tibetan border: this was, as Dr. Chester had said, a land of brigands and robbers. Here in this wild mountainous country, the Shang Chen Tibetan tribe fought furious guerrilla battles with the Druwasa; and the Tibetans under the lama Ra Nah fought with the Chinese. Missionaries were generally accorded safe passage through these dangerous internecine skirmishes, but overexcited warriors had been known to attack even women and children. It was Laura who noticed the mysterious retinue of soldiers in white accompanying the Walkers' party, and she pointed them out to her husband, who explained to his wife that these dim shadowy warriors were certainly an angelic host sent by God in answer to their prayers for safe travel. The Walkers crossed the frontier without incident.

On the road to the sacred Kawa Gabo Mountains they saw pilgrims prostrating themselves hand and foot, mile after mile, to their demon gods, and the Walkers were reminded of what Dr. Chester had told them of the exceptional spiritual desires of the Tibetan people. If only they knew to Whom to turn their prayers! Scores of antelope protected from the poacher's arrow by order of the Dalai Lama himself flashed down the slopes of piney mountains in advance of the tiny caravan. Sullen, massive China with its heathen multitudes was behind them, and ahead a kingdom commensurate in grandeur, in beauty, and in suffering with His ambitions. These were the days when the great missionary rallying cry "Onward to Lhassa!" was heard from every evangelical pulpit in America, and for the first time the Walkers understood the charismatic attraction of Tibet to all those who earnestly wished to see the world in Light. They passed caves in which were entombed living hermits, men determined to sit in darkened silence until enlightenment or death arrived, and the Walkers would have stopped at each and every cave and explained the simple, sublime Good News which would have liberated these spiritual isolates from their self-imposed prisons, had not their rendezvous with the Tigi awaited. The Tibetans, too, for their part, were fascinated by the handsome white man, his smiling woman, and their charming child. The Walkers spent a night in a forest lamasery where the monks had taken a vow of poverty so extreme that the abbot's drinking bowl was made from a desiccated human skull: when the Walkers explained their faith, the lamas insisted on reading Dr. Chester's Bible immediately. The fertile valleys teemed with yak and sheep, and the gentle breezes made the barley fields quiver like velvet brushed back by His hand. Here the headwaters of the terrible Salween, the raging Mekong, and the endless Yangtze were just gentle rivulets. What cruel irony that He Who made this magnificent land entombed its occupants in spiritual darkness! Raymond and Laura had never felt so alive.

Swift messengers on horseback had alerted the Grand Tigi to the missionaries' arrival, and showing them the hospitality for which he was renowned, he sent out his army to greet them. The Walkers had stopped for the night in a simple peasant home, where with typical Tibetan generosity they had been offered a mud floor and barley bread. Awakening in the morning, they found a grand army clad in silver and gold saluting them with the music of trumpets. Burned pines flashed in copper pans to perfume the dry mountain air. *This* was the welcome the Tigi offered his friends. Two days' further journey brought the party to the palace at Gartok, where the Tigi himself greeted the Walkers of Oklahoma as the emissaries of a great nation and a greater faith.

A month in the palace passed in the timeless manner of dreams: the Walkers slept at night in a room whose floors were covered in sumptuous rugs, and awoke in the morning with the pale light of the mountain sun breaking through the colored-glass windows. The Tigi had once summoned the greatest artisans of Gartok to decorate his palace, and the great masters had covered the walls of the Walkers' quarters in elaborate depictions of the animals, flowers, and myths of Tibet, which first frightened, then enchanted, young Thomas. The Walkers feasted, danced, hunted with falcons, and explained their faith to a fascinated and receptive audience.

One afternoon, for his amusement, the Tigi clothed Raymond in the finest silken robes from his wardrobe, while his wife and her servants dressed Laura. Raymond had brought his camera with him on the expedition and insisted on taking photographs. All of these photographs were lost in the flood of 1934 but one, which survived because Raymond sent it to his mother, who kept it on her Tulsa mantelpiece to show to the ladies of the Church Society. They never failed to stare in wonder. The photograph shows the Grand Tigi and his son, mustachioed and fierce, standing side by side, each fingering Tibetan prayer beads. They are wearing Raymond Walker's clothes, dark woolen suits and pressed white shirts with high collars, and on the Tigi's large head, Raymond's cowboy hat. Handsome Raymond Walker is beside them, wearing an ankle-length silk gown. A vague smile, almost a smirk, breaks over his clean-shaven face. Laura Walker is the only seated member of the party. Her hair has been plaited by the Tigi's handmaidens into long tresses, as is the Tibetan style, and held in place with gold and turquoise combs: the dark sleeves of her robe descend into flared white cuffs, and her hands are settled in her lap. Swathed thus in embroidered silk and rare jewels, she looks up at her husband with an expression on her pretty face that even the most jaded observer would admit was love.

On the last evening of their visit, the Walkers presented their gifts to the Tigi. They gave him canned Del Monte fruit, which the Tigi had never before tasted—pineapples, pears, and peaches, all in heavy syrup. The Tigi had been fascinated by Raymond's field glasses, through which one could see things that were not yet visible, and those, too, were offered as a gift. From China, the Walkers had brought a red silk veil for the Tigi's wife, which she accepted with lavish compliments and, imitating Laura's occidental style, polite kisses.

The next morning, accompanied again by the Tigi's army, the Walkers set off in a fine rain to return to Bantang. The journey lasted almost a week, over the same mountain passes. The rain grew heavier, and the color washed out from the land and sky. As they approached Bantang, the roads became muddy and rutted, and a sense of dark gloom came over the couple. Raymond thought of the high stack of correspondence which awaited him, and Laura of the endless mild instruction which Mrs. Chester was sure to offer. Every evening when they stopped for the night, the Walkers renewed their prayers to be of greater service to His Kingdom and to be used by Him for His Glory.

They arrived at the Mission Station just after dark. A cold sleet had made the last of the journey difficult, and they thought of the mugs of hot tea which the Chesters would offer them after they had settled into their robes and slippers. They would put Thomas to bed and rock him gently until he fell asleep, then they would tell the Chesters every detail of their adventure.

But the Mission Station was deserted when they arrived. The house was cold and the servants missing. The Walkers prowled the house suspiciously. Raymond was in Dr. Chester's study, which was almost exactly as it was when he had left, when he heard Laura cry out from the garden.

He dashed outside and found Laura in the garden, trying to usher Mrs. Chester back into the house. The older woman was dressed only in a soaking nightgown, and her long gray hair was down around her shoulders. The Walkers had never seen her before without her hair neatly in a bun, and her damp nightgown clung to her massive breasts, from which Raymond instinctively averted his eyes. How long had she been sitting in the garden, in the pouring rain? Raymond started a fire, and Laura rummaged through the old woman's cupboards to find her clean, dry clothes. Mrs. Chester sat by the fire, unmoving. Laura changed her clothes, and Raymond made tea. After an hour passed in the most unnerving, terrible silence, Mrs. Chester coughed slightly. "Dr. Chester has left me," she said.

For a second Raymond misunderstood. He could have imagined no more unlikely happening in all the universe than the voluntary uncoupling of this strong yoked pair. But Laura comprehended Mrs. Chester immediately. "Oh no, Mrs. Chester," she said. "Oh, no."

"He's left all of us," Mrs. Chester added.

They were able to get no more out of Mrs. Chester that night. Despite the Walkers' entreaties, she sat in silence for perhaps five minutes more, then laid herself down on the stone floor in front of the fire. Raymond covered her with a blanket, and she stared into the flames until, exhausted, she slept. Laura and Raymond stayed in their chairs all night long, dozing, praying, and tending the fire.

In the morning, Mrs. Chester was able to relate to the young Walkers the terrible events which had passed while the Walkers were off enjoying the hospitality of the Grand Tigi of Gartok.

Dr. Chester had left immediately to visit Père Antoine, traveling only with one Chinese helper. The journey had taken two days, and by the time they arrived, the Catholic evangelist was already starting to feel better. It was his servant who had sent off the urgent message which had summoned the doctor, and Père Antoine, a tough old soul, was vaguely embarrassed by all the commotion his illness had stirred. Dr. Chester spent a day in Père Antoine's mountain hut, then set off for Bantang.

He never arrived.

For almost a week Mrs. Chester had waited. Usually if he was to be away more than a few days, he would send a runner with a message. But poor communications were the norm here on the frontier: runners were often distracted by opium pipes, rice whiskey, or a mudslide washing out the solitary track which the Chinese called a road, and Mrs. Chester could do nothing but pray and wait. Then the message arrived—a letter, written in Chinese, from the leader of a notorious band of local brigands. Her husband had been taken prisoner and would be released only in exchange for gold.

Immediately Mrs. Chester set about amassing the ransom. From the local Christians, she borrowed on the credit of the Missionary Society in Kunming. By hook and by crook, she put together the extraordinary sum demanded, and was prepared to offer it to the thugs in exchange for her husband. Then, late that night, her husband's Chinese helper, who had accompanied him into the mountains, slipped into the Mission compound. The servant had escaped with an urgent message from the doctor. She was *absolutely* not to pay the ransom. He would not tolerate it! It would place every missionary in China in danger should word go out that missionaries could be kidnapped in exchange for easy cash. He would die or he would live—that, as always, was in his Master's hands—but he would not be ransomed. There would be victory in Jesus.

The next day, every Christian in Bantang beseeched God to spare the old scholar and evangelist's life. The kidnappers had proposed a complicated system to exchange messages, and by this system she sent back word: by her husband's own request, she would not pay the ransom. It was an excruciating decision, but she knew Dr. Chester. When Morris made up his mind on principle, he stood firm like a mighty rock. He would not waver, and neither would she. She would prove herself a wife worthy of his faith. Every hour now was spent on her aching knees in prayer. She would never have admitted it to anyone, but after a lifetime in His service, she felt that the Lord owed her and her husband this favor. But after three weeks, Dr. Chester's body was found by a shepherd in a cave less than five miles from Bantang. The old man had been dead no more than a day or two, and the kidnappers had evidently fled the cave immediately upon his death.

On receiving the news of her husband's death, Mrs. Chester built a small fire in the compound yard. There she placed her husband's nearly complete manuscript edition of the remaining unpublished books of the Tibetan Bible. These people, she decided, did not deserve Morris's gifts. They did not deserve the Lord's gifts. Then she lit the fire and watched the Bible burn. She had sat now in the garden under a raining sky for almost three days, bewailing the death of her husband.

Mrs. Chester told her story in a monotone, and then said hardly another word to the Walkers. Her red eyes accused the missionaries from Oklahoma: Raymond should have been the one visiting Père Antoine in the mountains, not Dr. Chester. What kind of people were these Walkers, who allowed a man of sixty-three to set out alone into the mountains, who had come to help the Chesters and instead destroyed them? Her sweet and tender Morris, the father of her children and the comfort of her old age! The Walkers offered an equally unspoken reply: it was the will of God.

Mrs. Chester remained in Bantang another week, until she joined a caravan of dealers in copper goods marching in the direction of Kunming. The Walkers begged her to stay a little longer and regain her health, but the woman was forceful as ever. She was returning to America, she said, to the leafy village in upstate New York where both her daughters lived, to inform them of their father's death. She would leave this hateful land forever. All the long week before Mrs. Chester quit the Mission, Thomas, aware of the tumult and sadness of the household, cried in his crib, and no matter how Laura bounced him on her knee the boy would not be comforted.

In this terrible way, God answered the prayers of the Walkers: they now were in charge of the Bantang Mission. Raymond swore never to submit his soul to the responsibility of another man but also never to forget the example of Dr. Chester's bravery, and he adopted as his own the other man's motto: "Jesus Wins All." The Walkers spent a year alone, preaching in their fashion and wandering the mountain valleys, then proposed to the United Missionary Society in Kunming that they quit the Bantang Station, in order to spread the Gospel to the tribal peoples along the Salween River, whom they had found were most receptive to the Word. When the Society refused their request, saying that the risks were too great in the tribal valleys, the Walkers resigned their commission entirely. Now the Walkers affiliated themselves with no one but

God; Raymond and Laura now were truly alone in the Orient. Raymond's mother went from church to church in Tulsa, reading her son's letters from the tribal country, and the churches of Tulsa sent donations to support the work. These churches would continue to support the Walkers' work for the next eighty years, as the Walkers pursued with monomaniacal zeal their extraordinary goal of bringing an entire people, the Dyalo, into the Light.

Like so many occidentals in the Orient, the Walkers had swung to the pendulum-edges of their souls.

# TWO

# EDEN VALLEY

TOM RILEY WAS SWEET on Judith Walker. Tom did not have a boy's face: when he didn't shave, he looked like something out of those old Marlboro ads, the ones showing a cowboy roping a steer and lighting a cigarette off the edge of a red-hot brand. It was wonderful to see this large, handsome man's shy face as he admitted that he had "feelings" for Judith, and wondered whether I thought she might reciprocate them. It occurred to me that Tom Riley, who must have been in his late twenties, might well have still been a virgin, given how seriously in all other respects Tom took his faith. I told him that I honestly didn't know what Judith was thinking, and Tom asked me—begged me, really—to find out. He seemed to think that because I was living in sin with Rachel I had some secret insight into the hearts of women.

Whenever I saw Judith in those weeks, I tried to steer the conversation toward Tom. I watched very carefully to see if she became embarrassed or shy when the subject of Tom came up—if she went red, or shifted in place, or rearranged her hair. The problem was, I kept getting false positives. Judith did all those things when I mentioned Tom, *yes*, but also when I mentioned John the Baptist.

"Tom Riley is *such* a nice man," I said to Judith one afternoon.

"Yes, he *really* is," she replied.

I reported this back to Tom faithfully, and for a minute he glowed.

Then he said, "That's *all* she said?" It was hard to get anything else out of him that day. I wanted to tell Tom that he should go and talk to Judith himself. But I was afraid that if I did that, he wouldn't tell me anything more about the Walkers. Also, I thought to myself, maybe this is normal for them. Maybe this is how evangelical Christians mate.

We went back and forth like this for a good ten days. I was paying so much attention to Judith that if she'd had half a mind, she'd have figured *I* was sweet on her. Then one day Judith gave me a clear sign. "How long do you think Tom Riley's going to stay here?" she asked.

Thinking quickly, I said, "I'm not sure, but he said he might be going back soon."

"Oh," she said with a sad, dreamy, faraway air. "That's too bad. I hope he stays for a long time." Then she blushed, and to cover her tracks, she added: "Need *somebody* to carry those boxes!"

The next day I told Tom, "She's crazy about you, big guy. The ball is totally in your court."

Then we got back to talking about the Walkers: I think Tom felt he owed me at this point, and he coughed up the intimate materials which make up the bulk of this chapter. But Tom started spending more time with Judith. I'd come by the big pink house and see Tom and Judith huddled in fervent conversation at the kitchen table, leaning into each other's eyes, or sitting on the stoop, eating a juicy mango and laughing. When I'd walk by, they'd hush up quick. Seeing them together made me think I had done a good thing.


In 1935, the British adventurer John Hanbury-Tracy crossed very northern Burma on foot on a mission to find the origins of the Salween River. The man needed more than three weeks just to cover a hundred miles, on the way surviving a snowstorm, a sunburn, two poisonous snake attacks, countless leeches, a falling boulder and a falling tree, a tiger bite, a bear scratch, malarial fever, *and* diarrhea—a travelogue which leads one naturally to conclude that either John Hanbury-Tracy was a man who should not have walked under that bamboo ladder back in Mandalay *or* that the very north of Burma is no place for a pleasure jaunt. Yet just fifteen years after John Hanbury-Tracy staggered out from the wild, it is *precisely* in the middle of this thick and miserable jungle that the Walker family resettled when they were expelled at gunpoint from China after the Communist revolution. It was in this jungle that Thomas Walker's first son, David, was born.

When the revolution took China, the Walkers, like a flock of disturbed pigeons, disbanded and then regrouped, this time in northern Burma, so close to the Chinese border it was hard to tell the difference between where they had been and where they were now, but for the color of the missionary visas in their passports. The Walkers called the long green valley "Eden," and sent word to their Dyalo brothers and sisters in China and in Burma that Eden Valley would be a Christian paradise, a place where God ruled. When Samuel Walker, Thomas's younger brother, first arrived in Eden Valley, the place had been infested, just lousy, with spirits, which explained why the tribal peoples, poor things, had all left this beautiful fertile valley untouched, with its central plateau perfect for rice, and hills which could be terraced, and a freshwater stream. So Samuel and Raymond (Thomas was still in a Communist jail) came to Eden Valley to exorcise those demons. Sleeping only under Samuel's canvas army tent, they prayed night and day. They wandered from the big rock at the head of the valley to the little rook at the foot, praying until their throats were hoarse and their arms trembled. In this way, they spent six whole days and nights, and when they were done, the valley was theirs.

When the men had cleaned out the valley, the women arrived, and one by one the Walkers built homes, carved out fields for the rice, and planted fruit trees. In the Walkers' wake, long ropy streams of Dyalo followed, crossing single file over the mountains. They carried all their worldly goods in bamboo baskets: the crowing roosters and the squealing piglets, the sharply honed knives, and rice to last until the next crop was harvested. Exciting times, with friends old and new arriving daily, the villages going up, the whole valley a beehive of energy and industry! Helena Walker told me that the water had been *so* sweet in the river which meandered gently through the valley floor, and Sarah Walker told me that this was a place where she woke in the morning and could pull from trees three steps from her door and in bloom eight months a year peaches, mangoes, oranges, and jackfruit, which her children ate for breakfast, the juice dribbling down their little chins. It was as lonely and as isolated and as perfect a place as you could find on the face of this earth, the Walkers said, this valley of theirs—and of course they knew it wouldn't last. They, too, had read Genesis.

Raymond was a gardener, and when he was forced to leave China, having to leave behind his orchard at the Mission in Abaze had been a bitter blow. For almost thirty years, Raymond had included a brief note at the end of his reports to the churches back home asking for seeds and clippings from fruit trees. Every month the postman had brought him another bulky package, and whatever he received, he had planted behind the house in Abaze. A Chinese horticulturalist from the China Inland University had once visited the orchard and pronounced it certainly the widest variety of fruit trees anywhere in the Salween River valley: a half-dozen varieties of apples, some for eating straight off the tree, others for pies, green and red; four types of oranges and three lemons; peaches; pears; apricots; plums; guava; nectarines; mangoes; starfruit and jack-fruit—and hybrids and crossbreeds too, including one which Raymond suspected was unique, a mango-guava cross. Visitors to the Mission in Abaze hardly had time to catch their breath before Raymond had them by the arm and was showing them the carefully tended acres. Whatever grew here, Raymond told his visitors, he clipped and gave to the Dyalo, so that now there were Dyalo villages on those high mountain slopes growing their own oranges and lemons where once for lack of vitamins there wasn't a man over forty with a tooth still in his head. Raymond had come to Eden Valley with a huge box of clippings from his most successful experiments. While the other Walkers loved the beauty and isolation of Eden Valley, Raymond was passionate about the dark, rich, loamy earth, from which was springing up a new orchard faster than he could have imagined, row after row of healthy, solid trees.

Eden also was the answer to Laura's prayers. The thirty years in China had seen the Walkers occupy a dozen houses, all of them drafty, dreary places, with dirt floors and sod walls; and Laura had lived in them prepared to leave at a moment's notice should the good Lord need the Walkers elsewhere. She had lived the last fifteen years in the Mission House in Abaze, which was filled with spiders and simply did not get clean no matter how she scrubbed it. Laura never complained about her choices in life, but for thirty years now she had read letters from her sister, who had married a large-animal veterinarian named Marvin and stayed in Kansas all her life, about wallpapering the parlor and sitting at night on the swing porch. Raymond and Laura almost never fought during those years, except over the subject of a home: Raymond maintained that to invest energy *now* in a house—energy which, he said, rightly ought to go toward saving the Dyalo while there was still time—was just plain silliness. "And *you* are not a woman, Raymond," said Laura. Faced with this incontrovertible truth, Raymond, who hated to see his wife unhappy, promised Laura when they left Abaze that wherever they went next, she would have the home she yearned for.

Laura never wanted a fancy house. She just wanted a large parlor with plenty of light where during the rainy season the grandchildren had space to play; and she wanted a good solid floor, so that if she woke up in the night and went downstairs, she didn't have to worry about snakes. She wanted two floors, even if she and Raymond would soon be getting older, because she had grown up in a house with two floors, and it just wasn't a home unless you went upstairs at night. The Dyalo, who used communal cooking areas in the center of the village, considered the idea crazy and a touch antisocial, but she wanted a kitchen of her own: for almost thirty years she'd had to walk outside every time she wanted an afternoon snack, and she'd had enough.

It was her son-in-law Paul, Sarah's husband, who built a home for Laura. Paul Kingston was a young missionary, originally from Texas, who had come to China just after the war to work in the Walkers' district with another of the hill tribes, the Lisu. Samuel Walker met Paul in Kunming—at the dentist's office, oddly enough, where both were having the same rear molar pulled, still odder—and invited Paul to the Walkers' annual Christmas conference. The tall, gangly Texan proposed to Sarah before the New Year. They were married a month later. Paul's grandfather in Austin had been an architect, and before Paul got the Calling, he himself had considered the profession: when he and Sarah got to Eden Valley, he took his mother-in-law aside and told her that he thought maybe he could help to build her a house to her liking, a pretty little place. No Walker man ever used phrases like "exposure to the morning light," and Laura, with real tears of gratitude in her eyes, accepted Paul's offer.

Paul had noticed a stand of teak only a half-day's trek from the valley, and the Dyalo were experienced woodworkers. They taught him how to cut teak and plane it into long boards, then how to temper the wood over smoky fires to protect the house from termites. But no Dyalo had ever thought to build a house with wooden walls—a Dyalo home had thin walls of thatch and woven bamboo—and organizing the labor in this wild country was a difficult job. Everything that came into the valley from Fort Hertz or Putao came by mule: the circular saw and band saw, the keg of iron nails, the stucco, the glazed tiles for the roof, the varnish, the enameling. During the rainy season, no caravan could pass in or out of the valley, but it was only during the rainy season that Dyalo men were at their leisure to help with the woodwork. The Dyalo wouldn't even consider the idea of working for wages; and if a man gives you his time as a gift, Laura felt, she really couldn't complain if he decided to take a week off. The Dyalo frequently decided to take a week off. As a result, Laura ended up learning a lot more about woodwork than she ever thought she could. She was more than fifty years old, and although everyone helped, in the end, Raymond, Paul, and Laura built most of that house themselves. It took them almost a year, in a country where homes went up in a matter of days.

Laura's house had two stories, just as she'd asked for, and six rooms, which she filled with flowers from her garden. She built a study for Raymond, so he could spread out his papers and read prophecy and help them all understand God's word, and she built that big living room, which was soon filled, just as she had hoped, with rowdy grandkids. From the windows, which were shuttered but of course did not have glass, there was a view over the whole valley; and if Laura woke up early, she could sit in the living room sipping a cup of tea—wild tea leaves grew not far from Eden Valley—which she had brewed in her own kitchen, and watch the sun coming up between the cleft rocks due east.

The house was on the slopes of a small hill, from whose summit the whole of Eden Valley was exposed. Seeing the valley always made Laura's heart beat fast: dark-green jungle nuzzled up against the silver-tipped fields; huge, huge clouds, the biggest she'd ever seen, floated serenely over the river, which flashed like liquefied lightning through the mossy rocks; and a family of hawks played on the thermal currents, riding high above the gorges. When she stood there watching Creation, her heart pounding away, Laura sometimes felt that as big as the whole world was, it could all fit into her palm. Laura and Raymond had agreed that if they died before the Rapture, this was the place where they would be buried, right here on the top of this hill.

Thomas, although the oldest, was the last of Laura's children to marry. Sarah had married Paul Kingston, and little Helena had married a Kachin preacher named Jesse Myang. It was the first time a Walker had married an Oriental, and Laura had been nervous about the match. But in truth, you couldn't ask for a better man than Jesse. You *certainly* couldn't ask for a harder worker or a more dedicated evangelist. The biggest surprise, though, had been Samuel, who to everyone's shock and delight had married two years after the family came to Eden Valley, winning the hand of a gloriously beautiful English nurse named Virginia whom he had met in Mandalay, where he had been shopping for books. Samuel was chubby and asthmatic and never had his big brother's charm—and look how God had taken care of him! When Samuel turned twenty-five, Laura had started to wonder if he would ever find a woman, as shy as he was, until Virginia came along, a statuesque blonde, buxom, with pale skin and bright-green eyes. Sometimes Laura wondered precisely what Virginia saw in Samuel, but this pale girl in her sundresses and floppy hats certainly saw *something*: she married Samuel after hardly more than a month of courting, and once she told Laura something about Samuel that Laura found terribly touching and, if she was honest with herself, a little improbable—that Samuel was the most interesting man Virginia had ever met, that she and Samuel could spend hours talking. The only thing that troubled Laura about Virginia was a certain lingering doubt about the intensity of Virginia's faith. Virginia ran a medical clinic for the Dyalo of the valley, and she went to the church services on Sunday, but Laura had the sensation occasionally that Virginia did not weep for the lost tribesmen as she and Raymond wept. Also, one time Laura had visited Samuel and Virginia unannounced, and on the veranda of the house which Samuel had built on an isolated bend of the river, she had seen her daughter-in-law lying quite naked in the tropical sun, her pubic hair the very same pretty blond as the curls which cascaded over her shoulders. Laura did not mention the incident to her husband, but she wondered in a letter to her sister whether lying in the sun like that was a Christian act or not. She just wasn't sure.

The last piece in the puzzle of Laura's contentment was Thomas. How complicated her son was! She hardly knew him nowadays. When the Walkers left China, only Thomas did not escape in time: he spent almost a year and a half in a Communist jail. The experience changed him: he was stricter now, and sterner, and just a little less tolerant of weakness and sin than the boy she had raised. About two years after the Walkers arrived in Eden Valley, some of the Dyalo at the head of the valley had started growing opium. Once Thomas might not have taken it so very seriously. In the old days he had always said that he preferred to convert ten new Dyalo than to convert the same man twice. But now he stormed up to the poppy fields, and bare-chested and bathed in sweat, he laid into the waist-high flowers with his machete. When one of the Dyalo men protested, Thomas turned on him. There were other villages, Thomas said, and other valleys, other places. But not here.

Laura worried because Thomas drove himself so very hard. Raymond, Samuel, Paul, Jesse—all the men still went out and preached in the villages, went out on foot into the other valleys, looking for souls to be saved. But only Thomas went out for weeks on end, a bag of rice slung over his shoulder, and when he came home from these long trips, he was moody and distant. Laura sensed that he did not approve of her house, or Raymond's garden, or Samuel's books. Only Thomas had not bothered to build himself a home. He slept at night in Samuel's old tent, and bathed in the river. His body, always long and lean, looked haggard to her eyes.

A year passed, and then another, Thomas saying nothing, scowling, coming and going on his long trips. In the end, he drove himself so hard that, just as Laura had feared, he got sick. Virginia the nurse said that it was hepatitis, and possibly dengue fever in addition. He turned the most horrible yellow color, and burned under Laura's hand; he passed several delirious nights, and Laura was certain that only the intervention of the Great Physician kept him alive.

When the fever broke, Laura sat nervously on the edge of his sickbed and asked whether he wouldn't like to spend some time at home, some quiet time back in Oklahoma, because if he stayed here much longer, living like this, she was sure that he would die.

"Mother, this *is* home," Thomas said, his voice weak but firm. "This *is* my home, and I have work to do."

Laura trembled. Since her son had first set out in the hills alone, she had deferred to him, as she had deferred to Raymond and, but for her decision to serve the Lord, had always deferred to her own father. So many others had told her that she was a strong woman, living the way she did in these savage desolate lands, but she knew the truth.

"No," she said. "I am your mother, and you *owe* me this. The Dyalo can wait. They are not your mother. I am, and you will not make me watch you die, not so long as you love me, just to show the world what a goddamn good Christian you are."

This was the first and only time in Laura's life that she would ever take the Lord's name in vain. The curse lingered in the humid air of the sickroom like the sound of a resonating bell. Thomas stared at his mother. The long muscles of her neck strained hard, and her jaw was set. Four children and thirty years of frontier living, hauling buckets of water, riding on muleback, nights outdoors, and long windy days had robbed her of her beauty. Her hair had turned a steel gray, and for convenience she now cut it herself with her old shears, barely even bothering with a mirror just so long as it was out of her eyes and off her neck—this, the woman who in her youth had ordered by mail from Chicago a book entitled *One Hundred Hair Arrangements for the Modern Lady*. On her last home furlough, Laura, sitting with her own mother, had realized with a start that they could now be sisters. They shared the same web of lines around the eyes, the same grooved cheeks and old yellowed teeth. Laura had lived a harder life than her mother, who had been a pioneer on the plains. Once she had considered old Mrs. Chester dour for wearing the same black gowns day after day. Now Laura had only three dark dresses in her closet—but that, she thought, was the life she had chosen, and every life, even a life of Service, was bound to have regrets. Now her son proposed to multiply her regrets a thousand-fold, and Laura didn't know why.

---

When Thomas was a boy out preaching with his daddy, Laura recalled, Raymond was accustomed mid-sermon to pick his young son up, swing the child over his head, and sit him down on his shoulders. *My boy will never be as big as me*, Raymond would thunder from the makeshift podium. *That's how soon God will call us all to judgment!* Other children might have been terrified (Laura would have been), but Raymond had patiently explained to Thomas that the Apocalypse was a joyful fact rather than a cause for lamentation, and Thomas loved his moment of glory, when all those sad Dyalo eyes met his over the crest of his father's slicked-back hair.

Thomas grew bigger than his father waiting, and his father picked up Samuel and thundered, then Samuel grew heavy and Raymond picked up Sarah, who made the crowds laugh by playing with her father's glasses, then little Helena, who howled in fear; but even as he grew into young manhood, the sense that daily life was inconsequential stayed with Thomas, this wonderful sense that it just didn't matter, the "it" being *anything* but getting right with God.

Late in the afternoon, cold wet rain falling, long way from home, long way to there, Raymond to Thomas, dawdling on the trail: "Do you have a tail, son? Let me see your tail."

"Dad, I don't have a tail."

"You sure? I think I see one growing. You're old enough now for a tail."

Thomas bent and twisted his seven-year-old body in a fruitless effort to spot the nascent tail which he was sure was this time miraculously sprouting from just above his coccyx. "Dad, I don't think I have a tail yet."

"Then *don't drag it*! God wants you moving. You can rest later."

Both father and son knew "later" meant much later, after the end of the world.

Thomas's parents had told him, as a child, that he was here, on Earth, in China, in this-here Dyalo village, to witness the Gospel, witness some *more*, witness *again*, witness it *better*, *tell* the Good News, and his testimony as a boy never failed to thrill his audience or produce converts. *That* was what mattered, and that was the *only* thing that mattered. Conversion was the great game at which he as a child naturally excelled, and with every baptism, Raymond and Laura, after thanking God, showered their boy with praise. Thomas was thirteen years old before he fully realized that there were other white people who were *not* missionaries. By his middle teens, Thomas had begun to preach alone, and he singlehandedly won whole valleys to Christ, liberating thousands from the bondage and cruelty of demon worship. He told the people that they could be free, that they need not live like beasts in chains. When he preached, the Dyalo listened, and when he got back to the Mission and reported to his parents that there had been over seventy baptisms on this swing through Sound of Water Valley alone, Laura told him: *You are God's gift to the Dyalo. God Himself has sent you to help these people.*

During the war, Thomas worked with the Army Air Force, organizing search-and-rescue missions among the tribal peoples for flyers downed over northern Burma. The work was dangerous, because the front lines of the Japanese armies in Burma crossed the region to which he had been assigned—but there was no one else, literally no one else in all the world, who could speak Dyalo well enough to organize the peoples. Even in uniform, Thomas Walker did not stop preaching the Gospel. He convinced his military superiors that the conversion of the tribal peoples was necessary to military goals, and air force pilots flew low over the jungle, spotted the huge crosses the Walkers burned in the jungle, and dropped down parachute-loads of freshly printed Dyalo Bibles, a spectacle of such unprecedented wonder that numerous Dyalo tribesmen were inevitably won to Christ simply by the manner in which the Book arrived.

After the war, Thomas went back to the States on furlough, where a half-year spent touring congregations of like-minded believers reinforced his growing sense that to the general patterns of life he was the exception: he and his siblings alone had been raised in China; he and his siblings alone in all the world of white people spoke Chinese, Tibetan, and Dyalo like natives; and among the Walker children, he was the undisputed leader. The girls, Sarah and Helena, both worshipped their handsome older brother; Samuel, absorbed in his books and translations, deferred to Thomas on everything Thomas considered important. Even Raymond and Laura Walker listened when he spoke: they had passed half a lifetime in Dyalo country, but he had passed his whole life there.

When he told them that the people of a certain village were ready to hear the Word, and that the people of another village were wicked and would never listen, his parents knew that he was almost always right, in the way that a canny politician knows every nook and cranny of his district.

Sometimes he even *looked* Dyalo, his mother thought. The Dyalo had a facial habit, a way of tilting the head to the side and rolling up the eyes, a gesture that meant resigned confusion. When Thomas Walker got lost on the trail, he tilted his blondish head to the side and his facial features went slack, and his mother would say with a confused sigh, "I've given birth to the only green-eyed, blond-haired Dyalo boy in all the country."

In the fall of 1951, in the last days before the revolution drove the Walkers out of China, Thomas was summoned by the Christian residents of the isolated Himalayan hamlet of Leopard Roar.

There the village headman explained the problem to Thomas: the handsome son of the village's wealthiest Christian family was proposing to marry a heathen girl from Squirrel Mountain village, two days' walk over the hills. This violated the clear commandment laid down in Corinthians, "Be ye not unequally yoked together with unbelievers," and the headman, who was also the pastor of the fledgling church, saw no ambiguity in the situation. But the Fish family remained defiant. Reasonable persuasion had devolved into heated argument, then threats. Neighbors no longer walked to the fields together. Now, the headman said, the church elders were on the verge of refusing fellowship to the offending family. The young church of Leopard Roar was foundering, and the elders had summoned Thomas to set the sinking ship aright.

So Thomas went to Squirrel Mountain village, thinking to convert the bride. But that day God did not give Thomas the gift of preaching, not at all. She had just come from bathing with her sisters when he first saw her, and on her hip she still balanced the clay bathing jug. He thought of Scripture, "But it came to pass in an evening-tide, that David arose from his bed, and walked upon the roof of the king's house: and from the roof he saw a woman washing herself; and the woman was very beautiful to look upon." Her damp sarong exposed her slender shoulders. This is how he would always remember her.

Thomas spoke for a long time that evening, but, entranced by the girl's liquid stare, he could persuade her of absolutely nothing. Thomas thought she was bored. But Thomas had no sure idea at all what she was thinking. He reckoned himself a sensitive man—this was the key to his success as an evangelist—and for certain sensitive men, an inscrutable woman is as terrible a provocation as red lips is to another. He went outside. It was a clear night. He could see a thousand stars, and behind these stars, he knew, lay heaven. It seemed a faraway place, and cold.

Thomas went back to Leopard Roar village, where he spent a week trapped by late-season rains. There was little to do but listen to the splash of heavy waters against the bamboo tiles of the headman's roof, occasionally stirring the ashes of the fire pit back into life to warm the iron teapot.

The groom was a young man named Tanzay. Tanzay had met Anye at the New Year's Festival in Squirrel Mountain, and they had danced together, she in one direction around the fire, he in the other, their fingertips grazing with every pass. Anye had assented to the match: no Dyalo maiden marries against her will. The headman's hut, where Thomas was staying, was snug and well built, but there were seven of them in there, the headman and his wife, the headman's mother, and the children, and at night between the pounding of the rain, the headman's snores, the children's dreamy cries, and the old woman's mutterings, Thomas could hardly breathe. Leopard Roar and Squirrel Mountain were only two days' trek apart, and Thomas was sure that the moment the rains abated Tanzay would leave for Squirrel Mountain, where he would find Anye and understand her and know her.

It wasn't in the end a very difficult thing to convince the Fish clan to send Tanzay off. Thomas was, after all, almost Dyalo, and this time God gave him a honeyed tongue. On the northern fork of the Salween River, there was an entire precinct of Dyalo who knew nothing of Christ's love. When the hard rains tapered down, Thomas went back to the Mission at Abaze, and Tanzay set off to preach the Word in the north country, where the Dyalo still lived as slaves.

A month passed, and Thomas decided to return to Squirrel Mountain village. When he saw Anye again, he knew that he had done the right thing. He took her into the garden, and had the Dyalo language had a word for "love," Thomas would certainly have employed it; but, given the constraints of the language, the most he could say was that he wanted her. "I knew you would come back," Anye said. "I want you too." Returning to the family gathering, with an almost imperceptible nod of her head Anye indicated to her parents that she would accept what Thomas had proposed, that she wanted this man more than the other. Then Anye, a well-brought-up daughter, retired from the room and allowed her parents to negotiate with Thomas for her bride-price.

Perhaps if Thomas had not been so caught up in the bargaining, he might have heard the news that Yunnan Province had fallen to the Communists and realized that the time in which a foreigner might safely leave China had passed: when he returned to Abaze to buy the oxen, pigs, rice, and silver he had offered to give for Anye's hand, he was arrested at gunpoint and accused of being an American spy. Thomas spent a year and six months in a Communist prison and was then expelled from China. He had been denounced by the villagers of Leopard Roar.

Thomas never again saw any of the Dyalo villages on the nearly vertical slopes of the canyons formed by the lower reaches of the Salween River. Every so often, when Thomas and his family were settled in Eden Valley, gaunt refugees from China would come staggering across the mountain passes with terrible stories of Communist oppression. From one such refugee, the second cousin of the headman of Leopard Roar village, Thomas learned that Tanzay never came back from the Wa country. No one ever was able to tell him what happened to Anye, although for years and years he asked everyone he met.

Thomas followed his mother's advice and went back to Oklahoma for a year to recover his health. He lived with his grandparents there, and at the age of thirty-four acquired a driver's license and a library card. Laura had been right: this was the place for him to get strong. Although he found it strange to eat eggs, potatoes, and bacon for breakfast in the mornings, every morning that's what his grandmother gave him, and his weight and color returned. Thomas's lifelong obsession with current events began in his grandparents' house, with long careful morning readings of the *Oklahoma Sun*. His father had always said that they were living in the End Times, but this had been a feeling in his bones rather than something founded on hard facts and reason. Now Thomas could see, reading the newspaper and then studying in the library, that there was real, solid evidence that the time of judgment would be soon. The Seven Churches had come and gone, the Seven Seals would soon be broken, and the Seven Trumpets would sound. The Seven Vials of Judgment had been opened—and now he read in the newspaper that a new Israel had been born and a war was brewing in the Holy Land, just as Prophecy had said. The more time he spent in the library studying these matters, the more he respected his father's good judgment and sound common sense.

Thomas came back from his home furlough twenty pounds heavier and a married man. When he introduced his new bride, Norma, to the family, Laura took a liking to her instinctively, immediately. She was no delicate fainting flower, that was for sure. Norma was pregnant, just as Laura had been, by the time her ship had pulled out of San Francisco Harbor, and Thomas had offered to wait with her in Rangoon until the baby was born. But Norma insisted that they go straight to Eden Valley. She was too excited to wait. "Whither thou goest, I will go; and where though lodgest, I will lodge: thy people shall by my people, and thy God my God," Norma said.

When Norma arrived in Eden Valley, the first thing Laura thought when she saw her was that Thomas had married himself a tomato woman: Norma had a huge frizz of bright-red hair, the kind which in the humidity seemed to stick out in absolutely every direction; her round cheeks and forehead were red from exertion; even her fleshy arms and hands were a bright pink. The first thing Norma said when she was introduced to the family was, "You must be Laura! Thomas loves you *so much!*" The second thing she said was, "And you must be Raymond! You are Thomas's absolute *hero*." The third thing she said was, "Have you folks got any bug spray?"

That night, at her Welcome to Our Home dinner, Laura had never seen her son look quite so adorably uncomfortable, as if he was praying extra-special hard to be Raptured up into Heaven *right this minute*. Now,

Thomas had told her all about Eden Valley, Norma said, he had told her all about China and Burma and the Dyalo and the tribal life, about the way the light looked at dawn over the mountains with the roar of the tigers and panthers and elephants in the hills—that man could sell sand in Sinai, she told her new in-laws, like she had told her friend Evangeline after that magic night talking to Thomas on the porch of her parents' home in Wheaton, Illinois; but Thomas had never mentioned, not even one itty-bitty little time, the extraordinarily horrific superabundance of bug life here in the jungles of northern Burma. Not that she was complaining, mind you, but you people have some *crazy* bugs around here. There were big bugs, little bugs, and bugs that you didn't notice when they bit you but itched up something fierce later with these huge red welts that Thomas kept telling you "Don't rub," which was as silly a thing to say as she had ever heard—

"But you can't scratch those! They'll just get worse," Thomas protested.

"Well, what the Sam Hill am I supposed to do, then? They itch."

—and bugs that you didn't see in the day or hear, but sure made a racket at night when you were trying to sleep and which Thomas here didn't seem to notice at all; and bugs which didn't ever want to duke it out with her one-on-one like an honorable bug ought to, but would come at her like an army, everywhere, just one big black cloud of swarming bugginess, until all she could do was flail her arms helplessly and cry in frustration. *Oh! And another little thing you forgot to tell me about, yes, you, don't look down at your feet, they're not going anywhere, YOU! I don't remember you telling me about the enormous snakes, the poisonous little guys or the pythons or the boa constrictors so big they could eat me up like I was a little mouse. Don't remember one word about that! Didn't'cha think I'd notice 'em when I got here?*

*A little thing like a python crawling up my skirt?*

And Raymond and Laura, listening to Norma, they laughed so hard they could bust, those big Walker hands pounding on their knobby knees, because if ever there was a woman who should be out here in the jungle with the Dyalo, Norma Walker, *née* Smith, of Wheaton was she. Norma was great. She treated the jungle that had nearly broken so hardy an explorer as John Hanbury-Tracy as nothing more than summer camp.

She was five months pregnant and spent half her days laughing and half her days crying, but she was always in motion, helping Thomas build their home ("You want me to live in a tent? I—don't—think—so. I'll get eaten by a bear." "Honey, there aren't any bears here." "That's what you said about the snakes. Get moving, mister."), helping Laura make window boxes, going up to the nearest Dyalo village and without knowing one word of Dyalo making friends with every kid there, so that just one week into her tenure in Eden Valley there was a constant stream of children asking at Raymond and Laura's door if Miss Nomie could play with them, "Nomie" being as close as a Dyalo mouth could come to "Norma." Everyone loved Norma. She came with a box of clippings from her father's backyard for Raymond and told him that if they blossomed, she'd make him real apple compote like she used to make back home. Two years later, she did. When Paul made an overnight preaching trip, she spent the night in Sarah's house, just the two of them, and for years to come, the words "rubber gloves" alone were enough to make both of them laugh like schoolgirls passing notes. And above all, she was a natural missionary: that big open smile, the eyes ready to laugh or cry as needed, a gift for listening the equal of her husband's gift for talking—people from all over this valley and the next wanted to tell her their problems, and when she told them that she knew a little secret, you'd have to have had an awful cold heart not to want to hear more.

Laura was so happy that Thomas had found a woman like Norma.

Norma gave birth right on schedule, no problems at all, to a beautiful baby girl named Ruth-Marie Walker, named for Norma's two heroines. Just two years later ("That girl is fertile as a turtle," Raymond said in private to Laura) Linda-Lee was born, named for Norma's mother and grandmother, and then just two years after that, on July 13, 1961, David Luke Walker, after Thomas's heroes. By all accounts, he was a quiet baby, an undemanding toddler, and a charming and inquisitive child. He sang in the valley choir, led by his aunt Sarah, and was an excellent student in the village school, where his grandmother educated Dyalo and Walker children alike. When all of her children were finally married, when the grandkids were rolling on the floor, when she could hear "Jesus Loves Me" sung in Dyalo from the church up the river, Laura thought to herself that until she was called Home, this was as happy as she'd get.

With the accession of General Ne Win's socialist government to power in 1962, the Walkers' happy days in Eden Valley were numbered. By 1965, the Burmese government had ordered the expulsion of all foreign missionaries, and the Walkers, settled in their northern paradise, waited for the day when the eviction orders would arrive. The Walkers prayed for one more day and one more week in Eden Valley, and for a time, God listened to their prayers, and granted them the Visa no general could revoke. Turmoil in Rangoon, civil strife, a sympathetic Christian governor who chose to ignore certain inconvenient orders—for almost five years the Walkers were able to stay in Eden Valley in defiance of the law. In those years, no Walker left by caravan for Putao or Fort Hertz, lest they draw attention to themselves, and they truly lived as Dyalo: the Walkers ate only the rice they themselves planted in their own paddies, and when in the hard winter of 1967 the rice crop was bad, like the Dyalo they scrounged in the jungle for roots. The experience made Eden Valley all the more precious: now that the Walkers could say that unlike all the other missionaries who had ever lived with tribal peoples anywhere, they were of the people they served. Had young David or his siblings or his cousins been stopped on a mountain trail, they would have said that they were Dyalo youths from Eden Valley.

When David was eight, his father found a mewling tiger cub abandoned in the forest behind Eden Valley. Bright eyes, thick golden fur, a cub the size of a Maine coon: a child's delight, a midwestern mother's nightmare. "No, sir, I will *not* have a wild animal in this house," Norma Walker said, exactly what she had said about all the other strays that Thomas and the kids had previously found in the jungle and proposed to raise under her roof—the civet, the leopard, the monkeys who would eventually steal her grandmother's pearl earrings, the baby deer, and the goral. "No, sir. We are not rearing up *tigers*. A tiger will eat the baby."

The five children began to wail, producing a polychromatic fugue on the theme of "But, Mom!" Thomas said, "But, Nomie, just look at the little guy!" and the clever tiger cub climbed into her lap and fell sound asleep. Norma fidgeted a moment and relented, as she always did, on the condition that when the thing got just a little older, Thomas would get rid of it, put it back in the jungle, do *something* with it. To David's other chores was added the task of tiger-mothering, and six times a day and all through the night he fed the cub goat's milk from a baby bottle, until the cub was big enough to eat a warm rice-and-milk mash. Against all odds, the cub thrived, and although David's parents had told him that only people could know and love Jesus, David nevertheless secretly baptized the cat when it was six months old.

But tigers grow quickly, and one year after the big cat had joined the household, Thomas agreed with his wife that the tiger was a real and present danger: although in his affectionate behavior Elijah Cat (the name was David's choice) presented himself in every way but size a normal housecat, in recent months he had gone from goat's milk to goats, stalking and killing them as an ordinary housecat might kill mice. Thomas was not entirely sure, however, just *how* he was to go about evicting the animal, tigers being notoriously resistant to gentle persuasion.

Then, one foggy morning in March 1970, Thomas stepped out of the house he had built to pee off the porch, as was his wont, and noticed foreign men in dark uniforms carrying guns. That was the day the Walkers were cast out of Eden Valley. In the end, the Walkers' eviction from Eden saved Thomas from the necessity of action: Elijah Cat was just another thing lost when the Walkers were forced to leave, missionaries being somewhat more tractable than tigers, and the only Christian tiger in all of northern Burma was left to roam the faraway hills, far from the shelter of the fold.

The last thing Laura saw of Eden Valley as she was led out at gunpoint over the hills with her family was the smoke from her house and Raymond's orchard, which the soldiers had set on fire. She began to cry. Raymond, wearing the last of his surviving wool suits, gathered his wife in her tattered housedress under his long arm and in a clear low voice reminded her that soon they would be living in a Mansion. He stroked her gray hair gently, and with the back of his hand wiped tears from her cheeks, and when she seemed to have calmed enough to listen to the Word of God, he quoted Scripture: "How doth the city sit solitary that was full of people! how is she become as a widow! she that was great among the nations, and princess among the provinces, how is she become tributary!" The notion that others before them had suffered as she did now consoled her somewhat, and with a heavy step Laura left behind the only real home she would ever have.

# THREE

# MAY THE FORCE BE WITH YOU

HELENA MYANG was David Walker's aunt, not mine, but it didn't take long before I started to think of her as Aunt Helena, and once by accident I think I even called her "Aunt Helena."

She was everyone's favorite aunt, just hip enough with her kooky yellow sunglasses and hoop earrings and the way she cussed when she stubbed her toe—you wouldn't think an old lady would even know those words, much less an old *missionary* lady—that if you're a young Walker, you might think that maybe there is some hope in your genes after all. But Aunt Helena was also not so far off the family reservation that she didn't understand where you're coming from, having had the same experiences herself, when you complain that you're almost thirteen, fifteen, seventeen, and *bigger than your father* and Dad still won't stop pointing at you in the middle of his preaching and saying that his boy there won't ever be big as him, that's how soon the end of the world is coming. Because Thomas did in the end grow into his Dad, believing the same things as old Raymond, chiefly that this weary world would soon be coming to an end, and using his father's tricks and tactics to convince the Dyalo to get right with God before the gates of Heaven were locked down; and David grew into *his* Dad, thinking that his father just didn't get it, the way the younger generation thought about things and that things here in this new country—Thailand, in David's case—just weren't like the way things were in the places where Dad had been young and at the top of his game. So David would complain to Aunt Helena, and Aunt Helena would listen to him patiently and lovingly, because he was her favorite nephew, and she'd tell him that one day, and it wouldn't be long, he'd be all grown up and he could go where he wanted and do as he liked, the important thing being to remember that his Dad loved him, a response which satisfied David precisely as much as that response has satisfied any frustrated adolescent anywhere.

Aunt Helena said that if I wanted to understand where David went when he went just where he liked, I should talk to a man named Rabbit, who lived in Boulder. Aunt Helena had his phone number in her little red phone book. He had gotten in touch with her after David's death, and the two of them had passed a tearful hour on the phone, remembering David. Rabbit was totally cool about my confusion with time zones— Rachel's grandmother wasn't the only one who found that an unusually tricky arithmetical operation—and thus my disturbing him at three in the morning: he said he was up anyway, dubbing mix tapes. I told him who I was and what I was working on. Then we got to talking about David.

Rabbit called him the Big Bamboo. "You ever see a picture of David? Long, tall, skinny, like a stalk of bamboo. It was Jerry who got the Bamboo's head right," Rabbit said. "Jerry just had an effect on him, you know? Of course, Jerry had an effect on all of us, but there was something special between the Big Bamboo and Jerry. Bamboo went on tour as messed up as any of us, and then Jerry just played six-string therapy out there, until the Bamboo felt like it was time to go back and do what he had to do. Man, I loved that guy. I can't believe he's dead."

I wasn't sure if Rabbit meant Jerry Garcia or David Walker, but I guess both were pretty tough blows.


Hot season, 1973, and Randy Cooper, whose father worked at the American embassy in Chiang Mai doing something that involved water buffalo, could not believe that David was such a dickwad that he had never ever seen a real movie in a real movie theater, indeed, had never seen a movie in his entire life.

"I *told* you," David said. He was twelve years old. "We used to live in the jungle. I mean, really in the jungle, where there wasn't even electricity and stuff. I had a pet tiger. I *told* you."

"Still a dickwad, Tarzan."

With Randy Cooper's explosive "dickwad," David realized that *everything* had changed. Since the family's arrival in Chiang Mai a little over two years earlier, David had been trading on the story of his adventures in the jungle, his account of the family's lonely homestead in the farthest reaches of northern Burma reaching a stirring crescendo with his account of his pet tiger. The story had produced big eyes in its first-grade recitals, and contemptuous "No ways" in the more skeptical sixth grade, until David produced for his classmates a photograph of himself with Elijah Cat in his lap. Aunt Helena showed me the photo: a bare-chested boy with a sweet goofy smile and an awful homemade haircut, sitting cross-legged on a bamboo floor with an honest-to-God tiger cub bent backward over his thigh. All four of the tiger's paws were in the air, and David was rubbing its belly. So it was all true after all. David had been enrolled in the fifth grade (at age level, to his grandmother's pride), when they came over from Eden Valley, and through the end of sixth grade, that photograph, explaining David's oddness and proving his extraordinary pedigree, had been the difference between dorkhood and grudging popularity.

But even the most wonderful story, told too often, loses the power to compel; and David's, which was his little part of the story the Walkers told of themselves, now provoked only withering glances of indifference from the other kids at school, who had heard the jungle stories when David didn't know how to play dodgeball; when he admitted that he had never heard of the Rolling Stones; when he couldn't ride a bicycle; and when he wasn't sure just who the president of the United States was—although David could have easily identified a dozen varieties of snake and pronounced them poisonous or benign, ably assisted in the construction of a thatch-and-bamboo home, identified all of the signs of the Rapture, or recited more lines of Scripture than anyone in school cared to hear, in both Dyalo and English. Indeed, by seventh grade David was no longer even the possessor of the most exotic story in class: Sarabeth Morgan's parents had been aid workers in Laos, and Sarabeth had grown up in a Hmong village, until the family was driven out by the war. She had seen a massacre, and had lost an adopted brother. She had arrived in Chiang Mai just this year, and her fresh stories made David's tales seem wilted and antique. David felt that it was time to put the photo of Elijah Cat back in the album and begin to accept that Eden Valley was gone forever, and that he lived now in Chiang Mai, where people went to the movies if they didn't want to be dickwads.

Not very long after his encounter with Randy Cooper, David decided to defy his father's unspoken but omnipresent code of personal conduct and go see the English-language movie of the week at the Kamtoey Theater, where was showing an entirely forgettable and now almost entirely forgotten blaxploitation film called *Blacula*, which the very same Randy Cooper, who brooded over the seventh grade like an incubus, the week before had said was so funny it almost made him piss himself.

Thomas had never specifically told his eldest son that he was not allowed to visit the Kamtoey Theater, but David knew his father was far too subtle a psychological tactician to prohibit outright a forbidden pleasure. Not long after the Walkers arrived in Chiang Mai, Linda-Lee had begun reading *Cosmopolitan* magazine, which she borrowed monthly from a classmate at school. Thomas didn't tell Linda-Lee that if she looked at that magazine one more time she'd be headed straight to the burning pits of Hell, which in Thomas's mind was not very far from the truth; but when he happened to notice a copy of *Cosmo* in Linda-Lee's book bag, the fifty-one-year-old Thomas began very publicly to read the magazine himself. Linda-Lee came home from school one day to find her father on the couch absorbed in an article about trimming the pubic regions, and at dinner with the whole family Thomas asked Linda-Lee if she had read that same fascinating article about how to seduce a man in six minutes or less? The funny thing was, Thomas continued, that was precisely how Mom had won his attention all those years ago, and was it working well for Linda-Lee? Linda-Lee went quiet as a puddle of water at the table. The very last thing the fifteen-year-old girl wanted to do was publicly compare her mother's quondam abilities as a seductress with her own. Can you imagine, Thomas went on, that people actually paid attention to this *silliness* when other people on this planet still lived as slaves? Norma went *tsk-tsk* wearily, and Grandpa Raymond shook his pa-

triarchal gray head from side to side. You could almost hear the bags under his eyes go *swish-swish* in disapproval. Linda-Lee wished that the
ever-present gaping maw of Hell would swallow her up right then and
there.

So to go the Kamtoey Theater, which if discovered would have subjected him to his father's mockery, David was forced to lie to his father,
which if discovered would have subjected him to his wrath. In preparation for his first visit to the cinema, David announced to his mother that
he had joined the swim club, which met from four to six on Tuesday and
Thursday afternoons. (Except at the height of the rainy season, when the
pool, for reasons no one could explain, turned a violent cucumber green
and widespread student opinion held that to dip so much as a toe in the
water would lead to an agonizing death by slow-creeping gangrenous rot,
which would pass *upward* from the feet, if you catch my horrifying drift, a
terrible thing which *really* happened to some poor kid in the tenth grade.
In the rainy season, David thought it prudent to play volleyball.) But at-
tendance at athletic clubs was optional, and David explained to the
swim teacher that he was expected that evening at a church youth group
meeting.

Thus having fashioned himself a solitary afternoon in the hot season, David went to the Kamtoey Theater, by bicycle, directly and absolutely alone, first dodging traffic on the Charoen Muang Road, then
over the Nawarat Bridge, crowded with bicycles, motorcycles, trishaws,
tuk-tuks, and handcarts piled high with bags of rice and cement, past the
aromatic flower market with its mountains of roses, orchids, jasmine, and
lilies, then into the old city itself through the Tha Pae Gate. The whole
way there, David swore to himself that he would never forget the Dyalo
again, not even one time, not when the hills which ringed Chiang Mai
were throbbing with demon-besotted Dyalo who needed *his* personal assistance, whose souls were crying out for liberation—although David did
wonder just how two hours of swimming or volleyball, activities which
no one disapproved of, would have *helped* the Dyalo. The question had
bothered him enough that he'd asked his grandfather what he should be
doing to help the Dyalo if he wasn't going out into the hills and preaching as his dad had done at his age. Grandpa Raymond had nodded in
that slow, thoughtful way he had, and said that at the very least, David

could pray for the Dyalo. "I take prayer extremely seriously, David. Prayer is often our most effective tool in the Fight." David was impressed by the serious, manly way his grandfather spoke to him, and decided that he could just as well pray for the Dyalo in a movie theater as in a swimming pool.

But the hard truth of the matter was that the very instant David settled himself nervously into the very last row of the Kamtoey Theater, he forgot his vows altogether.

David sat in the red-velvet seat, his heart racing and his skin prickling with a fine nervous sweat. He had a theoretical knowledge of film from his mother, who had told him that a film was like a photograph the size of a wall that moved, but the whole notion struck him as somewhat incredible. He wondered how he would describe the film to his classmates tomorrow. Maybe he would say, "It was so funny I peed myself," although he was not precisely sure how a moving photograph would be that funny, exactly; or he would say, "It was so scary I almost barfed," although again, the connection was obscure, between a picture which moved and the kind of cold terror he had felt when, pulling up the bucket from the well not long before the family left Eden Valley, he had found a cobra spitting back. That discovery had in fact provoked David to vomit.

The more David thought about barfing, the more he felt just a touch queasy. The Thai don't believe a movie should be a barrier to a decent meal and rightly consider popcorn proper fare only for pigs, so generations of cinemagoers had come into the theater laden down with meatballs and grilled chicken on skewers, soaked with sweet sticky sauces; salted dried fish from the vendors lined up outside the theater; and bowls of noodles drenched in fish sauce, vinegar, sweet kaffir lime, spicy ginger, lemongrass, and galangal, the whole odoriferous concoction to be slurped down all through the show with the aid of chopsticks, whose click-clack against the ceramic bowls could be heard even at moments of highest cinematic tension. The red carpets and thinly upholstered seats had absorbed forty years of spills. The smell was overpowering, although to a nose not distended by guilt and anxiety, not entirely unpleasant. Later in life, David, wandering through the covered spice market or just passing by a street stall, would be instantly transported by a familiar smell back to the Kamtoey Theater and the sweet, illicit afternoons of his adolescence.

David thought about going home. His butt wasn't stapled to the seat. He figured that he had seen enough of the theater to fake it at school from now on, but not so much as to estrange him from his family. That was the hardest thing to explain to the other kids at school, just *why* he had never been to the movies. He had only recently begun to suspect that his family, in its enthusiasms and convictions, was different from other families; and, indeed, the Walkers lived more intensely in the service of the Lord now than they had even in Eden Valley, treating Chiang Mai as little more than a mirage offered up by the Deceiver to distract them from what they needed to do.

When they had first come to Chiang Mai and all of them were still living in a two-room house lent them by a wealthy Christian tailor, how admirably flexible in the face of adversity the Walkers proved themselves to be! Raymond and Laura were more than seventy years old, Thomas more than fifty, all of those children, not one Walker speaking a single word of Thai, little money, twenty years spent in the deepest jungle— and the only thing the Walkers knew for sure was that *they would not forget the Dyalo!*

"This was no accident, our coming here! Oh no! God's planning is coming together, and soon the Day will come. The wind of God had blown us down from China in the north," said Grandpa Raymond.* "And when the storm picks up, don't you worry, the Dyalo will come running in for Shelter. We'll be patient like a seed in the earth."

By giving those old enough to preach a goal, namely the conversion of the Dyalo of Thailand, Raymond distracted them all from the sorrows of exile. And all those old wild wandering Walker impulses, long suppressed in twenty years of jungle domesticity, came out again, to the exclusion of almost all other cares: Thomas, together with Uncle Samuel.

---

*The grandkids just loved Raymond but, nevertheless, when alone could not always resist the temptation of making fun of his many endearingly dramatic phrases: "the wind of God" blew across "the river of time"; men climbed "the tall mountain of sin," only to fall into "the deep abyss of suffering," in which was heard "the thunder of repentance"; the only deliverance from "the wolves of Satan" was "the sweet honey of Heaven"; "the black night of Eternity" was promised to all who had not been scared by "the fire of the Word," supported by "the solid oak that is His Promise," or touched by "the flames of His Love." Even Norma, when alone with the kids, could not resist laughing when her youngest son, Paul, did his imitation of Grandpa Raymond preaching.

Uncle Jesse, and Uncle Paul, devoted themselves to learning these strange new hills. Talk at the dinner table was of preaching and baptisms, conversions and wavering villages, shamans who fought the work and headmen who—*Praise!*—were coming close to the Light. The Dyalo in these hills were strange and different, their dialect outlandish, but the Walkers knew them. Even Raymond with his bad hip couldn't keep from going into hills and limping from village to village, as he hadn't done since he himself was a young man, and when the men came down from ten days, two weeks, a month in the mountains, caked in mud, their faces were flushed red because they had felt His power. David didn't even need to ask what his father would think of his decision to see *Blacula*. *If you have time on your hands, son, pray for those folks in Mae Salop*. That's what his dad would say.

David had almost convinced himself to leave the theater when the lights went down. He gripped the arm rails of his seat. The roller coaster rolling slowly upward, a plane in heavy turbulence, a doctor probing the genitals, that familiar tightening of the scrotum and cloaca. He wondered: Why had he bothered to lie to his mother? As if God couldn't see him sitting here? As if God couldn't afford a ticket to the movies, God who had made the universe? What had he been thinking?

Why, he wondered, had nobody told him that movies were in the dark?

Then bats. That was the first thing he heard. From up above, the hysterical shrieking of a flock of bats swooping down from above, a flock of idiot bats who nested in the rafters of the old theater. Confused by the unexpected and untimely alternations of light and dark, the bats flapped and dove, as strange lights began to play across the screen, accompanied by loud music, which David recognized from school assemblies as the Royal Anthem. On the screen, the bright colors coalesced into the form of a man, and then a crowd, then dissolved and disappeared just as quickly, before David could quite decide what he was seeing. Then David realized that it was just as his mother said: the screen was all *one moving photograph*. He saw the king of Thailand on the screen. In his anxiety David had hardly noticed the others in the audience, but now, looking around, he realized that he was the only one still sitting. He stood up.

David knew that when presented for the very first time with a photograph, many Dyalo, particularly the old people, have trouble interpreting it. It would only be colors and lines to them. They would hold it right up close to their eyes and then far away, then upside down or sideways, and would call their wives over, and say, "Do you see anything here?" and David would say, "Don't you see? That's a nose and that's eyes and that's a mouth there." And still the old Dyalo just wouldn't get it, until all of a sudden, like someone examining those optical-illusion puzzles which show *either* a candlestick *or* two faces, they'd say, "Ah-hah!" and they'd figure out what was going on—although each new photograph would still require long scrutiny before the "Ah-hah, isn't *that* clever!" moment.

Now David found himself in the same confused position. There were photographs of the king on the walls of every shop in Chiang Mai, but *this*—this was another thing entirely. What his mother had never mentioned was that the photograph was constantly *changing*. The king would appear in one place and then in another, on the left side of the screen and on the right, an older man and a younger man, dressed in a suit and then in the ochre robes of a Buddhist monk, and then in a military uniform, and then in the elaborate royal gowns. David would only begin to figure out who the king was, and then the king would disappear again. Sometimes the king would move, but sometimes the camera rotated and advanced, even gained altitude and perspective, while the king stayed in the same place. There was the king humbly reciprocating the bow of an old peasant lady; then the king in a military jeep. The king was driving, his regal face a study in concentration. Now the king was on elephant-back heading up into the hills. Bats flew across the king's face. The king's jeep was driving toward the camera, and David involuntarily ducked and then a second later stood up straight again, feeling foolish. Then the anthem swelled to its dramatic crescendo and the screen went black. The bats who lived in the rafters of the Kamtoey Theater retreated to their nesting place.

David sat back down in the dark, breathless. This was more than he expected. He had only seen the minute-long tribute to the king of Thailand which precedes the showing of every film throughout the kingdom, but David was confirmed in the very secret suspicion that he shared with every other thirteen-year-old in the world: that God and his parents really did wish to deprive him of the best pleasures in life.

All this even before the show began.

My sources told me: David grew into a tall, skinny, strong young man, with his father's moss-green eyes and his mother's tomato-red skin. Because he grew so fast in adolescence, his pants and shirts were always half an inch too short for him, making him seem taller still, and because in Thailand no doorway and no chair is made for somebody almost six feet three inches tall, he developed a permanent slouch, bending slightly at the waist and curling down at the neck. His dark hair was inevitably uncombed. They told me: David was good with languages, like everyone in his family. By the time he was done with high school, his Thai was nearly perfect, like his English, almost as good as his Dyalo—the language in which he thought and dreamed. He wasn't an excellent student, but he got by. He was well liked in high school but didn't have a best friend. He went on chaste, chaperoned dates with another missionary's daughter. He would juggle whatever small objects were at hand. He was one of those kids with a bottomless pit for a stomach, and sometimes he'd eat dinner at home, then at Aunt Helena's house, then stop at the noodle stall for a bowl of noodles.

*Jai-yen.* That was the Thai phrase the Walkers used to describe David. It means "cool-hearted," which means easygoing, mellow, not too excitable, the kind of guy who saves his energy for things that count. If you've been saving birthday and Christmas money now for almost four years, and you've just got a new Honda motor scooter for your seventeenth birthday one week ago, and you've parked it in front of the market, and some drunk in a pickup trying to parallel park smashes into the side of it, knocks over your brand-new bike, breaks the rearview mirror, and scratches to heck the yellow paint job—and the first thing you do when you see the guy is smile, then you're *jai-yen.* David smiled, not just because he was in Thailand, where, of course, you smile when someone smashes up your bike, but also because that was the kind of guy David really *was.* It was just a motorbike. With those long, floppy limbs, and that Adam's apple one size too big for his adolescent throat and bobbing like a tea bag, the mussed-up hair, and the uneven stubble covering his chin but not yet branching up seamlessly to the mustache, the XXL T-shirts ("Chiang Mai Baptist Church 1975 Christian Youth Outing!"), the shorts with all the pockets; with the way he had of cricking his neck from side to side, that slow, thoughtful way of talking in his low but unsteady voice; never in a hurry, never sweating, even in the height of the hot season, when even the bronze Buddhas in the temples had to wipe the perspiration from their golden brows—all in all, he was just your calm, good-natured kind of kid. The kid you didn't have to worry about, because he had a level head. The kid you didn't have to take care of, because he'd make himself a sandwich or get himself some noodles or pick up Laura's prescription at the pharmacy without even being asked. The kid you didn't have to remind to do his homework, because he was pretty much on top of the situation. The kid you didn't have to tell to come home before midnight. (That was his sister Linda-Lee.) The kid who didn't get caught coming out of one of those massage parlor places. (That was David's cousin, whose name has been withheld because it was a long time ago.) David was the kid who bought his mother a goldfish tank for Mother's Day, because she'd had one, she once remarked, as a little girl, and there was nothing so calming as watching fish swim.

And in a household with three teenage girls—Ruth-Marie and Linda-Lee and David's little sister Margaret, who was twelve going on twenty-two—David was a relief. Sometimes, Norma thought, her head could just explode with the chaos in her household, especially on those hot, steamy tropical days, when she'd think that if she'd stayed in Wheaton, it would be twenty-eight degrees right now with a soft, quiet snow falling. But here she was in Thailand, her husband off in the mountains somewhere charming who-knows-who into doing who-knows-what; Ruth-Marie and Linda-Lee were having another one of their knock-down, drag-out fights; Margaret just bought her first tube of lipstick; little Paul had a fever; Laura wanted to show her *once again* how to can mangoes—and bedraggled and sweaty, she'd knock on the door of her son's room and say, "David, can I just come in here and close the door behind me?"

Of course, David's room would be a mess; the kid didn't—he couldn't—keep anything neat: heaps of papers from school on the floor, all his old clothes piled up and perhaps a little ripe, puzzles and games in the corner which he had long outgrown but which his grandparents in America still thought were to his taste and sent him, the guitar which he was forever plucking lying on his unmade bed, sheets tangled on the floor. But for Norma, the room was dry land when the good ship SS *Walker Family Mission* seemed in danger of going under. Five kids in the jungle was *easy* compared to five adolescents in Chiang Mai. And the nice thing about David was, he got it. He really did. He'd laugh his rumbling not-quite-sure-what-my-voice-box-will-do-next laugh and say, "They're driving you nuts, huh? Come on in, Mom, you can hide out in here."

Just a really good calm kid.

But of course there was another side to things as well. That family was a pressure cooker, like the rice steamer in the kitchen, always on, always hot. Aunt Helena, who is the family's informal psychologist and the only Walker I met who in any way could see things from an outsider's perspective, said that in retrospect the big fight wasn't about those trips to the Kamtoey Theater at all. There was simply so much *pressure* on David, she said. She told me that I couldn't imagine what it was like to grow up the oldest son of a great preacher, the grandson of another, with so much real achievement on a boy's shoulders, and so many people's hopes. When David was a little boy, nobody ever asked him, "What are you going to be when you grow up?" They asked him, "Are you going to preach the Gospel like your daddy? Are you going to save souls too?" And what could David do but smile his sweet little-boy smile and say, "Yes, when I'm big enough." They told David, "God has chosen you." Somewhere along the way, the people in David's life just started telling him how beautiful it was that he was giving his life to Christ. When all the other kids at school started after-school prep sessions for the SAT, thinking about college back in America, Thomas just said, right in front of David, what his own dad had said a long time ago: "Why bother? It's just tits on a bull." Norma thought maybe David might want to go to Bible college for a couple of years, as she had; she had never regretted her education. But that was the most extreme suggestion anyone in the Walker family offered David for his future.

From the moment David staggered out of the Kamtoey Theater for the first time, he lived a divided life. There was his life as a Walker, in which it was understood that preparing the Dyalo for the Rapture was the absolute and overwhelming goal of his young existence. Then there was his other life, his real life, the life at the Kamtoey Theater, where every Tuesday at five he forgot entirely for two hours to pray. For almost six years David kept his two lives strictly separate. Sometimes when he left the Kamtoey Theater, having seen policemen and lawyers, doctors and politicians, hippies and pimps and gangsters and adventurers and detectives and reporters, sometimes on the way back home to the big pink house with the brass placard that read SOUTH CHINA CHRISTIAN MISSION, he thought he was barreling down a dark tunnel so narrow and ✓ confining he could not even lift his arms.

Thomas's sister Sarah was on the subscriber list to a newsletter called *Christian Family Alert!*, a mishmash of advice on Christian living and snippets of biblical commentary and interpretation, mixed up with stories about cute things the kids and pets did, together with household tips and advice. When she was done reading *Christian Family Alert!*, Sarah usually passed it along to her sister-in-law Nomie, who, in those few calm quiet moments that she could steal from her household, liked to read the newsletter at the kitchen table, sipping green tea and clipping out the recipes, because the thing she had been meaning to get for the longest time was a good cookbook, in English, filled with the kind of midwestern recipes on which she had been raised, and the recipes in *Christian Family Alert!* were actually pretty darned good. When Nomie was done, she left *Christian Family Alert!* in the kitchen, where her husband read it over his morning tea.

Now, the ironic thing was, Thomas tended to dismiss most everything in *Christian Family Alert!* If people in America would get half as upset about the unconverted masses of the world, half as upset as they seemed to be about what was on the dang television, if they'd get so upset that they'd just get down on their knees for twenty minutes a day and ask the Lord to save the Dyalo and all the other lost peoples of the planet—that, Thomas figured, would achieve something useful. Thomas read *Christian Family Alert!* more out of sociological interest than anything else, to see what the folks in the Home Country were thinking these days, and having read the magazine, he usually spent a good forty minutes once a month at the dinner table complaining that he didn't see why Nomie read that thing anyway, until Nomie pointed that in the first place, she didn't subscribe, Sarah did; in the second place, he was eating a very fine zucchini casserole thanks to that magazine; and in the third place, she didn't think *Christian Family Alert!* made its way out of the kitchen, up the stairs, down the hall, and beside the toilet every month all by itself, thank you very much.

On the release of *Star Wars, Christian Family Alert!* sent out to its subscribers a "Special Action Bulletin" warning Christians of the danger that popular film posed to their children, what with its vaguely messianic slant, its mysterious magical "force," its Manichean battle between good and evil, and its complete omission of any deistic references. The Walkers were all very eager to assure me that the odd thing was, this was *precisely* the sort of thing about which Thomas usually could not and would not get himself all lathered up. Nobody knew just why that film, which he had never seen and had no intention of seeing, rubbed him so the wrong way. But he had read about *Star Wars* in *Christian Family Alert!*, and the movie stuck in his throat like ashes.

"What is going on back home with this *Star Wars* stuff?" Thomas asked his family over the dinner table. America was always "home" to the Walkers, although of all those at the table, only Nomie had ever spent more than eight consecutive months there. "Can somebody just tell me what people are thinking? Don't they know what is going on over here?"

Long silence at the table. With Dad, sometimes the best strategy was just to *stay quiet.*

"Do you know what they said in China when we first came with the Word? Linda-Lee, what did they say?"

" 'Two thousand years,' Dad. They said, 'Two thousand years we've been waiting for this Word, why didn't you come sooner?' "

"That's right. Exactly right. We *cried* because they wanted to hear the Word so badly. There wasn't a minute we weren't out there preaching, your uncles, your grandfather, me, because the people were so eager to listen." Thomas shifted to his didactic mode. "So what we are seeing now, you see, is a complete and total reversal of roles. Even as the Dyalo people are going toward the Lord, the people in *our own country* are turning their backs on Him. Sad, really. Crisscross, you see. A film like this one, *celebrating* everything that we have spent such a long time fighting, a film like this one would have been unthinkable when I was a boy, when America was still a Christian country. When I first started working with the Dyalo, we had a whole country praying for us, and you could feel the difference. It was like having wind in your sails. Now it's not the same. A boat can't sail without wind. And you know who suffers? Paul, tell me who suffers because of this."

"The Dyalo, Dad. The Dyalo are suffering because of this."

"That's right. That's exactly right. People in America go around watching your *Star Wars* or what have you, and thinking that there is something else in this world more powerful than Jesus Christ, and they forget to pray. Just forget, if you can imagine that. I remember when I used to go up in the mountains and tell the people about Jesus. There wouldn't be enough hours in the day to baptize all those who were ready to be baptized—we'd have them lined up—and now, well, just look at the difference. Still the same Gospel, same as it's been for two thousand years. Still the same people, same old Dyalo. I'm still me. What's the difference? I'll tell you all the difference. Not the same *prayer backing* in the Home Country. They're sending us out to fight the battle and not giving us the tools we need. And you know why not? Because their minds are being filled with trash. David, are there kids at your school who have seen this movie?"

David looked down at his plate and made a little rice mountain with his fork.

"David, that was a question for you. I asked if there were kids at your school who had seen this movie?"

"Yes," David said.

"And what do you say to them?"

" 'May the Force be with You.' "

The fight that followed was a turning point in the Walker family dynamics. David, frustrated to the point of tears, tried to tell Thomas that

*Star Wars* had nothing to do with the Dyalo, nothing to do with demon worship, that it was just a movie, a good one, that he had seen it three times and loved it, and that if his father wanted to know why the Dyalo didn't listen, perhaps, just perhaps, it was because he kept pointing at his son, and saying that his son wouldn't ever grow as big as him on account of the end of the world, when his son was two inches bigger already; and Thomas, hurt and angry, wondered just how David could be wasting his time on trash like that when he had grown up himself in a Dyalo village and seen those hurting people who needed his prayers and love, and how long had he been lying to the whole family? It took Nomie two days of shuttle diplomacy to make the peace, which was finalized over breakfast two days later, when Thomas asked David if he'd be going upcountry with him the next day. That Thomas had asked and not presumed was a sufficient gesture for David, and he said that he would. Nomie thought to herself that boys were *so* much easier than girls: had the offended party been Ruth-Marie or Linda-Lee or Margaret and not David, she would have been staring at two months of sulking, pouting, and slammed doors, *minimum*. David really was a good, calm kid.

But with the fight over *Star Wars*, something had changed. Before, David had considered his involvement in the big world a source of guilt and shame; after the fight, David went to the movies openly. He was now a senior in high school, and following the fashion of the time, he allowed his hair to grow long, which irritated his father, not because it was a countercultural gesture (in fact, Thomas, who had simply missed the 1960s, would hardly have recognized it as such), but because it reminded him of the queue worn by the cruel Chinese Mandarins of his youth, who forever impeded His progress with the Dyalo. David, who had been plucking out hymns on his guitar since he was a boy, started a rock-and-roll band with three of his classmates called Waterwheel, and stopped going up into the mountains with his dad on weekends. He went out with some kids from school and came home reeking of cheap whiskey, which would have provoked a monster fight had Grandpa Raymond not taken Thomas aside and said that as a boy in Tulsa, before he found the Lord, he'd certainly taken his fair number of nips from the bottle. Just give the boy an aspirin, Raymond advised. David bought himself a record player and started playing such horrific music on his speakers that Nomie no longer knocked on his door and asked if she could hide in his room.

David graduated from high school and spent half a year with his big feet flopping over the ends of the fake-leather couch in the living room watching the goldfish Olympics, until his Aunt Helena, who'd been telling him all along that one day he'd be big enough to do whatever he liked, told him that now that he was big, he ought to get off his duff and do something. She called *her* Aunt Jean in Tulsa—this would be Laura's other sister, these Walkers had aunts like China has heathens—and had her send over pamphlets and brochures from the local community college, and she convinced the whole family that the best thing was if David went off for a while. Grandma Laura, who always felt that it wasn't entirely a good thing for the kids to lose touch with their heritage, especially supported the plan. She wasn't quite sure what to make of it all, however, when Aunt Jean wrote the family in Chiang Mai to say that six months after David had arrived in the States, he had left Tulsa to follow a rock band called the Grateful Dead. Laura was only partially comforted by the thought that given the group's name, at least David seemed to be involved with good Christians: if Laura's long experience had taught her anything, the only people who were particularly happy about the prospect of being dead were those who had been saved.

Let me tell you. If you think it's tough to ferret out the doings of an unknown anthropologist in a village of unlettered tribesman deep in the remotest jungle in the heart of Southeast Asia, just try finding out exactly what David was up to on the Lot of Dead Tour twenty years ago. If you find someone who remembers it all that well—actually, I couldn't find anyone who remembered it all that well; and those who do remember something tend to have memories that sound a lot like this: "Oh yeah, that was the show when the boys did 'St. Stephen' and Mickey did a cosmic drum solo, and then this girl Moonbeam who was a twirler and this guy Miguel who was a taper and I decided to go to Boulder to see this guy she knew who could hook us up with some jimsonweed." Then try doing it all over the telephone from Chiang Mai, dealing with more than your fair share of people who for one reason or another are just a little suspicious about calls from strangers. For this reason, given how hard it was to get the lowdown on David during his Dead Tour years, I think I should here and now give a big "Hey now" to my friend Rabbit, whose help and assistance lacking, no story would have been possible.

Rabbit—full name, Gray Rabbit, legally changed from Jeffrey McLean—was old school: in his Boulder home, he told me, he has over two thousand bootlegs, from the band's very early days in San Francisco to Jerry's very last terrestrial show, including the European tours and Egypt.* I asked Rabbit how many shows he had seen himself and elicited only a low groan, which I think meant either very many or very, very many; and when I began to think about what those very, very many Dead shows really meant, I began to think in terms of *planets* circumnavigated in that gray-green Volkswagen van, license plate MAGICMN.

Rabbit told a typical Deadhead story: on the road first in 1975 at the age of eighteen, when the Dead first blew his mind wide open; off the road finally in 1997, when a bad case of trucker's back and a profound distaste for Phish convinced Rabbit that Boulder was a nice-enough town, if you had to live somewhere; and in the middle, largely continual traveling. Rabbit was an American nomad who from the comfort of his Caravan, at once cozy *and* mobile, like a Mongol in his yurt, roamed across endless scorching deserts and over white-crested mountains, down lonely highways bordered by fields of corn and wheat and cotton, on the soles of his Birkenstocks always a few stray grains of sand from the shores of one great ocean, to be washed away only when Rabbit swam in the waters of the other. And through all that wandering, there was only one place where Rabbit was at home, free from the withering glances of the highway patrolmen who pulled him over, called him a vagrant with no fixed address, looked at him from behind mirrored shades, and suggested that he best be heading upstate soon, adding a maddening, sneering,

---

*Nevertheless, his collection is not complete, and if there's anybody out there who would like to trade tapes with Rabbit, he said they should feel free to find him at his Web site, www.my magicneverends.com. He is particularly looking for tapes or MP3s from Jerry's band, 1985–1987, because some creep broke into his VW Caravan and took his tape box, including also two Led Zeppelin rehearsal tapes which are extremely rare and he'd like back.

condescending "*son*"; only one place where he was free from the suspicious eyes of disapproving Pakistani AM/PM clerks, who, taking in his
straggly beard, long hair, and tie-dyed T-shirt, assumed that Rabbit was
trying to steal those Pringles, although Rabbit supported himself perfectly well making and selling the best damn devil sticks on the lot,
thank you very much, best damn devil sticks there *is*.\* That place where
every eye was friendly and every mouth was grinning was the Lot. No
matter where Rabbit had roamed or how long it'd been since he'd seen a
show, Rabbit came home when he pulled over into the parking lots outside the coliseums, amphitheaters, and fairgrounds where the Grateful
Dead were playing; when he smelled the incense and saw the rows of yellow school buses, VW vans, trailers, pickup trucks, brightly painted RVs,
campers, and tents; when he heard more people banging on their drums
than all the rain chiefs in Africa invoking the water devils in a drought.
Home is the sailor in from the sea, home is the hunter down from the
hills. That's what people even said, the Deadheads on the Lot, when
they saw that their friend had made it down safely from Santa Fe to
Austin, one more leg of their unending trip completed: *Hey now, Rabbit.
Welcome home.*

Rabbit first met David sometime in 1981. This was the best that
Rabbit could do, specificity-wise, and he knew it was 1981 for sure because he had just gotten back on Tour after taking 1980 off on account of
his failed experiment in domesticity. Somewhere in his wanderings, Rabbit had gone to the Show single and come back to the van married.
Everything in between was a blur. His bride was a fellow Deadhead, a
pretty little earth goddess who wore flowing faded paisley skirts and
homemade macramé tank tops, who spent two years in the Rabbit

---

\**Devil sticks*: This was certainly a phrase which confirmed some awful fears back home in
Chiang Mai when included in one of David's not-so-frequent letters. In truth, a reasonably innocuous object: two short balsa wood sticks of equal length, wrapped tightly in pleather; one
much longer, betasseled stick, slightly heavier, also wrapped in pleather. The object of the art
was to balance and bounce the long stick between the two smaller ones, an occupation not entirely unlike juggling in its demands for coordination, balance, and grace, and a wonderful thing
to do when jittery on account of being just a little too stoned. Rabbit and David made money
by buying two dollars' worth of balsa wood, colorful pleather, and duct tape, and with forty minutes of careful cutting and wrapping produced an object which was sold on the Lot to yuppies
and high school kids for ten dollars apiece, thus in three sales realizing a ticket for the Show.
Oddly enough, devil sticks are now sold to tourists in the Chiang Mai night market, *billed as an
authentic Dyalo tribal art*. David Walker, it is reasonable to presume, was the vector of transmis-
sion.

mobile before telling Rabbit that either they got themselves a den or Rabbit would be wandering alone. Rabbit loved his little Sugar Magnolia and tried out life in Babylon, as the followers of the Dead called the sober stationary world, but the sight of his parked Caravan sitting out front every day got to be too much, and Rabbit bolted, never looking back. He got back on Tour in 1981, and in the way that Dead Tour tends to bring you together with all different types, from policemen to Wall Street bankers to farm kids to hippies, he got to talking with this really nice kid with an incredible story—"the most polite kid you ever met," Rabbit said—just outside Indianapolis, who was looking for a ride to the show in Buffalo.

That kid, of course, was David Walker.

Dead Tour! It just seemed *so right*. Where else in America, Rabbit asked, could a kid like David announce that he grew up in a near–Stone Age village in northern Burma with a tiger cub for a pet preaching the Gospel to illiterate tribesmen who hunted with poison-tipped arrows— and have folks just look at you, say "Cool," and remind you not to bogart that joint? On Dead Tour, David was hardly even considered odd, not compared with Mean Jim, say, who'd followed the Dead since being discharged from three tours in Nam, slept with a foot-long hunting knife under his pillow, and *worshipped* Phil Lesh, the bassist, in the most literal sense of the word, right down to the shrine, the candles, and, rumor had it, the occasional sacrifice.

David had a bumper sticker right on the back of his big green backpack: "Life Is Better When You're Dead," and David put it there because it was so true. The Walkers don't like to admit it; they talk about it as David's time of *soul-searching*, when he was *lost*, the *lonely* time before David *got right with God*. But don't believe a word of it. Just talk to Rabbit. David *loved* Dead Tour. He woke up every morning, and that kid who had been told all his life that God put him on this Earth to save the Dyalo from the bondage of demons, he was surrounded by ten thousand of his closest friends who couldn't have said whether a Dyalo was a primitive tribe in the Tibeto-Burman hills or one of those spiffy new Japanese imports with the great mileage. The only *demon* on tour was the narc. And that kid who had been told that *Star Wars* was a sin, the only time on Dead Tour he heard the word "sin" was in connection with spilled bong water.

I asked Rabbit what it was about life on the road, and he just sighed, a soft, lilting sigh, not entirely dissimilar to Thomas's much later when I finally summoned up the courage and asked about Jesus. David couldn't believe how big the country was, just couldn't believe it. He had seen Nevada when the Dead played Vegas, but he had never seen New Mexico. Never saw Alabama. Never saw Idaho—and folks said it was *beautiful*. But they were there and waiting for him. He had time. Sometimes, he'd wake up at three in the morning unable to sleep, and he'd decide to go *right now*, without waiting for dawn, just to see what was between here and Austin, where in two days' time the Dead were playing a four-show set.

Dead Tour was David Walker's Yale College and his Harvard: David met people on Tour he never knew existed—and this was a kid who'd met witch doctors and Burmese generals; but he'd never met someone like the slender young woman who spent almost six years in the company of the New York City Ballet before she broke her leg. She told David that she knew she was done dancing ballet from the moment when she was lying in a hospital bed, her leg in a cast, and realized that the best time dancing she'd had in the past six years was when she went on a date with a guy who took her to see the Dead play Madison Square Garden. David never forgot a face: he remembered everyone he met and he greeted them by name, often wrapping his long limbs around them in a spontaneous bear hug. *Hey now, Moishe*, the former professor of political science at Northwestern, who'd been on Tour almost five years. The former Green Beret. *Hey now.* The son of the senior senator from Indiana. Pretty girls from every county in the country, girls who spoke with twangs and lisps, harsh nasal northeastern vowels, soft southern whispers. For the first time in ten years, David could tell the story of Elijah Cat and expect big, big eyes. *Hey now.* People who were obsessed with making sure that every note that Jerry played was recorded on tape. "It's a responsibility, man. In a hundred years—the people won't *have* Jerry anymore. This is what they'll have."

David had a propane stove, and he made rice stir-fry which he sold on the Lot for a dollar a plate, and vegan burritos and tofu enchiladas, and he rolled incense, and Rabbit taught him to make devil sticks; when he got his own van a year or two later, he went down Mexico way and bought copperware, which he sold to yuppie Deadheads in places like San Francisco, Boston, New York, Philadelphia, and Seattle. David would stay on Tour months at a time, usually driving from show to show with Rabbit, then disappear for a while the way people on Dead Tour tend to do, maybe because that nice couple he met at the Nashville show had a little communal bio-organic beet farm somewhere up in the mountains and they invited David to spend a week which turned into a month which turned into six. Winter was coming, Dead Tour was over for the year, but Jerry Tour—the Jerry Garcia band—was just starting up, and when the people on the Lot saw David, wherever he went, they said: *Hey now, Bamboo. Welcome home.*

Every few months, David would call Chiang Mai, from Buffalo or Memphis or Des Moines or Phoenix or Spokane or Mobile or Malibu or Eugene. When Norma answered the phone, the same strained conversation predictably ensued:

"Are you eating okay, David?"

"Yeah, of course I'm eating okay, Mom."

"What are you doing all day?"

"I'm just, you know, traveling around the country, and listening to music, and being with friends."

"Are you in a cult? Do you need help? You can tell me if you need help." *Reader's Digest*, which Norma read weekly, had recently run an article about cults and cultlike behavior.

"No, it's not like that."

"We love you very much, David."

"I love you, too, Mom."

"We're praying for you, David. All of us."

David would hang up the phone and he had the strange sensation that for the duration of the call his soul, his very soul, had been sitting in the big, pink house in Chiang Mai and was having a difficult time returning to his body. His soul was floating out over the Pacific Ocean, dawdling and indecisive. He could imagine, being the good, kind kid that he was, the conversation over the dinner table that night. Norma would tell Grandma and Grandpa and Dad at dinner that David called that afternoon, and everyone at the table would lean forward.

"So when's he coming home?" Grandpa Raymond would ask.

Mom hated to say she didn't know, so she always said soon.

"Oh, I hope so," Grandma Laura would say. "I hate to have him so far away."

"That boy's not coming to this home until he cleans up his act, no sir," Dad would declare. His sister Linda-Lee, with whom David occasionally exchanged letters, had told him that Dad said that a lot. "He cuts his hair, gets himself some clean clothes, starts to act like a man, then he can come home. Not until then." Still, almost every night, Linda-Lee had said, it was Dad who gruffly asked his wife: *Hear anything from Davy lately?*

And when the Walkers of Chiang Mai prayed, Linda-Lee had said that they all put prayers for David's safety right up at the top of their list, even Raymond, who had prayed above all else for the conversion of the Dyalo for some sixty years now.

That strange, mildly disorienting feeling of having lost his soul somewhere over the ocean persisted for perhaps five minutes after every phone call with his family, and then the sadness would be drowned out in the general tumult, chaos, and weirdness of the Lot. How could David explain Dead Tour to his family when he couldn't even explain it to himself?

I thought I knew David by this point. I really thought I did. I'd known kids who'd gone off and followed the Dead in college, kids like Henry Sifton, who straight out of school and armed with perhaps the least useful bachelor's degree in Middle Eastern studies ever earned, went on Tour with a half dozen of his friends in a huge yellow school bus which he and his friends called the *Little Red Bus*; and Emily Something-or-other, who in junior year went hippie chick. She started wearing long, flowing skirts and made the big mistake of using an herbal deodorant. Dead Tour was such a cliché that nobody said one word about David but I didn't have an inward flash of recognition and perception, a palpable sensation that David could have gone to school with me, could have even been me: out of college, I had hit the road myself, not on Dead Tour but in India and

Indonesia, floating from Karnataka to Tamil Nadu and up to Calcutta, through Bangkok and Malaysia down to Sumatra, places which I found every bit as thrilling and exotic as David found Montana and Indiana. Who couldn't sympathize with David's flight from parental expectations? I figured he couldn't have been *that* different from me.

But I was dead wrong. David was nothing like me, not at all. Of course he wasn't: David was a Walker.

For the rest of his short life, David would tell all the people who asked and plenty of people who didn't about the moment that he got right with God. He could never bring himself to say that his life on Dead Tour was sinful; but, he would admit, there had been a time in his life when he was blind to his responsibilities. But the glorious thing about God, he would tell his Dyalo audiences, the truly glorious thing, was that God wanted you to come Home as badly as you wanted to go.

He had been on Dead Tour for almost four years when Jerry told him it was time for him to go home, on a warm August night in Eugene, where the Dead were playing a five-show set, not three weeks after David had celebrated his twenty-fourth birthday.

What a treat Eugene had proved to be! Whenever the Dead played Eugene, Rabbit's hometown, Rabbit stayed with his family, who did not much approve of Rabbit's way of life but had long since stopped fighting it; Rabbit had invited David to park his van in front of the hutch for a few days. Of course, Rabbit's mom had insisted that David stay inside the house, and the last few days, David had the very finest hospitality the elder Rabbits could offer: Mrs. Rabbit had made him two hot meals a day and not just carrots and lettuce either. Mr. Rabbit had shown David his fine collection of fishing ties and lures. The gentle atmosphere of home-cooked meals, cozy beds with fresh-washed sheets, and hot showers had relaxed David, to the point where when Rabbit announced that fateful, final afternoon on Dead Tour that it was time to head down to the fair-grounds, David had almost decided not to go. The senior Rabbits had a big-screen television and cable in the basement, and David was seriously considering whether it wouldn't be nicer to watch a little tube with Mr. Rabbit than to see Jerry one more time. He'd been to two shows now in Eugene, and, truth be told, although he didn't much like to admit it, the boys hadn't been playing their best lately: Jerry had been out of tune, no disrespect, I mean, Jerry out of tune is *still* Jerry, but Jerry, I mean, it's just a fact, he had been out of tune; Phil was on Planet Phil, as always; and Bob was doing this new thing where he . . . he just seemed to *wail*. Only Mickey was on top of his shit. But in the end David decided to go, chiefly because there was a rumor going around that the band was going to play "St. Stephen."

It was the warmest, gentlest of summer afternoons, big cumulo-nimbus clouds floating overhead, the kind his grandmother called "angel pillows," with just a hint of a northern breeze breaking up the still heat. The Lot smelled of barbecues and beer and pot and mud. David didn't have a ticket and didn't have the money to buy one, so he took a pizza box from the floor of the van and with a bright green crayon wrote on the back: "I need a miracle!" He tied the pizza box around his neck with a shoelace and started walking the Lot. He would never walk the Lot again.

David stopped for a lemonade with some folks he'd met in Seattle a few weeks earlier, a housepainter named Mike and his girlfriend who'd driven down for the show in a beat-up Bug. The housepainter had also heard the rumors about "St. Stephen." When David got to his friend Se-quoia's RV, he accepted an invitation to step inside for a bong hit and play with Sequoia's new kitten. David spent some time watching a teenager with a homemade "Grateful-fucking-Dead" T-shirt juggle fruit, and by the time the kid had three apples, two oranges, a mango, a grape-fruit, and a pineapple in the air, David had to admit that this was some serious juggling talent, and he gave the kid a dollar. It was almost time for the show, and the Lot emptied out. Maybe he wasn't going to get a ticket. That happened, too, sometimes, and a big-screen television *chez* Rabbit made things easier to accept. He was philosophical about it either way. He could hear clapping from inside the fairgrounds, as the warm-up band took the stage. A few latecomers arrived and ran for the entrance. David watched them enter the fairgrounds. The sun was high in the sky, and a cloud passed over it. David started to give up hope of seeing the show, and headed back toward his van.

Then a young man with long hair and sideburns in the front seat of a pickup truck called out, "Hey, Miracle! I got a ticket for you."

David walked over to the truck. "You're not going?"

"Nah, she's sick. We gotta go." He pointed to a young woman shivering in the front seat of the pickup truck, her arms tightly crossed in front of her chest.

The woman groaned menacingly, and the man turned in her direction. "Listen, you're not goin' to ralph, right?" he said. "My brother just got this fucker deep-cleaned—upholstery, carpets, everything."

David felt a sudden sympathy for the woman. "You want to wait a little while, see if she gets better?"

"Nah, we gotta go," the man said. "It's gonna be a frickin' great show too. I just know it too. I always know. We drove all the way down from Portland, and—"

He waved his hand in a what-can-you-do gesture, handed David the ticket, and drove off. David shouted thanks in the direction of the retreating vehicle, and then thanked God.

The Lord, David would later tell his listeners, the Lord works in the strangest ways. But that is surely the essential point, he would say: *He works!*

By the time David had wandered back the length of the Lot, the Dead had taken the stage.

The guy in the parking lot was right, David told his audiences: It *was* a great show, proving once again the wisdom of the old Deadheads, who said that you needed to go to *every* show to see a *good* show, and you needed to see every *good* show in order to see a *great* show. The day was so hot that Bob started spraying the crowd down with water from the stage—and in the audience, someone thinks: *Those are little drops of Bob himself, floating out of that rubber hose, little refreshing drops of Bob himself.*

It was somewhere in the second set, just after "Uncle John's Band," when the miracle happened, and what could it be called but a miracle? David heard the angels singing. He was lying on his back in the grass, his long arms at his side, a damp towel across his eyes, his fingers dug into the earth, his mind wandering, when Jerry introduced a familiar melodic line into the musical chaos for the which the Grateful Dead are known. Jerry was playing something that David recognized from his childhood—and how did Jerry know *that* tune? But Jerry knew so many tunes, country and folk, the blues, Spanish *canciones*, even an occasional Scottish hymn. Jerry played out that melody a little more, playing so sweetly that it could have been Grandma Laura singing as she bathed David in the running waters of Eden River when he was four years old. David sat up straight and listened more intently.

Then the angelic chorus began to sing in four-part harmony:

*There were ninety-and-nine that safely lay*
*In the Shelter of the fold.*
*But one was out on the hills far away,*
*Far off from the gates of gold.*
*Away on the mountains wild and bare,*
*Away from the tender Shepherd's care,*
*Away from the tender Shepherd's care.*

The angels mingled their majestic voices with Jerry's reedy tenor, and David began to cry. David felt his soul separate from his body and he knew that he had died and was being welcomed into Heaven. Now he had come Home. He thought of his grandfather wandering through Chinese villages, desperate to tell the people what he knew. David could feel his soul floating vaguely over Oregon, and from his perch in Heaven where the angels sing, David could see the white shore of the dark Pacific, and then huge waters and stormy seas, then a line in the ocean where it was night, and far in the distance, across the ocean and high in the hills, David could see Dyalo villages in darkness.

In the story the Walkers told of themselves, this was the miracle that brought David back home.

The creature that got off the plane a week later, although definitely David, was not at all the person Norma had expected.

She had not expected that her sullen, good-natured, shy, slouching, adolescent son, a boy capable of spending whole days on the couch watching the goldfish, would be transformed into the young man who *exploded* off the plane. There was no other way to put it. Right there at the arrivals counter of the Chiang Mai airport, David picked up his Grandma Laura, all eighty-odd years of her, right off her feet. Norma knew that Thomas had been nervous about how to greet his own son;

but David overwhelmed the anxieties by enfolding his father in his long arms—*my*, Thomas looked little next to David; he must have grown, and that long hair and beard only made him look bigger—hugging him with such ferocious intensity that when finally the two untangled themselves, Norma noticed that her husband's light green eyes were damp. David winked at his mother over Thomas's shoulder. She really hadn't expected all that hair.

Norma was so glad he was home. But everything about him was different. He walked differently: the last time Norma saw David, he used to shuffle. Norma could not count the number of times that she had said, "David, pick up your feet. David, don't walk like a turtle. David, stand up straight." Now David strode through the airport terminal out into the hot Chiang Mai sun, spreading his long arms like the wings of a huge bird. Then they got to the house, and David strode inside, his long arms sweeping back and forth in huge arcs. Only when David had entered the house, in the process hugging, kissing, and embracing no fewer than twenty aunts, uncles, sisters, brothers, and cousins, not to mention a goodly portion of Chiang Mai's Christian community, sometimes taking two or three relatives into his long arms at the same time; only when he had flopped himself down in his old place on the couch and asked if there was anything to eat in the house, did Norma really recognize her son.

A few days after his return, the Walkers had a party for David. A party in the Walker way of thinking was simply normal life plus a cake, and it was Norma who baked the cake that night and made the frosting. After the guests had gone home, David told his family about the miracle that brought him home, about the moment when he had heard the angelic chorus singing.

When David said that he was sure that he had died, Norma shivered. *Am I the only one here who thinks this is weird?* she thought. She had heard Raymond's story ten thousand times; but that was *Raymond*, and long ago, and in the war. But to hear the story from David's own mouth, to hear David—*David!*—who had always understood her so well, so much better than anyone else, speak of rising up into Heaven and hearing angels singing hymns, for just a moment Norma felt lonely, lonely and more than a little frightened, looking around that room and wondering just who these people were that were her family.

The next morning, when Norma woke up, David was already gone. He left a note. "Great to be home. Back soon. Love you all & bless. David."

He wasn't home again for almost a month, no phone calls, nothing.

David came back suntanned and a little bedraggled, his sweaty hair showing the first hints of dreadlocks. Norma was determined not to show how bothered she had been by his absence.

"Oh, honey, I'll put a plate on the table for you," she said. "Lunch will be ready in a jiffy."

"Thanks, Mom. I could eat a horse." David had an odd grin on his face, and was whistling tunelessly. He was an enthusiastic but incompetent whistler.

Norma went about rearranging the plates on the table to make space for David. There was a plate for Laura, who hardly ate anymore, then Raymond, then Thomas, then a place for herself, near the kitchen, then David's little brother Paul, who ate enough for a small army, then a plate for David's big sister Ruth-Marie, who was pregnant again, and then a plate for David, slouched against the doorway. He really needed some new clothes; those things on his back were almost rags.

"Honey, do you want to take a shower before lunch?" Norma asked.

"Are you saying I smell?"

"Nothing a little lye wouldn't fix."

"I bathed in the village this morning," David said.

"Next time try using soap and water."

David still had the same grin on his face. Norma finally had enough. "Honey, just a word saying where you're going and when you're coming back, that's all I ask. I worry."

But David hardly heard her. He was still grinning, that same odd grin. "Mom, do you remember Moo Bat Yai? With Headman Honey?"

"Of course I remember Moo Bat Yai. Headman Honey is up there."

"I was in Moo Bat Yai. I couldn't leave."

"But why? For a month?" Norma's heart began to pound faster.

"Twelve."

"Twelve?"

"Twelve. Headman Honey. His wife. His oldest son. A guy from the Fish clan—you don't know him, he's new. His wife. And the rest from down the hill, four in the Wood clan, and three from the Rabbit clan."

"Oh my," said Norma. "Have you told your father yet?"

"Not yet."

"Go now. He'll be so proud he could die."


Norma was right, as usual. Thomas was so proud of his son that he could die. For the two years following his return, David wandered the mountains, carrying nothing but a small backpack and his guitar. Norma could not help but hold her breath when David was gone, but she loved the moment when he walked back in the door. On Thomas's map of the Dyalo villages of northern Thailand, the purple pins, which indicated a wavering people, and the black pins, which indicated the deepest heathenism, steadily turned white, one after another.

David had been back in Thailand for a little over two years, Norma told me, when Laura had her stroke. She was sitting in the garden on a bamboo-and-rattan chair that her grandson Paul had made for her as a Christmas present when she felt a little weak on her left side. That was all she felt, just a little weak, but when she tried to stand up, she collapsed on the crabgrass lawn, and it was almost an hour until Norma found her lying there. She didn't mind the wait, Laura told the family later, because that's when she saw the very first of her crosses. At first she wasn't sure if it was anything more than the play of light and shadow on the cement foundations of the house, but as she lay there, wondering just what was going wrong with the left side of her body and feeling very frightened, she realized that it was a cross, and she could even see the grain of the wood if she looked closely. When she looked even more closely, she saw stains from His blood.

The family took her to the hospital, and took her home, and she spent her last year sitting in her rocking chair. For the rest of her life, Laura saw the crosses regularly. She saw them in the dust motes playing in the late-afternoon light, in the irregular formations of early monsoon clouds out the windows, in the dirt on the floor, even in the folds of the fake-leather couch. Laura had thought, leaving Eden Valley, that her happiest days were behind her, but she was wrong.

"She was so happy," Norma said. "She couldn't talk much, but she had such a big smile, that was the best time of her life. There was a real peace in the house right before she died. Do you know what her last words were? Her last words were, 'Thank you.' Isn't that a beautiful way to go Home?"

"It is," I agreed.

Norma was silent for a long minute.

"It was hardly after that at all that that woman . . ."

Just eleven months after Laura died, two young Lisu boys found David's partially decomposed body in a remote valley to the northwest of Chiang Mai. He had fallen a great distance, then been shot twice in the back. He was buried beside Laura in the family plot at the Chiang Mai Foreigners' Cemetery.

PART THREE

THE NATIVE'S
POINT OF VIEW

# ᴘᴀᴋ ɴᴀɪ

THERE WAS NO NATURAL END to Walkerology, and in the spirit, if not the endurance, of the heroic Sir Richard Jebb, who studied all—and only—the seven surviving plays of Sophocles for upwards of sixty years, I would have been content to study the Walkers for a very long time.

But then the Walkers stopped talking. Just what happened I'm not sure. For a happy month, I interviewed Walker after Walker, taking them aside with my notebook and tape recorder, asking questions. They'd been eager to talk to me; a few even said that they wished their kids were as interested in the family history as I was. But then, sometime in mid-April, nobody seemed to have time to talk to me anymore. I don't think that I offended anyone. *Maybe* I said the wrong thing. I don't know. Aunt Helena went back to the States to visit her children. Tom Riley stopped having breakfast with me, saying he'd put on ten pounds since we'd started meeting and he'd call me when he lost the spare tire. The truth, I suspected, was that things were going so well with Judith that he no longer felt the need for my services. I figured he'd call when they had their first fight. Everyone was still nice to me on the phone and very polite and still said "God Bless You" before they hung up, but everyone inevitably had other commitments or was going off somewhere really exotic without me or on prayer dates with other Christians, to which I, of course, being a heathen, had not been invited.* It's possible, I suppose, that middle April is just a very busy time for missionaries, as it is for accountants, what with Easter and the existential despair which inevitably accompanies the humid days toward the end of the hot season. I even stopped by the big pink house one day uninvited, but only Ah-Mo was around, and in her broken Thai she explained to me that Thomas and Nomie had gone-gone, far-far, and wouldn't be back for a month.

They hadn't even said goodbye.

It might seem strange, but in the absence of the Walkers I fell into deepest gloom. It was right before the Songkran holidays. Brown clouds covered the city. But it would not rain. I took a shower in the morning, another at midday, then one in the early evening, and a final one before bed; and after every shower, I dusted myself liberally with mentholated prickly heat powder. All day long there were tantalizing moans of distant thunder on the horizon, falsely suggesting that soon, very soon, *achingly soon*, the explosion of the monsoon would be on the city. Or worse: standing on the crabgrass lawn outside our concrete house under the swaying palms, I would feel a fast wind stirring up, and then a single, immensely large *plop* of rain would tumble on my upturned forehead. And then—nothing. The thunder would roll over again, the dogs would dart for shelter, the palms would sway in the wind, and then—nothing.

Meanwhile, I was almost broke. All that time with the Walkers, I wrote nothing. I did not pitch a single story. I would rather have been Left Behind than write one more word about another local jazz quartet, wood carver, pub, pizzeria, or tailor. The Thai gazillionaire who had once asked me to write short summaries of English-language business books had been implicated in some incomprehensible Thai financial scandal; I sent an e-mail to his secretary, offering to summarize books about criminal justice, but got no response.

Rachel's questions about the year to come were growing more insistent. She wanted us to figure out where we were headed and what we planned to do with ourselves. If we didn't take action soon, she faced an-

*Not one of the Walkers ever attempted in any way to preach the Gospel to me. There was an occasional flutter of curiosity about my own religious beliefs, which the Walkers assumed I held as intensely as they hewed to theirs, but otherwise they betrayed a complete indifference to the state of my soul. You tell me why.

# FOUR

# RAIN

SO MUCH OF LIFE consists of long puttering spells: when I look over *my* letters from those first few weeks of the rainy season, I find e-mails to and from my editor at the *Bangkok Times*, who asked me to write about the artist-in-residence at the University of Chiang Mai. To my mother, I wrote that Rachel and I took a class one Saturday afternoon in Thai cooking, and another in Thai massage. There was a letter to my grand-mother, in which I told the story of the fourth-grade teacher at Rachel's school, a quiet Burmese woman, who broke her wrist in a tuk-tuk acci-dent. Mr. Tim, I continued, asked me to take over her class while she convalesced, and for a week I taught school, an experience so exhausting that I didn't think once of anthropologists or missionaries, just savages.

None of these e-mails was exciting, but the events they depict were the real events that made up my days. Not one e-mail mentions Martiya or the Walkers; but not a day in that early monsoon passed when I didn't rifle through Martiya's letters (which ended shortly after her arrival in her new hut), or look through the extensive notes of my conversations with the Walkers. But as it happened, almost a month passed in which I made no progress, until I ran into Thomas Walker in the parking lot of the supermarket on the Chiang Mai–Lamphun Road.

I had never before seen Mr. Walker outside of the big pink house, and the sight of him in those waist-high slacks staring at the steel sky from under the supermarket awning took me aback: I was used to seeing him putter in a narrow triangle between the living room, his study, and the dining room; and although I had heard stories of him in China, in Tibet, in Burma, in Oklahoma; although Mrs. Walker had told me he was headed off to Mandalay—I hadn't really believed that he existed outside that house. Now he held a large bag of groceries in his left hand and was looking for his car keys, the man who in his youth had stolen sweets from the pockets of the future Tigi of Gartok.

I waved as I walked across the lot, but he seemed not to recognize me until I was right upon him; then he smiled and said, "Well hello, young man! I was telling Nomie just the other night that she must have scared you away!"

"Not at all," I said, and suddenly I could think of nothing else whatsoever to say. Judging by Mr. Walker's silence, he was in the same position. The two of us stood there for a moment bobbing our heads, and I think that if it hadn't started to rain at that moment, Mr. Walker would have excused himself a second later and retreated to his car, and I would have gone to buy my coffee and bananas.

But it did start to rain. There were three huge cracks of thunder like the sound of the giant wooden blocks that the Thai slam together to frighten crows in the rice field. Then, with no transitional drizzle, rain so fierce that I could not see the other side of the parking lot.

We stood for a few moments watching the downpour. Mr. Walker had done his shopping but was going nowhere, not in this weather. He said something to me, but the rain was too loud for me to hear him, and he shouted it over again. I finally understood that he was saying, "Let's go get a Coca-Cola." Mr. Walker's long fingers gestured in the direction of the tarpaulin-covered noodle stand abutting the supermarket, where long pale ducks hung on hooks above vats of boiling water.

We sat under the plastic tarpaulin drinking our Cokes. I asked about Judith and Tom Riley, and whether he and Mrs. Walker had had a good trip, but Mr. Walker just smiled back at me in mute incomprehension. The rain was that loud. Soon, the parking lot began to flood, and by the time we were done with our Cokes and the rain had dwindled to a last few furious drops, the water in the lot was nearly knee-high, every car in the lot submerged to just under the headlights.

Mr. Walker snorted through his nose. "Ever seen rain like this?"

"Yesterday," I said, but Mr. Walker hardly seemed to notice.

"Rains like the dickens here four months out of every twelve. Every day it'll rain here until September. Parking lot here gets flooded, I've been seeing it now some twenty years. It's not a mystery what you need to do to prevent this flooding, let the customers get home. All you have to do is build the lot on an incline, dig out a drainage ditch, and cement in that hillside. But they've got a different mentality here. *That's* the difference between a Christian and everyone else, you see. Only Christianity tells a man you've got to take precautions and come in from the rain, build a solid home, because the rains are coming."

I could have been any vague acquaintance who had met Mr. Walker by chance in that parking lot and drunk a Coke with him, and he would have been delivering the same speech, which I could only hear through David Walker's bored adolescent ears: "Is Dad giving the Flooded Parking Lot Speech *again?*" Not that I entirely disagreed with Mr. Walker: a parking lot *shouldn't* flood every time it rains.

"You see, your animist or your Buddhist—they don't believe they have a *relationship* with God. They don't know how to *find* Him. So their fundamental point of view on life, you see, is powerless. It doesn't occur to them that they can change things, make things better. Dyalo knew we could help them, though. Right from the start. Back when we first came, family after family asked us, 'Two thousand years! Why did it take you so long to come with God's word?' And we—"

Mr. Walker stopped talking, and his eyes looked past me out into the parking lot. He rattled the ice cubes in his glass of Coca-Cola.

"I'm sorry?" I said, thinking that he had asked me a question which I had failed to hear.

He sat silently for long enough that I thought of telling him it was nice to see him again and going into the store to do my shopping. But then Mr. Walker, with a note of absolutely uncharacteristic nervousness in his voice, said, "So did you find out anything about that woman?"

For a moment I wondered why he was so nervous. Then I realized that it was Norma. He was nervous that Norma might even *suspect* that he was discussing Martiya. I had never spoken to him without his wife in the next room, or without wandering into his study unexpectedly. But that's why, when he had seen me, he had asked me to have a Coke with him—so he could talk about the woman who had murdered his son without his wife nearby. I felt a sudden surge of sympathy for the man: a lifetime of outstanding bravery, and in his old age, Thomas Walker lived in fear of his wife.

And then I realized something else: the answer that he had given me when I asked why Martiya had killed David hadn't satisfied him either. He had told me that the devils and demons had made her do it—but he wasn't convinced. Like those Melanesian Islanders who interpreted the cargo planes of the United States Navy as benevolent deities descending from heaven and built their own landing strips to attract the generous bird gods, he had fit David's death into his own system of the universe. But no *schema mundi* was big enough to accommodate this sorrow. Mr. Walker was hoping that I could tell him something he didn't know.

"A friend of Martiya's sent me a pile of her old letters," I said.

"And?"

"I don't think they have much to do with your son." I told him about the letters, about Martiya's hut, and Pell.

"I knew old Farts-a-Lot," he said.

"You did?"

"Biggest pain in the backside you ever met. Last saw him a few years back. He was a Christian for a while, backslid. Couldn't keep away from the *lao-kao*." He used the Thai word for rice whiskey. "Did you know she used to come by the house?"

"When?"

"Back in the early days here in Thailand. Back in the 1970s."

*Back when David was alive.* Before David went away on Dead Tour. "Did she come by the house often?" I asked.

"Oh, yes sir, she used to come by the house all the time. She used to come to our house and ask us questions, and we'd tell her about the Dyalo as best we could. I met her at the bank."

"The bank?" These little prompts kept Mr. Walker talking. I think they were a psychological device by which, should the necessity arise, he would be able to justify the conversation to Norma: "Why, honey, I was just answering the young man's questions. Curious little guy."

"Yep. I was standing in line with my daughter Linda-Lee, we were chatting in Dyalo like we do, and this woman starts staring at us. *Farang* woman, and she says to us, not in the best Dyalo, but we could understand, she says, 'You are Dyalo speakers too!' I could hear her American accent, so I said back to her in English, 'Of course!' We got to talking, and when we heard about her work we invited her back to the house for dinner."

After David's death, all of the Walkers would say that they saw something rotten or malicious in Martiya when she first showed up at the house in the fall of 1977, but in truth only Norma said anything at the time.

The other Walkers, when they sat around talking about her after she left, decided in the collective fashion of large families that they liked her, probably in the same kind of way they more or less liked me: the Walkers could never really be at ease with anyone who hadn't vigorously accepted Jesus Christ as his personal savior—that was simply too big a chasm in understanding to overcome—but they found her lively and interesting, with an odd take on the Dyalo, as when she described them as "strictly exogamous from the clan." Laura Walker, who despite a lifetime of acquaintanceship with the Dyalo had always found them a foreign people, was especially taken with the confusions of the young anthropologist, and sent her home with a freshly baked loaf of banana bread. Raymond Walker remarked on Martiya's beautiful green-gray eyes. The younger Walkers—David, his siblings, his cousins—liked Martiya too: they had never met anyone like her, somebody so clearly of their generation but not of their world. When they said grace before dinner, twelve-year-old Margaret noticed that Martiya did not close her eyes. Seeing Margaret and catching her staring, Martiya had smiled—an expression so inappropriate to prayer time that Margaret wondered whether God would still bother to bless the meal. If God didn't bless the meal, Margaret later asked her mother, would it still be worth eating, with protein and calories and stuff? Margaret also noticed that Martiya wore dark red lipstick, which interested her intensely.

All that evening Martiya peppered the Walkers with questions.

"You mean that you think the spirits are actually—I don't know—

what's the word? *Real?* They're not just something that the Dyalo invented?" she asked, in response to some remark which began, no doubt, "Two thousand years!"

"Absolutely real," Thomas said. "No question about it."

"Have you *seen* a spirit?" Martiya asked.

"Never seen Africa but I'd bet that it's there. The Dyalo aren't the first, not by any means, to be oppressed by such devils. In the first six chapters of the Gospel of Mark alone, there are ten references—ten!—to the casting out of devils. The New Testament is just chockablock with devils, demons. Now think about that a moment. The Jews in ancient Israel, the Dyalo in the eastern Himalayas, thinking the same way, with the same beliefs—that's a mighty strange coincidence. People in every corner of the world believe in spirits, ghosts, what have you. It's not a coincidence."

"And these spirits are *enslaving* the Dyalo?"

Thomas sighed at the simplification of the complicated relationship between the Dyalo and the spirits who controlled them. "I'd certainly say the spirits are bullies and brutes. They're ugly creatures, no doubt about it. And the Dyalo are sick and tired of being told by these ugly creatures what to do. When someone who's bigger than you and meaner than you and stronger than you tells you what to do—wouldn't you call that slavery?"

Martiya thought for a moment. "In the village where I'm staying, the people say that Old Grandfather spirit *protects* them. And they have ancestor spirits. They don't talk about being enslaved by them."

Thomas snorted. "First, according to the Bible, which is quite clear on this point, human spirits don't linger on the Earth, but only those unclean demon spirits which occupy the body *before* death. That's one of God's promises to us, that when we're done here, he'll take us Home or send us to our punishment. So I think that's a confusion the Dyalo are making. Those aren't the spirits of the ancestors the Dyalo are worshipping but *deceivers*—spirits taking human form to confuse the Dyalo. Now, about Old Grandfather. *Hah!* When I was a kid, there used to be a Chinese warlord, came by the mission every few weeks. Said he'd protect us. We asked him, 'What happens if you don't protect us?' He said, 'My soldiers will cut off your heads.' That's how Old Grandfather protects the Dyalo."

"What did you do?" asked Martiya.

"Do?"

"About the warlord."

"Oh, yes. Dad here"—Thomas gestured toward his father, who sat at the head of the table, smiling gently—"well, Dad here told that warlord, 'Go on and cut off our heads. Cut off anything you like. God sent us this money so we can work with the people, not to give to you. But if you want, I'll give you something worth much, much more than gold.' Well, that warlord, he wasn't happy about that, not one bit, let me tell you. What is he going to do with our heads? The next day, the warlord came back, and Dad said the same thing. We *knew* the Lord would protect us. Day after that, the warlord came back and asked to be baptized in the name of Christ."

Like me, I imagine, Martiya was not quite sure how to respond to the Walkers' more extraordinary stories. "Did the warlord explain what happened, why he changed?"

"The man was filled in the night with the Holy Spirit. He said that any God which made people so courageous must be worth believing in. We've seen things like that happen more times than you can count."

The table fell silent a moment. Raymond cleared his throat. "You're asking very important questions, young lady. And let me tell you, when we first came to China in 1920, a very long time ago—"

Laura interrupted, "Oh my, yes."

"—I had an attitude very similar to yours, I thought that spirits were only something you read about in the Bible, something that only bothered people in biblical times. I certainly didn't realize the *magnitude* of the problem. It took me a considerable period to realize that defeating the spirits *in our day and age*, right here, defeating them through the aid of our Lord and Savior Jesus Christ was the significant spiritual challenge of our time. But Grandma Walker and myself, we saw case after case of it, wandering through those villages, until we finally had to put aside our white colonial master attitude and admit that these people might know something about something. We arrived in village after village and were told when we tried to set up our tent, 'Oh no! Don't put up your tent near that rock! There's a nasty spirit who lives there, he'll get angry with you.' Or, 'Don't talk too loud in the rice field. The rice spirit *hates* loud noises.' We learned."

Laura Walker shook her head. "Oh yes, it was *terrifying* for them in those days," she said. "For us too! When the spirits saw us coming to baptize somebody, they would be furious. They would fight back with everything they had. Somebody would come to us and say, 'Yes! I want to be free of the demons, I want to be baptized in the name of a God who loves me,' and we would make an appointment for the morning to baptize them, and in the night they'd be attacked by the spirits, they'd come to us in the morning with bite marks, bruises, bleeding. 'What happened to you?' I'd say. 'Spirits attacked us in the night,' they'd say. After all that we couldn't deny the *severity* of the problem."

"I can see that," said Martiya, having sought, and found, a neutral phrase. "What do you think the spirits *are*?"

It was Thomas's brother Samuel who took up the bait—Samuel now in his early fifties, balding, a round face and spectacles, Samuel who had passed the better part of his life quietly reading and translating the Bible into Dyalo, verse by verse. He said, "Miss van der Leun—"

"Martiya. Call me Martiya. Please . . ."

"Miss Martiya, we're not anthropologists. We're practical people. We see a problem and we're trying to fix it, if we can. We're certainly not experts like you."

"I'm not an expert!" said Martiya.

"Well, compared to us, you certainly are. Nobody knows what the spirits really are—maybe they're fallen angels, that's certainly a possibility, or maybe some other being created in the spiritual realm. The biblical evidence certainly associates the spirits with Satan. But you know how I've always thought of the Dyalo spirits? They're like a bureaucracy. Like a giant powerful bureaucracy, which imposes a million and one rules on the Dyalo. Fines them a pig or a chicken or something worse when they do something wrong. Punishes them, kicks them around, treats them like dirt. You ever try and get a residency permit here in Thailand? Go from office to office, lose two whole days? It's like that *all the time* for the Dyalo. If the spirit of the big rock makes your kid sick, ask the spirit of your ancestor to protect you. So you slip him a bribe, a chicken, a pig. Maybe he'll help you, maybe not. If not, you go to another spirit, try and bribe *him*. So it goes."

"Exactly!" said Thomas. "Exactly! And then we come along and we say, 'Folks, we know the Man at the top! You want to plow that new field? You don't need to sacrifice a pig or say this ritual—just talk to the Boss! Who loves you! Who *wants* to help you! We'll teach you how to talk to Wu-pa-sha directly!' "

Wu-pa-sha was the creator of rice, rain, life, and thunder, at the very summit of the Dyalo spiritual hierarchy.

By the end of the evening, when Norma served her pineapple upside-down cake, the group was prepared to laugh together.

"So I move into the place, I take a deep breath—and I get about exactly five minutes of solitude, no more," Martiya said.

"Yep!" said Raymond. "They're not a people to leave you alone!"

"First, it's the kids who show up. All of them. Every kid in the village thinks the place is his."

"That means they like you," said Laura.

"First morning in my new hut, one kid is crawling up the mosquito net, another is on my desk—right on top of it!—and a week later, one of the little twerps comes tumbling in right down *through the roof*. Kid looks up at me, doesn't say one word, picks himself up with a kind of shocked look on his face"—Martiya imitated the child's face, raising her eyebrows and sucking in her lips—"and walks out of the place. Big hole in my roof."

"Oh no!" said Laura.

"But the kids aren't the only thing. I bought myself a mirror here in Chiang Mai. I thought one morning, 'You know, I better check everything is still in place.' "

"Yes!" said Norma. "That used to drive me insane in Eden Valley. No mirror, not one in six years, I just wanted once in a while to *see myself*!" Norma turned to her husband. "You see, it's not only vanity."

"In my case it is, actually," Martiya said. Everybody laughed.

"Well," she continued, "I should have guessed, but that mirror has attracted every teenage girl in a ten-mile radius. 'Martiya, may I use your see-myself square?' That's what they call it, the *tai-tin mah*."

"The what?" said Thomas.

"The *tai-tin mah*."

"Oh! The *tai-tin mah*!" corrected Thomas, changing the tone of the final syllable from flat to rising.

"*Tai-tin mah*," Martiya repeated.

"It's hard!" said Norma. "You'll get the hang of it. Believe me, it was years before I could say 'Hello, my name is Norma and that water buffalo there is my husband' in Dyalo."

Martiya laughed. "In any case, from morning until night that hut is *filled* with girls. 'Oh, you look so pretty!' I told them all that the thing would steal their souls, it's *danger, danger, stay away*, but they just giggled. But that's not the worst of it—no sir—it's the boys. They're like flies on—" Martiya stopped herself, recalling suddenly that she was in the company of missionaries. "They can't keep away. One day I come home from a day of interviewing the shaman about Dyalo magic, and there must have been fifteen teenagers in my little place, hormones so thick I needed to wipe the place down with a sponge.

"That's not enough, there's *also* the drinking men. Nobody told me, but my place is the local tavern. Lately, half of the village men have decided that my hut is the place to meet for drinks in the evening. I walk in, any time of day, half a dozen men are seated on the floor around one of those pots of rice whiskey—you know, with the big straws? Smoking those smelly cigars and drinking whiskey. So I'd say that the new-hut thing hasn't worked out all that well."

Thomas explained to Martiya that the attraction of her hut was almost certainly that it was associated with no clan. "Have you ever had a dog, young lady?" he asked.

"Growing up, yes."

"He ever bark at the other dogs?"

"Sure."

"Same for spirits. That's why those men are in your house. You take your dog for a walk in the neighborhood, he barks at some dogs, sniffs some other dogs, lies down on his back and pretends he's dying for other dogs. You have an aggressive, mean dog, better to leave him at home.

The Dyalo think that your clan is the pack of spirits which follow you around like a dog *all the time*, fight with the other spirits. Over the years, the Dyalo have figured out that you just can't introduce some of these spirits into another spirit's house. Dangerous stuff. But your new hut, young lady, it's neutral territory. That's why they're coming to your place. You best take care, though. Those spirits can be dangerous."

"I'll be on my guard."

"I'm quite serious. You're a long ways from home, and there are things in those hills you don't understand."

Martiya came by the house regularly her last year in Dan Loi, Mr. Walker said: once a month, every six weeks, the doorbell would ring and there she'd be, smiling, full of questions, lively as all heck—who wouldn't like her? Sometimes of course the Walkers were busy, as folks will be, but Mr. Walker always tried to make time for Martiya and would sit with her for hours in his study.

Mr. Walker proved himself among the very best of Martiya's informants on the Dyalo. Sitting with me in the parking lot of the supermarket, he made a list of the things that he had discussed with Martiya. I copied them down with a stub of pencil on the back of a receipt. That Mr. Walker remembered these interviews in such detail suggested to me both the excellence of the man's memory and the considerable time he had spent privately reconstructing the chain of events that had led to David's death.

There was a question about iron knives: "Do you guys have any insight at all into the business about pregnant women and knives? Why can they use bamboo but not iron knives? It's driving me insane." And a question about the Dyalo calendar: "I'm confused by the calendar . . . It's a lunar calendar? But it forms a *solar* year?" "Sure, because you've got the New Year's feast days at the end." Martiya asked about rice planting and how the fields were distributed; about Dyalo marriage (which inevitably digressed into discussion of the difference between a heathen marriage and a true, Christian marriage); bride-price, and the conflict in the missionary community about whether bride-price was to be suppressed, the Bible being largely silent on this crucial issue (Mr. Walker: "We like to let them do what they think is best, but we discourage the bride-price. Christians shouldn't buy and sell each other, that's just what I think"); sex and eating taboos, of which there were at least one zillion; Dyalo notions of village, jungle, and field, where one ended and the other began, who lived in each, and why the Vampire clan at the foot of the village were considered jungle people and not village people; the New Year's feast; the magical rites associated with hunting, gardening, rice planting, and opium growing; and conflict in the village and its resolution.

Martiya inquired about how rice was distributed in the village after planting, and the proceeds of the opium planting; what roles men and women played in the household economy—

"But why don't you ask the people in *your* village these questions?" Norma asked her once.

"I've got notebooks full of answers from them. But it's always so interesting to hear your responses. You guys are almost Dyalo, you know."

"Four generations, you do get to know folks."

—and the Dyalo names for trees, stars, flowers, plants, and animals, the last being particularly useful, what with the Dyalo's trouble understanding photographs and drawings; the history of the Dyalo, all the way back to the complicated Dyalo origin story, when Wu-pa-sha made the first Dyalo man and his sister, as well as the Dyalo story of the flood, which confirmed in the Walkers' eyes what they had known all along, that the Bible was perfect and true; the ways in which the Dyalo buried their dead; where the Dyalo believed the spirits of their ancestors went; how the Dyalo treated malaria; the precise recipe for the poultice used in treating broken bones; and the superiority of the Dyalo treatment for lumbago to its Western analogue.

But most of all, Mr. Walker told me, Martiya asked about the *dyal*, the rice-planting ritual for which the Dyalo were named. Her interest in the *dyal*, Mr. Walker told me, was almost an obsession.

Mr. Walker stared at his Coke bottle. Now the rain was just a soft mist.

"So you see," he said, "that's why Norma never liked that woman."

I didn't see at all. "She didn't? Not even then?"

"No."

"Did she ever say anything about her? Was there ever an incident or anything? Or was it just a feeling on her part?"

Mr. Walker stayed quiet a little while. "When you live with a woman a long time, you get to know what she's thinking, and I've lived with Norma for a long time. I always tell the people, the bond between a man and a woman, I always say it's not just a transaction or a partnership or what have you, it's the basis of a Christian life. The love of man and wife, it's a reflection of God's love. That what I always say. But it's a strange thing, though, because the firmer the bond is, the more united a man is to his wife, the more fragile that bond becomes. Do you see what I'm trying to tell you, son?"

I nodded. "What did Mrs. Walker say about her?"

"Sometimes I'd invite Martiya to stay in Ruth-Marie's room, now that Ruth-Marie was out of the house, if Martiya stayed late talking and she didn't want to drive in the dark or go to a guest house. Norma didn't like that at all, she always thought that Martiya was maybe a little superior. You know women, son, they have their territories. I always tell the people . . ."

But Mr. Walker didn't tell me what he always told the people. He just stared at the flooded parking lot.

"Mr. Walker, I'm sorry, I don't understand," I said. "Why didn't Mrs. Walker like it when Martiya spent the night?"

"Well, Norma had her ideas. Martiya was a very attractive young woman, and you know women, Norma was very sensitive."

"Jealous?"

"You could say jealous. Son . . ."

He didn't finish the sentence. His voice was tight. I sought a way to phrase my awkward demand. Inspiration arrived: "Mr. Walker, did you *sin* with Martiya?"

Mr. Walker looked at me. I was afraid that he would say, "Son, that is absolutely none of your business." But he didn't. He just held his handsome moss-green eyes steady with mine until I blinked and looked away. He sat straight up and tall. Later, Rachel would ask me why he kept talking, and I told her that it was my impression that Mr. Walker was a man who loved honesty and hated evasion. He said, "David was a champion, too, you know, a great champion of the Lord, and he sinned also. I love

Norma, you know that, son. I love Nomie more than words, but even a great champion sometimes sins."

It took me a moment to realize that he was talking about David, the biblical hero, and not his son.

I'll never know the details of Mr. Walker's sin. Perhaps in those long afternoons in Mr. Walker's study, with Norma out at the market, the kids at school, and his parents at the church, Mr. Walker laid a hand on Martiya's slender thigh. Perhaps she let it rest there; or perhaps she said, "Mr. Walker, you are a happily married man!" Or perhaps Mr. Walker's sin consisted only of desire. Whatever happened, it was too much for Norma.

Mr. Walker shook his head, but he kept looking straight at me. "But I've been punished for my sins, son, don't you ever think that I haven't been."

A trilling sound set Mr. Walker's hands into motion. He started tapping his breast pockets and his pants, until finally he produced the cell phone and began stabbing at it with his gnarled fingers, squinting anxiously at the display, muttering to himself. "Gift from the kids," he said, as the thing continued to sound. Finally, unable to find the correct button, he just handed the phone to me.

I pushed the appropriate button and said hello.

It was Norma on the other end of the line. She hardly seemed surprised to have called her husband and found me. "Oh, honey, what have you done with my husband?" she asked.

"He's right here," I said, and handed the phone to Mr. Walker.

The two of them conversed a moment in Dyalo, until Mr. Walker handed the phone back to me. "Is it done?" he asked.

I examined the display, confirmed that the line was cut, and returned the phone to its owner, who slipped it into the breast pocket of his shirt.

"I hate that thing," he said. "The kids told me that if I want to keep driving, I need a cell phone. For the emergencies. But they make the things so darn small—"

We had been talking now for almost an hour, and Mr. Walker began to gather his bags. By now, the waters had receded. Everything looked cool and clean and shiny.

Not long after Martiya returned to Berkeley, David Walker went to see *Star Wars*; not long after that, he went off to follow the Grateful Dead. When Martiya came back to Thailand, she didn't call on the Walkers; and northern Thailand is sufficiently large, and Martiya's village sufficiently remote, that they had no idea she was there at all. David came home in 1985, on fire to spread the Word. Three years later, he found Martiya in her village; and two years after that, he was dead.

Norma's call had broken Mr. Walker's patient mood of recollection. He took his groceries in hand and started off in the direction of his car. He had gone about two paces when he turned around.

"David was a good boy," he said. "Tell me what we ever did to her."

PART FOUR

POSSESSED

# ONE

# THE CURIOSITY

NOT LONG AFTER MY CONVERSATION with Mr. Walker, I had reason to visit the Chiang Mai University Library, on business not related to this account. I have always felt that university libraries must be some of the most erotic places on Earth. They are, after all, filled with young people, most of them attractive, and most of them bored out of their skulls. The Chiang Mai University Library is no exception, but it is an eroticism of a particularly sweet sort: a young girl with her long black hair pinned back in an elaborate bow looks up from a chemistry text and with an exasperated sigh pines for distracted Noi across the table. Will he invite her later for noodles? Outside the windows, the palm trees sway, and on the lawns little groups of students giggle. On the wall, the queen of Thailand, the patroness of learning herself, smiles serenely: she, too, was young once, and remembers those precious first minutes at the Royal Palace all those years ago when she was introduced to a handsome young prince who hardly paid her any mind at all!

I finished my business after a few minutes, but something about the place made me reluctant to go straight home, and on a whim I went to the anthropology shelves. The ethnographies were organized geographically, and my eye wandered from continent to continent, from the ferocious Yanomano of the Amazon to the elegant, erudite Dogon of the Sahara to a slender volume explicating the life of a Sicilian village in the

1920s. Chinese villages lay side by side with the Kwakiutl of the Pacific Northwest; Siberian shamans cohabitated with the Pygmies. I felt dizzy for a moment. Spend five minutes in the anthropology stacks of a major university library and gasp at the size of the world, the sheer wonder and diversity of its inhabitants! What sturdy, impressive men and women wrote those volumes! Before I had met Martiya, I had never thought of them at all. Each one had mastered an obscure language, submerged himself or herself in the foreign; those shelves were a testament to curiosity. Every book was the product of an obsession.

The library catalogued the works of Bronislaw Malinowski apart from those of his fellows, which, now that I think about it, is not wholly inappropriate: perhaps it was a kind of homage on some anonymous librarian's part. For it was with Malinowski that the art of ethnography began. I slipped his greatest and most famous work down from the shelves and began to read, surrounded by those sweetly courting undergraduates. And although what follows might seem another digression, it isn't: Malinowski's ghost was there in Dan Loi with Martiya van der Leun.

Born in 1885 into a distinguished family of Kraków aristocrats and intellectuals, Bronislaw Malinowski was originally educated in the hard sciences of mathematics and physics. Sometime in his early twenties he suffered a physical crisis and was advised by his physician that the nervous strain of his studies could overwhelm his fragile constitution. Famous photographs of the man in later life suggest immediately, even to my untrained eyes, why his doctors were concerned: he was a thin-lipped, owl-eyed creature with a long, beaky nose, hollow cheeks, and a very high forehead receding into thin, worried hair. It is the face of an intensely intelligent sparrow or badger. The striking thing about many of these photographs is the contrast between this nervous, high-strung little man and his surroundings: Malinowski is photographed on the most mellow tropical beach imaginable. He is dressed in a round pith helmet and shorts. Tall palms sway in the distance. The sand is white, and a gentle wave is breaking on a gentle shore. Malinowski is surrounded by the natives, who regard him with affectionate, tolerant, bemused stares: the women stand topless, with large pendulous breasts reaching almost to their grass skirts; men and women, black as coal, sport enormous, simply stunning afros. Some of the afros must be a *foot* of hair in every direction—which makes sense, given that the people of the Trobriand Islands didn't have scissors. The sun is very bright. Malinowski looks miserable.

Malinowski found himself in those tropical islands—the Trobriand Islands, as it happened, off the coast of New Guinea, a place which even the Australians considered impossibly remote and horrible—having been beguiled, as the natives might have said, by the magical influence of a great sorcerer, the Englishman Sir James Frazier, whose contagion was transmitted via Malinowski to Joseph Atkinson, then again to Martiya van der Leun. Having been denied the pleasures of mathematics and physics by his doctors, it was to Frazier's *The Golden Bough* that Malinowski turned for diversion and consolation; and it was after reading Frazier, with his long lists of fascinating and barely comprehensible primitive rites and rituals, that Malinowski conceived a desperate urge to see a preliterate culture with his own eyes. For unless we understood our *own* culture, Frazier convinced Malinowski, we could not possibly understand ourselves; and we simply cannot understand our culture from the inside. "We cannot possibly reach the final Socratic wisdom of knowing ourselves if we never leave the narrow confinement of the customs, beliefs, and prejudices into which every man is born," Malinowski wrote, explaining his desire to live in the South Seas. By removing himself entirely from his own society and living with the people of the Trobriand Islands, Malinowski proposed to come to know *himself*. The greater the immersion in Trobriand society, the more profound his own insights would be. The result of such immersion would be an ethnography, on the one hand, a real contribution to the world's knowledge of its inhabitants, an exhaustive description of a people; and, on the other hand, a transformation of the observer's soul.

That, at any rate, was the theory.

But there is something in those photographs of Malinowski on the beach that isn't quite right, a kind of vague grimace on Malinowski's face. The man looks . . . constipated. Hideously so, as if it's been weeks since he snuck off to fertilize the jungle, and he's carrying around way more tribal soup than he's comfortable with, and it's hot, *really* hot, the kind of hot that makes you feel woozy, and it's not even ten in the morning yet; he's sunburned, and he's cranky, and there is sand everywhere, and those people were banging on drums all night long, don't they know any other rhythm than *thumpety-thump-thump*, and the nearest effective purgative is on the other side of the Pacific Ocean.

Could the opium from his medicine kit be interfering with his digestion? Perhaps.

The impression offered by the photographs is not mistaken. Malinowski—the most famous ethnographer in the history of anthropology, a man said to be possessed (by his contemporary R. R. Marat) of the uncanny ability to wriggle his way into the soul of even the shyest savage—was, in fact, miserable. In 1967, Malinowski's widow, doing the reputation of her late husband absolutely no favors, published the diaries he kept while working in the Trobriands. The truth was out: it seems that Malinowski didn't love anthropological fieldwork quite as much as everyone thought. Malinowski, to judge by his own words, *loathed* the Trobriand Islands, and *detested* the Trobriand Islanders. "As for ethnology: I see the life of the natives as utterly devoid of interest or importance, something as remote from me as the life of a dog," Malinowski confided to himself. The natives are variously referred to in the diaries as "fuzzy-headed savages" and "brutes." There are stories in which Malinowski strikes recalcitrant locals. Fieldwork, even for the great Malinowski, was terribly boring, frustrating, dangerous, difficult, enervating, and lonely. Forcing himself to quit the mosquito nets every morning and interview one more damned naked savage about the magical rites found in the coral gardens takes the full measure of Malinowski's discipline. "At bottom," Malinowski wrote, "I am living outside of Kiriwina . . . strongly hating the niggers."*

There is in this something that confirms common sense: no liberation of the spirit should come easy.

The Curiosity saved him. Malinowski, however much he may have disliked island life, spent the better part of five years living with the Tro-

---

*After the publication of the diaries, students of the history of anthropology returned to Kiriwina and asked elderly natives to recall Malinowski. In stark contrast to the self-portrait offered up by the diaries, Malinowski seems to have been a beloved figure among the villagers: endlessly inquisitive, charming, patient, willing to talk with anyone about anything for hours. Only his intelligence was put in doubt: the man barely knew which end of the tuber to put in the ground.

briand Islanders because the Curiosity had seized him. He had noticed a Very Strange Thing—and if he wished to understand it, there were no books of which he could avail himself, no authorities to consult. The only way to satisfy the Curiosity and understand the Very Strange Thing was to stay on the island and ask more questions. The literature of anthropology is absolutely thick with such stories: the exotic location, the deep boredom, the malarial fever, the muffled cry—"As God is my witness, I will get off of this rock!"—then some small element in the local culture that quickens the pulse. The unpleasantness of the local life is forgotten or ignored as the Curiosity takes hold; a hitherto-unknown hot monomania bubbles and steams in the anthropologist's previously tepid soul.

The Very Strange Thing that Malinowski noticed was a practice called *kula*. It is a captivatingly simple idea. For the inhabitants of the village in which he was ensconced, Malinowski noticed, far and away the most beloved of a man's possessions were his necklaces and armbands; indeed, so valuable were a man's necklaces and armbands that they were never, ever, worn, the armbands in any case being too small even for a child. Whatever the appeal of the necklaces and armbands, it was certainly not to Malinowski's eyes an aesthetic attraction: they were brutish-looking handmade things, bits of shells strung on a rope. In his book, he published pictures of the necklaces and armbands: they are the sort of things that David Walker might well have found on sale outside a Grateful Dead show, handmade by a girl named Moonbeam.

But how the Trobrianders loved their necklaces and armbands! They gloried over them for hours, and told stories of their illustrious lineage, how they had come to possess them and who had possessed them before; the necklaces and armbands were comforts in times of sorrow and additional reasons to take pleasure in life in times of abundance. A dying man would ask to be presented with his necklaces and armbands as proof that all the aching and struggle had been worthwhile; when a Trobriand Islander in a philosophical moment thought of the things that really, *really* mattered—not just the day-to-day grind of fishing and gardening and canoe-making, not just the frivolity of feasting or lovemaking—but when he took stock of the things that *counted*, one of the things he would surely think of were his necklaces and armbands.

Then he would give them away.

It was all *very* perplexing to Malinowski. It was the strangest thing that he had encountered in his entire life. It made him curious. One day, a villager would boast that *his* necklaces and armbands were the finest in all the Trobriand Islands; the next day, he would prepare his long outrigger canoe and head off into the pounding surf. The Trobriand Islands are roughly arranged in the shape of a doughnut, and distances between islands are considerable; voyages by canoe between islands were long and hazardous, and certainly uncomfortable. Yet not to go was unthinkable. A man and his kin would paddle off in their long canoe, sailing for days under an unflinching equatorial sun to arrive at some village on some other island along the perimeter of the doughnut, where the man from Malinowski's village would find one of his long-standing partners in *kula* and present him with a necklace or armband. If the direction of travel was counterclockwise, the man got an armband; if clockwise, a necklace. What's more, although it breaks a man's heart to give away his favorite necklace or armband, he must do it with high style—disdainfully, haughtily, as if such a treasure were no more than a trinket. The conch is blown. There is a feast. And then the man returns home. Sometime in the future—never right away—the gift is repaid. The men from the faraway village on the faraway island arrive in Kiriwina, and if they originally received an armband, they now present an equally fantastic necklace; if they received a necklace, they present an armband. The conch is blown. There is a feast. In this way, necklaces and armbands forever circulate in opposite directions around the circle of the Trobriand Islands, pausing for a time in this village or that, then moving along.

The Curiosity took Malinowski. Only necklaces could be exchanged for armbands, and nothing else. They were not money. To possess a beautiful necklace or armband conferred status upon a man, but only for as long as it was in his possession. The Curiosity would not let Malinowski go. How did the villagers *see* these necklaces and bracelets? Why did they risk their lives on these long voyages only to give away what they so treasured?

To understand *kula*, Malinowski spent almost five years on those islands off the coast of New Guinea. Judging from his diaries, the intensity of his dislike for island living never abated; but, then, neither did the

Curiosity. Malinowski's final analysis of *kula* is the magisterial *Argonauts of the Western Pacific*, and it is a sad book. His analysis runs to some five hundred pages, and covers in depth everything from the appropriate hand gestures with which the necklaces and armbands are offered to the magic spells required to avoid the Flying Rocks of the open sea. But, oddly, and to my great frustration, the simple question—why? why do they do it?—remains unanswered. Suppositions have been offered elsewhere in the anthropological literature. But one has the sensation on finishing *Argonauts* that Malinowski had come to see the *kula* as so normal an activity that, although it certainly merited describing, it no longer needed explaining. For the reader alone, the Curiosity remains.

Now one more digression tacked on to this already digressive path.

In the final chapter of *Argonauts of the Western Pacific*, entitled "The Meaning of the Kula," Malinowski, although he could not explain the *kula*, nevertheless argued that the *kula* is not a novel form of human activity, and that in the fullness of ethnographic time, it will not prove unique to the Trobriand Islands. Ethnographers will find that other societies also practice the *kula*, or at least things very much like the *kula*. He wrote: "And we may be on the lookout for economic transactions, expressing a reverential, almost worshipping attitude towards the valuables exchanged or handled; implying a novel type of ownership, temporary, intermittent, and cumulative; involving a vast and complex social mechanism and system of economic enterprises by which it is carried out."

We need not look far. My stepfather is a gastroenterologist by day but by night a passionate collector of rare and first editions of books concerned with polar exploration and the nautical exploration of the Pacific Northwest. My stepfather devotes enormous time and energy to his collection, and invests substantial sums of money in it. I will provoke no family quarrels by saying that when my stepfather reflects on the things in his life that give him real pleasure and satisfaction, those gilt-edged, leather-bound volumes are not very far down on his list. In his library there are editions so precious they cannot be touched or read; such books often have a surrogate *reading* edition, a perfect facsimile of the original, but are worth substantially less. There are books valuable precisely because the pages have never been cut and therefore *cannot* be read ("*a reverential, almost worshipping attitude towards the valuables exchanged or handled"*). He has Shackleton's memoirs, and George Vancouver's, and a first edition of Apsley Cherry-Garrard's *The Worst Journey in the World*, signed by Apsley Cherry-Garrard himself. My stepfather is a member of a community of equally committed collectors of rare books devoted to polar exploration and the nautical exploration of the Pacific Northwest (as it happens, two distinct but overlapping sets) whose members trade letters and e-mails and phone calls. They travel great distances to meet with one another and discuss and exchange rare books (*"involving a vast and complex social mechanism and system of economic enterprises by which it is carried out"*). It is something of a closed circle, this little world, and books pass from one collector's hands to the next. A collector will buy a book, hold on to it, sell it to another collector, and then, much later, buy it again (*"a novel type of ownership, temporary, intermittent, and cumulative"*).

Now imagine trying to explain the point of all this to an illiterate Trobriand Island anthropologist, who has no idea what all the scribbles on the page mean, has never seen a book, and has no idea at all that he lives on a spherical planet with two ice-capped poles explored by brave men whose endeavors make for thrilling reading. The Trobrianders have never even *heard* of ice. Malinowski, whose pale skin was little suited to the tropical sun, was no less handicapped than this imaginary Trobriand anthropologist in his first attempts to beat back the Curiosity, which was like a brushfire in his soul: he knew nothing of Trobriand magic and magical ways, of Trobriand myth and cosmology, of the relations between distant Trobriand islands and tribes who engaged in this reciprocal gift-giving, of the wily ways of the sea and how to pass through the dangers of the deep in an outrigger canoe. All of these were essential to understanding the *kula*. No wonder the most difficult question of all—why?—escaped his penetrating analysis.

Martiya was hardly better suited to her self-appointed task of understanding the Dyalo when the Curiosity took her; but of course I was hardly better suited to my self-appointed task of understanding Martiya.

I did not find out what the *dyal* was for a long time, but rather than make the reader wait, I will interrupt briefly to explain this interesting custom, which will form such an important part of Martiya's story. I wish to preface this description with a reminder that I am not an anthropologist, have never seen the *dyal*, and do not speak Dyalo; what I offer here is at best a second- or third-hand description.

The Dyalo language makes a formal distinction between the plant and the spirit that animates it; but the distinction is tonal and hard to reproduce in English, so I will make the same emphasis through capitalization: rice is a plant, a physical thing; but Rice is a spirit. The two exist in much the same relationship as humans and their souls: the spirit animates the thing, is eternal while the thing is not, passes from one thing to the next, has personality and will. Spirit and matter live in symbiosis: without spirit, matter is lifeless; without matter, spirit is restless, frustrated, and cruel. The Dyalo believe Rice "makes good" the rice at the moment the rice seed is planted. The rice seed, after all, is an inert thing: it sits for years in the rice barn and does nothing. But placed in the earth at the right time of the year, the seed germinates, and a miracle ensues: the rice plant grows. This miracle is the work of Rice. And the *dyal*, the villagers of Dan Loi believed, was what was necessary to convince Rice to do his fruitful work.*

The Dyalo plant rice seed at the very onset of the rainy season. It is the hottest and most humid time of year. The previous few months have seen the fields prepared for planting: the Dyalo have tromped through the hills and chosen good sites. They have slashed the jungle down and cut the trees. What remained or was too tough for their machetes, they have burned, and for weeks, the mountain was black with smoke. The jungle itself, a Dyalo proverb says, is Rice's first demand.

The very survival of a Dyalo family depends on the success of the rice planting. Bear in mind that rice is among the most difficult of all crops to raise successfully, especially in the mountains: mountain soil is often poor in nutrients, particularly nitrogen; the climate is unstable; and rice is a notoriously temperamental grain. Over the course of ten

---

*Linguists disagree about the meaning and etymologies of the words "*dyal*" and "Dyalo." The debate, roughly summarized, boils down to whether "*dyal*" means "the rite of the Dyalo people," or whether "Dyalo" means "the people who do *dyal*"—that is, whether the people are named for the rite, or the rite is named after the people.

thousand or more harvests, the Dyalo have noticed that rice fails with terrifying frequency. Two Dyalo, encountering one another on the path, do not ask, "How are you?" They ask, "Is your Rice happy?"

Planting rice is a two-person, four-day job, more or less. The lead member of the planting team, who is always male, works with a dibble stick, a long bamboo pole attached to a metal plow head. His job is to dig the holes into which the woman, following behind, will drop a handful of rice seed. When the Dyalo had planted the opium poppies in December, husband and wife had worked as a team, an arrangement that seemed sensible enough to Martiya, the marriage, and by extension the immediate family, being the basic unit of Dyalo economics. For the rice planting, however, the men and women throughout the Dyalo country pair themselves up according to a very different system—the *dyal*.

Here is how the *dyal* appeared to Martiya her first year in the village.

The *dyal* began with the quiet departure of all of the married men from the village. One morning, the village awoke as normal. Martiya had breakfast with Lai-Ma, as usual, then went to talk to George Washington about the difference between the jungle spirits and the village spirits, one of the fundamental distinctions in Dyalo spiritual life, a continuation of a conversation of several days' standing. So quiet was the departure of the men—no goodbyes, no ceremonies, no sacrifices, no chanting—that Martiya hardly noticed them slip off into the forest; but by evening, the village was only women and children, with the exception of George Washington himself, and a few men too old to travel, who sat around looking dejected and sullen.

That evening, the women dressed themselves in their finest clothing. They prepared elaborate meals. The mood in the village was suddenly light and gay. One of the women began to sing, and another woman, from another hut, joined her: the song was passed from hut to hut, one woman taking up the melody, others repeating the chorus. That evening, strange new men began to arrive in the village—Dyalo men who had left *their* villages to come to Dan Loi. Some of these men Martiya knew: they came from nearby Dyalo villages; but others were strangers, and when she asked about them, she learned that they had traveled upwards of a week. Some had even surreptitiously crossed national borders. Yet they entered the village with odd familiarity, greeting the women as old acquaintances.

For the next week, the women of Dan Loi and their *gin-kai* (the phrase, appropriately enough, means "rice partner") planted rice during the day and feasted at night. For the duration of the week, the *gin-kai* lived as surrogate husbands: each lived in the house of the man he replaced; together with his "wife," they worked his fields; they ate the foods his "wife" prepared. They were addressed by their women always in the verbal form reserved for intimate family. These rice-planting partnerships, Martiya learned, were not transient things: men and women would *always* plant rice with the *same* partner, season after season, year after year, but it was taboo to see these planting partners the rest of the year.

At the conclusion of the week, the *gin-kai* took their leave of the village. The rice crop had been planted. By nightfall, the men of the village began to return. The *dyal* was thus concluded.

The *dyal* was like hitting the anthropological bingo: by the time the last man had wandered home, Martiya saw in the *dyal* not only a doctoral thesis but an article in *Anthropos*.

It was Martiya's strong suspicion that the women and their rice mates were sexual partners. Martiya didn't know the right word to describe the rite. Was it adultery? A kind of bigamy? She wondered: Was sex an obligatory part of the *dyal*, or something that just sometimes happened? Why did successful planting require such a liaison?

Although the institution of the *dyal* had no parallel in Martiya's personal experience, she was aware that similar practices were to be found in other parts of the world. In Martiya's small library of books, she had a paperback abridged edition of James Frazier's *The Golden Bough*, where, in a chapter titled "The Influence of the Sexes on Vegetation," Martiya read about similar rites. The Pipile of Central America "kept apart from their wives 'in order that on the night before planting they might indulge their passions to the fullest extent; certain persons are even said to have been appointed to perform the sexual act at the very moment when the first seeds were deposited in the ground.' " Similarly, "in some parts of Java, at the season when the bloom will soon be on the rice, the husbandman and his wife visit their fields by night and there engage in sex-

ual intercourse for the purpose of promoting the growth of the crop."
Analagous rites could be found also in Leti, Sarmata, in the Babar Islands, in Amboyna, and among the Baganda of Central Africa—and
even in Europe, where Frazier notes the custom, found in Ukraine and
Germany, of asking married couples to lie down and roll over the newly
sown fields "to promote the fertility of the crops."

It was one thing to read about such things in Frazier; another thing
entirely to see them with her own eyes. What piqued Martiya's curiosity
most intensely was the total reluctance on the part of the villagers
of Dan Loi to discuss any aspect of the *dyal* with an outsider. One by
one, Martiya had delicately asked questions of her favorite informants
throughout the village; but even the old women who would gladly chat-
ter for hours with Martiya about every other facet of village life, from
childbearing to inheritance law to intimate secrets of the Dyalo bedroom, shied away when asked to discuss the *dyal*.

The more Martiya studied the *dyal*, the greater the importance of
understanding the custom seemed to her. It was a counterexample to
some of the most important rules of Dyalo life: it was the only time in
which the normally strict rules governing associations and the segrega-
tions of clans were relaxed. Partners in the *dyal* came from every and any
clan, and were mixed up in no easily discernible way. The rice harvest
was one of the only rituals, rites, or festivals in the Dyalo calendar binding far-flung Dyalo villages together. Martiya asked herself: How were
the planting partnerships formed? Was the *dyal* a way of legitimizing and
discharging sexual tension within the community of Dyalo villages? Fi-
delity was generally prized by the Dyalo and adultery commonly considered shameful—did the Dyalo make an exception for the *dyal*? In her
time in the village, Martiya had already seen several feuds erupt as the
result of an adulterous liaison, including one which had led to violence.
Did jealousy ever ensue as a result of the *dyal*? How did husband and wife
greet each other at the end of the *dyal*? How and when was the *dyal* explained to children?

What did the Dyalo think happened when the rice was seeded? Why
didn't the opium, the maize, or the gardens require similar rituals? If a
woman became pregnant as a result of the *dyal*, how was the offspring

treated? The sexual act at the heart of the *dyal*—was it ritualized? Was it accompanied by any particular prayers or magic rites?

What was the connection in the Dyalo mind between the *dyal* and rice planting? Did the Dyalo believe the *dyal* necessary to the fructification of the rice? Or simply desirable? If necessary, how did they explain the failure of other peoples to perform the same rite?

*What was the native's point of view?*

Martiya hadn't the faintest clue.

The only answer the Dyalo offered when she asked about the *dyal* was that this was what it took to keep Rice happy. And if Rice wasn't happy, *the Dyalo would be hungry!*

# TWO

# THE MINISTRY OF GHOSTS

KAREN'S TRIP TO THAILAND in the winter of 1983 was just what her sagging soul had needed. Martiya met her at the Chiang Mai airport in a borrowed jeep, then drove her up to Dan Loi on the one-lane red dirt road, Martiya *accelerating* into the curves, one hand holding the wheel, the other hand tapping Karen's knee, Martiya saying, "Kit-Kat! It's *so* great to see you!," the old jeep making scary, creaking noises, suggesting to Karen that even if Martiya had wanted to hit the brakes, it wasn't entirely a sure thing that the vehicle would obey. Martiya had the habit of taking her eyes off the road to point out some thatch-roofed village on the far horizon and give commentary: "We're coming up on Moo Bat Yai, it's an Akha village, interesting headman, you've *got* to meet him, he's got three wives and they are driving him insane, funny thing is—the Akha aren't usually polygamous. Oh! See that hill there?" All the way up to Dan Loi, as the jeep barreled blindly around the curves with clouds of red dust trailing behind, Karen held her breath.

But when they got to the village, the place was just one huge bougainvillea in bloom, that's what it felt like: bougainvillea everywhere, sprouting weedlike from the ditches beside the road, draped like a bright crimson curtain over all the huts. Martiya hadn't mentioned the bougainvillea in her letters, how colorful the village was, and how warm the winter sun. Just being with Martiya and walking through the village with her reminded Karen of the apartment on the north side of campus with the handwriting on the wall.

Martiya had done what everyone else just dreams about: she had dropped off the face of the earth and, despite having fallen so impossibly far, had landed on her feet.

Karen spent most of her first day in Dan Loi thinking about faculty meetings in Madison and that lonely kitchen with the formaldehyde floor, and scraping the ice off of the windshield when she went out to start the car in the morning; then she went with Martiya down to the communal cooking hut, where Martiya laughed with all the village women as she sat down and made dinner over an open fire, chopping garlic, onions, and chili peppers with a huge machete, then stir-frying everything up in a wok. Karen could understand nothing of the language, of course, but it was clear that Martiya was fluent: only someone quite fluent in a foreign language could laugh so unhesitatingly at the jokes. After lunch, Karen and Martiya went back up to Martiya's hut, where they sat outside on the patio in the early evening, drinking one of the bottles of white wine which Karen had bought at the duty-free shop. Martiya pointed out the Hmong village on the far side of the valley and there was nothing, really nothing, so green as the green of the rice fields. *Have you seen it?* Karen asked me. *Then you know.*

The sun set, and all evening long as Karen and Martiya talked and talked and talked, the kiss-me birds sang in the trees, *whoo-tuk-tuk, whoo-tuk-tuk*. Later, as Martiya and Karen sat on the porch smoking a joint the way they used to back in Berkeley every night, fireflies swarmed through the village, an endless trail of flickering green lights swooping and diving through the warm night air. A little yellow moon hung in the sky like a man grinning in his sleep on account of a pleasant dream, and somewhere in the village someone started to sing, a tender baritone singing in that strange language, a song so sad that the whole village grew absolutely still.

"You didn't tell me this place was so amazingly beautiful," Karen said.

Martiya just smiled.

Over their tea the next morning, Martiya and Karen watched the silver mist burn off the valley. It was cold season, although it wasn't cold for someone living in Wisconsin; but Martiya wore a big oversize sweater which made her look little, her arms lost somewhere in the long sleeves, and she tucked her legs underneath her, cuddling herself up into a ball. She was still as pretty as Karen remembered—not beautiful, but definitely striking, with those big eyes and high cheekbones, and the tumbling dark hair offsetting the small features. Against Martiya and the villagers, Karen felt big and slow and swollen, as if she had been inflated in the years since she had left the Philippines. No matter what, she had to get back out into the field.

Karen told Martiya about all the people they had known in graduate school and where they all had ended up: Mike Pendleton was at Brown with tenure, and Sarah Lutz wrote a great paper on the Sigoni, really interesting stuff, she's a big talent, too bad about the acne, and that weird guy who did pre-Columbian? Who chewed with his mouth open and left those gross notes for Karen in her mailbox? Harvard. Yup. *So* unfair. Then Karen told Martiya all about Ted, and Martiya listened with her head cocked at a feline, feminine angle, so attentive you'd think she had spent the last few years here in the mountains just asking herself, over and over again, "And gosh, how *are* things going between Karen and Ted?"

"I never liked Ted that much, to tell you the truth," Martiya finally said.

"Really?" Karen had always thought that everyone liked Ted. That was one of the things that she had liked about Ted, the way everyone liked him.

"There was something . . . something too clever about the guy, like he was trying to get away with something."

"That's it. That's it *exactly*," said Karen.

"And remember that business with the tipping? At restaurants?"

"My God, that used to drive me nuts. That little plastic thing he had in his wallet to work out the percentages. I got so embarrassed when he took that thing out."

"And he had such shifty little eyes."

Martiya made such a dead-on imitation of Ted's beady little eyes sliding back and forth that Karen started to giggle, and when Martiya started to imitate the way Ted's fishy one-size-too-small mouth twitched, Karen started to laugh. Then a few seconds later, when Karen started to cry, Martiya gave her a big hug and stroked her hair, and said, "It's okay, Kit-Kat. It'll be okay."

Can you *believe*, Karen asked me, that this woman would spend the last ten years of her life in jail, for *murder*?

*Murder!* Karen paused dramatically on the word. I jumped at the unaccustomed pause in the conversation.

"Karen, hang on one sec—there's something I'm not understanding here—something I just don't get."

"Shoot," said Karen.

"You went off to visit Martiya in . . ." I checked my notes. "In 1982."

"Eighty-three."

"Eighty-three." I corrected my notes. "But Martiya left the village—she was done with her fieldwork—in 1977. She went back to California."

"Uh-huh."

"Okay, all that I understand. Here's the thing I don't understand. You told me that a year and a half, two years later, she came *back* to Thailand. That would be . . . 1979 or so."

"That's right."

"So the thing I don't get is—why did she come back to Thailand?"

The question was not spontaneous. I had written it down on a Post-it note and attached it to the telephone in anticipation of Karen's call. I had thought about this a lot. I knew that Martiya spent two and a half years in a Dyalo village, and returned to Berkeley in 1977; and I knew that after eighteen months back home, Martiya decided to return to Thailand and *live in a Dyalo village*. As courageous as the decision may have been, it was also very unusual: Martiya was, by all accounts, a smart, ambitious student, a leader in one of the very finest doctoral programs in the world. Her thesis adviser was the legendary Joseph Atkinson. And at an age—thirty-one—when pressures to succeed and form a life and make a place for oneself in the world are not inconsiderable, Martiya decided that her life, her real life, the place where she wanted to be, was a tribal village in the north of Thailand. She was no longer interested in being an academic: she returned to the village no longer under the aegis of the Anthropology Department. The government no longer covered her expenses. Joseph Atkinson specifically advised her not to go. And this time, she went without a return ticket. So I wondered: Why did she go back?

*Well*, Karen said, redirecting the great eighteen-wheeler that was her conversation, she had asked herself the same thing. And this was *her* take on the situation.

Everyone in anthro knows it, it's an open secret, but coming home from the field is as tough as going out. Maybe even tougher. When you go out on the road, you're you; and when you come back, you're not you anymore, but they're still them. You get off of that plane thinking that the world is a big strange place and your brain is just churning, trying to figure it out, and even if the place where you're coming back to is the *Department of Anthropology*, your brain is still churning faster than everyone else's. It's like a chainsaw hitting a steel spike.

It had been hard for Karen coming home from the Philippines, but one thing had made it easier: Ted. She had met Ted just two days after she got back to Berkeley, and being swept-off-your-feet, can-I-possibly-get-enough-of-this-man madly in love—especially in love with someone like Ted, who knew how to love a woman, she had to say that about Ted, he did know how to love a woman, except that he didn't seem to know how to love just *one* woman—it was like somebody had turned up life's intensity meter all the way to maximum. Ted had listened to Karen talk about the Philippines for hours and hours, the two of them lying naked on Ted's bed, and Karen had to admit it, although she hated to, Ted had been a good listener. Christ, Ted was so goddamn smart, that was the thing: Ted had just homed in straightaway on what made her village *hers*, and how it worked, and what was interesting anthropologically, and what was interesting humanly, and after spending ten straight days in bed talking with Ted, it was like Ted had *been* there with her.

But Martiya didn't have Ted—and although not having Ted could only be considered a blessing in a woman's life, sometimes Karen wondered whether Martiya would have ended up Martiya the Tragic Murderess, if Martiya the Frustrated Grad Student and not Karen had sat next to Ted that day in the library. Because for Martiya, the hardest thing about coming home was that when she finally got back to California, after almost two and a half years in Dan Loi, nobody seemed much interested in the Dyalo at all. This was a keen irony, because after two and a half years complaining to Karen in letter after letter that she was bored, as soon as she left that village, she could think of nothing else.

She had figured that, at the very least, the other anthropologists in the department would want to ask her a million questions, but most colleagues just used her return as an excuse to tell stories about *their* experiences in the field—and those stories, unlike her own, were very boring.

Joseph Atkinson gave Martiya exactly three hours of solid, serious attention. He invited her out for dinner a week or so after she got back, and took her to a good restaurant in San Francisco, some place with flickering little rainbows on the very white tablecloth where the candlelight refracted through the heavy crystal. The food struck Martiya as tasteless, after Dyalo food, and a little heavy, but she didn't complain: at least Atkinson was giving her the chance to tell Dyalo stories. Martiya knew she wasn't conversing, she was delivering a monologue, but she had wanted to tell someone all this stuff for such a long time. She talked about the huge New Year's feasts, when the village exploded in dancing for three days, with wild drumbeats all through the night, and the complicated games by which the Dyalo young men paid court to the Dyalo maidens; and she told him how thrilling it was when, after almost two years, she could finally start to understand Dyalo poetry. When old Sings Soft had recited Dyalo love poems on a warm summer night under a full moon with all the village crouching low, not daring to breathe or even sigh, she had cried. She had seen Dyalo children born and Dyalo die, and they had started coming to her, of all people, for medical advice. She had so many more stories to tell, too, about the Yunnanese opium traders who came on muleback, and the flash that came when Martiya finally figured out the east-west/life-death/sunrise-sunset symbolic system that— well, it pretty much organized *everything*—and the time that the shaman who looked like George Washington exorcised her when she had this persistent headache, and *damned* if she didn't get better right away. But then she and Atkinson had dessert and coffee, and although Martiya would have liked to talk more, Atkinson took her home, and from that point on, whenever Martiya tried to tell a Dyalo story, Atkinson just said, "Save it for the thesis, kiddo."

Like all graduate students returned from fieldwork, Martiya was given the opportunity to lecture on her findings. There were exactly eighteen attendees for her lecture, entitled "The Ministry of Ghosts: Bureaucratic Form and Function in Dyalo Spiritual Life," and two of those attendees, Martiya well knew, went to *every* lecture, on account of the little buffet the department set up afterward, with takeout from the Chinese restaurant on Shattuck Avenue. A third was Karen. Even now, when Karen lectured on animism to her undergraduate students, she found herself using examples from that lecture. If Martiya had stuck with it, Karen said, she would have been a superstar.

No one who lived with the Dyalo, Martiya began, could fail to note the very frequent references in Dyalo conversation to the things called *tsi*. The word meant, more or less, "spirits" in English, but the word had a somewhat greater range of meaning in Dyalo: in certain contexts, the word meant "god," as when the Dyalo spoke of Wu-pa-sha *tsi*, the creator of the wind, water, rain, and thunder, while in other contexts, the word had a strictly technical sense, as when the Dyalo spoke of someone afflicted with "*wu-neu tsi*," or a headache.* All of the various *tsi* were invisible to the Dyalo, at least with the eyes, but nevertheless were absolutely real to the people of Dan Loi. To deny the existence of the *tsi* was to deny one of the most basic aspects of the natural world. Not long after she arrived in the village, Martiya asked how many *tsi* there were in the world. "There are as many *tsi* in the world as clouds in the sky or grains of rice in the fields," was the response: the *tsi* were uncountable, and the question made as little sense to the Dyalo as the question, "How many bacteria are there in this room?" Lots.

Martiya was very small behind the podium, but she spoke with a wonderful authority.

Martiya continued: Some of the *tsi* were associated with places, like the *tsi* who dominated the mountain on which Dan Loi was situated, the *tsi* who ruled the village, and the *tsi* who lived on the big rock behind the village. Almost every place had its own proprietary *tsi*. Other *tsi* were as-

---

*And then there was the usage invented by the Walkers to describe their God: Ye-su-tsi.

sociated with natural phenomena like thunder or rain; and still other tsi with biological entities, like rice, trees, various animals, and even human beings. The tsi associated with human beings the Dyalo called ts'aw-wo—a word which Martiya translated as "souls," and such tsi might be associated with men and women both living and dead. The latter category is what the occidental refers to as a ghost.

One of the consequences and fundamental underpinnings of the Dyalo spiritual system was the odd and provocative idea that, to the Dyalo, there were no accidents.

Martiya's thinking on these matters was substantially influenced by a rereading of the great English ethnographer E. E. Evans-Pritchard and his studies of witchcraft among the Azande of the Sudan. The peculiarity of Azande thinking, Evans-Pritchard argued, was that, like the Dyalo, the Azande had no notion of bad luck; rather, they ascribed all ill fortune to witchcraft, from the most trivial, a stubbed toe, to the most grave, a sulky wife or death. Whatever went wrong, went wrong because a witch had cursed the action. The Dyalo were not great believers in witchcraft—although witches did exist among the Dyalo—but the Dyalo, like the Azande, were unable to admit the possibility of accident, simple bad luck. Indeed, there was no word for "luck" in Dyalo. If an otherwise inexplicable bad thing happened, it happened almost always because a spirit was angry; if a spirit was angry, it was because somebody had angered a spirit.

Things that to the occidental mind were clearly bad fortune or happenstance, the Dyalo automatically interpreted within a chain of spiritual cause and effect. In Martiya's village, a young woman stumbled and fell into a cooking fire, burning herself badly. A man in the village raised pigs; a pig wandered off into the forest and was lost. A village woman, an expert weaver, produced a garment that snagged on a branch and unraveled. In all three cases, what Martiya would have called bad luck, or misfortune, the Dyalo called the work of the spirits. Why did a young woman known for her grace stumble at precisely that spot and fall into the fire? To fall at another spot would have been benign. A spirit seized her and pushed her. Hundreds of pigs were raised in the village; every now and then a pig would be lost in the forest. But they were almost always found again. Why not this one? A venturesome spirit took the pig's soul. The weaver was a woman of the highest skill. Her garments from twenty years ago were still in use. Why not this one? She had been distracted by a spirit. The young woman who stumbled was thought to have angered the fire spirit by eating corn near the fire pit. The owner of the pig erred by allowing the pig to wander in the vicinity of the Old Grandfather shrine: it was inevitable that something would go wrong. The weaver's mother had been careless, failing to present the household spirits with their breakfast.

"Think about this for a minute! Just think!" Martiya said. "If you think that everything that goes wrong in the world is caused by some bad spirit—and if you think these bad spirits are all around you—think how nervous you'd be all the time. You can ask the spirits to do this or that, but you can never be sure that they'll listen. Think how different your mental world would be if you thought that even moving a rock in your taro patch could anger the spirit who might make your taro come in badly, or give your daughter an incurable illness, or just put your wife in a really bad mood for a month. The fact that the Dyalo live in this world, surrounded by invisible enemies everywhere—and they do it with so much good humor and such grace—they're the bravest people I know."

Karen recalled the quiet that came over the room when Martiya was done speaking. Then a woman in the audience raised her hand. It was clear from her straggly appearance that she was a Berkeley resident rather than a member of the department, and this woman explained that she had come to the lecture attracted by the word "spiritual" on the flyer. She asked Martiya how her time with the Dyalo had affected her personal spiritual practice.

"My personal spiritual practice?"

"Yes, how you relate personally to the Goddess and other spirits."

Martiya thought about the question a moment, and then said, "I learned that I liked to slit the pig's throat and watch him bleed."

The little woman blanched.

To Martiya's intense surprise and displeasure, the scholarly community of the University of California at Berkeley had not, in fact, been waiting with bated breath for the results of Martiya van der Leun's expedition to Dan Loi. The frustrating thing was not that this was a big blow to her ego—on the contrary: she was smart and sensitive enough to realize that anthropologists had come home from expeditions to the farthest corners of the globe every single week since Malinowski had come home from the Trobriands; and that another graduate student coming back was not grounds for a university-wide day of rejoicing and celebration. No, what really frustrated Martiya was that she still didn't understand the Dyalo, not at all, and all the time she was in Dan Loi, her Curiosity had been growing day by day, and she had imagined that when she got back to Berkeley she'd be able to put all her field notes out on the table with some really smart people, and she'd finally be able to figure out all the things about the Dyalo that she couldn't figure out in the field.

She had a thousand questions. She didn't know why she had been moved into Farts-a-Lot's house and not some other. She didn't know what happened to the shaman when he entered his trance. She didn't really understand why the Vampire clans at the foot of the hill were poor; and she didn't really understand why it was so shameful for husband and wife to plant rice together in the rice fields. She had given Lai-Ma her running shoes, and it took almost a week to convince Lai-Ma that she hadn't meant to offend her. She didn't know why Lai-Ma had been offended. Most of all, she wanted to understand the *dyal*. She wanted to know why the Dyalo engaged in this complicated ritual to plant rice, and what they were thinking when they engaged in it. She thought that there were answers to all these questions, which literally kept her awake at night, but she didn't know them. She didn't even know what *kind* of answer would satisfy her. She only knew that for all of her hard work in Dan Loi, she hadn't yet grasped the Dyalo point of view, understood the Dyalo relation to life, or realized the *Dyalo* vision of the *Dyalo* world.

So that was the first thing that really bothered Martiya: all the time in Dan Loi, whenever things got tough, really tough, she had thought to herself that she was just the sharp end of the steel spear of scholarship, and that when she got back to Berkeley, all the other scholars and anthropologists and students of human behavior would help her understand the things she couldn't understand herself. Instead, Martiya found herself positively *shunned* in the department for having visited a preliterate society. The winds of anthropological fashion had shifted while Martiya was in the field, and preliterates were out: the hot young anthropologists were heading off to study South African diamond mines and Swedish ceramic factories and the corporate headquarters of AT&T. That's where the excitement was, and when Martiya tried to interest her colleagues in a rousing discussion of magical rites preceding the rice planting, she met with a palpable lack of interest. Instead, what they talked about in the graduate lounge and at the dinner parties and in the coffee shops were tenure and jobs and grants and absurd theories by trendy French *philosophes*. There was a time when nothing had thrilled her more than department gossip and the pitched battles between the various academic camps. Now, back from three years in Dan Loi, these debates bored her to death, and she could not make a connection between the generalities of theory and people like Lai-Ma, George Washington, and Farts-a-Lot.

One evening several months after coming back from the field, she went out on a date with another of her classmates. He was just finishing up his thesis, which dealt with the influence of the Catholic Church in a village in southern Mexico. She had read a draft of his thesis, which argued that the villagers had incorporated traditional magical practices into the Catholic liturgy. The facts that her classmate had assembled were fascinating, and reading the thesis, Martiya had been able to imagine the hot, dusty plain of Chiapas, the whitewashed adobe church, and the ecstatic peasants in tears carrying the cross through the village just as their forefathers many generations before had carried the icons of Aztec gods. But when Martiya asked her friend just what the natives *felt* as they carried the cross, it was clear from his stream of jargon and theory that he had no deeper insight than Martiya. She felt as if she were talking to a blind member of the Department of Art History, who could recount every detail of Caravaggio's life and describe every symbol in every painting, but who had never actually seen the canvases or felt the power of his art. The encounter left her increasingly sure that what she was looking for was at odds with what the Department of Anthropology could offer, at odds with what the *discipline* of anthropology could offer.

Martiya invited Karen for coffee, and the two women talked. It was an irony, Martiya said: eighty years after Bronislaw Malinowski told all the anthropologists to get off the veranda of the mission house and go and live with the natives, the only people in all the world who seemed to share Martiya's obsessive interest and fascination with the Dyalo were a family of missionaries huddled in Chiang Mai, waiting for the world to end.

*Uh-huh*, said Karen, who years later would feel extremely guilty about her response.

Karen spent a little more than two weeks in Dan Loi.

She followed Martiya's routine. In the early mornings, Martiya took Karen around the village, stopping in at one hut after another. *This* was how fieldwork ought to be done, Karen thought: patiently, over years. A little Dyalo village was a microcosm of the world, and every hut had its drama: in one hut, an old woman lay dying; in another, a young girl, frightened by the prospect of moving to her new husband's village, sobbed at her mother's side; and in a third, a husband teased his wife, the couple laughing. Karen had never seen this side of Martiya before, when in those dark huts that powerful, passionate personality diminished itself and a calm tenderness stole over her flashing eyes. It was *inspiring*, Karen said, all that intelligence and curiosity focused on this tiny village. Martiya still bubbled over with questions, even after all those years in the mountains.

One sleepy morning, Karen decided to lie in bed a little longer as Martiya went out about her rounds. Martiya's hut was not what Karen had expected. She had remembered Martiya's epistolary descriptions of dreary and primitive Dyalo huts, but on her return to Thailand, Martiya had built for herself a new house, simple but comfortable, two light and airy rooms under a high-arched ceiling. There was a bedroom, and now, in the early morning, Karen lay in bed and watched the sunlight filter in through square windows to fall in long white rectangles across the bamboo-tiled floor. The view extended out over the whole of the valley, light green mountains darkening in the distance, each bend in the mountains suggesting to Karen intrigue and mystery. For a few moments, Karen imagined staying with Martiya here in the mountains: getting someone to sell the Ford Pinto and wire her the money, not even bothering to resign her lectureship, just staying, building herself a hut, if not in this village then in the next one over.

When she was awake, Karen went into the other room of the hut, where Martiya kept her desk. This room, which Martiya called her study, stared out at the village itself. Long silk *tai-lue* tapestries, one red with blue, one yellow with green, one black with silver, hung along three walls; the other wall was dominated by a floor-to-ceiling bookcase. Martiya, Karen said, read voraciously, and every month her father sent her books from California. On Martiya's desk, there were three lilies in a glass bowl.

Karen was seized by a sudden desire to snoop, and she began to look through the volumes of hard-sided notebooks on the bookshelf. Martiya seemed to be writing a book. On the flyleaf of one of the notebooks was written a title, "The Dyalo Way of Life," and from what Karen could tell, the book was a memoir of daily life with the Dyalo. Karen thought of Colin Turnbull's famous memoir of life with the Pygmies, *The Forest People*. Karen read Martiya's memoir all through the morning, and when she was finished, she was convinced that the completed manuscript, still only a fragment, would be one of those rare literary documents that created for the reader the life of a whole people. She had spent several days now in a Dyalo village, but nothing that she had seen made the Dyalo come alive like Martiya's account. Hearing Martiya's footsteps on the terrace, Karen returned the notebook to its proper place and went with her friend to make lunch in the cooking hut.

After lunch, every afternoon in the heat of the day, Martiya and Karen went swimming. There was a small clear pool at the base of a steep waterfall an hour's hike from the village. Although the pool was small, the water was deep, and local legend held that at the very bottom of the pool was a rock in the shape of the seated Buddha. To touch this rock was a means of making merit, of ensuring oneself in however small a degree a more favorable reincarnation. Karen was a strong swimmer; even so, she was never able to swim down deep enough to find the rock and examine it. But Martiya claimed to be able to do it. The trick, Martiya said, was to dive into the pool from the rock ledge that overhung the waters. Martiya dove and disappeared into the darkness, and Karen became slightly nervous waiting for her friend as the waters smoothed over and became calm, with Martiya still someplace deep underneath. Only when the waters were perfectly still did Martiya burst up out of the water, panting for breath, the sun reflecting off her dark hair and lean, flat face.

A day or two before Karen was scheduled to return home, Dan Loi was blanketed in a heavy mist, which Martiya told Karen was almost unheard of at that time of year. But there it was: the village and valley were enshrouded in mist so thick that Karen could no longer see the summits of the near hills or even the shrine of Old Grandfather just down the road; the village became perfectly quiet except for the sad cawing of the kiss-me birds and the gentle drip of water from the heavy trees. It was a mist so thick that Karen would not have been surprised at all to see a dinosaur strolling down the red-dirt lane. Martiya told Karen that she liked the mist: it reminded her of rainy season, cozy mornings with her book, and of rice planting. But Karen thought that the mist transformed Dan Loi into just about the spookiest place she had ever seen, the way the villagers wandered out of the mist, then disappeared back into it. In the end, she was glad to get out of there.

That visit to Dan Loi was the last time Karen saw Martiya. She had meant to go back to Thailand again, but not long after returning to Wisconsin, one of her grant applications—to study rainmakers in West Africa, an idea that came to her in Dan Loi, while watching the shaman—was finally approved. Between her own fieldwork and then the new job in Texas and then meeting Paul, which was altogether another story, and then the kids, the years slipped by. She and Martiya continued to write to each other, but with time the letters passed across the Pacific less and less frequently, until finally the correspondence came to a halt. Then a man named Gilles called, saying that Martiya was in jail.

"I thought he was crazy," Karen said. "I tell you, I didn't believe him. I thought he was trying to get money out of me or something. I mean, he sounded so *weird*. But then I got so curious, and I wrote him and he wrote me back that she had killed a missionary, so I wrote her, and I wrote her again, and she never replied, and then you wrote me, and God, I feel *so* bad. I should have done something to help her when I had the chance."

# THREE

# BAMBUSA VULGARIS

GILLES BLOUZON FOUND THE HOUSE WITH MARTIYA—an old teak house with a gabled roof that curled at the eaves. They'd been roaming on Gilles's motorbike, nothing more than a Sunday drive, and when he saw the old house, with its stupendous view of the plains, Gilles said to himself, "This is the house where I wish to pass my *retraite*." Buying property is a complicated business for the foreigner in Thailand, but Gilles was patient: it was in his *retraite* that he, like every Frenchman, imagined that his real life would begin. He signed the papers with a vision in his sleek, seal-like head: a sunny afternoon in cool season; Gilles in the garden, pottering away; and Martiya looking out on him indulgently from the window of the kitchen, where she was preparing a tasty Dyalo *daube*. But when Martiya left him, Gilles took stock not only of this failed romance but also of the general trajectory of his life and decided to leave the University of Chiang Mai, where he had spent the last five years as a professor of botany, a specialist in the life cycle of bamboo. He found a position at the University of Grenoble, and returned to France. This was in 1988. The teak house was shuttered and boarded up. A family of owls nested in the eaves.

When Gilles left Thailand, he had resolved to sell the house; but selling property in Thailand is almost as complicated a business as buying it, and he held on to the house for almost ten years. This was good fortune: only months before Gilles was scheduled to begin his *retraite*, he was interviewed for *The Guardian* by a pretty Englishwoman named Vivian who was interested in the biological effects of deforestation in Bangladesh. Gilles married Vivian not long thereafter. I recognized Vivian's name, as will many of my readers: she is now *The Guardian*'s Southeast Asian correspondent. She famously reported from Tianamen Square, and was the first journalist in Asia to interview Pol Pot's second-in-command. Gilles and Vivian now made their headquarters in the house that Gilles found with Martiya.

I stood beside him in his garden.

"All *that*," Gilles told me with a sweep of his hand. "All *that* I planted."

Laterite blocks formed walkways through the jungle-like profusion. Gilles named species with a flick of his forefinger as we walked: ficus, banyan, monkeypod—these were the shade trees already on his property when he arrived; but it was Gilles who planted the Persian lilac, the jasmine, the jacaranda, the perfumed frangipani and the lantana, with its pungent smell of smoke and garbage. We paused beside a lipstick tree, and Gilles pointed out a flame tree, a flame vine, and a fire bush. Bougainvillea bloomed in purple, magenta, orange, white, pink, and crimson. A passion flower drooped—"He needs less sun," Gilles said, "I am going to transplant him"—but the golden trumpet, the pink trumpet, and the blue trumpet were all in blossom. Lilies and lotuses in tall vases floated on murky green waters.

But the flowers, the trees, the shrubs, the vines, the exotics, the water plants, the palms—coconut, palmrya, taliput, and fishtail—were all preamble to the *bambou*. Land being cheap in Thailand, Gilles had bought almost a half acre of adjacent property on which to indulge his passion.

"*Bambusa andinacea*," he said as we walked, petting the stalks fondly as another man might stroke the muzzles of his favorite dogs. "The giant thorny bamboo. *Bambusa pallida. Bambusa polymorpha. Dendrocalamus giganteus.*"

The list went on.

"Have you ever seen a bamboo flower?" Gilles asked abruptly.

His excitement mounted, and it was easy to see what might have attracted Martiya, and subsequently Vivian, to the man. But I could also see why Karen Leon might have thought that he was a weirdo.

"The bamboo, she is a sexually timid but intensely passionate grass," Gilles continued, not waiting for my answer and pointing at an abashed-looking green stalk. "*Bambusa vulgaris*, this one, she flowers once every one hundred fifty years, and when she flowers, she flowers everywhere! All of the bamboo, after decades and decades of calm, now suddenly decides it is time to wake up and flower. And then, once it has flowered and reproduced and the baby bamboo shoots, all of the old bamboo all over will die. All at once. How does bamboo everywhere know that it is time?"

"I don't know," I said.

"Of course you don't know! *Nobody knows!* I've been studying the bamboo a lifetime, and *nobody knows*. It is one of the most fantastic mysteries on Earth. Bamboo in Brazil and Bamboo in China, exploding at once in bamboo flowers. Nobody alive today has ever seen *Bambusa vulgaris* in flower! It last flowered in 1860. But it's coming! In just a few years—I hope I will be alive—it will flower again—I'm waiting—after all this time—the explosion—I think that I can feel it coming! But it will be a catastrophe, and nobody is ready. It will be a terrible thing.

"A terrible thing!" he repeated. "We have some records, some documents, from the last time the bamboo flowered. But this time it will be much worse. When the bamboo flowers, it happens all at once, and everywhere that there is *Bambusa vulgaris* will drown in bamboo flowers. What do they look like? What do they smell like? No one knows. One thing we do know. The rats will love them. The bamboo flowers in the hot season, when everything else is dying and *BOOM!* the rats will eat like the pigs, they will gorge themselves, they will stuff themselves, and then they will reproduce, because that is what rats do when they are full. And when the rats reproduce and reproduce and reproduce—it means *famine*. And of course, nobody is prepared."

Gilles shook his head at the improvident nature of his fellow man. His lecture on bamboo ended abruptly, and Gilles took me inside the house, where he would, he said, make me a *tisane* from things grown right in his own garden. Such a *tisane*, he promised, would increase my mental acuity, which I suppose he found lacking.

Silk curtains held back the late afternoon sun, leaving the *sala* bathed in mustard-yellow shadows. Above us, a row of winged angels met in intricate aerial embraces, the delicate little things unmindful of the heavy wooden beam across their backs. All his life Gilles had traveled—there is, after all, no wild bamboo in France—and from every corner of the bamboo-occupied globe had acquired pretty things: Javanese batiks hung low across the teak walls, fresh roses were haphazardly arranged in a vase which Gilles explained was once the spirit urn of a little-known tribe in northern Côte d'Ivoire who lived surrounded by the most *merveilleux* bamboo groves in all West Africa. We sat crosslegged on the floor around a low wooden table drinking Gilles's bitter *tisane* from celadon mugs. I was feeling sharper already.

Every time Gilles said the word "bamboo," his tongue flickered out from his mouth very slightly, and Gilles said the word "bamboo" very often. He was nevertheless a handsome man, all the charm in his face centered in his melancholy, sympathetic eyes. His hair was high and receded, and he had the first hints of long descending jowls. It was fully a man's face, and again I could imagine the appeal to Martiya of this worldly character when she first met him at a lecture he gave to the American University Alumni Association on, of course, the mating habits of bamboo. It was 1984 and Martiya was thirty-seven years old, Gilles perhaps ten years her elder.

The relationship proceeded with all of the amatory languor of *Dendrocalamus strictus*; yet by Gilles's description it was nevertheless a warm and tender affair. Gilles in those days drove a motorcycle, and every weekend he rode up to Dan Loi. He spent hours telling her more than I suspect she wanted to hear about the bamboo, but she reciprocated by insisting that he master the intricate details of the Dyalo rice-planting cycle. It was from Gilles that I would later learn how the *dyal* worked.

Every year at the start of the monsoon, Gilles returned to France for a month, to visit his aging parents and his son, and it was his practice to come back to Thailand with several cases of wine. It was, he said, the one thing from France that he missed while living in Asia. "And the cheese," he added, after a moment's thought, and had I not pressed him to continue his story, I think that list might have gone on. Gilles was not a great connoisseur, but it gave his methodical, scientific nature pleasure to record when each bottle was drunk, and under what circumstances. This was the closest that Gilles had to a diary. In anticipation of my visit, he had pulled down his wine logs from his years with Martiya.

The first night that Gilles met Martiya, he wrote: "*15 March 1984. Sancerre. Chiang Mai. With Martiya van der Leun, anthropologist.*" By the fall, Martiya had become "M," as in: "*21 September 1984. Bordeaux Blanc. Chiang Mai. With M. to celebrate my new motorbike.*" The wine diaries were an odd, unwitting witness to the rhythms of Dyalo life. Martiya and Gilles toasted the Dyalo new year together every February: "*15 February 1985. Champagne. Dan Loi. With M. Dyalo new year. Banging on drums.*" All through February and April, the Dyalo slashed the jungle and burned fields to prepare them for planting; when the fields were ready for planting, the village held the first of the *dyal* feasts: "*17 April 1985. Macon Villages. Dan Loi. With M & George Washington, start of rice planting season.*"

"Why didn't George Washington make *dyal?*" I asked.

"The shaman *never* makes *dyal*, of course," Gilles said. "How would that be, if the shaman made *dyal?*" Gilles shook his head and pointedly refilled my cup of tea.

All through the rainy season, the Dyalo weeded the rice fields, and occasionally Gilles, who liked digging in the dirt, would go out to help. He'd return in the late afternoon, covered in sweat: "*17 May 1985. Very cold Sancerre Blanc. Dan Loi. With M, chicken curry, spent day working in fields.*" One night in June 1986, the headman shot a wild boar and gave a portion to Martiya; it was stewed and accompanied by a Burgundy. Every year, with the first mangoes in spring, Gilles opened a Sauternes. When Gilles found the house in which he anticipated taking his *retraite*, the couple drank a Muscat. By September, the maize was harvested ("*16 September 1986. Bordeaux Blanc. Dan Loi. With M, corn chowder, new corn*"), shortly thereafter the rice ("*12 October 1987. St. Julien. Dan Loi. With M. Rice harvest*"), and in December, the opium harvest coincided with the birthday of the king of Thailand: "*18 December 1985. St.*

*Julien. Dan Loi. With M. King's Birthday.*" They drank a Graves on 18 December 1986, for the same occasion, and a St. Estephe in December, 1987.

The wine log went on and on: a bottle of wine once a week and a man with whom she might share the ordinary pleasures of life—that seems to have been Martiya's relationship with Gilles. It was a relationship of opposites: Gilles was methodical whereas Martiya was impulsive, an excess of phlegm balanced against an excess of choler. It wasn't bad. Toward the end of the affair, Gilles told me, he had begun to consider marriage. But it wasn't meant to be: the last bottle the couple drank together was just before the start of the planting season, April 1987. Gilles was headed back home for a month with his aged parents. They drank a Côtes du Rhône.

The room in which I sat with Gilles was not the perfect rectangle it seemed: the northern wall was a few inches longer than the southern wall. It was a distortion, Gilles explained to me, that was not visible to the naked eye, but once Gilles had pointed it out, the room did appear very slightly wider at one end than the other. The room seemed to pulse slightly and breathe, as if the eye longed to correct the very slight imbalance in the proportions. The effect was, as Gilles had said, immensely calming.

On a low wooden table near the door, there was a photo of a handsome young woman with auburn hair. I would have imagined that she was Gilles's daughter, but Gilles had earlier mentioned that he had only a son, a banker in Paris, so I ventured a guess that it was Gilles's wife. Gilles confirmed my suspicion: Vivian was in Hanoi covering a conference of Asian-Pacific leaders.

The brief discussion of Vivian's career brought us back to Martiya.

"Was she ever lonely?" I asked.

He shook his head. "She was a very self-sufficient woman, the most self-sufficient woman I've ever met. She could go weeks and months in the village and be very happy. I cannot do that. I need to talk to people, to tell stories. But Martiya was fine by herself."

Gilles leaned forward and rearranged the lilies in the vase.

"You can't imagine it was an easy life she led in that village," he said. "Even if she had the money to buy her own rice and pork and vegetables and did not go to work in the fields. But she had to carry those huge buckets of water up the hill every day—it gave her the most beautiful shoulders and arms, that work, like marble. Just to wash her clothes took her a half a day. She never allowed herself to wear dirty clothes, that was something she would *not* do, and she always wanted to wear nice clothes, those lovely Dyalo skirts and blouses, and so every day she was washing. And cooking in that village! She was an excellent cook, but it took *time* to cook as the local women did. It was the way my grandmother of course used to cook, making everything by hand in the kitchen, all afternoon, chopping, chopping, chopping.

"Then there was her work, her real work. That's why Martiya spent so much time cooking, because that's where she could talk to the women. She'd spend three or four hours with the women, and then she'd spend three or four hours back in her hut, going over what they told her. Martiya trained herself to remember those conversations. She would talk to someone for an hour and then remember everything. But later she'd want to write down everything the women said, and think about what they said, and organize her notes, and then—this was the very hard part—really listen to the notes and to the voices, close her eyes and try to really *hear* what these voices had told her. You need *time* to listen like that. We don't listen like that ever. We miss so much of what everyone says.

"It was almost a compulsion for her to stay in that village. She hated to be away from Dan Loi, something physical. I remember we once attempted a vacation together. I took her down to Phuket, because I am very fond of the seaside, and it was like traveling with a ghost. She wouldn't eat, she had trouble sleeping, she didn't talk to me. We had a big fight, she said, 'I'm sorry, Gilles.' I said, 'Can't you even try?' She said, 'I am trying, I don't know what's wrong with me.'"

"You know that when she was young she used to travel quite a bit, don't you?" I asked.

"She told me about her adventures, but that was not the woman I knew. When I knew her, her world was that village. But there is something thrilling about *une femme obsédante*. Her passion for that village gave her something very addictive. I would come to her hut, and she'd be so excited. 'Gilles, it's fantastic what the shaman knows,' she would say. And that was just the shaman. There was always something. You know, she wanted to write a book about the Dyalo. She was not in a hurry to write it, but she worked on it, and she allowed me to read it every so often."

"How was it?"

"She had something to say."

"Martiya never thought about publishing that book?" I asked.

"Of course she did. Martiya was very ambitious. But she wasn't in a hurry. She had her own sense of time, and she wanted to finish the book, and she knew it would take her a long, long time."

Gilles sipped his tea. Then he said, "Do you know where that book is now?"

"No."

"If you find it, I would like to have a copy. It would be like meeting an old friend."

Gilles invited me to walk with him a few minutes. He took such a stroll every afternoon.

Before we left the house, Gilles closed every one of the windows, then checked that they were closed. He confirmed that the gas was off. "This is a wood house, you know," he said. He had a handful of papers that he wanted to leave on his desk. He changed shoes, and although it was easily eighty degrees and humid, he wanted to wear a light jacket. But when we were walking, he moved at a good clip. Our destination, Gilles said, was a small temple, perhaps a kilometer away, whose frescoed walls he admired.

He talked while we walked. In November 1988, Martiya heard rumors of an extremely unusual marriage in Wild Pig village, between matrilineal first cousins, and she decided to hike up there to investigate. Gilles accompanied her. When the couple arrived at the village, Martiya learned that the rumors were false: the marriage was prohibited by Dyalo custom and never happened. But as the day was late, Martiya suggested to Gilles that they spend the night in the hut of the headman.

The headman was a newcomer to the village named Hupasha, a handsome man on the cusp of middle age; his dark hair was streaked with gray, and Gilles could recall, even many years later, his kindly, intelligent eyes. He spoke only Dyalo, and although Gilles could understand a little of the language, he could not follow the headman's thick Burmese accent. Gilles quickly grew bored and, after the simple dinner of rice, chilies, and vegetables, excused himself to the front porch. Gilles read by the light of a hurricane lamp as he waited for Martiya to come out. Occasionally, he heard laughter from the inside of the hut. Gilles fell asleep without Martiya.

He woke up when she came out later that night and lay down beside him. "I asked her what she had talked about all night. She said that she had been talking about her childhood. 'And what was so interesting about that?' I said. She told me that in her whole time with the Dyalo, the headman was the first to ask about her childhood."

The next day, Gilles and Martiya went back to Dan Loi village.

"That man was Martiya's lover," Gilles said.

"I thought that was the first time she met him," I said.

Gilles stopped walking. We had been walking quickly and he was breathing rapidly. His matter-of-fact tone had concealed more intense emotions than I realized. There are only two emotions one can recall, even after a long time, with perfect and unerring accuracy: embarrassment and jealousy.

"It was the first time; they would be lovers later," Gilles said. He started walking again.


A few monks in yellow robes tended the temple garden, and Gilles was friends with all the stray cats who lived in the woodpile. "That one is a very bad cat," he said, pointing to a small yellow tabby.

"Why?" I asked.

"A bad character." He rubbed the cat's forehead affectionately, as it curled around his shins and purred. "A very bad character. Like me."

From the pockets of his coat, Gilles pulled out a tin of anchovies and another of tuna, both imported from France. (Gilles later explained to me that he didn't care for the smell of fresh fish in the house.) He opened the tins and offered the cats some food. "*Tiens*," he said. He spoke to the cats in French for a few minutes. He told one cat to share and told another cat that he was beautiful. Then he came and sat beside me on the steps of the temple.

Despite the very great distance between a Dyalo village in northern Thailand and Berkeley, Gilles said, Martiya had remained close to her father. Not a year or at most two passed without an extended visit from one to the other, and in the last several years of his life, Piers spent part of his long academic vacations in Dan Loi. After his death, a handwritten outline for a proposed grammar of Dyalo—a language whose acquisition and mastery Piers referred to as his "hobby"—was found in his office in Dwinelle Hall. Whenever Piers took leave of his daughter to return to California, he inevitably took Gilles aside and, in his crisp, Dutch-accented but otherwise impeccable French, asked Gilles to "look after my girl."

In May of 1987, a massive heart attack on the tennis courts took Piers's life. Martiya went back to Berkeley.

Martiya called Gilles from California in tears. She had spent the day going through her father's things. In his study, his briar pipe remained half packed with ash and tobacco, his silver pen lay uncapped and open across a proposed submission to *Ethnolinguistics* which the editor had asked him to review. The journal made Martiya think of her father's silly weakness for puns: he had always referred to *Ethnolinguistics* as a Piers-reviewed journal. He had left a sweater on the back of his chair, a gray cardigan. She put the sweater on and wore it around the house, padding from room to room. She kept only her father's pipes for herself. Martiya put the house on Etna Street up for sale.

In this way, Martiya severed her last connection to Berkeley and returned to Dan Loi. Just one week after her return, she turned forty.

Back in Asia, Martiya complained to Gilles that her cottage was smaller than she had recalled, and darker. She told Gilles that the hut, which she had once considered cozy, now seemed as tight as a coffin. Gilles remembered visiting her and being startled by the manic energy with which she burst out of the bedroom and into the study. The hut wasn't small, Gilles said: it was almost as large as the *sala* of his house. What's more, it opened up onto a spectacular vista: just beyond the threshold of the hut was her large patio, beyond that all the village, and beyond *that* the huge dip of the valley, those foothills which if followed would lead to Burma, to China, and to the highest mountains in the world. Now Martiya complained that there was no place for her here: she was tripping over her books, her desk, her chair. The chimney smelled. She could not even turn around.

The sensation of claustrophobia continued even beyond the tight confines of her hut. It had been twelve years now since she had first set foot in the village, and, disciplined as ever, she continued in her routine: she pursued her longitudinal studies of village life, visiting every day with village families, continuing to observe the panoply of Dyalo rites, attending law cases. Yet even in the rice fields, where she stood with the shaman George Washington, chasing out the jungle spirits who threatened Rice, with nothing around her in any direction at all but open mountain air, she felt trapped—the same sensation of panic, and nervous sweat, and nausea rising up in her as she felt in her study.

Martiya told Gilles that she had not realized how much her father's presence in that house on Etna Street had offered her. She had never said to herself, "I have moved to a small Dyalo village in northern Thailand where I will stay forever." She had always said to herself, "I am doing fieldwork, extensive fieldwork, in Dan Loi, and when I am ready I will leave." To leave meant to return to her father's home, to Berkeley, there to begin again. Now contemplating her life, she asked herself, "Where would I go?" That she had no answer terrified her.

Gilles remonstrated with her when she complained. "A woman of your intelligence, of your abilities, has options, Martiya. You do not have to stay in that village. You could finish your doctoral thesis in two months and become a professor. It is still possible. We could go to France. The world is so big, and you're still young."

But Martiya didn't listen. Did Gilles understand what it meant to be *alone* in the world? She had no family at all but some vague relatives of her father's in Holland. She was forty years old. She had been in the village more or less since the age of twenty-seven. She had no skills, knew nothing of the world really but this little village. Martiya's normally bright face was now habitually drawn and gloomy. She complained that her attempt to see the native's point of view was a failure. She could not escape herself. She understood nothing of these people, and what's more, her sustaining curiosity had failed her: what she did not understand, she no longer cared to understand. She had no place to go.

At the onset of the rainy season of 1987, almost precisely a year after Piers's death, Gilles had dinner with Martiya in Dan Loi. He was about to leave for his annual visit to France. She was, he said, calm, and had proposed that the two of them take a vacation together when he came back. This was a breakthrough, Gilles thought, the first sign of progress in almost a year. Neither Gilles nor Martiya said it, but it was understood by both that this vacation would be the first step in constructing a new life together, away from Dan Loi.

"Do you want to go now?" he asked.

Martiya said no. "I want to see the rice planting," she said. The rice planting was one of Martiya's favorite moments in the Dyalo calendar. That night they had a bottle of wine, and Gilles noted the occasion in his wine log.

That bottle of wine, a Côtes du Rhône, proved the last that Martiya and Gilles would share.


Two of the cats began to fight over an anchovy, hissing at one another. *"Il y en a assez pour tout le monde,"* Gilles said. *"Ça suffit."*

Gilles went back to France, and spent a month, as usual, with his parents and son. Usually when he was away, he and Martiya would exchange a few letters, and Martiya, when she was in Chiang Mai or elsewhere, would call him; Gilles couldn't call Martiya, after all, in the village. But this year, Gilles heard from Martiya only once: about two weeks before he was to return, she called him in the middle of the night, awakening him and his family. When Martiya realized the hour at which she called, she excused herself and said that she would call the next day. She didn't, and Gilles had no way of reaching her. Her voice had been agitated, and Gilles was worried.

"Why, exactly?" I asked.

Gilles hesitated, then said, "I thought she might be with another man."

Gilles decided to cut his trip back by a week. Although he could not call Martiya, there was a telephone at the café where she usually read her mail, and he left a message for her there that he was returning. He told her to meet him at the airport. But when he arrived at Chiang Mai, there was no sign of her. The next morning, Gilles went up to Dan Loi.

The monsoon had broken that year with unusual force, and the road to Dan Loi had been washed out. Several kilometers from the village Gilles was forced to abandon his motorbike and hike into the village on foot. He arrived just as the evening sky was turning black. The great bowl of the valley spread out from Martiya's front porch like the pit of an exhausted mine. Martiya looked up at Gilles as he entered the hut, and for a long terrible moment didn't seem to recognize him.

"Gilles," she said. "I should have—I'm sorry . . ."

Gilles had never seen her this way before. She began to tremble. Gilles went to her but the look in her eyes stopped him. She breathed deeply and calmed herself. She offered Gilles a seat and, seeing his soaked clothes, began to make tea. She lit the small gas burner with a match, poured water into her old kettle, and placed it on the blue flame. When the two were settled with mugs in their hands, she looked at Gilles, then swung her eyes away from him. Her moment of composure was gone, and she began to tremble again.

"What's happened?" Gilles said. "What's the matter?"

Martiya said nothing. A moment passed, then a minute.

Martiya broke the silence. She told Gilles that it wasn't his fault, but that there was another man.

"I had no idea that I could be so angry," Gilles said. The declaration contrasted with his calm face, his tone of voice, and the tins of tuna. "But I looked at her, and it was like being angry with one of *them*."

He gestured at the cats.

"You know what she said to me?"

I shook my head.

"She told me that the headman of Wild Pig village came to her hut. She said that she made *dyal*. She told me that she had made rice. She told me that she had gone into the headman's fields and made rice. I said, 'And?' And she said, 'Isn't that enough?' "

Gilles was silent for a long while. An adolescent monk strolled past us and nodded at Gilles, who nodded back.

"It wasn't what she was saying. It was her eyes," Gilles said.

"What was it about her eyes?"

"That evening in Martiya's hut was the strangest moment in all my life. Because I knew that woman, I knew her very well. But I don't know if she recognized me at all. There is only one word I can use to describe her eyes. *Possédés.*"

Gilles went back to France a few months after he last saw Martiya. He wrote to her, asking her to get in touch with him should she need anything. Otherwise, he promised, she would not hear from him again; and, he wrote, he hoped she would leave him alone as well. He heard nothing from her, and Gilles, who had learned from the *bambou* to bend in a hard wind and not break, was sufficiently a man of the world to interpret her silence appropriately.

Several years after his return to Chiang Mai, Gilles fell into conversation with a young Thai botanist at the university. Knowing nothing of his connection to Martiya, the younger man mentioned the story of the anthropologist who had murdered a missionary in the hills. Gilles knew at once that he was referring to Martiya. Gilles would have visited Martiya in prison, but he couldn't find her. He tried the same tactics that I had: lawyers, judicial records, old friends, even Karen Leon. My visit to his *bambouserie* had been the first piece of news he had had of Martiya in years.

PART FIVE

# THE
# PENDULUM-EDGE
# OF THE SOUL

# ONE

# THE HIKER HUT

IN A SMALL CEREMONY at the end of May, Rachel's class—with the exception of Nat—was graduated from the first grade. To underscore the festive mood of the moment, Miss Rachel ordered pizza from Pizza Hut, a food better than which none of the students could imagine. As Miss Rachel's consort, I had been invited to attend the celebration, and Rachel and I listened attentively as the kids told us about their summer plans: Morris was going back to America for the summer, where he would stay with his grandparents, then would be returning to Thailand in the fall. He imagined his summer, it was plain to see, as an endlessly glistening string of ice-cream cones. "My grandmom, she let me eat so much!" Morris said, eyeing the last slice of pizza in the cardboard tray. Najda, her father, and his two wives would all be spending the summer in Chiang Mai, where the family would await the birth of not one but *two* younger siblings. Maria's father, who worked for the DEA, was being transferred to Bogotá. Within a year, she'd be speaking perfect Spanish, just as she now spoke perfect Thai. Nat would be repeating the first grade, but the prospect of another year of the same-old, same-old hardly seemed to faze the boy. He ran around the classroom blithely, chewing, for some reason only Nat knew, on his sandals. Summer vacation! When you're six years old, the summer is an abyss of time, and not one of Miss Rachel's students really imagined that the fall would ever come.

Miss Rachel, however, had seen the fall coming all too clearly, and she had made it plain that her time as a first-grade teacher in Thailand, exciting as the adventure had been, was over. She wanted to go back to the States, and go back to school: her experience in the first grade had made her dream of cool, sleek offices populated with bald-headed, suited adults. We had had any number of serious conversations about the future, then we had fights and arguments and tears. The end of anything is always painful. At some point, we both knew that Rachel would be going home without me.

Up until the moment that Rachel left, we maintained the fiction that she was going home *before* me, not without me, that I was just staying in Thailand to arrange a few loose ends. But at the airport, Rachel said, "I'll see you soon, won't I?" and began to cry.

"Of *course*," I lied.

I spent the rainy season alone in our concrete house. It rained all day, every day. I fell into irregular hours, waking up at noon, falling asleep at dawn. I stopped going to yoga. I saw no one but people whom I had contacted on the off chance that they knew what Martiya had done. I wrote a series of listless, dull reviews—of films I can no longer recall, of restaurants whose food I described in a string of glossy clichés. I don't think I even bothered to visit the restaurants. I wrote a profile of the general manager of the Westin Hotel. It was work. I went back to my concrete house, and once, twice, three times picked up the phone to call Rachel and tell her I would be on the next flight to the States. But every time, some stray detail of the story brought me back, something I read in the notes I took when I met with Tim Blair, or an odd phrase from the loose-leaf binder of Martiya's letters.

The last six weeks of the school year had seen the story drift idly. Gilles Blouzon returned, as he did every year, to France, promising to be in touch. He wasn't. I called a dozen prominent figures at Chiang Mai University, trying to pursue the rumors that Gilles had heard; I found nothing. Martiya's village, Dan Loi? Try finding that hamlet on the map, or try finding someone who knows where it is: the Dyalo villages of northern Thailand are unincorporated entities—they splinter and fragment; villages spring up out of nowhere; others disappear. A number of trekking agencies offered to take me by elephant back through a dozen different hill-tribe villages in a dozen days, but not one could guarantee me that they knew where Martiya's village could be found.

I tried to convince myself that the thing was done. This was not only Rachel's advice, but Josh O'Connor's also: he had been shocked to hear I was still pursuing it. Josh's gelateria had been a huge success, and so had the Herbalife products. He bought himself a candy-apple-red Cadillac, hired a driver, and now tooled around Bangkok conducting business from his backseat by cell phone. He could hardly remember Martiya van der Leun. Even my mother told me to let it go. "It's important to have a balanced life," she said. She had been hearing me talk about Martiya the better part of a year.

In early September, I ran into Judith Walker and Tom Riley in the city center. We went for a cold drink at the same diner where Tom and I used to meet for breakfast. Judith and Tom were getting married, and if there exists a pair of human faces more excited and contented, I've never seen them. I gave them my congratulations. After a few minutes, Tom's cell phone squealed, and he got up to take the call outside. When he came back, he explained something complicated to Judith involving Bill and the jeep. The upshot was that he had to go. Judith's face fell, and as much to console her as for the pleasure of her company, I invited her to have another Coke with me.

"Well, okay," she said doubtfully.

But Judith and I ended up talking for a few hours. She played with her shoulder-length hair while she talked. "Do you like it?" she asked. "I'm going to grow it out for the wedding. Tom says he likes it short, but he's never seen me with long hair." Then she told me about her wedding gown, which would be ivory; her bridesmaids' dresses, which would be teal; and that she and Tom planned on going to the Holy Land for their honeymoon.

I asked Judith how old she was, and she told me that she would be nineteen on September twenty-third.

"So you never got to know your uncle David."

"No, not really. I was just six when he went Home. I remember a few things. I remember he was really tall, and had long hair, and he could do all sorts of animal impersonations. He could do an elephant and a horse and a monkey. When he had to baby-sit me or the other kids, he'd put us all in a circle and we'd make a zoo."

I had never really understood why Judith was living with her grandparents, and I asked her about it.

"It was just a little after Uncle David was called Home that my mom and dad decided they wanted to spend more time in the field," she said. "They've been living in Laos since then, near the Vietnam border. They're medical missionaries. I spent a couple of years with them there, but we decided that when it was time for high school, I'd live here with Grandma and Grandpa."

"That must have been tough, being away from your family and living with your grandparents," I said.

"You have no idea!" Judith laughed. "I love Grandma and Grandpa to death, but they're old and they're strict. Tom is the first boy they ever let me even be alone with. I didn't go to one party in high school."

"Who's the tougher one?" I asked. "Your Grandma or your Grandpa?"

"Oh, Grandpa, definitely. If it was up to Grandpa, I'd just stay home all the time. I'd probably never even have gone to school. Grandma sometimes says, 'You've got to let that girl breathe.' But I understand, they're just worried, you know? Because of David." Judith's voice grew low, and she looked around the room. "Don't tell anyone, but sometimes in high school I snuck out the window at night."

Judith sat quietly for a minute. Then she said, "Mischa, do you know why that woman killed Uncle David?"

"No," I said. "I'm trying to find out."

"Can I tell you something?"

"Of course."

"And you promise you won't think Grandma and Grandpa are bad people?"

"Of course I promise."

"I once heard Grandma and Grandpa have a fight about David. A big fight. It was just a little after I got there. I wanted to go out after school and Grandpa didn't want to let me, and I don't know how it happened, but Grandma and Grandpa started fighting—I don't think I should be telling this to you."

I didn't say anything, and Judith kept going.

"In any case, they were fighting, and Grandma started yelling at Grandpa, 'You're going to drive her out of this house, just like David.' And Grandpa, he got so mad. He said, 'Don't talk to me about David. If you had done what any decent Christian woman would do, David would still be here today.' It was awful. I was upstairs in my bedroom, and even with the door closed I could hear them in their room. Grandma said, 'You brought that woman into this house. Don't ever forget, you brought that woman into this house.' I always wonder still what they were talking about. Later that night I heard them singing hymns downstairs."

A few minutes later, Judith stood up to go. She looked at me searchingly for a moment, and I could see her grandmother's shrewd eyes inset in a still young, unlined face. "Last year it was this girl Sarah Kennedy's birthday? At school? She had a party at a guest house in the mountains, and I think you should go up there."

"Why?"

"Because I think the owner of the place used to be Martiya's guide in the mountains. His name is Vinai. I think he knows all about her."

Judith looked around the room again.

"But if you go, *please* don't tell Grandma and Grandpa that I told you about it. Because I told them that I was going on a Bible retreat."


I left for the Hiker Hut that same day, traveling by motorbike.

When I first began driving in Thailand, one of the teachers at Rachel's school—Mr. Robert, a devout Buddhist, as it happened—gave me a piece of pointed advice. *Distrust everyone*, he said, *for no one— absolutely no one—on the Thai highway is your friend.* A people renowned for their calm and delicate nature, the Thai are nevertheless among the most aggressive of all the world's drivers, yielding lunatic pride of place only to the pacifistic, vegetarian Hindu.

But the Thai system allows for a certain flexibility: my little Honda Dream hugged the far left-hand margin of the highway, and the unwritten rules of the Thai road allowed me to cruise along as slowly as I wanted, past bamboo shacks where old ladies in sarongs sold coconut milk and fanned themselves with giant palm fronds. On either side of the road leading out of the lowlands, there were rice paddies being worked by very little women in broad hats and high boots, trudging slowly across immense flat fields, bent at the waist. A Thai proverb summarizes the life of a peasant farmer: "Back to the sun, face to the earth."

Then the road snaked into the mountains. A twenty-minute climb; I passed three elephants, led by mahouts, walking trunk in tail; my ears popped—and northern Thailand exploded in light. The plain of Chiang Mai had been a gloomy checkerboard of rice and sludge; the mirrored temple roofs had reflected a dark sky. But as soon as I hit the hills, the weather changed. Sweet flimsy mountain clouds floated across an open sky, and I could smell wild jasmine, honeysuckle, hibiscus, and something strangely like lemon tea. The paddies were terraced on the mountain slopes like a wedding cake made of mud: each glossy layer reflected the emerald hills, the azure sky, and the wild palms. At the very top of the wedding cake, short crabbed trees in radiant red blossom marked the place where the jungle began. Somewhere along the way, a mountain summit had been leveled to make way for a stupendously large yellow Buddha, who looked out impassively from his high perch over the mountains and the plains, his cherry lips ladylike. Mysterious dirt roads forked out every now and again, leading off to God-knows-where. I wanted to follow them all.

When I came to the hot springs, following the instructions that Judith had offered me, I made a left turn and crossed a small bridge that led onto a narrow red-dirt road. This took me up through little villages filled with rooting pigs and houses on stilts with tin roofs. Small children looked at me gravely.

Then the country changed again, the green turning golden with altitude. Some parts of the hill were on fire, and other slopes were black and charred. This was the real mountain country. A little brown stream wandered by the side of the road. A young boy led a humped bullock by the nose. I decided to defy the odds and took off my sweat-drenched helmet. A warm wind tousled my hair.

I came to a long, low teak building nestled on the side of a hill, looking out over an exuberant field of yellow sunflowers. A sign read THE HIKER HUT, in both English and Thai. Sprawled in a hammock in the shade of two big trees, a small silver-haired man plucked at his guitar. He didn't look up as I approached, and only when I was two-thirds of the way up the walk did he stop strumming. He put the guitar aside, rolled himself up to standing, and with an air of lazy cool asked me in English with only the slightest hint of an accent if he could help me.

It's very disconcerting the way the Thai laugh and smile at bad news. When I told Khun Vinai that Martiya was dead, he smiled. Maybe his smile meant: *She suffered for a long time and it's best this way.*

But maybe it meant: *It served her right.*

Or maybe it just meant: *Huh.*

The Hiker Hut was a collection of little huts, each in the traditional style of a different hill tribe. There was an Akha house, with its roof like a plump hive of mountain grasses; and a Lisu hut, with an elegant long front porch; and a cylindrical Karen house, tall and stately. There was a Mien cottage, a Hmong hut, and a Palaung long house, large enough for a convention of Palaung stockbrokers on a junket.

I, of course, stayed in the Dyalo hut.

The thin cotton mattress was the only concession to Western taste; the Dyalo, I well knew, typically slept on the floor. But in all other re-spects, Khun Vinai later told me with pride, so perfectly authentic were his tribal huts that once a visiting British television program was able to produce an entire documentary about the lives of the tribal peoples with-out ever leaving the property.

I spent the better part of the afternoon lying in the hammock that Khun Vinai had vacated, reading the Bible. After all those meetings with the Walkers, I had realized with a shameful start that I had never read much of the Good Book. *His eyes were as a flame of fire, and on his head were many crowns; and he had a name written that no man knew, but he himself. And he was clothed with a vesture dipped in blood: And his name is called The Word of God.* That's from Revelation. I wondered what that sounded like in Dyalo.

There were two other guests at the Hiker Hut, a young blond couple. From the hammock where I had installed myself, I watched them mount the hill and climb into their Akha hut. I had dinner with them that evening. I didn't really have a choice: there was only one restaurant in the village, managed by Khun Vinai's wife, and it would have seemed strange if I had said no. They were both from Denmark, and they told me a lot of things I didn't know about the hill-tribe villages: all of the villages in this valley, Henrietta said, were part of a program sponsored by the king of Thailand to substitute other crops for opium. The whole thing was an American idea. That's why there were so many strawberry and tomato fields. Later, I tasted the strawberries. They were bitter and chalky. I had my doubts.

After dinner, we walked back up the hill, and I excused myself to my Dyalo hut, pleading exhaustion. I took a shower and dried myself off and dusted myself with mentholated prickly heat powder and wondered what I was supposed to do with myself now. Then I heard a soft shuffling step on my stoop, and a knock on the door.

# TWO

# THE HAPPIEST WORDS
# IN ALL THE WORLD

I KNOW THE HAPPIEST WORDS in all the world.

The happiest words in all the world are "Opium Man," when accompanied by a little knock on the door of your hut and the old Akha man's shuffling step. "Come in," you say. Then the Opium Man lies down on the bed with you, both of you on your sides, facing each other, a little paraffin candle between you. Only a lover lies in bed with you like the Opium Man. He pulls a sticky pouch of black opium from his pocket, and lights the candle and prepares the pipe, heating the opium over the open flame, working it carefully until it is a perfect sizzling ball, then plunging the bolus into the pipe. It is not even necessary to lift your head while you smoke: the Opium Man holds the pipe while you inhale. I know all about the Opium Man, because opium makes you endlessly inquisitive. I speak to the Opium Man in my halting, hesitant Thai, and he replies in his thick Akha accent. The Opium Man can be talkative or silent, as he wishes, because he has the self-assurance that comes from being truly desired. I know about his little village and his pigs, his daughters and the bride-price he is expecting for them; I know that it is difficult for the sad Akha to follow the Akha *zha* when they wander down from the mountains to the Thai villages of the plains, where the lowland merchants cheat them and the children mock their rustic ways. The Akha man, himself a smoker, asks me questions, and I tell him about Martiya van der Leun.

When Vinai knocked on the door of the little hut, the pipes that I had smoked in anticipation of his arrival had wrongly rendered him a familiar figure, an old friend. He stood half a head shorter than me, and I am not particularly tall; but when he lay on the bed with the Opium Man, he sprawled and seemed big. He said he was a member of the Rotary Club of Chiang Rai, and asked if I was a Rotarian also. He seemed disappointed when I said I wasn't. I had decided that he was as distant and elegant as a headwaiter, then he belched; I had decided that he was tight-lipped, then he spoke for hours. It is a cliché to speak of the inscrutable Oriental—but clichés exist for a reason. Talking to Vinai, who was himself Dyalo, gave me some sense of how difficult it must have been for Martiya to penetrate the life of a Dyalo village. All those strange smiles.

Khun Vinai took my place on the bed. He was distracted, and said something about roofing tiles. He had driven all the way to Chiang Rai that afternoon, but the tiles he was looking for hadn't been available. He had wasted his afternoon.

The Opium Man made him a pipe, and Khun Vinai smoked it down in a single lungful. He held the smoke a long time, and then exhaled long tusks that hung below the ceiling of woven grass. He relaxed visibly. This was not the first time that I had smoked opium—I had, after all, lived in the Golden Triangle for almost two years—but the drug this time was different. The last time that I had smoked, with Rachel, a half-dozen pipes had rendered me pleasantly sleepy and lethargic. But now I was almost trembling. The only light in the hut was the Opium Man's candle, casting long pale shadows on the thatch wall.

Finally Vinai spoke, "Martiya, she is my good friend. It is too sad story, Martiya's story. I miss her too much."

Then he lapsed back into a long silence.


Khun Vinai propped himself on one elbow and looked at me. From my angle on the floor, I saw his bare feet, horny and calloused; then his short legs in a pair of khaki trousers; then a polo shirt with a little alligator above his heart; then a well-shaven Dyalo face, with mellow dark eyes, an unlined forehead, and a head of uncombed spiky gray hair.

Once he began to talk, all his reserve melted. Like many a man who reckons that he has made a success of his life, he was eager to tell his story. For twenty minutes or more, Khun Vinai narrated in my direction, occasionally making eye contact, but more often than not directing his conversation to a spot above my head on the bamboo wall. He spoke fluent English, but for an unflagging reliance on the present tense. I listened patiently, waiting for him to get to Martiya, and eventually he did.

As Khun Vinai spoke, I took notes:

— born in Dyalo vill., north of Burma's Shan state. So remote, hunt monkeys in forest with poisoned bow and arrow

— youngest of five children, only child in his family to survive to adulthood. Mother afraid spirits, sure that Khun Vinai die as well, insist he flee

— no possessions but the clothes on his back & his grandfather's gourd pipe, fled across the border to Thailand. Just fourteen.

— CHIANG MAI. Made a living—manual laborer and porter. Learned Thai, and some English also, contact w/ westerners

— Good w/languages—brought him 1974 to Martiya vdL's attention

— A dollar a day to go Dan Loi!!!

— How $ me then! Today—Toyota tr., then—no eat

The next morning, I would translate the last line of the notes above as: "You have no idea how much money this was to me then. Today, I drive a Toyota truck, but in those days, I barely had enough to eat."

On his left wrist, Khun Vinai wore a Rolex. Although his watch probably came from Chiang Mai's counterfeit bazaar, just like my Cartier, poverty had clearly taught Khun Vinai the value of things.

Khun Vinai told me he spent almost two years with Martiya in Dan

Loi. He was like Martiya's shadow in the village: the two spent day after day together, interviewing the villagers or taking genealogies. When Vinai realized just what Martiya was trying to do in Dan Loi, when he had finally figured out just why Martiya was asking all those questions and just what Martiya was writing down in her notebooks, Vinai became an enthusiastic partner in her work. When her Dyalo became conversational, Martiya would interview the women privately about those things which they will not discuss freely in front of men; and he would talk to the men. At night, they would compare their findings.

When Martiya was ready to go home, she took Khun Vinai aside. She said, "Vinai, you did half of the work up here, I think you should take half of the leftover grant money." At first he refused. But Martiya insisted. "She takes a fifty-baht bill, lights a match, and burns the money," he said. "She is about to burn another bill, when I say okay. I take the money. It is almost twenty-five hundred dollars. That's how I start Hiker Hut."

Khun Vinai took the pipe from the Opium Man, inhaled, and passed the pipe back. "I owe Martiya everything," he said. "I always tell people that without Martiya, I probably am dead."

Martiya went home to California, then came back to Thailand. Over the next decade, Martiya and Khun Vinai saw each other frequently. They developed a friendship. When Khun Vinai married, Martiya was present at the wedding feast. Khun Vinai recalled Martiya dancing all night around the bonfire, and then in the morning, because Khun Vinai had no close female relatives in Thailand, he had invited Martiya to participate in the ritual kidnapping of the bride from her family's hut. This Martiya had done with great style, shrieking like a real Dyalo woman as she grabbed Sang-Duan from her bed. Then, when Sang-Duan gave birth to Khun Vinai's first child, a lovely girl, Martiya had been present also at the soul-gathering ceremony, where the child's souls were bound up in her body on the twelfth day of life. It was Martiya who accidentally gave the girl her nickname, when she remarked, innocent of yet another Dyalo taboo, that the girl had kissable lips. Sang-Duan's mother had been horrified by the remark, but Vinai thought Martiya's gaffe hysterical, and the name stuck: the girl was Kiss-My-Lips. A few years later, Khun Vinai's first son was born, and a few years after that, another girl, and Martiya helped gather up the souls of those children as well.

Khun Vinai paused as we exchanged places. I took up his place in front of the Opium Man, and he took mine, on the floor. The Opium Man set to work preparing my pipe, kneading the black bead of opium between his fingers, melting it over the open flame, then kneading it again. He was a perfectionist. The door of the hut was open, and by the bright light of a full moon I could see the valley in the distance, and silhouettes of palms. I heard the wind passing lightly over the rice fields.

Khun Vinai first met David Walker at the funeral of Sings Soft, the great poet and singer. People came from every village in northern Thailand and even beyond: nobody seemed to organize anything, but within three days of his death the village was flooded with newcomers, most of whom made camp on the far side of the village, not far from the Old Grandfather shrine. Even David was there. Only Martiya was missing, and Khun Vinai wondered where she might be: Martiya loved Sings Soft as much as anyone.

The funeral went on all day and all night, Khun Vinai said.

"We take a water buffalo, and we put a spear in his heart like this. And when he is dead, we pour water down his throat like this, so he make no sound. Because Sings Soft hates ugly sounds. And we say, 'This is so our friend Sings Soft can eat in the Land of the Dead.' We say, 'Sings Soft, you are dead. We don't want you anymore. Go to the Land of the Dead.'"

The villagers washed the water buffalo and covered it with rice from Sings Soft's fields. They made a feast, and all day long they ate and drank rice whiskey. Then, just as dusk was falling, they took a hawk which a young boy had caught in the forest, and released the bird. The bird flew away. The villagers said, "This is so all nine souls of our friend Sings Soft head straight to the Land of the Dead. Bird, take the souls of our friend Sings Soft with you."

All night long, the villagers drank and sang. Sings Soft had written marriage songs, death songs, funny songs, songs for boys who wanted girls, songs for girls who wanted boys, songs to accompany the hunt for wild pigs in the forest, songs for the harvest of rice—and after each song, someone would sigh softly and say something like, "I remember that song. It was when my youngest sister was married. She's gone to the spirits now, poor thing, but what a lovely song that was!" Then somebody else would sing another.

Then one man shouted, "David Walker, do you know any of the songs of Sings Soft?"

David stood up. He said, "My friends, I know no songs from Sings Soft."

"Then sit down," shouted one drunk man from Big Rock Village. Everyone laughed. "I know a song from Sings Soft," the drunk man said, and proceeded to sing one of Sings Soft's bawdier songs, the story of a young boy who fell in love with a pig.

Now a Dyalo funeral involves large quantities of rice whiskey and beer, and sometime after moonrise but well before the end of the party, Khun Vinai sat for a minute on one of the big rocks near Old Grandfather's shrine. He wondered just where Sings Soft's souls were at that very moment, whether they had already gone to the place where souls go, or whether they had lingered on to hear the beautiful things the people had to say. Khun Vinai had settled into his thoughts when he heard a rustling in the bush. When he looked up, Martiya was there.

"Martiya, my friend," he said. "Why aren't you at the soul-saying-goodbye ceremony of our friend?"

"I have been listening from behind Old Grandfather's shrine," Martiya said.

"But why haven't you come out into the open and sung a song for Old Grandfather?"

"Vinai, my friend, you don't know? I am not at the funeral because I have been seeing my *gin-kai*, and the villagers think that I am unclean."

Khun Vinai was shocked. "You have been seeing your *gin-kai*?"

"Yes."

"Why?"

"I couldn't stay away from him."

"Where did you see him?"

"In his fields. In his hut."

"But don't you know that—"

"Of course I know, Vinai. Lai-Ma told me that if my shadow falls on her fields, the harvest would fail. They're quite scared of me. Some of them wanted to kick me out of the village."

Khun Vinai didn't know what to say. He had heard stories of other women who had seen their *gin-kai*, but had never met one. He was frightened now to be on a lonely rock with Martiya. She saw the fear in his eyes and said, "Go back to the funeral."

Khun Vinai stood up to go. Then he did a very brave thing. He said, "Come to Hiker Hut soon," and Martiya promised that she would.

When Khun Vinai had returned to the funeral, the villagers were again demanding that David sing a song of Sings Soft, and David was saying all over again that he didn't know any. Then the shaman said, "Our friend Sings Soft was too happy to listen to a song, same as to sing one song himself. Sing a song now for his spirits, before he leaves us."

And the people said, "Yes, sing."

And David said, "This is a song of my ancestors for the dead." He sang:

"*I am Wu-pa-sha's* bi'na-ma*; *there is nothing I want.*
*He brings me to sleep in the soft grass of the green rice fields;*
*He leds me to the clean water drinking spot.*
*He brings me back my lost souls;*
*He shows me good customs for his honor.*
*Even though I walk through the valley of the shadow of death,*
*I fear no bad spirits: because You are with me.*
*Your* ka-beh† *comforts me.*
*You give too much food to me, even if my enemy comes.*
*You rub coconut oil on my head; my cup is too full.*
*So every day of my life I will always have good things of Wu-pa-sha*
*and I will live in the well-built house of Wu-pa-sha forever.*"

People asked David Walker to sing another *farang* song, and he said no. Then one by one, some still murmuring the songs of Sings Soft,

---

*bi'na-ma: water buffalo used for work and milk (but not for food or sacrifice).
†ka-beh: long wooden pole used by the Dyalo to drive water buffalo.

others too tired to recall another verse, the drunken villagers fell asleep.

The next day, a number of the guests asked David about the beautiful *farang* song, and he spent the day preaching not far from Sings Soft's grave, with the result that three villagers asked to be baptized.

The Opium Man handed me the pipe, and I smoked again. The smoke was sweet, with a taste a little like caramel toffee. With every pipe, I felt as if I were gradually rising higher in the air. My breathing was slow and steady. The Walkers had told me that the Dyalo, upon accepting Christianity, were required to stop growing poppies and smoking opium. *If Christianity could convince a man to do that*, I thought to myself, *well then! That's some religion indeed.*

Khun Vinai told me that he didn't see Martiya again for almost a year after Sings Soft's funeral. That was the year that Kiss-My-Lips was sick. One night Sang-Duan woke to hear Kiss-My-Lips groaning and thrashing about, trembling and bleeding from the mouth. This was the first of her seizures. Khun Vinai had a modern outlook on things, and he took her to Chiang Mai for treatment at the hospital, and while the doctors ran their tests, Sang-Duan insisted on pursuing traditional Dyalo remedies—medicinal herbs and shamanic intervention. Whether it was these or the doctors' prescriptions, the seizures stopped, and life settled into its normal rhythms: banana pancakes in the mornings; box lunches for trekkers; and at night, the Happiest Words in All the World.

Then Martiya came to visit Khun Vinai.

It was just as Gilles had said: there was something about her eyes. They were wild and unfocused, then distracted and staring. Yet Vinai also said that he had never seen her so beautiful. Her cheeks were pale with a hint of bright pink, and her lips were scarlet like the flame tree.

Sang-Duan looked at her husband.

"I cannot turn her away," Khun Vinai whispered to his wife in the kitchen.

That evening, Sang-Duan served Martiya, and the family ate together from common dishes.

Khun Vinai had never seen Martiya more charming. She told stories from her childhood which made the children howl with laughter, and her imitations of the villagers were so spot-on that Khun Vinai would have sworn that Farts-a-Lot or the shaman George Washington was right in front of him. Only Sang-Duan was not amused by Martiya, looking at her all night long with the same distrustful stare.

That night, Kiss-My-Lips suffered another seizure. In the past, her seizures, although terrifying to watch, had passed quickly, after only five minutes or so. But this seizure, it was clear, brought the young girl to the edge of death before she came to. When finally the worst was over, and the girl was sleeping calmly, Sang-Duan turned to her husband.

"Vinai, you must," she said.

"How can I?" he asked.

"You must. I will not live with Rice. Do not bring the anger of Rice into the hut of our children. For I fear Rice, as I fear Lightning, and I fear Death."

Khun Vinai did not sleep the rest of the night. He watched the sun rise over the hills, then went to Martiya's hut. He found her awake, sitting cross-legged on the terrace, staring out over the fields.

Martiya saw the look on his face, and said, "And you too, Vinai?"

"I can't," he said.

Martiya gathered her bags and went back to Dan Loi village.


Khun Vinai stood up, and the Opium Man, seeing that his work for the evening was done, followed him. Khun Vinai did not linger at the door. He said, "Goodbye, my friend. We'll talk more tomorrow." Then he and the Opium Man were gone.

My bed was not particularly comfortable, but I think even on a down mattress with silk sheets I would have lain awake for a long time: insomnia is another of the effects of the drug. I found myself thinking about Martiya alone in that Dyalo village. How must she have occupied her days? How can an anthropologist do fieldwork if she can no longer talk with the people she intends to study? What *else* was there for Martiya to do in that village?

Her life, I imagined, had been reduced to her *gin-kai*. She was alone in the mornings, then she carried water back to her solitary hut. She ate alone. She read all day. Then, on those nights when she wasn't with Hupasha, she must have lowered the wick on her hurricane lamp and climbed into bed not having spoken to a soul since the morning. I thought about Martiya's letter to Tim Blair. She had met a man, she wrote, and was madly in love. Having no one with whom she might share her thoughts, she had decided to write to Tim himself. What she didn't tell Tim Blair was that her lover was *all* she had.

I finally fell asleep that night, and I dreamed of Martiya. Opium produces dreams of unusual vividness, and this dream was as real as any event of the daytime. I was in the kitchen of my house in Chiang Mai, making coffee, and Martiya was there also. I have never seen a photograph of the woman, but I knew that it was Martiya. I was excited to talk to her. "You must be Martiya van der Leun," I babbled. "I'm so happy to finally meet you. I've been looking for you everywhere, you have no idea how hard it's been to find you. Would you like a cup of coffee?" Martiya didn't say anything, and I stared at her. Her face was pale, and she was trembling. She was terrified. "It's okay," I said. "Have some coffee and you'll be fine." Then she began to whimper, but I couldn't make out what she was saying. "Just speak up a little," I said. "Please." But she wouldn't speak louder, and when I woke up, the only word that I was sure that I had understood was "Rice."

# THREE

# ᖴAᖇ Oᖴᖴ ᖴᖇOᗰ
# Tᕼᕮ GᗩTᕮS Oᖴ GOᒪᗪ

THE NEXT DAY, Khun Vinai went back to Chiang Rai, still looking for roofing tiles. I spent the rest of the day in the hammock. I had nothing to do but wait—and watch the hills. By dusk the mountains were gray and the far mountains were indigo, and the farthest mountains just silhouettes. Sunset was a reddish-yellow spectacle, dramatic and fast. Then the night was moonless and almost perfectly dark. I heard bullfrogs in the paddies, and vast choruses of crickets, and the kiss-me birds croaked their mechanical *whoo-tuk-tuk, whoo-tuk-tuk.* It was dinnertime, but I wasn't hungry. Khun Vinai's truck drove up, and later, from the lodge, I heard voices, and a television. Then I saw a yellow light swinging back and forth. The light wandered from the porch of the lodge toward the car shed, then arced back up the side of the hill. Then the light came closer and I realized it was Khun Vinai, carrying a flashlight. When he got to the hammock, he sat down on a small chair just behind my head. He turned off the flashlight, and we sat for a long time in darkness.

After her arrest but before trial, Khun Vinai said, Martiya's visitors were limited exclusively to her lawyer, her family, and representatives of the American consulate. The pretrial detention lasted for almost two years.

Then, after her conviction, Martiya, like all new prisoners, was forbidden guests for another year. So it was almost three years before Khun Vinai was allowed to see her.

Josh O'Connor would visit Martiya a decade later at the new prison just past the ring road. But the old prison, where Khun Vinai saw Martiya, was an altogether tougher place: Khun Vinai had never been in prison himself, but he knew women who had, and they talked about crowded cells, sometimes filled with upwards of fifty or sixty women, cells so small that the inmates were forced to sleep on the floor in shifts. The toilet was just an open trough along the far wall. The women cooked for themselves over a kerosene stove in the corner, and daily life was a constant battle against fleas, cockroaches, lice, and rats.

On the first day that he was allowed to see her, Khun Vinai went down to Chiang Mai. The prisoners entered the visiting room on their knees. It took Vinai a second to recognize Martiya, although she was the only *farang*: the prison authorities required that the women shave their heads for the first five years of their incarceration. She was "thin as a snake," Khun Vinai said, and her face was lined. She had very large ears. She recognized Khun Vinai, however, and her face flushed. She crawled in his direction, and as she crawled, she began to cry. Then she arrived at the table and lifted herself up on the stool, carefully keeping her head below his.

"Vinai," she said, after a moment. "Oh, Vinai."

Khun Vinai forced himself to smile. He had no idea at all what to say.

"Vinai, it's not your fault."

"No," he agreed.

"It's just that when they said there was a Dyalo man, I thought you were . . . I thought he had come."

Vinai didn't understand. "Who?" he said.

"Hupasha."

Vinai let her cry. He wasn't offended. The Dyalo have no taboo on staring, and he examined her strange, bony skull; her pale, thin face; her ruined hands. Only her eyes were familiar: when Martiya eventually wiped aside the last of her tears, her light blue eyes met Vinai's. No Dyalo woman in a Thai prison would have met Khun Vinai's gaze so fully.

Sang-Duan had prepared a box of food for Martiya, and Vinai was glad for the distraction. "This is for you," he said.

Martiya accepted the gift gravely. She examined the fresh mangoes, the bananas, the bag of mountain rice, and the six-pack of Coca-Cola. "These will be wonderful," she said. "Thank you."

Martiya was no longer crying. She even smiled, and there was something protective about her smile, as if Khun Vinai had just come out of the prison cell on *his* knees. The two sat without talking, neither knowing just where to begin.

"How are your kids?" Martiya finally asked.

Khun Vinai seized on the topic gratefully. "They're fine," he said. "My little son, he loves elephants too much. The other day . . ."—and as Khun Vinai talked, Martiya grew increasingly agitated. She began to shift her weight from side to side and to nod her shaven head. The corners of her eyes narrowed. Then she interrupted him. She leaned forward and laid her pale hands on his forearm.

"Vinai, tell me—is Rice happy in Dan Loi village?" she said.

"Rice is happy in Dan Loi village," he said.

"And the people still make *dyal?*"

"Yes," he said. "They still make *dyal.*"

She closed her eyes and exhaled. Her shoulders slumped. "Good," she said. She relaxed. She sat without moving. She didn't look at Vinai. They sat in silence for a few minutes. More than once, Khun Vinai started to speak—and then checked himself. Martiya didn't move.


Twice in my life I have seen a ghost.

The first time was in South India, in the holy city of Gokarna. Every morning I took my *chai* at a stall near the temple, where I exchanged smiles with the same gentleman, a gray-haired man in a loincloth. Once I mentioned this elderly figure to the *chai-wallah.* He asked me to describe him, and when I was done he roared with laughter. *That* man had been dead some twenty years. I thought that perhaps the *chai-wallah* was only teasing me, but others in the village confirmed what he had said.

The second time I have been in the presence of a ghost was that night on Khun Vinai's hammock.

Khun Vinai told me that he ended up spending several hours with Martiya in the visiting room of Chiang Mai Central Prison. The guards allowed them all the time they wanted, and Martiya spoke at length.

The night was so dark that I couldn't see Khun Vinai's face. But there were two voices beside me, and one of them was the voice of a dead woman.

"I didn't have a choice," she finally said. "Vinai, if I hadn't done something, they would have taken the *dyal* away. They wanted to take Hupasha away. What else could I have done?"

She looked at her hands.

"Hupasha came to me one night. I was in my hut, but I wasn't expecting him. I hadn't seen him in a week or two. He'd go away, and I'd miss him so much. That's when I knew he had my souls, because I missed him so badly. So when he came that night, I was very happy.

"But Hupasha wasn't himself, I knew right away. We always had a little game. He'd shout, 'Tie up your dog!' when he came to my hut, and that made us laugh, because I didn't have a dog. But that night he came and he didn't say anything, he just came up to my hut and asked if he could come in. I asked him why he was talking to me like a stranger, and he didn't say anything. So I asked him if he was going to talk to me or if he was just going to sit there like a rock all night long. And he told me that he had decided to become an Adam-person.

" 'You too?' I said. And I started to laugh, because, well, I had thought it was a big deal what he was going to tell me. I thought his daughter had died, but *this* just didn't seem to me a terribly big deal. People change, even Dyalo men, although I wish they wouldn't. But he was very interested always in what the Adam-people said, and he always liked to hear David Walker and the others preaching, talked to them about their ideas. Good for him, I always said. I mean, it would certainly be wrong if I was interested in the foreigners and he wasn't. He wants to read the Bible, that's fine. I never wanted to control him or tell him what to do. He was far too smart for that, far too *strong* for that. So I just said, 'Congratulations. Don't scare me like that next time.'

"But I thought about things for a moment, and I asked him how was he going to keep Rice happy if he didn't make *dyal*. He said that he wouldn't keep Rice happy. And I said, 'You aren't? What are you going to eat?' Because that's such a basic Dyalo idea, that you need to keep Rice happy. And he said that now he would ask Ye-su-tsi to make the fields grow. 'What does Ye-su-tsi know about Rice?' I said. But he didn't say anything.

"I asked him why he was doing all this, and he said he no longer wanted to be a slave to Rice. That he wanted to be a free man.

"Then he said he wouldn't see me anymore in the fields because it would make Ye-su-tsi angry if he made *dyal*. He said that Adam-people don't make *dyal*. So I said, 'Okay, we won't make *dyal*,' but he said that it didn't matter, that I was still his *gin-kai*. That they only give honor to Ye-su-tsi, and sing Ye-su-tsi songs.

"I asked him who taught him this, and he said it was David Walker.

"So he went home and I went back to work, and I waited for him to come back to my hut again, because I figured this all would blow over, and one week went by, and then another. I started to feel a little worried, and then another week went by. I decided I would go up to Wild Pig and see him, and talk to him again.

"I found him in his rice fields. What beautiful fields we had made! He was so handsome working. It was a glorious day, with a clear, hot sun. He saw me and he stopped working, and I knew before he even said a word that he wanted me. And I wanted him too. He was a beautiful man, simply beautiful. Things would be fine. But he said, 'Martiya, why are you in my rice fields?' I'll never forget his voice, it was so cold.

"He said that, and I got angry.

"I said, 'I gave up my life to learn your language, so that I can talk to you. And then you came along, and I give up my man to be with you also, one good man, who had all my souls, who would have taken me away from here. This village was all I had, and I gave up this village for you, too, this village which I wanted. They came to me and said: *It is either us or Rice*. And I said, 'Give me my man.' And now you say that the rice fields we made together are *yours*?'

"He didn't have anything to say to that, there was nothing he could say. He walked away. I walked home through the fields. I had planted the rice, and now it was high.

"That night I was all alone in my hut, and I began to shiver. My teeth were chattering. My whole body was trembling, and the next thing I knew, Lai-Ma was there. She was frightened of Rice, but she came.

"She was stroking my head. She said that I was taken by the spirits in the night. And I said, 'I was?' And she said, 'The spirits caught you and you fell down, and you screamed.'

"I guess that's when I first knew how angry Rice was. How angry Rice could be."

"I wish I could say that I was very brave, but I wasn't. If Lai-Ma hadn't been there, I don't know how I would have eaten, how I would have got water, how I would have bathed myself. I spent most of those days sleeping. That little hut was so small. And I couldn't breathe. My chest ached. The only person I wanted to see was Lai-Ma. She was so kind. When I was with her, I calmed down, just a little. But she had things to do. She had her fields.

"And so I would sit there at that desk. I had these conversations with myself. I'd say, 'Let's go. Let's go now. Don't wait.' And then this voice would be in my head, it was my voice, but dark, it would say, 'Martiya, where would you go? How could you leave?'

"I didn't think I could live without Hupasha, without the rice fields. I thought about the *dyal* all the time. What a mistake he made, to give up Rice.

"The first time we made *dyal*, Hupasha came to my house. I didn't expect him. I hadn't seen him in a year, but I had thought about him. He took my breath away, he was so handsome. He shouted, 'Tie up your dog!' and then he didn't say one more word. Took me to his rice field. It was a dark night, he led me on the path, up over Big Hill, in the direction of Wild Pig village. I couldn't see a thing, just held on to his hand, we walked for hours. Then the moon rose, just as we got to his rice fields. Just an empty field. I never felt so happy in my life. So this was the *dyal*, I thought. This was it.

"We planted rice by moonlight. I followed him. He walked in front of me. Hupasha would step forward and rear back and pound the dibble stick into the earth, drive the thing a foot or two feet deep into the earth, and I would breathe in and step forward. We had a rhythm, the two of us, and my part was so delicate and simple, just to take the seed and let it drop; then we'd step forward.

"Then he reached for me. And I saw Rice. Either you know Rice or you don't. Rice is like steam rising from the fields, like silver flames. I didn't know where I ended, where he began. The field was on fire with Rice. His touch, his smell—where does such a good thing come from? I had never before understood what the Dyalo meant when they said, 'Only a woman can make rice.' Later they would tell me, 'Stop making *dyal*. Walk away from *dyal*.' I couldn't.

"I made *dyal*, and I got home to the village and all I thought about was *dyal*. And it's not true that you can only make *dyal* once a year, at planting time. Rice is always there. I used to ask, 'What happens if you see your *gin-kai* when it's not the *dyal*?' 'But, Martiya, that is not our custom.' 'But if a woman sees her *gin-kai*, what would happen?' 'Martiya, she would be a slave to Rice.' I never thought to ask why that would be a bad thing.

"That is the *dyal*, and how could Hupasha want to leave it all behind him? How could he? I'll never understand that, not until the day I die. What is better than Rice?

"I had so much still to learn about Rice. I had just begun to understand Rice, when Hupasha left.

"I must have spent weeks, then months like that. At night I dreamed of being with Hupasha. Of Rice. I'd wake up sweating. Then I'd fall back asleep and have the same dreams all over again."

"One day David Walker came by my hut. It was toward sundown when he knocked on the door. I saw him through my window. He knocked again, and when I didn't answer, he pushed the door open. He stood in the threshold.

"He was large, much larger than I was—and as he stood in the doorway of the hut, with the sun setting right behind him, the hairs on his arms were very fine and golden. I remember looking at those hairs, and thinking no wonder the Dyalo were so impressed by him, he looks like a tiger to them. Once I went out hunting with Fat Belly, years and years ago. We went deep in the jungle and I saw a tiger. It couldn't have been much farther away than that wall. They say that there are no more tigers in northern Thailand, but I saw one. And when you see a tiger in the jungle—you don't see anything else. That's what I thought about when I saw David.

"David didn't say anything for a moment. Then he said that Hupasha had asked him to come. I asked him why, and David said that he needed to talk to me. I said, 'Talk,' but he asked if he could come in.

"He was so big, and there wasn't quite enough space in the hut for both of us. We were both sweating because it was such a hot night. His teeth were very white, and I could see the pores in his skin. I could feel the heat coming off him. I was a little frightened of him, to tell you the truth. I asked him the last time he saw Hupasha, and he said that he had seen him just the night before. He had been up there talking about the Bible with him. And I said, 'David, will you tell me something?'

"David nodded yes, and I asked him if Hupasha was really a Christian. Or whether it was just something that Hupasha invented to get rid of me. That's what I really wanted to know.

"David thought for a long time. He said, 'It was hard, what he had to do. Choosing for the Lord was the hardest thing he ever had to do. I think he wants to be a Christian—and I think that's enough. God put the desire there.' I thought about that a minute, and I said, 'Does he want me back?' and David said, 'Martiya, all I know is that he never, ever wants to go back to Rice.'

"'But he loved Rice!' That's what I said. I said, 'David, you have no idea how happy we were together. It was the most beautiful thing in the world, when we were together and made rice. I think we would have been together forever, if you hadn't come along.'

"David leaned forward. I could smell him. He smelled like earth and clay. He said, 'Martiya, I need to tell you something. I talked to him yesterday. He wants to go back to Burma and tell them about the Lord.'

"I felt like a candle was melting inside me. But I still didn't cry. 'Was this your idea?' I said. David looked at the ground, and he said, 'He asked me what I thought about it, and I said that everyone needs to know the Lord.'

"'But how is he going to eat? Where will he get rice?' I said, and David told me that the Christians had made a rice fund for the evangelists.

"That's when I knew I had really lost him. If Hupasha had decided to go, I knew he would go. I was all alone with Rice. David said, 'I admire you, Martiya. You've been living here alone for such a long time. I know how hard it is to live without the Lord.'

"But I don't think David realized how angry I was. I said, 'Why did you do this to me? What did I do to you?'

"David stood up. He looked at me for a long, long time. Then he said, 'Martiya, will you sing with me?' And he seemed almost as surprised saying these words as I was hearing them, like the words had come out of his mouth by accident. It was the hot season, and we were both so sweaty, his face was red and slick, and my clothes were so heavy. He stretched his arms out wide and leaned over me. Then he began to sing:

'There were ninety-and-nine that safely lay
In the Shelter of the fold.
But one was out on the hills far away,
Far off from the gates of gold.
Away on the mountains wild and bare,
Away from the tender Shepherd's care,
Away from the tender Shepherd's care.'

"He took my hands. He held them tight and pressed them up against his shirt. I could feel his heart beating. He was out of breath, and I could see veins throbbing in his neck. 'Did you hear them?' he said. And I said yes, I had heard them, too. Then he walked out the door, leaving it wide open behind him.

"I couldn't believe I would never see Hupasha again. I thought he would come by the next day or the day after that."

---

"I watched the village prepare that year for the *dyal*. It was obvious to me that the Christians regretted their decision, and were very jealous now of the animist half. They made Fat Belly the pastor of the church—Fat Belly! In charge of *anyone's* spiritual life! I think that really says it all. The animist half, though, were very serene. They had lived in these hills forever. Their faces said: This is our life, this is the way Dyalo live; we don't need Ye-su-tsi. We know how to please Rice.

"It had to be the same in Wild Pig village. So when I saw the preparations, I was sure that Hupasha was going to come. And so I started to prepare for the *dyal* myself. I wanted to look beautiful.

"When I learned about the *dyal*, the people always used the phrase 'The *dyal* is the Lesson of Ten Thousand Harvests.' Can you imagine? They were making *dyal* long before Jesus was born—maybe not the Dyalo exactly, maybe not the *dyal* exactly, but somebody was making some ritual like this, to please Rice. Rice is old, older than you can imagine.

"But Hupasha didn't come.

"I got in my jeep and I drove down to Chiang Mai. It's a long drive, but I remember a feeling that if I didn't get out of the hills, get out *now* . . . I decided to go for a drink. I went to one of those bars on the river, with the music. I was so grateful to be with strangers, with people who had never heard of the *dyal*, of the Dyalo even. I ordered a drink, and then another. One of the tourists asked if I wanted to get stoned, and I did. We stood outside on that balcony smoking, looking out over the river, with the reflection of the moon. I started to think, just for a moment, that I was going to be all right, that things were going to work out.

"And then I was sick. I ran to the bathroom as fast as I could, a dirty little bathroom in a dirty little bar, and I threw everything up—and is it strange if I say it felt wonderful? I threw up until I felt empty inside. I stood up from the toilet, I must have been in there ten minutes, twenty minutes, and I looked in the mirror, and this old woman stared back at me. I wondered who she was, and of course she was me. I was an old woman. I knew at that moment that I was no longer a beautiful woman, not even a pretty woman anymore.

"That's when I noticed the bathroom attendant. She was standing behind me. If I was an old woman, she was ancient. She must have heard me vomiting. She must have thought I was disgusting. But she looked so peaceful and serene and contented—and that's amazing, if you think about it. This woman *lives* in a toilet, that's her life, from morning until night she lives in the toilet and gives out hot towels and rubs the necks of rich women and listens to them pee and shit and vomit, and I've never seen in all my life such a simple, contented, happy face. She had a cross around her neck. And that cross—I stared and stared.

"At that moment, I knew that I could have everything I wanted. And I can't tell you how much I wanted to take a bath. I hadn't taken a real bath in years, only showers in the village. I wanted to wash myself in clean water—to begin again, just to start over. I wanted to find David right away. I wanted to tell him that he was right. It wasn't a rational decision, I hadn't thought it all through, I just *wanted* it.

"I went to the Walkers' house. It was only a twenty-minute walk or so, and it felt glorious. But the closer I got to that house, I started to hear this very small voice in my head. This voice said, 'Is *this* how you treat Rice?'

"Then I saw that house, with that huge fence around it, at the end of the block, and it was black. I went through the gate and up to the door, and I rang the bell and nobody came for a very long time.

"Then the door opened. It was Norma Walker, and I didn't know what to say. I had only thought about David, about meeting David, and explaining to him what happened in the bathroom. I asked if David was there.

"Norma looked confused. She must have been asleep. She's a big woman, like her son, and I felt so small.

"Norma stared me up and down, then finally she asked if I knew what time it was.

"And I didn't, I really didn't, so I said no. She sighed and said it was four-thirty in the morning. I told her that I was looking for David, and she shook her head and she said that David was in the field. I felt like an idiot, because of course David wouldn't be here the first night of *dyal*. Then I thought of Thomas. But she shook her again and said, 'No, my husband is with my son tonight.' I didn't know what to say, so I asked if she remembered me, and she said that she knew just who I was, and she stared at me with those dark eyes, like I was a wild animal. She had never liked me, I knew that. Then she asked what she could do for me, and suddenly I was so thirsty that I thought I would die. I couldn't think of anything but a cold glass of water. So I asked if I could have a glass of water.

"She didn't say one word. She just backed away from the door and disappeared into that black, empty house. Then she came back and gave me the glass and said that I should come in for a minute. I didn't want to go in, but I did anyway. And we sat down in that living room, with those poor goldfish going back and forth. I drank my water, and I started to wonder what I was doing there.

"Then she asked me again what she could do for me. And I wanted just to tell the truth. So I told her that I came to be baptized, and I started to cry. She didn't say anything at all. She just sat, and I looked at her face. I saw David's face in hers, just heavier. The same dark eyes, the same long nose, those same thin lips; those two were cut from the same cloth. She said, 'Now?' and I said, 'Yes,' and she said, 'You want *me* to baptize you? *Me?*'

"And I didn't say anything. I was still crying. I wanted to tell her about Rice.

"Norma looked at my face. She looked at me slowly. I hadn't seen her in a long time, not since before I went back home to California. Then she asked if I had anything I wanted to tell her, if I wanted to get square with the Lord.

"And I told her that I had made *dyal*, and that I was frightened of Rice. And she nodded, and she said that baptism meant I was square with the Lord, but she didn't think I was square with the Lord at all. And I stopped crying, and I said that I needed to be baptized, that's why I had come. I wanted to tell her that whatever she was thinking, it didn't matter now, but she cut me off. She said that she loved her husband, that from the first moment she saw him she'd loved him, he was the most handsome man she'd ever seen. Norma told me that she'd never loved another man, and she never would. And I said, 'He's a wonderful man, Norma,' but Norma wasn't listening to me. She said she'd made her peace with the kind of man he was, an imperfect man, and she didn't want me back in their life, that those days were over. She asked me to leave her alone, please leave her and her family alone. And I said, 'Norma,' but she was already out of the room.

"I walked out of that house perfectly sober. I walked away from that house thinking that I had to do something. I walked away from that house thinking how close I had come to angering Rice."

"You see, I told you I didn't have a choice. Even now, I know it was the only thing I could have done. I knew that without David they would worship Rice again.

"He was headed up to Wild Pig village, and I went up the path ahead of him, and I got to that first bridge. I was able to untie one of the ropes and although the thing looked solid enough, I knew that when a big man walked on it, the bridge wouldn't hold. Then I waited. As it happens, that bridge overlooks a very beautiful rice field, and it must have been toward the end of rainy season. So the rice was high, and I was very calm and peaceful. It was a windy day, and the rice was blowing back and forth, like waves of silver and green. There is nothing so beautiful as a rice field. Then David came, and it was silent. He didn't shout, and I looked, and he had fallen, fallen, fallen, down below. I went home.

"I went to bed that evening and I slept, and I woke up the next morning, and I felt like sleeping again, and I slept most of the next day as well. It was the next night when I had a very strange dream. I dreamed about David. He came to me, and he sang again at my door.

"I woke up the next morning and I didn't know what to do. Because I did not want to be cruel, not at all. He was a nice boy, just dangerous, very dangerous. So I took my hunting rifle, which I'd used exactly once since the blacksmith made it for me, and I went out to the bridge and I looked down, and I took very careful aim. I shot him twice, just to make sure.

"Then I walked home through the rice fields."

# EPILOGUE

I WENT UP to Dan Loi village with Khun Vinai.

We drove as far as we could and then we walked. We had nearly arrived when a mechanical buzzing startled us, and we stood aside to allow a young man on a motorcycle to pass us on the narrow path, bouncing over rocks and swerving to avoid a fallen log. This was the first suggestion I had of how much the village had changed in the years since Martiya left it. The village still straddled the same ridge, fringed in every direction by the rice fields, then fields of purple taro, sunflowers, yellow sorghum, and tall corn. But tin roofs instead of thatch now covered about half the huts. A number of them sprouted antennas.

Still, I thought I recognized the place. There were the other roofs, of woven cogon grass. There was the cooking hut. Pigs rooted between their stilts, and chickens squawked nervously under bamboo baskets. Gray, mean-looking dogs with yellow eyes barked at us. A few women wearing the famous Dyalo costume—the low trailing skirt and the brilliantly colored tunics—threshed rice into wicker baskets. Small naked children, brown and lean, stopped playing as we came through the village, but only for an instant: I could have been any Western trekker on holiday.

It had been more than a decade since Khun Vinai was last in Dan Loi. The familiar huts were full of strangers. The headman who had consoled Martiya on the loss of Pell was dead. The woman in his hut knew him only by name. Miss Dan Loi, once the prettiest woman in all Dan Loi, had moved with her husband and their children to a new village; they left no forwarding address. This was no surprise: the Dyalo are wanderers, and it is rare for a Dyalo family to stay in the same place for very long. George Washington had died three years before, the oldest man anyone in the village had ever seen. I began to wonder, wandering through the village, whether Martiya had ever been here at all.

But Lai-Ma and Farts-a-Lot were just where Martiya had left them.

Does one shake hands when introduced to a Dyalo stranger? Bow, as in Thailand? Dance a jig? I had no idea, and so I stood there with an embarrassed half-smile on my lips, moronically shaking my head up and down. Lai-Ma and Farts-a-Lot! I had hardly believed that they existed, and now they were in front of me: Lai-Ma, a small, wrinkled creature, barefoot, in a magenta tunic, her hair wrapped in a headband; and Farts-a-Lot, smaller than I had imagined, and with a sweetness to his lopsided, toothless smile that I hadn't expected from Martiya's letters. Lai-Ma and Farts-a-Lot had a habit I recalled from my grandparents: one began a sentence, and then the other finished it. They were like a pair of garden trolls come to life.

We climbed up the shaky stairs and sat on small stools. The hut was dark and low; it smelled of smoke, sweat, incense, and chili powder. The place kept cool even now in the heat of the day. From a line suspended diagonally across the large room hung the family's wardrobe: a few shirts, a pair or two of black cotton trousers. On the wall there was a calendar from 1997 with pictures of the mother of the king of Thailand. And not much more, really: a hoe, a large covered cistern, some smaller jars, a bamboo mat rolled and propped against the wall, a few blackened cooking implements, and a row of bottles filled with rice whiskey.

"Was this the hut Martiya lived in?" I asked Khun Vinai. "When she first came?"

Vinai said something to our hosts which made them laugh. He turned back to me and said, "Yes. Right there." He pointed to a patch of uneven floorboards near the far wall. Martiya had slept in that corner for almost a year, unrolling her mat at night, leaning cross-legged against the wall during the day as she transcribed her field notes.

Then Lai-Ma said something which provoked a response from Farts-a-Lot. Khun Vinai sat up straight. It was also in that corner, he said, that Martiya lived at the end, when she had no place else to go.

Lai-Ma and Farts-a-Lot spent hours telling their story. Occasionally, Khun Vinai would remember that I was there and summarize ten minutes of animated conversation in a sentence or two: "People were afraid to be Adam-people with David gone. People quit the church."

Then I would ask, "Who quit the church? Did so-and-so stay a Christian?"

This would provoke another half hour of urgent conversation, at the end of which Khun Vinai would say, "No, so-and-so didn't stay a Christian."

"Why did he quit?"

And the cycle was repeated.

The four of us spent most of the day like that. At one point, I leaned up against the southern wall of the hut. This produced an anxious moment. Farts-a-Lot said something to Khun Vinai, who said, "Don't touch that wall."

"Why?" I asked.

Translation. Back and forth. Waiting.

"He says it makes the spirits angry," Khun Vinai finally said.

A trio of young boys from a neighboring Karen village, fishing for river shrimp, found David Walker's body. Their parents informed the police. A squadron came through Dan Loi, and then several hours later passed through the village again, carrying the bloated corpse on a stretcher.

And then there was nothing. The villagers had seen the body and that was all the information they had: there are no newspapers in the mountains, no journalists. At first, they assumed that David's death was an accident: an old bridge had collapsed. No one knew what this meant. The sight of David's body being borne on a palanquin through Dan Loi village had frightened the Christians. If not even David Walker—who presumably knew how to please Ye-su-tsi in ways infinitely more sophisticated than they did—could keep a terrible death away, just how strong was this *tsi*?

But from the shaman, George Washington, Lai-Ma heard a more disturbing rumor: that David Walker had been shot.

The rains were heavy that year, the harvest was meager, and not long after Lai-Ma and Farts-a-Lot had emptied their baskets into the rice barn, the structure collapsed. Big Teeth's opium crop was half what he had hoped: he would be forced to buy his youngest son an ugly bride. Bad luck pursued Christian and heathen alike. Pastor James, who before his conversion was called Fat Belly, lost two pigs in the jungle. Garlic Breath was stricken with diarrhea. Two children died that winter, one by drowning, the other of a mysterious fever.

The deluge was followed by bitter cold. At night, the water cisterns froze over, and even at midday, in the exceptional clearness of the winter light, the villagers could see their breath. Villagers reported nightmares, animals acting strangely. Wives complained of bad-tempered husbands, and husbands lamented volatile wives. No one could explain it, but the communal cooking hut began to stink—as if something had died and was rotting in one of its corners. No one could find the offending object. Food cooked in the hut was generally agreed to have a bad taste.

Pastors Moses and James read from the pulpit, the congregation sang. But the church had registered its last convert, and its flocks began to thin.

They left for any variety of reasons. Stupid Squirrel had converted chiefly in the expectation of saving money: with a family as large as his, he had been forced to buy pigs frequently to sacrifice. Seeing that the Christians made do without any sacrifices at all, he had converted. But he hadn't reckoned on the Christian ban on opium planting: a man is hardly called Stupid Squirrel for no reason, after all. David had a particular genius for framing these dilemmas within the grand context of biblical history, but, of course, David was gone.

Another who succumbed was Miss Dan Loi. Miss Dan Loi had joined the church chiefly to avoid the *dyal*: just as Martiya had always suspected, some women in the village found that rite a horror. Even seven months after David was dead, she had remained steadfast in her faith, planting with the other Christians, praying over the fields. But as the first seedlings sprouted, Miss Dan Loi and her husband noted a deformity in their harvest. Miss Dan Loi hated her duties in the *dyal*, but clearly Rice wasn't happy, and if Rice wasn't happy, she knew, her children would go hungry. In the old ways, the Dyalo had known how to treat such problems: how to feed the deformed Rice glass after glass of whiskey, and trap the drunken spirit in a bamboo cage. If David had been alive to lead them in the appropriate Christian prayers, she and her husband wouldn't have needed to turn to George Washington—but with David gone, what choice did they have?

Pastor James knelt down every Sunday alongside the members of the accursed Vampire clan, and Old Limping Lady, and others. And Hupasha remained a Christian. Every night Martiya expected to hear the news that he had renounced his faith, to hear his footsteps on the porch of her hut. She asked for news from every traveler who passed his way, and the same news always returned: they had found him distracted with the Big Book.

It was at the end of that terrible cold that Farts-a-Lot, waking up early, noticed the flames coming from Martiya's hut. When he burst inside, he found her sprawled asleep and pulled her from the cottage just as the ceiling collapsed. Martiya tried to break free of Farts-a-Lot's arms and go back inside, but he held her back. Over his shoulder she watched the hut burn, and with it her row of spiral-bound, hard-sided notebooks, perhaps forty in all: almost fifteen years of field notes, essays, and a manuscript draft, now nearly completed, of *The Dyalo Way of Life*.

Martiya had no place to go. Lai-Ma and Farts-a-Lot took her back in, as if she were starting over, as if her life still lay before her, and the old songs of Sings Soft were still on every tongue, and Pell was waiting for her back home.

Days later, the shaman summoned the elders of Dan Loi to his hut, and there informed them of his professional opinion: that the string of misadventures in the village was not random, but rather the work of a disgruntled spirit—the spirit of David Walker.


The villagers of Dan Loi became convinced that George Washington's hypothesis squared with the facts: that one (or several) of David Walker's souls had not been carted off with his corpse, and that, far from its loved ones, it was wandering through village, making mischief.

Over a series of tense nights, the shaman entered into his trance and tried to reason with the spirits. I have no idea what happened to the shaman when the spirits seized him. All I can say is this: both Lai-Ma and Farts-a-Lot, like the others in the village, were convinced that the shaman was visiting with the dead David Walker. And David Walker had a tale to tell.

How did the shaman come to know the facts? He knew that Martiya kept a hunting rifle. He knew about Martiya and Hupasha. Maybe he looked into her face and saw the story written there.

Or maybe he went into his trance and communed with the dead.

Everyone agreed that action must be taken. Debate raged in the village. The headman, who had never even after all these years wholly trusted Martiya, proposed settling the situation in the simplest of all possible ways, with a bullet in the back of the head. Had a Dyalo man or woman shot David Walker, this is surely how the situation would have been resolved. Dyalo justice was very much of an eye-for-an-eye sort; there are no jails in a Dyalo village.

The villagers approved the headman's proposal, and only the lack of a willing executioner got in the way. No man in the village wanted to shoot Martiya himself, and although there was a Lahu man willing to do the job, it wasn't clear who would pay him.

Besides, if one dead *farang* was bad, wouldn't two be worse?

Lai-Ma and Farts-a-Lot did not recall who in the end proposed denouncing Martiya to the police. Lai-Ma thought it might have been Stupid Squirrel, and Farts-a-Lot thought it was Pastor James. But the villagers were agreed on the plan: it was not the Dyalo way of handling things, but Martiya was not, after all, Dyalo.


The day had gone from cool to hot to cool again. I excused myself from the hut. The last light breaking over the dark green mountains was gold and orange. The huts were cloaked in brilliant ringlets of fiery bougainvillea, and in the valley below I could see Karen maidens all in white, in sharp relief against the green fields. Everything was quiet. I made my way around the bend of the village, along the path that led through the ancient bamboo groves, until I found myself on a large rock overlooking the whole of Dan Loi. This was the rock, I realized, on which Martiya herself had whiled away so many hours at just this time of day. From this high rock, there could have been no more exotic and incomprehensible place than a Dyalo village: the sloping thatched huts, the rootings pigs, the shrine of the Old Grandfather, just barely visible in a clearing in the woods. Then, in a language not one word of which I understood, someone began to sing, breaking the stillness of the evening.

I wondered what the song meant.


My story—the story of my involvement in Martiya van der Leun's murder of David Walker—for all practical purposes ended there. I ceased to pursue witnesses, I never went back to the big pink house to sit again with Norma Walker and her husband on the matching fake-leather couches. But I expect that they are still there, that their grandchildren are off spreading the Word, that Thomas Walker is looking out on the horizon and seeing the storm clouds of the Apocalypse approaching.

One last detail will complete my story.

Not long ago, I received an e-mail from Josh O'Connor. He wrote that he had received word from the editors of both *Ethnology* and the *Southeast Asian Journal of Social Science*. Almost two years earlier, he had done as Martiya had asked: he had typed up her two remaining manuscript papers, both ethnographies of life at Chiang Mai Central Prison, and sent them off. Now, after a pause so long that Josh had completely forgotten the contents of the papers themselves, he had received responses from the editors. Both papers had been accepted. The anonymous reviewers were congratulatory. The critics had no idea of the circumstances under which Martiya had written, and imagined her an academic anthropologist conducting fieldwork in the traditional manner. "A deep and profound sympathy for the subjects," wrote one critic; and another, "A superb and detailed contribution to the ethnographic *corpus* detailing the conditions of incarceration for women."

When the papers are eventually published, they will represent the totality of Martiya van der Leun's contribution, after almost thirty years in Southeast Asia, to the anthropological literature.

Enclosed with the acceptance letters were two small checks. And that was why Josh O'Connor was writing to me. Did I have any idea, he asked, what he should do with a check addressed to Martiya van der Leun? Did I think he could cash it?

## A NOTE ON THE SOURCES

This novel began not as fiction but as a history of the conversion of the Lisu people of northern Thailand to Christianity. Then one afternoon, I woke up from a long nap with a plot in my head, and my history became a novel. At that moment, I abandoned any intention I had to tell a true story. The Dyalo do not exist, except in these pages. None of this stuff happened to anyone.

In the service of my original project, while living in Chiang Mai I spent hours talking with a number of missionaries. I would like to thank David Morse, Eugene Morse, Helen Morse, Joni Morse, the Reverend Andy Thomson, Gam Shae, and Jesse Yangmi for their generosity and time. My greatest debt, however, is to the late Gertrude Morse, whose wonderful, rich, and moving memoir, *The Dogs May Bark: But the Caravan Rolls On* (Joplin: College Press Publishing, 1998), informed so much of the writing of this book. Mrs. Morse gave me a glimpse of the profound faith, the reckless daring, and the absolute confidence required of a great missionary.

I also would like to thank Otome Klein Hutheesing. Ms. Hutheesing is an extraordinary scholar—and, as those who know her will gladly testify, an equally impressive woman. Her ethnography *Emerging Sexual Inequality Among the Lisu of Northern Thailand: The Waning of Dog and Elephant Repute* (Leiden: Brill, 1990) brings to life the secret world of a

Lisu village. The time that I spent with Ms. Hutheesing gave me my clearest idea of how an anthropologist sees the world.

My description of the rice-planting cycle has relied on Edward F. Anderson's *Plants and Peoples of the Golden Triangle: Ethnobotany of the Hill Tribes of Northern Thailand* (Portland: Dioscorides Press, 1993). This is far and away the best introduction to the modalities of hill-tribe agriculture, and I recommend it heartily to anyone proposing to travel in northern Thailand. A reading of Mr. Anderson's ethnobotany will transform your understanding of the region. Another invaluable book for the traveler is Christian Gooden's *Around Lan-na: A Guide to Thailand's Northern Border Region* (Halesworth: Jungle Books, 1999). Mr. Gooden is fearless—he traveled the very remotest regions of northern Thailand on a motorbike, with his wife *and their two-year-old daughter*—exceptionally erudite, and a great storyteller.

Those who wish to stay home, however, can do no better than Richard K. Diran's marvelous photo collection *The Vanishing Tribes of Northern Burma* (London: Seven Dials, 1997). See if you can find the photos of Farts-a-Lot, Lai-Ma, and Hupasha!

The conversion of tribal highlanders to Christianity is a subject of considerable interest in the contemporary anthropological literature. I recommend very highly the whole of vol. 27, no. 2 (September 1996) of the *Journal of Southeast Asian Studies*, entitled *Protestants and Tradition in Southeast Asia*. I benefited particularly from Cornelia Ann Kammerer, "Discarding the Basket: The Reinterpretation of Tradition by Akha Christians of Northern Thailand" (pp. 320–49); and Edwin Zehner, "Thai Protestants and Local Supernaturalisms: Changing Configurations" (pp. 293–319).

I read, and reread many times, E. Paul Durrenberger's monograph *Lisu Religion* (Northern Illinois University, Occasional Paper no. 13, 1989). I can't claim that I really understood it, but his description of real Lisu rites, particularly medical rites, gave me the confidence to make my Dyalo as—well, *weird* is really the word I'm looking for—as I wanted them to be. Next time you pass through a good university library, spend a half hour in the stacks with Mr. Durrenberger's ethnography. You will be rewarded with a pleasant sense that the world is much, much larger, and much, much stranger than you imagined. (I suppose Lisu readers would have pretty much the opposite reaction.)

Research for this novel has introduced me to a wonderful genre of literature—the anthropological memoir. Two practitioners of this art stand out above all others: Nigel Barley and Hortense Powdermaker. I say with no hesitation whatsoever that Mr. Barley's *The Innocent Anthropologist: Notes from a Mud Hut* (New York: Penguin, 1983) is the best book of its genre, perhaps one of the best books *ever*. I also loved his succeeding books, *Not a Hazardous Sport* (New York: Penguin, 1988) and *Ceremony* (New York: Henry Holt, 1986). Mr. Barley taught me, to the extent that an outsider and neophyte can ever understand, just what an anthropologist does all day long, and how hard it is to do it.

Hortense Powdermaker is precisely the woman I would most like to sit next to on a very long plane flight: intelligent, experienced, with a sedate, dry wit. It was through her memoir *Stranger and Friend: The Way of an Anthropologist* (New York: Norton, 1966) that I was introduced to Bronislaw Malinowski and the South Pacific island of Lesu.

Also very useful was Peggy Golde, ed., *Women in the Field: Anthropological Experiences* (Berkeley: University of California Press, 1986), particularly Kathryn Brigg's essay, "Kapluna Daughter."

ACKNOWLEDGMENTS

Having Lorin Stein edit my prose was a humbling experience—but also very exciting. First, he cut whole chapters—and he was right: I didn't need them. Then he suggested I cut dull pages; and while I was at it, a particular subplot or two that were just a little overwrought and labyrinthine. I believe what he wrote in the margin was "Snoozin' here." (On another occasion, he wrote, "No, no, no!" directly across the text; also, "Why, Mischa, *why?*") He eliminated wordy paragraphs, verbal tics, imprecise adjectives, just about *all* the adverbs, shoddy dialogue, and most of my pompous interjections. He was always right. Occasionally, I would get myself worked up into a righteous authorial lather and *STET* a deletion or two. After a few weeks, I'd go back and look at his suggestions again—and discover that he was, as usual, totally right. Lorin is also responsible for the novel's title, and he translated Psalm 23 into Dyalo.

There is nothing, absolutely nothing, that a novelist needs more than acres of grassy time in which to write. My mother gave me that gift. I was broke almost from page one of this novel, and all through its creation she supported me, telling me all the while the things that a child most wants to hear: that what I was doing was valuable; that I wasn't wasting my time; and that everything would work out in the end. What more could a son ask for?

The rest of my family played their part also. It was my sister, Claire, who introduced me to the novel-writing game; without her encouragement and example, I would never have thought to write this one. She read it at least a thousand times over, and every time she helped me make it a little better. My father, David Berlinski, who also read it a zillion times, gave me the model of literary excellence to which I will always aspire.

My agent, Susan Ginsberg, is a lot like Rice—a mysterious, almost supernatural force without whom the Berlinskis would be hungry.

Now I must say a word about the love of my life, Cristina Iampieri. When Cristina invited me into her studio apartment in Torino, I don't know if she quite reckoned on spending the next two and a half years not only with me but with a murderous anthropologist who hated to see *anyone* before ten; an extended family of missionaries; and an entire tribal village. Our apartment was not much larger, I should add, than the book now in your hands. In the mornings, she made all of us espresso, pot after pot; she rarely said anything about the water buffalo droppings in the kitchen; and I think Thomas Walker had a little crush on her by the end. But who wouldn't love her? She is wonderful and beautiful and incredibly patient; she has been the best of friends; without her, I couldn't have written a word. *Grazie.*

Culture 21/22
NATIVE CUSTOMS 24
"just a tribe... 136
calm, good natured 137
DAVID 146
MOTHERS 148
DAVID 150
xx "THE MOMENT" 151
angles (?) 154
DYNASTY 165
"NATIVE VIEW" + INNOCENT 165
"SCALY SKIN of SELF" 165
WHY (166)
ICE CREAM 167
"CRISIS" 170
"Semi-encouraging GRIN" 174
room of your own 174
POINT of VIEW 179
White colonial MASTERS 217
things don't understand 221
* KNOW OURSELVES 131
POINT of VIEW 251
Despair 267